Palatka

Ann O'Connell Rust

The Floridians Series Volume II

Amaro Books

Published by
Amaro Books
5673 Pine Avenue
Orange Park, Florida 32073

First Printing 1989
Second Printing 1993
ISBN N0. 0-9620556-1-1 (Soft Cover)
ISBN N0.1-883203-00-7 (Hard Cover)
Library of Congress Catalog Card No. 89-84402
Printed in U.S.A.
Cover Artist: Linda Taheri

Books by Ann O'Connell Rust:
Punta Rassa
Palatka
Kissimmee
Monticello
Pahokee

Books by Ann O'Connell Rust:
Punta Rassa
Palatka

IN MEMORY OF

Bill and Mutt Rust
Julia and Harold Hulpieu

ACKNOWLEDGEMENTS

The author wishes to thank A.F. Rust, Editor/Copy Editor, and Jim Brown and staff of Empulse, Gt. Barrington, Mass. Also the historical societies, friends of libraries, book clubs and book stores, which have been so supportive.

AUTHOR'S NOTE

The setting of this story if Florida — 1878 and 1879. The background is authentic, but all the characters are fictional. The following towns have since had name changes — some many times.

ROSE HEAD — is now PERRY
ROWLAND'S BLUFF — BRANFORD
TATER HILL BLUFF — ARCADIA

The town of CROSSTOWN is fictional but the author placed it in the same vicinity as the present day CROSS CITY.

CONTENTS

REFLECTIONS

The upcoming wedding of Berta McRae and Layke Williams had Old Town in a dither.

"Berta deserves this happiness - now you know that, Luta. After all, being widowed for over four years and having to work just to keep food on the table was especially hard on her," Trudy Stucky stated emphatically to Luta Brewster as they sat doing their handwork on the Stucky Hotel's front porch. The sun was already warning of its plans for the day. Trudy, the proprietor of the town's only hotel, or boarding house as the townspeople referred to it, and Luta, the wife of Old Town's blacksmith, were friends and neighbors and had been for as long as Luta and Bud had been married.

Luta nodded in agreement. "And she had such a genteel upbringing. You know, Bud and me thought she'd take those four little children back to Georgia after Reuben died, South Spring being so far from town..." She passed the embroidered piece she was working on over to Trudy for inspection and waited for her praise. Her previous plans for it had been for her own enjoyment, but when Berta and Layke announced their wedding date, she decided to present Berta with the pillow cases and matching dresser scarves.

Luta continued while waiting for Trudy's comments. "What with just the old colored families on the place, well, we were truly surprised when she told us that she was going to carry on Reuben's dream for their ranch. We truly were."

Trudy returned the pillow case and gave the enthusiastic "hmmms...and isn't that lovely!"

"You know there's no one I'd rather embroider these for than Berta, 'cause I know she'll appreciate them. Did you ever see that set she made for her parlor in the candle wick pattern, Trudy? Well, I never in all my life saw the likes of it. I thought Bud's Ma could out-do anyone I ever knew in embroidering and drawn work, but those pieces of Berta's beat anything I ever saw - they truly did. She should have entered them in the state fair."

There was no jealousy in Luta's observation. Handwork was her passion. Trudy thought as she continued rocking, "Well, we all have to have our own specialties so's to hold our head high. Now take Earline Haglund - she undoubtedly makes the best pecan pie I ever sank a tooth into and loves to hear everyone brag about it. And Buddy...well he's gotta be the best hand in the world for a sick person or an animal, for that matter, next to a bonafide doctor. If the truth were known, I'd rather have him than most I've seen, and that includes Doc Dorsette and all the others from Crosstown to Gainesville."

"Good mornin', ladies. It's gonna be another hot one. Yes, another hot one." Bo Lutes made his morning greeting as he was leaving McCoy's Dry Goods Store. He was a trapper from down Ft. Fannin Springs way, three miles downstream and on the other side of the Suwannee.

"You gonna be back for the wedding, Bo?" Trudy inquired. "Wouldn't miss it, Miss Trudy. Wouldn't miss it for the world. This town's finally got itself on the map of Florida, thanks to Layke's capturing the Skinner Gang and helping rescue young Jonah - and then the hanging. Yep, it sure got its name in every paper in the whole state of Florida." He tipped his hat, mounted his horse, positioned the supplies he'd just purchased from McCoy's and headed south to the ferry landing to return to Ft. Fannin.

They both thought but didn't say, "And if Layke hadn't been the one who rescued Jonah, he and Berta probably wouldn't be getting married." There never was more hatred coming out of anyone as bad as out of Jonah McRae - and every bit of it aimed at Layke. Jonah had never accepted his father's death and would have done anything to keep Berta and Layke apart. But he sure changed his tune about his ma and Layke after he was kidnapped by the gang, and the despised Layke Williams was the one who saved him. Yep...he sure changed his attitude when he got the reward money and all that attention from the townspeople. Why, they treated him just like a hero, they did, 'cause he was brave enough to go after that terrible gang all by himself. Jonah took to smiling and acting real friendly like. Before all the commotion he almost never cracked a smile.

"And how about that Graves girl from down La Belle way being taken in by the traveling medicine show folks - the deMoyas? How about that, Trudy? I'll declare, Buddy and me were shocked." Juanita Jane Graves reportedly ran away with the Skinner Gang...or was she kidnapped? No one seemed to know for sure. The deMoyas had been kind enough to allow her to join them after the Skinner brothers were hanged, and when Layke and Berta had invited them to come to their ranch, South Spring, to make their wagon repairs before going on the road again, she had joined them. The whole town was aghast and the tongues wagged. "Imagine...that girl living at South Spring...imagine that!"

"Ain't it amazing, Luta?" Trudy inquired. "You know not a year's gone past since Layke rode Bucko into Old Town and tied him to that very hitching post there." She gestured to the twelve-foot rail fence Leander had sunk for her before the Conflict. "I never thought when I first laid eyes on his handsome face that my life and everyone else's would have been in for such a change, did you, Luta?" Trudy got all drifty eyed.

"Well, like you said when you first met him, 'Luta that young man sure has a hurt in his lonely heart.' Remember? And we wondered if there was anyone in town who could help him ease it. Well, we don't have to wonder anymore - I never saw such a change come over a man, did you?"

Bud called to Luta from the stable that was on the other side of McCoy's and sort of cattycornered, facing the boarding house.

"Now what!" Luta exclaimed as she eased down her handwork and rose to return her husband's wave. "I'll be there directly, Buddy. Are ya inna hurry?" she shouted.

"Oh fiddlesticks! Trudy. The way he's carryin' on I'll for certain sure ruin my stitches." She disgustedly put her pieces in her apron pocket and walked very erectly toward her beckoning husband.

Trudy chuckled and thought, "Mr. Buddy Brewster, it had better be a good one, or Luta'll get riled up if you're the cause of her delaying this gift for Berta. Yessiree...it'd better be a good one." She continued to rock, not taking her eyes off of the closed door that was directly beside the stable door and the entry to the Brewsters' living quarters. She knew Luta would be out of there and back on her porch in jig time if Bud's summoning wasn't important enough for her to set aside her needlework.

Trudy heard the Brewster door close hard. "Yep, she's riled up!" Luta came walking toward her, starch in her spine, and started with the "Well-I-nevers" even before she got to Trudy's porch.

"What on earth, Luta? Gracious me - what's the matter?"

"Trudy, I'll declare. Men have gotta be the most helpless creatures on God's earth - well I never!" She looked at Trudy hard, her brown eyes were sparking, and Trudy got to chuckling - couldn't seem to stop even when Luta started sputtering. "Buddy Brewster is undoubtedly the most particular man, I do declare, Trudy. That waistcoat I made - you know the one for the wedding...the blue brocade that came in on the *Suwannee Lady,* Trudy, you know - has that sorta curlicue design all over it. Well, Mr. Bud Brewster informed me that I got it too tight, and he's havin' some kinda conniption fit. You'd think that just 'cause Layke asked him to stand with him at the weddin' that he'd been crowned the king of England or something!"

Trudy was laughing so hard she almost fell off of her chair. Then Luta joined in and they both started their remembering - remembering of when Layke first got to Old Town and all the happenings since that dry, dusty evening in November of '77.

It was like only yesterday Trudy, reflected. He and his cow dog, Tag, arrived in a cloud of flying sand. When he got off of Bucko, she noticed his limp and found out later that he had been injured in the War and lost his two brothers in the battle of Chattanooga. She remembered that he said he wasn't hungry - just wanted a nice hot bath. But afterwards he came down those stairs with spring in his step and minus his dark brown beard. Oh, how handsome he was! Those all-color eyes sparkled with new life, and was he ever hungry! Why, he cleaned up that platter of taters, pone and slab, and Trudy chuckled as she pictured Tag doing the same when she and Layke gave him his supper on the front porch.

Frankie, Luta and Bud's son, brought his harmonica over to the porch like he did most every night and joined his pa, and the McCoy brothers, Palmer and Davis. Soon Luta joined them, and the men began the telling of the tales, as usual, while she and Luta snapped beans for the next day's dinner.

They told Layke about the widow, Berta McRae, needing help at her ranch, South Spring, and Trudy hoped she'd hire him on, because they needed new settlers to move into the area to add to the twenty or so families that were already spread up and down the Suwannee close to Old Town. But that wasn't the only reason Trudy wanted Berta to hire Layke. She knew how desperate and lonely Berta was and that she needed a man around to help with the cow hunt and spring drive to Punta Rassa.

When Layke retired early, Palmer told the congregation what

Bo Lutes had just told him about the mysterious cowman. It was a tale that was often told around the cow camps about when Layke gave up soldiering to become a cowman, and why he gave up his gun and got the reputation of being the best hand with a cow whip in the whole state of Florida and sorta wandered from ranch to ranch...searching...with that hurt look always in his eyes. Palmer had them glued to their chairs.

"But those days will soon come to an end," Trudy thought. "Now that he'll be master of South Spring with Berta beside him he'll go some place in this state. Yep, Layke will be someone big, 'cause I can still see the gnawin' justa clawin' at him. But oh the price they'll hafta pay. I sure hope it's worth it...I surely do."

BOOK ONE:

BERTA AND LAYKE

CHAPTER I SOUTH SPRING

Everyone was jubilant at South Spring - the air was electric. Even the white fluffy clouds danced more energetically in their deep blue surroundings, and the hens clucked with more fervor in their enclosure, seemingly aware of the upcoming event...the wedding. "No need for concern, Layke," Etienne deMoya exclaimed, his dark Cajun eyes excited. "Plan as lengthy a honeymoon as you and Berta wish." Layke put his arm around his friend's shoulder as they proceeded to the barn.

"It will give me a chance to train Cherie for the high rope," Etienne added. He glanced at Layke for any adverse reaction and saw none. Relieved that his friend had accepted Juanita, or as he preferred to call her, Cherie, he wished that Maman Orlean and his brother, Pierre, were as accommodating. They were very vocal in their reluctance to admit her as a member of their traveling medicine show, but Dom, his father, had shown little reaction. Aimee, the youngest and only daughter of the family, was so excited that she immediately began planning Cherie's costume for the tight rope act and had started referring to her as "sister". But Layke was noncommittal.

Layke's attitude toward Juanita was indeed of a mixed nature. He didn't trust the girl and believed that she had run away with the Skinner Gang and had not been kidnapped as she'd claimed. From what Jonah had told him, she was a wild one. He told Layke that he'd been more afraid of her than of the Skinner brothers, and that she had an evil streak the likes of which he'd never seen. But Layke could see that Etienne needed his approval, so refrained from adding his suspicions to Orlean's and Pierre's and decided not to mention to the smitten Etienne what Jonah had said.

"You can rest assured that Maman Orlean and Aimee will be honored to take care of Wes and SuSu while you're away. I'm sure you've observed how they've already warmed to them."

"I'm not the least hesitant about leaving South Spring, Etienne. Everything will be in good hands, I'm sure."

Layke was not concerned about the deMoyas' care of Berta's children, or the ranch for that matter, because he knew they were a very capable family, and he wasn't nervous about meeting Berta's relatives in Jacksonville. But he was very concerned about their proposed visit with the Wilpoles in Rowland's Bluff, up river and on the Suwannee. He had ridden range for the Wilpoles for three years prior to settling in Old Town and felt he had done a good job for Santa Fe, their ranch, and had been liked by the family. He had written John Wilpole about his planned marriage to Berta, his new position as master of South Spring and their desire to visit them while in Rowland's Bluff.

But Layke wasn't sure how Mrs. Wilpole would react to his new position. She'd probably think him a young upstart. "Master of South Spring...indeed!" she'd probably say.

He'd noticed that she was a very social sort and held her role as Mrs. John Anthony Wilpole with an elevated regard, but he hadn't let her aires bother him. But because Berta would be with him, he had naturally invited her to accompany her husband for dinner at the Arthur B. Hotel, the nicest one in town. Now, that meeting did concern him. He wanted everything to be perfect for his love. The main reason for the visit was his hope of soliciting their support for a ranching effort that he and some of the leading ranchers had discussed on the spring drive to Punta Rassa, and yes, he was nervous.

"I'll not let it upset our plans," he decided, pitching the fresh hay toward the mound in the corner. He had to keep busy. He was usually a calm man; he'd been a soldier's soldier and brave under fire, but the closer it got to his wedding day the more nervous he became, and Etienne sensed his friend's plight.

For the first time since the War Layke desired to give himself totally. It was frightening, this newness, this longing, but he was confident in Berta. Her sensitivity to his needs reassured his every decision, and at long last he was at peace with himself.

He was the youngest of three boys, army born and army bred. Discipline had been harsh but fair in the Williams household. The Bull, Layke's father, was a tough career soldier, and his three sons had followed in his footsteps. They had all attended The Citadel, the military college of the South in South Carolina's low country. When Layke's older brothers were killed at the battle of Chattanooga and he was injured at the Bentonville battle against Sherman just before the end of the Conflict, the Williams dynasty was over. Layke could not resume his army career. He left the army and Tennessee, a bitter and restless young man, and began his wandering life. It wasn't until twelve years later, after embracing a cowman's life in Florida, that he met Berta and knew his wandering days were over.

Berta had asked Trudy to stand with her, and Layke had received Bud's assurance that he'd keep him in line 'til after the "I dos" at their small wedding; just the local townspeople had been invited.

They had originally planned to take the steamship as far as Rowland's Bluff for their visit with the Wilpoles, and from there the stage coach to Lake City, where they'd board the train for Jacksonville. But after discussing it with Berta, Layke decided that he'd rather drive the buckboard, as uncomfortable as it was. Berta had never seen that part of Florida except the area that was visible from the steamships while on her trips on the Suwannee River. He wanted to share everything with her, the stillness, the silence that radiated from the never-ending savannahs and salt marshes, that caused you to hold your breath in reverence and wonder, their overwhelming solitude enveloping you like a caring mother's arms.

Etienne continued to talk about Layke's and Berta's proposed honeymoon trip to Jacksonville to visit her Uncle and Aunt, and trying to get his friend's mind off the actual wedding, he filled him with colorful stories of his family's adventures.

The deMoyas' medicine show had performed in that area of Florida many times since the War, and he regaled Layke with the interesting sights of the northeast section of the state. He animatedly spoke of the beautiful sternwheelers and sidewheelers that plied the St. Johns River between Jacksonville and Palatka on Layke's and Berta's proposed route. They planned to board one for their visit with their friends Mary and Pierce Garvin, who owned the Bullseye Ranch, located between Lake George and Crescent City south of Jacksonville.

Layke had been corresponding with Pierce. They had come to know each other quite well during the spring drive to Punta Rassa, and when Pierce told Layke of the breeding experiments he and Jordan Northrup had been conducting at their ranches with certain strains of cattle, Layke asked if he and Berta could visit Bullseye for a personal inspection of the new breed.

Mary, being curious about Layke - Lordy, she could hardly wait to see him - wrote immediately to invite the honeymooners to be their guests. Their timing was perfect, she said, because

Jordan planned to stop over at Bullseye en route to the state fair in Gainesville, and it would give the three cowmen an opportunity to discuss the plans they had set in motion in Punta Rassa regarding the expansion of the northern markets.

What she didn't say was how anxious she was to meet Berta. She had heard so much about her from Pierce through the years, and frankly, Bullseye could stand some excitement for a change. "I think if I havta listen to one more conversation about cows at the dinner table, I'm gonna put cotton in my ears," she had said to Pierce just the other day. "Oh, I'm so hungry for another female to talk to! Lordy, I can't believe how I've let Bullseye take over my life."

****

"You must not sample...dees are special for Meester Layke's and Mees Berta's wedding day. Now, go - go - go...be weet de men een de barn!" They heard Orlean shouting playfully to Wes, Berta's youngest child. He came scooting around the corner of the house, sand flying out behind his sturdy legs, with Pierre racing right behind him laughing so hard he had difficulty keeping up. Orlean and Aimee had been cooking for days, and the unusual spices they used intrigued everyone at South Spring. She was very secretive about her Cajun specialties, and when Wes asked for a bite she shooed him from the kitchen. Pierre, hiding behind the parlor door, quickly grabbed a couple of hot, spicy tarts, juggling them so as not to burn himself, and ran toward the barn.

Layke called, "Hurry up you two. I've been wanting to sample those tarts for days." He said it loudly so Orlean could hear him. She clucked her disapproval at the four of them but had a smile on her weathered face as she turned to join Aimee in the kitchen to resume their baking. Layke playfully grabbed hold of Wes, and with his arm around his shoulder, they munched on the hot tarts, then went into the barn to begin mucking the stall.

Orlean and Aimee had taken over the family cooking so Berta could make her traveling suit and pretty undergarments. But she couldn't seem to focus on anything for very long. Her nervous mind hopscotched all over creation.

She had written her Uncle Jock and Aunt Lawanda to ask if

they might visit them while in Jacksonville and was looking forward to it, because she had not seen them since right after the War ended. They responded immediately and said they were delighted that she and Layke would consider a visit with them and suggested that they seek passage on the beautiful new steamship, *Robert E. Lee*, for their trip on the St. Johns.

"Oh, I can hardly wait to see the *Robert E. Lee*! It must be spectacular!" Berta exclaimed excitedly to Orlean and Aimee. "Gracious me! I'm more excited about getting away from South Spring than about the actual wedding. Imagine!"

"Oh, Mees Berta, you and Meester Layke weel love Jacksonveel and de beeg boat. You do jus' fine. Nevair you fear. Jus' fine." Orlean smiled at Aimee, who also sensed Berta's nervousness.

"Everything must be perfect," Berta excitedly said as she viewed herself, turning this way and that as the blue silk of the jacket caressed her pale shoulders.

Berta had very carefully stored her beautiful petticoats, chemises and wedding finery from her marriage to Reuben in the big cedar chest. They were in nearly perfect condition, but most did not fit well. She was thinner than when she had married Reuben, but somewhat larger in her still-small waist from carrying those large McRae babies. But she was very clever with a needle and was able to redesign the pale pink, brushed satin nightgown and matching robe. The heavy ecru lace on the bodice of the French blue silk gown was in need of some mending, but it was hardly noticeable, she decided after careful examination.

Orlean approved the navy blue serge dress and matching jacket that Berta decided would just have to do for shipboard. "Aunt Lawanda is such a dear, I'm sure she'll be more than happy to take me shopping for ready-mades in the fine stores of Jacksonville."

"De shops along Bay Street are aplenty, Meesy, and I nevair seen such aplenty hats. Dom always slowed de wagons when we rode down Bay Street." Orlean filled Berta's already swimming head with the sights she'd witness in the busy city.

"You know, I've not been more than ten miles from here since Young Reuben and Jonah were babes and I returned to Macon for that three-weeks visit. Can you imagine, Orlean?"

Berta lapsed into quietness as she remembered how frightened she was. It was right after the War when it was finally safe to travel that Berta and the children had returned to Macon. Reuben had known how homesick she had been, and they had discussed her return numerous times but had never set a date.

When she received word from Macon that her mother was gravely ill, Reuben knew that she had to return immediately, and he made the necessary arrangements. He went to Fannin Springs to telegraph her Uncle Jock and her father of her planned arrival, knowing full well that they'd have to have one of their help to meet her, because the trains were never on time, and they might have as long as a half day's wait at the stations.

It had been a gray day as they stood on the landing in Old Town. The wind had picked up and was rattling the cabbage palms that lined the banks of the Suwannee. "Funny - but I can still hear their incessant noise," she thought. Young Reuben kept pulling her, his small hand strong with determination. Jonah, who was really too heavy for her to carry, was squirming trying to join his older brother. There was no sign of the sternwheeler, and the boys were antsy.

Reuben's voice came to her so clearly. She could feel him beside her. "Now, hon, you mustn't fret. There is simply nothing you can do but put her in the hands of the Almighty. I just pray you are allowed time with her. Now, now, Berta...don't!" She wasn't going to cry, she remembered. She was almost as concerned about the tiring trip with two young babes and leaving Reuben as about her mother's condition, for she had been preparing herself ever since she had received word from her sister, Lamorah.

"Reuben, it's not that, really it isn't. You know Lamorah said she wasn't well the last time we heard, and I've been expecting it - really I have, hon. It's just that it's been so long since I've been home...or anywhere else, I guess, and I sort of feel scared, like I'm unable to handle anything. I'm just not used to being away from you. Guess I'm a little frightened, honey. I'm sorry."

She remembered touching his worried face and reaching up to kiss him gently on his cheek. Reuben held her free hand, took the wiggling Jonah from her and put his arm around her slight shoulders, holding her close to him.

There were several other townspeople witnessing the farewell, but they kept their distance so that she and Reuben could be alone. Word travels rapidly in a small settlement, and when Reuben had returned from telegraphing Berta's kin to expect her, he stopped by Stucky's to inform Trudy of Berta's journey. Trudy was already aware of Berta's ma's condition and knew that she would be going to Macon. Ben Thrower had stopped by on his way from South Spring and told her the news. There weren't many secrets in Old Town.

****

Layke sat on the edge of his narrow cot. Tag was asleep in the corner of the nearly empty room. All was right with his world at last, he thought. When he left the Tennessee hills, a thin, bitter, nearly destitute young man, there was no way he could have envisioned the happiness he had been allowed these last few weeks. To find a wonderful woman like Berta and to be able to stop his wandering were more than he'd ever hoped for. And the pride he felt in being privileged to manage South Spring - well - he felt overwhelmed.

He rose from his cot admonishing himself for his lazy daydreaming. Tag followed suit. He didn't get up quite as fast as he once did, but as before wherever Layke went, he still tagged along. They wandered down to the side yard to join Wes and SuSu, who spent every waking hour excitedly watching Juanita, while Etienne patiently taught her how to walk the tight rope.

Layke was not particularly fond of her, but, along with the other onlookers, marveled at her patience while listening to Etienne praise her every tiny improvement. When Layke witnessed her amazing endurance and tenacity, he felt that perhaps he had not given Juanita the proper respect.

Etienne and Pierre had strung a rope between the two large oak trees in the side yard. Etienne would lift dainty Juanita up, and Pierre was on the alert to catch her if she fell before reaching the other side. Each day the rope would be raised a few inches. Aimee, when not needed by Orlean in the kitchen, would also assist with the instructions, and her youthful enthusiasm could be heard all over South Spring.

Every morning after breakfast Juanita would accompany Etienne to the rope and begin her hours of intense practice. The only let up was midday during their dinner and rest time. Then back she would go for more of the same meticulous, labored movements with the unrelenting Florida heat clamoring to unleash her restrained frustration.

Proudly Etienne announced to the gathering, "Cherie's progress has been utterly unbelievable. By the time our honeymooners return and we begin our traveling, ma Cherie should be ready for the twenty-foot height and her debut."

Aimee ran up to her and hugged her, exclaiming, "Oh, Juanita, I'll have your costume ready by the night we open in Rowland's Bluff. Don't you fret. It'll take only a few more weeks of attaching the bugle beads."

The sisterly pride Aimee had in Juanita's accomplishments was shared only by Etienne. Dour Pierre, who never had a kind word to say to her, or a glance that was not a scowl, agreed reluctantly.

"Yes, Juanita, you've been doing real well," and he actually allowed a pleasant smile to escape.

Juanita was beside herself with joy when Etienne announced the news. She hadn't been feeling well lately and was having difficulty concentrating on her balance as the insufferable heat took its toll.

"Guess I just need a good spring tonic like Ma used to give me," she thought. "My, I haven't thought of Ma a single time since I left La Belle - not a single time." But she felt no guilt as she proceeded with her practice. Juanita never looked backward. She effortlessly blocked out the hanging and every other unhappiness in her young life.

She could feel her eyes tearing as she scanned the approving faces surrounding her, but Juanita knew the acceptance was fleeting, so she shrugged her proud shoulders and immediately averted her eyes.

Etienne's strong hand was hot on her arm. She felt his restrained yearning and understood his reluctance to show it. He could not allow his family to know how he longed to hold her in his powerful arms and love her as a man should love a woman. But he knew the time was not right. Until Maman Orlean and Pierre accepted her, he must be strong for all their sakes. Cherie was too important to him to allow this treasured love to be tarnished. It must be without a blemish, beyond reproach. He would continue to be patient.

So he smiled down and said simply, "Cherie, you make me very proud."

At that moment a vulnerable golden girl truly and unselfishly loved. It passed quickly. Reality and self preservation had been her accomplices too long to allow his loving warmth to penetrate her armor. She would not be his woman, she decided emphatically! She ran for the safety of the wagon.

Not again! Not so soon! R. J. Skinner's devilish grin alerted her subconscious of the impending danger and bolstered her determination. He was so real, this ghost of a man.

"Maybe R. J. didn't die after all. Maybe they just said he died. No! I saw him with my very own eyes. I saw his wet britches twirling round and round on that hanging tree. I saw it!"

****

Berta awakened very early. She lay quietly, barely moving in her thin muslin gown. Her mind restlessly flitting from one inconsequential happening to another, never fixing itself for even a moment.

"Dear Lord in the morning! Why am I so restless? This should be the most perfect day in my life...my wedding day."

She immediately thought of Layke. "I wonder if he's awake and if he's as restless as I? I wonder what your thoughts are on this special day, my husband?"

Lazily, she curled up under the light sheet and turned on her side facing the drab, faded wallpaper. She remembered when the cabbage roses had been so bright and cheerful that they helped lighten the otherwise dull life at South Spring. Berta allowed her thoughts to ease back to her wedding night with Reuben. It was vivid now, where as just a short time before it had been blurred, hazy, beyond recall.

Oh, she had been so very young and innocent, and goodness knows, she was totally inexperienced. "Reuben, bless his heart, knew it. And he was so understanding." She could still remember their drawing room with the low ceiling and walls covered with deep red brocade. The plush seats, when pulled out, made a very comfortable bed. She closed her eyes and slightly smiled, allowing the bygone impressions to form again.

She did not become Reuben's wife until after leaving Uncle Jock's and Aunt Lawanda's home in Jacksonville. They had nervously talked, non-stop all the way from Macon to Savannah, holding each other lovingly, tenderly, and had continued their journey on the Florida, Atlantic & Gulf Central Railroad from Jacksonville to Lake City. By then they were so comfortable with each other that their love-making was beautifully natural.

Berta sighed, then began smiling devilishly to herself, and said profoundly as she leaped from her bed, "Today's my wedding day, and there will be no delaying my becoming Layke's wife - of that I'm positive!"

She blushed as she covered her smile. "I'm grateful that you don't know what I'm thinking, Layke Williams. I'm sure you'd think me very unladylike, but I'm enjoying every minute of it," she thought as she removed her floral wrapper from the foot of the bed. She draped it over her bare shoulders and went barefoot into the kitchen.

Layke abruptly rose from the ladder-back chair, knocking it over in his anxiousness. Berta flew into his waiting arms. He kissed her eyes, her cheeks, then hungrily on her eager, moist lips. After a forever-seeming time, Berta breathlessly pushed him away.

"Is this a preview of what I may expect tonight, Sir?" He threw his dark mane back and laughed heartily.

"No, Madam, not even a smattering of what you can expect. I have ordered something for Madam Williams that is very special."

Berta looked very serious when she gazed into his laughing eyes and exclaimed, "This is undoubtedly going to be the longest day of my entire life, Layke Williams. I wish we could be alone right now ...this very minute."

"Not more than I, darling. Not more than I..."

When Wes came paddling into the kitchen, they were again in each others arms. She felt his small hand pull at her wrapper, and she broke away. Looking down at her precious towheaded son and back to reality, she said, "Wes, do you want Ma to scramble your eggs?" The magic was gone, but the lingering warmth remained.

****

Jonah had stayed in Old Town with Trudy. Berta was so busy making preparations that Trudy asked her and Jonah if it wouldn't be the best thing to do, and because the deMoyas would be at South

Spring during Berta's and Layke's absence, Trudy suggested that he stay with her until the honeymooners returned. She and Jonah had always got along, and this way she could look after him, for he was still not fully recovered from his ordeal. Besides, Jonah was hesitant to be around Juanita. He didn't trust her and was very vocal about it.

Young Reuben was to arrive early from up Rose Head way for the wedding, and he and Jonah could have a nice visit at the boarding house while Berta, Orlean and Layke completed their many tasks. Jonah had always been quiet, but Trudy Stucky had a way of bringing out anyone. He would talk his heart out to Trudy. She had seen a tremendous change in him since the kidnapping, and it was a change for the better, she thought. He was relaxed, and it wasn't because he was still weak. He smiled easily. It was as if a tremendous burden had been lifted from his young, inexperienced shoulders.

Jonah had missed his youth...no time for coming to town for the week's end...no time to visit friends his own age...no time to dream a young man's dreams. He was put into the position of the father's role at age thirteen when Young Reuben went to Rose Head, and he just didn't have the temperament or strength for it.

Maybe he did have some of his uncle Elon's devil in him, but with love and caring and guidance from a wonderful man like Layke, well, Trudy thought, Jonah McRae will be an asset to Old Town yet. The attention he's been getting from the townspeople has performed a miraculous cure already, better than any Elixir of Life. He's like a sponge. Every compliment and grateful comment has made him understand the good people around here and the role he's played in their happiness. Like Frankie said yesterday, "I've seen Jonah smile more in the last week than I've seen since I've known him, and heck, I've known him all his borned days."

As she pondered the situation sitting and rocking in the cool of the evening on her front porch she thought to herself, "Now he can be a young man and make all the mistakes he's supposed to and go back to school. I know his dad is smiling about the turn of events. Yep, Reuben would smile."

The young men of the area had started visiting on Trudy's front porch after supper to hear Jonah tell of his harrowing experience. He was getting to be quite a good story teller, too,

Trudy observed. "Pretty soon he'll out-do James Lutes." He was a celebrity, one of the few Old Town could boast of or lay a claim to, and he appeared comfortable in his new position.

When Young Reuben arrived, hot, tired and red-eyed from the long trip from Rose Head, Trudy didn't recognize him. He was a man grown, taller than Reuben had been with more of Berta's coloring. He had filled out real good, and when he flashed that big white-toothed smile and opened his arms to Trudy and in Reuben's wonderfully melodious voice said, "Why, Miss Trudy, you get prettier every time I see you. Come, give this old Scot a hug," she was in those steel-like arms as quick as a cat. She pushed him back and got a real good gander at that big, open, love-everybody, uncomplicated face.

"Didn't know you 'til you gave me that Reuben grin, I'll declare I didn't. You've up and grown up on us, Young Reuben."

He spun her matronly body around, swatted her on her behind and declared to the entire town that had gathered beside the porch to watch, "This is my best girl, who can still out-cook every living soul, or at least she used to lay claim to that distinction. Now, I want her to prove it," and he laughed along with the assembled crowd.

Bud Brewster spoke up and said, "Young Reuben, she'd skin ya alive if'n ya said otherwise. I just happen to know, cause my cat told me, that she's got a mess of the prettiest fried speckled perch you're likely to see and some hushpuppies to down 'em with. I'd bet Luta on it."

Trudy loved the sport they were having with her. She turned to Young Reuben and reached up on her fat tiptoes to catch his ear as she dragged him into her welcoming kitchen. She sent Frankie, who had followed them, up to Jonah's room to fetch him downstairs for his surprise. But no one had to fetch Jonah. He pushed past Frankie, and he and Young Reuben were in a brotherly bear hug even before Trudy got the fire stoked up for the coffee to heat.

They didn't say a word. Just round and round they went, hugging each other. Young Reuben had been gone for a little over two years and had not been back to Old Town or South Spring in all that time. He'd been doing a man's job for a man's pay all the time he'd worked on the Oliver spread just south of Rose Head.

Some said it was to be near Sam Oliver's youngest daughter, Leonora, but Trudy knew it was also to help Berta and South Spring that he loved. Young Reuben had a love of the land in his heart just like his pa. He was a good cowman.

He and Jonah sat wolfing down Trudy's bountiful dinner. "I'll declare, Jonah, it took a visit from your big brother to get you to eat again," Trudy interjected in between their palavering.

Jonah was retelling his tale, and Young Reuben made all the right gestures and comments just exactly like his pa would have done, Trudy observed. Young Reuben pushed back his chair, went to the corner of the kitchen and pulled a straw out of Trudy's titi broom and sat patiently picking his teeth while Jonah enthusiastically came to the climax of his tale, the part when Layke Williams picked him up in his strong arms and carried him to the grassy knoll beside the lake. Trudy was watching Young Reuben's face to see if there was an adverse reaction when Jonah mentioned Layke, his soon-to-be stepfather. None showed.

"Well, little brother, you had yourself quite a time," and he patted Jonah on the head in a fatherly way. Jonah opened his big brown eyes up toward the now standing Reuben.

"Did anyone tell you about the hanging, Young Reuben? I was right up there on the wagon," and as he rushed to tell him, Young Reuben put his hand on Jonah's arm.

"Hey, you've got to save some of this for after supper, Jonah. I've got to get Cloud over to Bud's. He threw a shoe just before I got here."

"That's a good idea, Young Reuben. Frankie can tell about the hanging real good. But you know him, it takes a week from Sunday to get to the good parts, he's so slow talking," and they chuckled together as Jonah walked with Reuben out to the porch and his horse Cloud. Trudy stood at the porch door and watched the two of them.

She wiped her hands on her soiled, spattered apron and returned to her kitchen. The Brewster cat was waiting patiently at her back door for the crisp fried perch tails and fins she knew Trudy would have for her.

"You've done a good job, Berta McRae. A fine job. Reuben would be proud of you."

CHAPTER II REUBEN

Reuben and the Swede - no one around Old Town but his family knew his given name - who owned the North Prong Ranch northeast of South Spring, and Charlie Beattie, who had a spread across the Suwannee and south of them and was more of a preacher and farmer than a rancher, were assigned to the "Cattle Guard", commonly called the "Cow Cavalry" during the War. Berta and the other wives were relieved that their menfolk were allowed time at home and had not been sent into the heavy fighting up north, but they knew that their job was dangerous, nevertheless.

Their main duty was to drive the cattle from central Florida to the railheads, where they were shipped to Charleston, one of the principal Confederate depots. Some of the ranchers in south Florida had managed to break through the Union blockade that had been thrown up around the state and sold their beeves to Cuba in exchange for coffee, tea and other hard-to-get goods. But most were driven on the old trails, the ones that had been used during the three Seminole Wars and widened by the U. S. military when they transported their supplies to the various forts. The cattle were headed towards railheads in Baldwin, Madison, Stockton and Sanderson and the other cow pens along the Pensacola-Florida Railroad and destined for Charleston and the starving troops.

Reuben, the Swede, and Charlie, plus some of the drivers who had been spared from General Bragg's Army, were detailed to take charge of the herds in and around Old Town and from as far south as the Ft. Meade district near Bartow, where they'd sometimes drive as many as 400 beef cattle all the way to Savannah instead of the closer railheads. It was a harrowing experience, for Union raiding parties were everywhere; they were desperate to stop the shipment of beef. It was 1863 and Florida was the one remaining source of beef for the Confederacy, because Texas and the rich grazing country west of the Mississippi were cut off by the Union. They felt their job was more important than joining up with the rest of the Old Towners under Gen. Finegan.

South Spring was a typical Florida ranch with a small, steep-roofed, heart-pine house and the usual out buildings: smoke house, barn, out-house and chicken coop. It was a smoothly run ranch even during the War. The chicken coop was attached to the barn and next to the vegetable garden. Berta always kept a couple of dozen layers around and a few bantams for the boys to play with, so there were plenty of eggs for eating and for the setting hens. Everything grown at South Spring was shared with the colored families, Rosie's rich milk included. Myrtice milked her and did the washing while her sister Willa, Big Dan's wife, tended the garden and helped Berta in the house. The jobs had never been delegated to either. They just seemed to fall into the jobs they liked doing best. When soap and candle making time arrived, they all participated.

As in the past they had planted a small patch of cotton for their quilts, sugar cane for syrup, a patch of tobacco, and had managed to keep a good garden, but coffee and tea were as scarce as hens' teeth and could be bought only on the black market from the suppliers who managed to get to the West Indies or Cuba. A drink was made from parched sweet potatoes or roasted rye, and they also boiled yaupon leaves to make a brew like the Indians had used in their ceremonies. It had been called "black draught" by the early settlers. But as Berta had said, "This'll do for now, but it sure doesn't take the place of a good cup of coffee or tea. "

The men kept them in fish and wild game and had resorted to trapping. Ammunition was scarce and was saved for any unexpected visit from a deserter or Union soldiers. Even the spinning wheel had been brought down from the attic and put to use once more. Ezekiel, husband to Myrtice, supervised the cane squeezing and making the home brew, and he kept a watchful eye on their mule, Lucifer, and the oxen, Jimbo and William. Big Dan butchered the hogs and smoked the meat in the smoke house down the knoll near his and Willa's house. He guarded those remaining hogs just like a new mom did her babe and hoarded every speck of salt they could manage to get from the salt works near the mouth of the Suwannee.

They were very alert, for you never knew when some half-starved deserter would come sneaking around the place; plus bear, panthers and wolves were a constant threat. It was a very tense time for all the settlers who were left by their menfolk.

When Berta first got to South Spring, just a young bride, she had asked Myrtice how long they had lived there. "Wees always been here, Missy," was her reply. But Berta could tell that Big Dan was part Indian, and she and Trudy had discussed their background.

A lot of families who had migrated to Florida during the first part of the century and homesteaded large tracts of land had brought their slaves with them. Trudy figured that the family who owned Dan's parents had been killed in one of the Seminole Wars, and the slaves had been taken captive. They were probably freed when the Seminoles were either driven farther south or killed, and the slaves returned to the Old Town area where they had lived previously. They had been there as long as anyone in and around Old Town knew about, and Dan was definitely part Indian - beautiful features and not as black as most. He was almost 6'4" but very graceful in his movements. He could break any horse around, and Reuben had said that he was an excellent woodsman. But he was oh so gentle. Willa wore the pants in the family.

Ezekiel was shorter than Dan but wiry and as lazy as they come. But Berta loved that man - he kept her amused. He was wily and clever but not devious. He'd tell Myrtice that he was going to the main house. She assumed it was to assist Berta and Layke. But he'd always find something to whittle on as he practiced a bird's call or a panther's scream. Reuben had seen his talent with a knife, so he'd had him finish the tables and chairs he'd made out of the beautiful red cedar, that was abundant all along the Suwannee. The demand for the cedar in the northern pencil factories before the War had been great and was a means of easy money for the area settlers. They'd fell the trees, rope the logs together, and with the help of a tug boat raft them down the river and into the Gulf to Cedar Key for shipment north.

Ezekiel took pleasure in making anything for Berta and Reuben. He had finished the chest where Berta kept her pretty things, inlaid designs in a scalloped panel on the top and scrolled the legs. Berta had never seen a prettier one, not in the shops in Savannah or anywhere. He was an artist with his old whittling knife. But to Willa he was just plain lazy. She could manipulate Dan and even her sister, but Zeke danced to his own tune. Willa never could understand why Berta got a smile on her face when she looked at Zeke. The fact that he lightened Berta's heavy load with his shenanigans never entered her mind. She just thought the young Missy was being misled by that lazy, no-account man.

The McRaes had been warned by the soldiers who came through South Spring to move in closer to Old Town for their own protection, but Berta, Young Reuben and Jonah remained at South Spring. They had discussed her moving into town to stay with Trudy, but she felt she was needed at home to look after everything. It was a frightful time for her. Confederate deserters, who'd steal anything in sight that last year of the War, were more feared than the Union raiding parties, and she and the old colored families were in constant fear, especially when Reuben was gone.

There was no way she could have envisioned that unforgettable day when Reuben and the Cow Cavalry, as it turned out, were on their last drive to Savannah and certainly no way she could have prepared for it. Jonah had been fretful since morning. She thought he was just teething, but come dusk he just couldn't seem to settle. Nothing she did eased his suffering. Aunt Willa could hear him all the way from her house, so toward dark she wandered up the knoll and rapped on the kitchen door as she called.

"Miss Berta, it's Willa. You be needin' hep with Master Jonah?"

No answer. Again..."Miss Berta, it's Willa. " Still no answer. She could hear the cows lowing in the large pens. Reuben had built them close to the barn in order to prepare a rich garden spot for planting. They were unusually restless, she thought, and decided to go back home to tell Dan that he'd better have a look, 'cause there might be a wolf or wildcat around. She didn't see her brother-in-law, Ezekiel, sneaking in the shadows beside the barn and snickering at her as he ducked inside. Outwitting his sister-in-law was almost as much fun as fishing or whittling when he should have been workin'. She knew he had to be the laziest nigger she had ever known and so informed him and her sister Myrtice every chance she got.

Ezekiel curled up on the mound of hay in the far corner of the barn and proceeded to go fast asleep. He had a satisfied smile on his face as he quickly eased into his favorite pastime.

"Now, now, Jonah. Now, now, honey," Berta said softly rocking him slowly and singing so that she didn't hear Willa's call and thinking that if she didn't get him settled down soon, she would just have to get Willa. Myrtice was good enough with the boys, but Willa was a take-charge person, and Berta just had more confidence in her.

She could hear the cows lowing. "Now what on earth?" she sighed tiredly. She got up from the rocker and turned to Young Reuben to shush him before he spoke aloud, for Jonah was almost asleep. She took his small hand and went into the kitchen. Peering out the window through the fading light she tried to see what was causing the commotion. She saw Willa walking toward her own house and started toward the kitchen stoop to hail her. But when she got there she realized she'd not be heard, so she returned to the kitchen. She had not seen Ezekiel sneak into the barn.

Jonah began howling.

"Well, young man, I'm at my wits' end," she informed the red-faced youngster as she placed him in his crib, sturdy legs kicking hard and not about to be consoled.

"Here, Young Reuben. You and your mama have to get those eggs before some hungry varmint beats us to 'em," she said lightheartedly. Just seeing Willa close by lightened her concern, and she dismissed the cattle's noise.

Berta and Young Reuben, hand in hand, opened the door to the chicken coop. When they examined the nests and found no eggs, she assumed that Willa had collected them. But it was strange that she had brought none to the main house, she thought.

"Well, maybe she's making a special cake or something - no, we're almost out of flour and no telling when we'll see any again. Oh, I'll ask her in the morning." But as she thought that, she could hear Jonah still screaming his lungs out.

"Maybe we'd better go down to Aunt Willa's, Young Reuben. Bet she's already gathered the eggs." She could see how disappointed he was. It was one of the chores she could share with him, and he was learning his numbers by counting the eggs and also learning how to hold things gently.

"Mama...Rosie. Rosie is upset," he said loudly. "No, Young Reuben. That's not Rosie. The cows in the pen are restless and...wait a minute. I think you're right. I think that is Rosie. Myrtice didn't mention that anything was wrong with her."

"Well, alright," she said smiling down at his up-turned face. She figured that he had not had the satisfaction of finding any eggs and counting them, so he wanted to go pet sweet, gentle Rosie in her stall. After all, he had spent most of the day listening to his younger brother cry, and she hadn't had much time with him.

"Poor Young Reuben. Have I neglected you?" she chortled as she hugged him to her and they unsuspectingly walked into the barn. Rosie was indeed restless. Berta's senses became very acute. The beeves were obviously disturbed - there were no eggs in the nests, and now contented Rosie was not herself.

She inhaled slowly as she began looking around holding Young Reuben's hand hard until he yelped. "Mama!"

"Shush!" she said, her forefinger moving quickly to her closed lips. He seemed to sense that he shouldn't prevail. Berta swallowed, slowly at first, then more quickly as she scanned the shadowed barn. She saw nothing, but she felt that there was something amiss. Her hand was trying to soothe Rosie as she looked to the left - nothing but tack and bales of hay. She looked toward the end of the barn - nothing. Suddenly hay fell from above, and she instinctively looked up toward the loft. She glimpsed the sole of a worn boot.

"Oh my God!" Her hand went quickly to her mouth. "What should I do?" She couldn't seem to stop her heavy breathing, almost gasping. She knew she couldn't panic. She began to talk to Young Reuben and Rosie. "Rosie, you're fine, girl. Just a sore teat, I think. Son, let's go see how Jonah is doing. Your father's due any minute," she lied, "and he'll want his supper hot and his baby quiet. Come on, Young Reuben," she pulled him with her, not daring to look toward the loft.

Ezekiel was awake now and quietly taking all this in as he huddled deeper into the hay. He decided that he'd best be mouse quiet until Miss Berta was back in the house. But he couldn't figure why she had said that the master was coming home soon. He knew that he'd left just a few days before and that this was to be one of the longest drives of the War, 'cause he had given him and Dan very strict orders about the do's and don't's of running South Spring.

As Berta and Young Reuben came dashing outside she was relieved to see Willa leading Big Dan toward her. They could see that she was frightened, but using their heads they didn't yell to inquire why.

Berta began acting out a charade. . a soldier and gun. Young Reuben began giggling, and Berta told him to shush. Big Dan understood and loped back toward his cabin to get his gun. When she screamed he stopped dead in his tracks...then whirled around.

She could feel the filthy hand hard on her mouth, and he had his smelly arms clasped tightly around her. Young Reuben was sent sprawling in the dirt as he shoved him away from Berta.

Willa ran to him and big as you please said, "Don' ya nevah harm dat baby, Mistah...not nevah! I'se don' care who ya is. Dat baby best not come to any harm!" She picked Young Reuben up and brushed him off while staring her hatred at the soldier before her.

Berta could see his ragged uniform and knew he was a half-crazed Confederate deserter. Even when Big Dan boldly walked toward him, he did not release her. He just kept shaking his gun with his free hand and yelling, "Don't ya take another step, Nigger. Can't ya see this gun?"

He dragged Berta into the barn. But Big Dan did not slow down and kept coming toward him. Berta knew he'd use the gun - he was desperate. They were now all in the barn. Willa clasped Young Reuben protectively to her, and he began to cry. The sun had lost its light, and it was now almost dark inside. All at once, out of nowhere, a booming voice spoke.

"Thou shalt not kill!" it said. Again..."Thou shalt not kill!" Berta could feel the soldier's arm go limp. He pushed her away from him. She scrambled toward Willa and Young Reuben, pulling him close to her.

Again the deep voice, "Thou shalt not steal!" once, then again. Big Dan's eyes were huge white orbs in his black face. He was looking everywhere to see where the voice was coming from, his head twisting, turning, his mouth opened in disbelief. The deserter saw Big Dan's fright, dropped his gun, and as he ran from the barn, fell, picked himself up, then fell again as he scurried away from that voice and continued as fast as he could into the wooded area east of the barn, not taking time to look back.

"Missus, you be all right?" Ezekiel shouted as he rushed out of the dark corner of the barn.

"Ezekiel! What on earth!" It finally dawned on her that it was Ezekiel mimicking the Lord, and Berta began to laugh. It was a relieved laugh, and Willa, who didn't take to her lazy brother-in-law, began slapping him on the back and laughing so hard she just about bent double.

Berta had known that Zeke had a talent for mimicking animals, birds and folks, too, but it never occurred to any of them that the voice was coming from him. She knew that he loved to sneak in the barn and crawl up in a dark corner. Myrtice thought he was up at the main house helping the Master and Missus, but he'd be curled up practicing Reuben's voice or Preacher Townsend's or anyone else he'd heard. Berta had always been amused by his antics, so she'd never let on to them.

When Reuben returned from the drive she was excitedly relating the story. When he asked what they would have done had Zeke not played God and scared the deserter away, Berta said that Big Dan figured that the gun wasn't loaded, 'cause if he had had bullets, then the varmint wouldn't have had to come around there stealing their eggs. He'd've been eating squirrel or rabbit. And sure enough, when he checked the gun, it was empty.

Reuben just shook his head, then raised it toward the heavens and thanked the Lord for his protection of these innocent children. If the scoundrel had had bullets he'd have saved them for his own protection from the wolves and bear that hovered in the woods and would have stolen the chickens just like he had attempted. But he decided not to inform Berta of his opinion, and together, arm in arm, they went to their room.

Dan hung that gun above his fireplace some fourteen years ago and it was there yet. Every time Berta visited them and saw the gun she relived that frightful night.

Reuben hadn't been home for more than a week when orders came to head for St. Andrew's Bay in the panhandle area of the state. By the time he and the twenty regulars had arrived, the U. S. Marines had already attacked the largest salt works and demolished the site. There were several more sites dotted all along the Bay, where as many as 400 barrels of salt were produced daily, for salt was as precious a commodity as beef, and knowing that that part of the state was the Confederacy's most important salt source in Florida, they headed for them without delay.

When they got to the first site, the marines had already arrived and had mounted a howitzer on a barge and thrown a dozen shells before Reuben and his men realized that they were outnumbered four to one and could not counter attack with just their Henry rifles. They high-tailed it out of there and barely escaped with their lives; two were wounded, and by the time they got to the nearest farmhouse for help, Joe Morris from down Otter Creek way had lost so much blood that he lasted only the night. It was Reuben's closest call during the War, he often said, and added that his wife had been in much more danger than he right there in South Spring.

****

Reuben McRae died the morning after his 41st birthday. He died a happy man. The spring drive to Punta Rassa had been his most successful, and all was right with his world. Berta and his four children were healthy, happy and, along with South Spring, his life. He had no enemies, no debts, and a future filled with promise. But he died a young man.

Reuben's birthday was filled with things he enjoyed most. He was surrounded by his family, the colored people on the place, Bud and Luta Brewster and son Frankie - Bethy had not arrived as yet - and Trudy. They arrived from Old Town early in the afternoon, a typical summer day, warm with a gentle breeze off the river.

He and his oldest sons had been fishing and caught a string of cats and bream and spent a lazy day on the river, while Berta, assisted by Willa and Myrtice, had prepared his favorite dinner: baked fresh ham surrounded by sugared sweet potatoes with glazed pecans, fresh blackeyed peas, turnip greens with roots, cut sweet corn with baby limas, pickled beets, watermelon rinds and tiny okra pods, baby green onions and Willa's golden corn bread. Myrtice had baked his favorite dessert, southern lemon pie, and heaped it high with Rosie's rich cream. Yes, all was right with his world.

Myrtice had spread a sparkling white cloth on the long table underneath the oaks in the side yard and set the table with Berta's wedding china and silver. SuSu helped her mother gather the snapdragons, zinnias and daisies from the front flower bed, that Berta arranged in the beautiful crystal pitcher that had been her grandmother Augusta's and brought from Georgia almost fifteen years before. SuSu was also detailed to keep Wes occupied - he was only two at the time - so her mother could supervise the preparations, and she was having trouble confining active Wes to the quilt that Berta had spread in the shade of the spreading oak.

Reuben and the boys finally arrived, and Berta sent them packing to the pump for a wash up. Big Dan relieved them of their catch stating, "Mister Reuben, here, I'll take dese scrawny lil fish off'n yore hands. Ya'd think that on yore day the Laud would'a sent ya some keepers. Why, dese ain' big enuf' fo' even ole mama cat," and he laughed along with the others who were having sport with Reuben. But he took it in his stride, as he always did, and joined in the merriment. He was even tempered like his mother and saw no reason to waste energy on something he couldn't control, a very practical man.

Berta called them together. "Oh, Willa, I forgot the lemonade. Would you be a dear and fetch it? Well, we're all together, Reuben." She took his hand, looked down at his smiling face and said, "Your family and your dearest friends wish you the happiest of birthdays, and may our bountiful Lord grant you many more." They all clapped as Reuben rose and put his hands skyward. "Oh, please, dear, don't make it a long one - everything will get cold," Berta admonished him.

Reuben was a talker and she dearly loved to hear him, but not today. She had worked into the night preparing the food and was understandably tired. She was very proud of his popularity as a dramatic reader at the church and school socials and knew how important the recognition was to him.

"Now Berta," he began, and they all knew he'd be especially long-winded, so she settled back as did the others on the smooth wooden benches. When he began with the "Many years ago - it's been 14 plus now - Berta and I arrived at our beautiful South Spring. " Young Reuben rolled his eyes at Jonah, stood tall, and with arms raised in a Reuben-like gesture began,

"Breathes there a man with soul so dead
Who never to himself hath said,
This is my own, my native land!"

"Shush, Young Reuben. This is your father's day and he is entitled to recite Sir Walter Scott if he wants to," Berta said, but soon joined in their laughter.

Finally Trudy said, "For heaven's sake, Reuben, let's eat! You can do your recitations afterwards. We'll even let you do Hiawatha.

Afterwards they all gathered on the front porch. The men smoked their pipes, and Reuben, at Trudy's request, recited her favorite from "The Lady of The Lake."

Hail to the chief who in triumpth advances!
Honored and blest be the evergreen pine!

When he got to the part, "*Row, vassals, row for the pride of the Highlands!*"...Trudy asked him to stop. Oh, how she loved it when he got to that part! Now was the time to give it to him. She had ordered "The Complete Works of Sir Walter Scott", and it had arrived on the stern wheeler, *Suwannee Queen*, only a few days before. She had been so afraid it would be late. When she presented it to Reuben, he cried unashamedly with joy, and Berta, to temper his emotion, signaled everyone to bring out their presents one by one starting with the Darkies.

Big Dan and Ezekiel brought up their gifts. Zeke had carved a beautiful pipe of cherry in the shape of a dolphin, and Dan had painstakingly woven a new bridle for Blackie out of supple, tanned leather. Willa had made a down-filled pillow, and Myrtice embroidered a pillow case for it with the McRae crest in burgundy, loden green and regency gold.

Bud and Luta gave him a can of his favorite aromatic tobacco that the McCoys had ordered all the way from Lake City, and young Frankie had reamed out a turkey bone, soaking it in lye water, to be used as a turkey caller for his hunting.

Diligently the river banks were searched for just the right bamboo fishing poles; straight and long, by Young Reuben and Jonah. SuSu, with the help of her mother, cross stitched a handkerchief. Berta had made a soft wool, maroon muffler with deep fringe to ward off the damp cold for when he'd be on the range searching for a bunch quitter.

The children had been asleep for hours, and the colored people had long since gone to their own homes as he and Berta waved their adieus, bidding their friends goodnight as they saw them on their way back to Old Town. He retired hand in hand with his love.

****

Berta awakened at first light as always and was surprised that Reuben was still asleep. "Oh well, he had a big day yesterday. I'll let him rest a little longer," she thought as she went to her kitchen to light the wood cook stove and start the water for coffee.

Wes hadn't awakened yet, so she'd have time to get the water herself and wouldn't need to awaken the boys, she decided, as she went out into the early morning mist. The dew-edged trees and the beaded grass sparkled with the new light. Her favorite time of day, she thought. Only the cocks and the early birds were awake already heralding their awakening messages for all their kingdom to recognize.

She had the bacon fried crisp and brown. The grits were on the back burner bubbling gently, and the aroma of coffee permeated the entire house. Still no husband.

"Well," she said aloud. "That lazy husband of mine had better get on his horse. The entire barnyard is alive, and all God's creatures are proclaiming this to be another glorious day."

"Reuben! You might be a year older, but that's no reason to start it off this way."

She looked at him dreaming away with a smile on his face. She thought he was playing 'possum.

"Alright, mister." She jerked off the covers and began to tickle him. But when he didn't respond she thought, "That bugger. I don't know how he can have so much control," fully expecting him to break out in his hearty laughter.

She looked at him again and slowly - quietly said, "Reuben?" Louder..."Reuben!" She began to shake him. No response...

"Oh my God! No...No...Reuben!" she screamed. Then Berta sat on the edge of their bed and started rocking back and forth...back and forth...moaning.

Young Reuben rushed in, still in his night shirt and rubbing the sleep out of his eyes.

"Ma! Ma! What's wrong? Why're you screaming?"

Berta just sat, rocking back and forth, moaning. She couldn't respond.

He looked at his pa. "Pa, what's wrong?" No answer. He was soon joined by Jonah and SuSu, and Wes began crying in his crib. He pushed Jonah aside as he ran for Big Dan's and Willa's.

When they got to Berta, she was still staring at the cabbage roses on the green wallpaper. No expression. SuSu was whimpering, and Jonah stood beside her patting her slight shoulder. He soon went to get Wes from the crib and began changing him and took him into the kitchen for his breakfast, in a daze, automatically.

Big Dan looked at Willa and shook his head, tears streaming uncontrolled down into his collarless shirt. Willa pursed her lips, took Berta's hand and trying to arouse some life in her, began to give orders.

"Now, Miss Berta, we gotta do what needs to be done. Don'

none of us lak doin' it - but it's gotta be done jes de same. Dan, go tell Myrtice to get Zeke up here right now. Ah wants him to fetch Miss Trudy." Dan moved to do her bidding.

"Young Reuben, hep get dese chilren fed an', oh, Ah see Master Jonah done tended to Master Wes."

Thinking out loud about the next step, Willa unthinkingly said, "Wees gotta get the McCoys to get fixin' on de coffin. " She could see Young Reuben start to cry, brushing his eyes and using his shirttail to wipe his nose.

"Now, Young Reuben, we ain't in charge of de Lawd's plan, so wees gotta do what he laid down fo' us to do - you unnerstan', don' ya?" He shook his head, brushing the tears away.

Zeke and Myrtice dashed in. Willa told Myrtice that she was to help her get Miss Berta into the other bedroom. When they tried to lift Berta, one on each side, the only thing she said was, "Reuben must wear the new green waistcoat, Willa. And the bridal wreath quilt I finished, he's to be laid out on that. Tell Palmer and Davis." She uttered not another word until Trudy arrived almost three hours later.

Myrtice took the children to her house so Dan and Willa could dress Reuben. Berta was lying in Young Reuben's bed staring into space...no motion. It seemed to take forever before Zeke and Trudy arrived. Right behind them were Bud and Luta. They rushed into the kitchen and were met by a stern Willa Roker. She wasn't about to allow anyone to upset the young missy.

Trudy spoke first. "What on God's earth happened, Willa? Zeke couldn't say anything but 'the Master's dead. . dead'. How could this have happened?"

When Willa realized that Trudy wasn't going to rush into where Berta was, she relaxed her protection and responded, "Don' know, Miss Trudy, mam. Don' know. He was live an' well yestiddy, an' dis monin' Young Reuben came arunnin' in de house a yellin' dat his ma could'n' talk an' sumpin' was wrong wid his pa. Dat's all Ah know. Wen me an' Dan got here, der she was - jes asittin' an' astarin' an' not sayin' nuttin' -jes asittin' an' astarin'..."

Trudy took hold of her arm, and together they went to Berta. Trudy turned to Luta and said, "She's in shock. Good! Best thing that could happen to her. Luta, we've gotta telegraph Reuben's kin, and only Berta would have that information. Get Wes! She'll respond to her baby, I'm sure." Luta asked Willa where the children were, then went to Myrtice's and brought Wes back with her. He was yelling his head off, and Berta heard him even before Luta got into the house.

"Wes! Wes! What's wrong with Wes, Trudy? Here my precious one," she said with her arms extended. Trudy looked at Luta, and Willa rushed to say, "He done had his breaffus, Missy. Master Jonah fed 'im. Dey's all at Myrtice's an' is doin' fine - jes fine."

At first she seemed perplexed. Then it all came home to her, and she began to cry and hug Wes, who just wanted to get down and squirmed until he got his way.

"Oh Reuben! Oh Reuben!" she sobbed. The three women, who stood at the foot of the narrow bed, glanced at each other, and their expressions conveyed that all would be well now. She had acknowledged his death...perhaps not accepted it as yet, but at least realized the fact and would be able to deal with it. The needed grieving time would make her strong.

Trudy knew that she couldn't delay any longer. "Berta, dear, we have to send word to your and Reuben's kin. Bud and Luta will go to Fannin Springs to telegraph them, but we must know who and where, dear. Please help us."

Berta sighed, got her breath and began giving them the information they needed. Luta asked for paper and a pen, and the business of Reuben's funeral and burial began to take place.

The McCoy brothers would have the traditional pine box made to size and as quickly as possible. The heat soon took its toll, and the burial would need to be within the two-day period.

The word spread rapidly. Charlie Beatty would preach, for Brother Townsend would not be coming to Old Town for another three weeks. The Swede, Bud, and Davis and Palmer Mccoy would attend him as pallbearers, and he'd be buried in the little graveyard directly behind the church. Word had been sent to Pierce Garvin, Jordan Northrup, Silas Redmon and Parker Meade and the other prominent cowmen in the state. Reuben had been highly thought of for his innovative and progressive ideas, and even the governor sent his condolences.

Once Berta realized her duty, she became the organizer that she would have to be for the next four years. When Hamilton McRae, Reuben's only brother, arrived at South Spring from

Georgia two weeks after the funeral to assist her in the financial matters of the estate, he informed her that they had no debts, but that there was a moderate amount of capital for her to continue the operation of the ranch. She'd need to hire a full-time foreman, and, according to the people with whom he had conferred, they were almost impossible to find.

Ham tried to talk Berta into selling out and accompanying him back to Lochmon or at least to Macon, where she still had friends and relatives and could live a "civilized" life. But she was adamant.

"It was Reuben's dream, Ham. Now how would you feel if Elaine sold Lochmon and moved back to Charleston after you died? Would you approve of that, Ham?"

He turned a subtle shade of red and lowered his head. "See, Ham. I'm not being unreasonable...a little impractical and pig-headed, yes. But unreasonable, no. Yes, I'll need an extra dose of courage. I needed that when I first arrived here. Reuben and I worked hard, Ham, very hard, and I'm sure my real test is just beginning." She stared off into space, and he was hesitant to interrupt but decided to pursue the subject.

"Is that how you think of South Spring, Berta? ...as a test of endurance?" He was surprised that a woman would think that way.

"In a way it is. You see, Reuben and I have both known that we're just pioneers in Florida and that our children and our children's children will have the ultimate test. They'll be the builders and history makers. We're just the ground breakers. That's all we are. But it's up to us - me - to build as firm a foundation for them as I possibly can. That's my job. That's what Reuben would have wanted, and it's what I want. I am fully aware that it will be difficult - just how difficult only time will tell - but it's a challenge that I'm already warming to. You see, Ham, I feel Reuben beside me, and I know he'll be right here when I need him."

He hugged her, then held her out from him. "You know, when you and Reuben were married and planned to move here to this wilderness, I said to Father, 'She'll not last out the year. She's a southern belle and won't be able to stand the hardships of a rancher's wife.' I'm glad I was wrong, sister dear. I'm so very glad," and they were in each other's arms.

Berta was glad her face was not visible. She was thinking the same about Ham, a decorated war hero, who could sport a chest filled with medals, and the owner and manager of one of Georgia's finest plantations. Only Reuben had seen that side of Ham. Only Reuben had had faith in his younger brother, who prior to Reuben's departure from Lochmon had been under the influence, as the Darkies said, and avoided any responsibility. Reuben with his love and faith and his keen insight had known of Ham's latent ability.

When Ham looked at Berta, he knew what she was thinking. "We've both grown with Reuben's love, Berta." And he brushed a tear away and turned abruptly so she could not see his emotion. Berta thought, "Reuben would not have turned from me or anyone. He was not ashamed of an honest emotion. He was the truest person I've ever known and will probably ever know."

"When things settle down, would you and the children please visit us at Lochmon? Elaine would be so pleased to meet you, and Maribea speaks of you often. You knew that she remarried after Matthew was killed in the War and seems very contented in Macon."

"Yes, Lamorah wrote me of her marriage after dear Matthew was killed. What a terrible war, Ham! I'm so glad you were spared - for all our sakes. We shall certainly plan on a visit to Lochmon. Reuben and I spoke of it often, and the children should get to know as much of their father as possible. Yes...we'll plan on a visit."

Hamilton left the next morning on the *Suwannee Queen,* but Berta and the children never did get to Lochmon.

CHAPTER III THE HONEYMOON

Juanita, lying sleepily on the straw-filled pallet, holding the copy of *Wuthering Heights* that Etienne had given her, watched Aimee dress her long, rich brown hair. It was so thick that she wondered how on earth she would be able to weave it into the figure eight French rolls in the back. Juanita felt so tired; she'd had a fitful night's sleep. She knew that she'd been completely immersed in her training for the tight rope act, so maybe that was the cause. Watching R. J. and Joe Bob hang did prey on her mind much more than she thought it would, but she just felt so tired this morning she was glad there was no practice.

As Aimee turned to her she said, "Juanita, I'll dress your hair if you'd like. I've always wanted to, ever since I first saw you."

Juanita lazily sat up and yawned, stretching her shapely arms in the air, and lackadaisically replied, "Oh, all right, Aimee, if you really want to." She picked up her book and resumed her reading. Etienne had been helping her with the difficult words, and each day after her practice she'd steal away to the south spring so she could read out loud. She thought Heathcliff was the most exciting character she'd ever read about. His devil eyes reminded her of R. J.'s, and she could hardly wait to get to the next chapter.

Aimee had noticed how withdrawn she had become lately. The only time she showed any enthusiasm was when she was reading one of her old books or practicing on the rope. "But then," she thought, "she had had a very frightening experience with those terrible kidnappers. It's no wonder," and she reached for Juanita's brush to begin untangling her hair, that was badly matted from her restless night.

When Orlean parted the canvas curtain that was nailed to the back of the wagon affording them some privacy, she peered inside the darkened interior. Noticing how quiet and still Juanita was, she questioned. "Are you not feeling well, Juanita?" as her knowing eyes studied Juanita's sullen face.

Juanita turned toward her - the cramped wagon left little room to maneuver - and smiled sweetly at Orlean, declaring to herself, "She'll never like me, not in this world or in the next. She's jealous of Etienne's feelings for me, the old crone," but she said aloud, "Oh, thank you for asking, Mrs. deMoya. I think I just need a good tonic, that's all."

Aimee's quick humor broke the strained atmosphere. "How about the 'Elixir of Life', Juanita? It cures all ills," she said with elaborate theatrics.

But Orlean deMoya did not join in their sarcastic merriment. She seriously looked at Juanita and asked, "You teenk you should chance de journey eento Old Town een your condeetion, Juanita?"

"Oh, I'm just feeling a little poorly, that's all. I'll be fine as soon as I have some breakfast," and she squinted at Orlean, trying to mask her true feelings, as the brightness of the glaring July sun intruded into the soft light of the wagon.

Orlean dropped the canvas curtain and stumbled as she began to run toward the house. She had to get away from the girl, the ungrateful girl, the girl who would bring shame to her family. "I was afraid of dees. I was afraid!"

She reached the porch and out of breath gasped, " Now Etienne weel nevair let her go - nevair!".

Orlean knew her son. Leaning her head against the porch post she heaved a sigh. "No mattair 'ose baby eet ees. A bank robber's, a rapist's, no mattair. He has great love of all life, and de life dat's no doubt growing witeen her ungrateful belly weel be as precious to my loving son as eef eet were 'ees own."

It was coming to pass what she had feared. She decided to say nothing of her suspicions to Dom and certainly not to Berta and Layke. Nothing must spoil their blessed wedding. She would bide her time, observing Juanita's every symptom. She could be mistaken, but she knew in her heart she was not. And the young, selfish, ignorant girl probably was not even aware of the miracle being visited upon her. The pity...the pity of the reckless.

She was also concerned with Aimee's obvious adulation of the undeserving girl. She would have to be especially clever in handling Aimee. She was a loving, affectionate daughter, but she also had an obstinate streak like her Uncle Pierre, wilful to the extreme about certain matters. Orlean was happy that one of them was her love of the family and the other, her performance on the tightrope.

She realized that the audience thought she and Dom put on an act when Aimee did her high rope act. They expected it from them, so they performed accordingly. But the truth was she and

Dom died inch by inch when their precious gift from God was closer to his Divine Countenance than prudent.

Straightening her weary, hunched shoulders and with her head erect and her eyes staring at the group that had gathered on the front porch she swore, "I'll not allow my fear and worry to veesit my friends on der wedding day," and smiled her masterful smile at the assembly declaring aloud, "De girls are dressing der hair an' should be weet us soon. Etienne, Pierre, see to de wagons for Master Layke. Dees ees hees special day, an' he should not have to tend to any chores. None at all, eh?"

Etienne and Pierre without question did as she asked, as they were accustomed to doing. Dom's bantam legs followed, always lagging a few steps behind his tall, long-legged, handsome sons of whom he was so proud.

With SuSu's help Berta finished the packing of her and Layke's trunk. On top she spread sheets of thin tissue paper and gently, reverently, laid out her mauve, tissue faille wedding gown. Every stitch had been laboriously sewn with love. The capelette was edged with pleated fluting, and tiny covered buttons gathered it to the fitted bodice. The double skirt was draped up to a bustle in back, and the same pleated fluting was stitched in rows into the long train. It had taken her two months to complete. Most of the sewing had been done after a sun-up to sundown, hard day's work on South Spring. She'd get the children to bed, and in the kitchen by lamp light she'd meticulously stitch her gown, dreaming all the while of her love - her life - Layke Williams.

The reverence SuSu displayed as she oohed and aahed over the beauty of her mama's gown saddened Berta. She had wanted to make a new dress for SuSu, but time would not permit, so she and Orlean redid her last spring's lisle dress with grosgrain ribbon around the edge of the skirt and sleeves. They had to let out the side seams on the bodice, but not much alteration was required. She was so easily pleased. It almost broke Berta's heart as she watched her frail, quiet daughter. The circles under her big, haunted eyes weren't as dark as last year, and her rich, red-brown hair had more sheen, Berta happily observed.

But Wes...he was already in Jonah's clothes of just before Reuben died; the pants required shortening but the waist almost fit. He would be as tall as Reuben's brother, Ham, but with Reuben's big frame, she thought, as she watched Orlean give him more milk and cookies. "Really, he shouldn't be having them so close to our departure. The jostling of the wagon sometimes makes him ill. Oh, well, this once won't hurt him," and she resumed her packing.

The wagons were loaded, and Juanita, Aimee and Etienne led the caravan of the three wagons over the same ox trail Layke had traversed just nine months before. As the pine- scented air filled his nostrils and the mockingbirds sang their welcome song, he turned toward Berta and patted her hand lovingly as he drank in the beauty of his wedding day.

"Oh Lord, I love the beauty of thy house and the place where thy glory dwells." He remembered the psalm Charlie had read the first Sunday he sat beside his beautiful Berta. He'd never forgotten it, nor could he, for His glory dwelled within him and this wild Florida land he had come to love and treasure.

"What are you thinking, Layke?" Berta asked softly.

"I'm thinking how the sun has shone on me since the first day I saw your golden hair and Tennessee cornflower blue eyes, Mrs. Bertrice Lillian Williams. And in you is truly where His glory dwells."

"My, my, Mr. Williams. How poetically you speak on your wedding day!" And she squeezed his taut arm that held the reins to old Blackie and smiled happily all the way to Old Town.

****

Church was finally over, and the townspeople excitedly walked to the boarding house. Everyone in Old Town had come to respect Layke, and his marriage to Berta was an event they had all looked forward to since their announcement after the hanging. Of course, some had known of the upcoming wedding - Bud and Luta and Trudy. But most had been unaware of the love between them.

Berta and the other wedding party members had changed from their wrinkled traveling garments and had completed their dressing by the time the guests arrived. Trudy had the punch table laden with miniature sandwiches of every description: tiny biscuits filled with crab salad, chicken salad, thin slices of smoked ham with spicy tomato sauce, tender backstrap of venison with onion sauce, hot and succulent. Orlean and Aimee had baked hundreds of flaky pastries filled with hot, spicy meat or egg custard drizzled with chocolate, delicacies the townspeople had never eaten nor heard of. There were hot, salted and roasted pecans placed in crystal bowls Trudy's ma had brought from Alabama as a young bride into this wilderness, and her heavy lace tablecloths, yellowed with age but still beautiful, covered the rough-hewn pine tables.

Trudy had Frankie and Jonah pick the wild daisies, fleabane and wild fern from along the river's edge to fill out her roses, that were too few.

It was the usual warm July day, but, thank goodness, they hadn't waited 'til the dog days of August, Trudy thought. The afternoon rains usually arrived on schedule, about four o'clock, and with them the cooler air, but a noon wedding wouldn't be affected. The tables did look pretty, everyone exclaimed as they entered the soft light of Trudy's parlor and dining rooms. The lace curtains that required mending after every careful washing were still pretty and diffused the sun's harsh rays.

Charlie Beatty wended his way through the throng of people toward Trudy to ask when he was to start the ceremony. Young Reuben was the message bearer, and two at a time his muscled legs climbed the stairs to deliver the message to his mother. Their reunion had been a touching one. Layke had remained in the buggy while Berta became re-acquainted with her first born. He liked the open-faced, happy young man before him and clasped his hand firmly to assure him of it. It was mutual, as Berta had known it would be. Young Reuben was just like his pa when it came to evaluations. Reuben had never known a stranger, and Young Reuben was privileged in the same way.

Trudy had Young Reuben, who looked handsome in his dark blue waistcoat, stand upon a chair above the guests to call attention to the descending bride and groom. She had placed Charlie beside the fireplace that was filled with ferns, and beside her grandmother's chiming clock. The golden chimes heralded the approach of Berta and Layke as they made their appearance.

The happy guests enthusiastically applauded and commented, "Oh, my, Berta, you're beautiful...just beautiful, and Layke looks so handsome!" Luta whispered to her Buddy, "I declare to you right now as God is my witness, Buddy, I've never seen a handsomer couple...not ever." She continued to gush over their appearance to Martha and Minna.

When Trudy reached Berta, she whispered, "I've never seen

a more beautiful bride, Berta, never in all my long years." Berta hugged her enthusiastically, kissing her quivering cheek.

Layke never took his eyes off Berta - not during or after the ceremony. He was in a complete daze, answering questions, making the necessary small talk and being polite to one and all, but his eyes never left her glowing face. The townspeople were so touched by his obvious adoration that they soon made their good wishes and good-byes to allow the happy couple to prepare for their trip to Crosstown where they would spend their wedding night before going on to Lake City to board the train for Jacksonville.

They changed into their traveling clothes, and when they came downstairs arm in arm, Orlean and Dom approached them assuring them that all would be well, for them not to worry about the children or South Spring, and they sent them off with a shower of rice for good luck. All along the street the townspeople did the same.

As soon as they were on the outskirts of Old Town, Layke reined in Blackie. He had been so quiet that Berta was a little concerned about him. It wasn't in his character to be that solemn. He slowly turned to Mrs. Williams and very seriously announced, "God, Berta, I'm scared! I know I'm not worthy of you. No man could be."

Before he could continue, Berta put her finger to his lips and confessed to her awestruck groom, "Layke, don't worship me, please. I'm flesh and blood just like any other woman. I have faults...I have a temper. You've been a witness to it a few times already. Now, a saint, I'm not, Layke Williams. You know that. I'm willful, and right this minute I'd like you to make me your wife." She smiled her devilish smile as they both remembered the day before the spring drive.

"Now, put a whip to Blackie and speed me away to our bridal suite before I embarrass you in front of anyone passing by this route. I'm also not patient, as you will come to know."

A relieved Layke did his lady's bidding, flicked Blackie's rump, turned to Berta and exclaimed, "I think I've married myself one helluva woman, Mrs. Williams. Make tracks, Blackie. My bride is impatient. Glory be!"

****

It was a three hour ride by buggy from Old Town, and they were both tired and hot, and had they not been so in love they'd have been irritable as well. The afternoon rains had miraculously held off until they arrived at the Hardwick Hotel in Crosstown, and they rushed inside as the wind began to pick up. Berta held onto her new navy straw hat as Layke rang the bell at the desk. Mr. Harold Hardwick, proprietor, rose from behind the dark, paneled alcove, his slick, dark brown hair and white starched collar in place, and summoned his son, Junior, to help with their heavy trunk. Then he asked if they'd like a bath drawn.

Berta shook her head, and Layke informed Mr. Hardwick that his wife was not feeling well after such a long, tiresome trip; perhaps after they rested it would be welcomed. He asked whether it would be too much bother if they had supper in their suite and said that about six o'clock would be fine. Mr. Hardwick allowed that that was quite customary for the visitors who requested the bridal suite and coughed as he gave Layke a knowing wink.

He and Berta stifled giggles all the way upstairs. The bridal suite left a lot to be desired. Berta had an idea that a great many couples frequented it who were indeed not man and wife, but in her euphoric state it was special to her, nevertheless.

Junior was leaving their room with a smart-aleck grin on his red, pimpled face, but he became quite sober when Layke tipped him handsomely and took him aside whispering into his wax-gummed ear, "Junior, if I think I hear you or any of your sneakin', curious buddies outside this door, you'll feel the end of my cow whip between your legs, and you'll have one helluva time pissing on tied-up cats, as I've no doubt you've done."

His dilated eyes assured Layke that he understood what he meant and that there would be no disturbance outside the bridal suite that night.

"What on earth did you say to that frightened young boy, Layke? I mean, my husband? He was scared to death."

"Never you mind, Berta - I mean, Wife. Never you mind, and not another word do I want to hear from you...at least for a while."

He turned and slowly walked toward her. Deftly he removed the hat pin from her dusty hat and put it on the dresser. Deliberately and steadily as they looked into each others' eyes, he unbuttoned her bodice, and she his coat. He kissed the hollow of her neck. Her eyes closed in ecstasy, savoring every moment.

"Oh, darling, I want you now," she cried.

He lifted his beautiful Berta and placed her on the still covered bed. With the frenzy of their love-making the disheveled bed covers became a source of amusement afterwards as they lay weakly in each other's arms.

Berta whispered, "Honey, cancel supper," and laughingly added, "Who needs food?"

"Hey, Wife, a husband has to keep up his strength when he's married to an insatiable wife such as you, Mrs. Williams." He stroked her warm, beautiful face and kissed the tip of her patrician nose.

"Don't you get frisky with me, Layke Williams. If, indeed, I'm insatiable, then obviously we've a long night ahead of us, and if the food your body desires is other than this beautiful, ravenous woman beside you, then perhaps you're not deserving of such a treasure," and she sat upright on the scattered bed covers, the thin sheet dropped from her as she coyly teased him.

"God, Berta, you'd tempt the saints themselves, you're so beautiful," and he pulled her to him. "You're all the food any man could yearn for, my darling," and he stroked her rounded breasts. She gave into his every desire, willingly, hungrily, 'til they were both spent.

They lay side by side catching their breath. Layke kissed her finger tips. Her eyes closed. She returned his light embrace and remembered his tenderness, but was enraptured by his unleashed passion of just a few minutes before. They didn't hear the hesitant rap on their door. Harold Hardwick decided to leave their supper outside, and as he descended the once grand, carpeted stairs, he smiled to himself as he remembered his own wedding night.

****

Berta and Layke had planned their honeymoon from a very practical standpoint. Layke had business to conduct at the Wilpole ranch, Santa Fe. They had originally planned to take the stage from Crosstown to Rowland's Bluff, where they'd visit the Wilpoles, and on to Lake City to board the train to Jacksonville, but after some discussion they decided to drive the buckboard; it was not much less comfortable unless they had rain.

There were so many places Layke wanted to show Berta, and

the stage followed a set route. He was well acquainted with the land around Rowland's Bluff and was excited at being able to share it with his bride. They decided to take their chances with the weather, so they took an extra tarpaulin to ward off the July storms that were almost an every-day occurrence. Mrs. Hardwick had packed a lunch, so there would be no rush to get to Rowland's Bluff, and they'd be able to take their time wandering through the hammock area west of the Suwannee. The stately pines towered over them as the buckboard seemed to find every pothole and sandy spot along the seldom used road. But Berta, in a daze, noticed not the bumps nor the blistering rays of the noonday sun. Her parasol and wide brimmed hat gave her some protection from its unrelenting rays.

Layke turned to her as he slowed Blackie down. "As we come around this bend, my darling, you'll see some of the most glorious land in this world...or the next. It's untouched beauty, Berta. I want you to close your eyes and prepare yourself for a spectacular wave of the Creator's magic wand."

He slowly drove around the bend, and Berta hoped, prayed, she'd not be disappointed. She wanted to appreciate and understand this man she married. He was so unlike Reuben. His passion for life overwhelmed her...excited her. He called Blackie to a halt. She licked her dry lips, and when Layke gave the word, she apprehensively opened her eyes. Never in her entire life had she experienced such a feeling of awe. Staring at her was a never ending expanse of bulrushes as far as the eye could see blending into the distant horizon - broken sporadically by round hammocks of cypress and sabal palms, noble in stature and seemingly undisturbed by thousands of years of solitude. She felt she had witnessed eternity.

She silently reached for him and he came to her...surrounding her with his sensitive, protective arms. "Oh, Layke, I was so afraid I'd not understand your love affair with the Florida wilderness, but I do...oh, I do, my darling. I feel we should whisper, so as not to invade the privacy of this virgin land. I know others have been here or there wouldn't be a trail, but don't you think that perhaps they felt as we do, that this land should be revered and the creatures that inhabit it left to enjoy their kingdom?"

"You are so precious to me, my dear one. Your sensitivity, your anticipation of my every need..." and he raised his head toward the heavens and said loudly, "Oh, Lord, I thank you for this woman of mine!"

And Berta and Layke, alone in the stark wilderness of western Florida, made love quietly, reverently, so as not to disturb the many creatures on whose land they were guests.

Later Berta spread the quilt on a thick grassy spot under an ancient live oak dripping with the mysterious grey Spanish moss. Mrs. Hardwick had prepared fried chicken, fried and sugared sweet potato slices, thickly buttered biscuits and a jar of her bread and butter pickles with little baby onions and okra pods, hot and spicy. Lemon butter cakes were for dessert, but as Layke put it, "Mrs. Hardwick certainly doesn't believe that two people can live on love alone," and he rubbed his too full stomach.

"I'll save the cakes for tomorrow on the train, hon," and they napped on the patchwork quilt under the oak's sheltering arms. Both wore satisfied smiles. They had never been happier or more content. Layke's concern about their reception by the Wilpoles had not even entered his relaxed mind.

****

They rode into Rowland's Bluff about 4 p. m. It appeared to Berta that Layke knew everyone in town, certainly at the hotel. He proudly introduced her to Mrs. Lombard, the proprietress of the Arthur B. Hotel. She looked Berta up and down, and Berta exclaimed to Layke later in the privacy of their room, "Layke, that woman undressed me with her very eyes."

He howled. "Why, Berta, whatever do you mean? Mrs. Lombard was just appreciating your spectacular beauty so she could go over to the Suwannee Saloon to tell all the girls what a catch I've made," and he roared with delight at his suddenly prim and proper wife.

She balled up her small hands and playfully pounded him with her ineffective fists.

"Oh, Woman, there's not a cow town girl anywhere who can hold a candle to you."

"And I just bet you know every last one of 'em, Layke Williams. I'll just bet you do," she teased as she resumed pounding on his muscled chest.

He grabbed both her fists, hurting her, and fervently told his feisty wife, "But I've loved only one, Berta, and don't you ever doubt that. Never doubt that, sweet Berta, no matter what happens."

When he released her, her hands throbbed. She began rubbing them to revive the circulation and was surprised at his intensity...but also delighted. "Reuben would never have done that," she thought, "Never!"

Layke turned abruptly and called over his shoulder, "I'll be downstairs ordering our dinner." As an afterthought he said almost under his breath, "I just hope that old lady Wilpole doesn't make a fuss about it. "

This relationship was so new to Berta. Every second of her being with him was like an introduction to a foreign, unexplored area, and it excited her dormant inquisitiveness. She realized that the quiet, serene life she'd had with Reuben was not really full...complete. And she never would have known it had she not met Layke. That frightened her. He frightened her.

"I felt that Reuben left me because I was undeserving, inadequate, and for all those lonely years afterwards I was numb, just barely breathing, doing my day-to-days. I could have missed living altogether had Layke not ventured into my empty life."

She continued rubbing her hands and felt intoxicated with anticipation. She caught her breath and thought, "He's so beautifully unpredictable, this husband of mine. I have a fascinating life ahead of me, I know...but it's also a little frightening."

****

She couldn't decide which dress would be appropriate, and as she brushed Layke's rich brown suit and laid out his brocade vest and good shirt she heard a rap on their door. Thinking it was Layke announcing his entry, she paid no attention. When the rap occurred the second time, she answered it, "Yes, who's there?"

She opened the door, and to her utter amazement there stood at least six cow town girls. It was obvious to her who they were. She was so astonished that when she asked them, using her most affected voice, "Yes, whom do wish to see, and how may I help you?" she couldn't believe the pretentious words had escaped her lips. They began to giggle in such a friendly manner that Berta soon dropped her reserve and joined them.

They began shaking her hand, patting her shoulder and

fingering her dress in such an unrestrained manner that finally she could not hold her curiosity any longer and invited them in. "Won't you please come in? I've not had the pleasure of meeting you, but my husband speaks of you often," she lied.

They giggled all the more and one by one entered the Williamses' suite. The redheaded one with too much rouge on her full cheeks appeared to be the leader and said, "I've not been here in the daylight before. My, my, it sure looks different," and the others joined her in their sport of Berta. She made up her mind that they'd not best her.

"And I've not been here in the night before, but I can assure you I'm becoming more excited about it by the minute."

The girl stopped laughing then. Realizing she was not going to best Berta, she began to shuffle her feet in embarrassment. She gulped and said softly, "Mrs. Williams...."

"My name is Berta."

"Please don't let on to Mister Layke. We was just funnin'. Me and the girls were just having a little sport with you...."

"Yes, I know. I'm grateful to all of you that my husband had the pleasure of your company when he was going through a very difficult period in his life and didn't know which path to follow. I'm sure you gave him many moments of pleasure." And she added with a broad impish grin on her sweet innocent face, "and I'm enjoying the results of your thorough training."

They nervously laughed with Berta as they quickly sought the door, not understanding the words she spoke but getting the gist of their meaning. She thanked them graciously for their visit and invited them to stop for a visit if they were ever in Old Town, where they owned a large spread called South Spring and where they would be most welcome. The girls sheepishly went down the stairs of the Arthur B. Hotel, keeping a watchful eye out for Mrs. Lombard, and made tracks for the safety of the Suwannee Saloon.

Berta closed the door, leaned against it and said to herself, "I don't think I've ever had as much fun. Should I tell Layke?"

After much deliberation she chose the royal blue taffeta to wear for their dinner with the Wilpoles - no drab color for a lively cow town like Rowland's Bluff. If the town wanted someone to talk about, well, she'd give them that person. She felt full of life and was as excited about their night out as she had been about her debut eighteen years before.

When Layke returned, he seemed somewhat despondent. She immediately went to him.

"What is it, my love?"

"It's nothing of importance, Berta. It's just that I expected more of a response from John Wilpole, that's all."

"What do you mean, Hon? Have they already arrived? I thought they'd not be here until later."

"Just John. Mrs. Wilpole will join us later. He had some business to tend to, and I ran into him in the lobby. He was so distant, Berta."

"Don't keep me in the dark, my dearest, please. I want to know what he said that's so disturbing."

He sighed resignedly and told her of his conversation with his old boss. When Layke had worked for the Wilpoles, they were developing a strain of cattle that they hoped would withstand the many diseases that the hot and humid Florida range inflicted upon them. He had worked very closely with Mr. Wilpole and his three sons and had been respected, he thought, and appreciated, he knew. But now that he was in the position of running a fine ranch like South Spring, John Wilpole seemed very distant and unresponsive in their conversation.

Berta understood immediately. She'd seen class distinction from the time she was old enough to join her parents at their political soirees in Macon and had been privy to Georgia politics when they entertained the state's most influential politicians in their lovely Melrose Street home. She knew instinctively how to play the Wilpoles' game. If her husband needed to be accepted into their privileged circles, she'd do her utmost to assist him.

She patted him in a wifely fashion and suggested he dress for dinner. She and Mrs. Wilpole, who was being driven into town to join them, would perhaps abolish any distance between them. She hummed confidently as she finished dressing, and Layke seemed to gain strength from her relaxed attitude.

He held her out from him. "Mrs. Williams, how very lovely you are! I would avow that you're the loveliest lady in all Rowland's Bluff tonight. Blue suits you," and he kissed her exposed shoulder. Berta sighed and thought, "Oh, how I've needed this!"

Reuben had given her his mother's amethyst and diamond earrings and a broach to match for their 10th Anniversary, and Berta chose to dress her golden hair in a high pompadour she had seen in the Godey books at McCoy's. Little Woman would be so proud of her, she thought. She often wondered what had happened to her after Aunt Bertrice died. She just disappeared, it would seem.

She searched through her jewelry case and gathered every ring she could find. "Opulence usually attracts their curious eyes, so tonight I'll be opulent. Add the sapphire from my 16th birthday...Oh my, it'll have to be worn on my little finger. 'Why, Miss Berta, you've sprouted up'," she could hear Little Woman say so plainly.

Now Rowland's Bluff was a cow town; there was no denying it. Cattle and boat building were its main industries. The wealthy ranchers, boat builders and turpentine kings who needed a place to entertain their visiting friends, politicians, and the wealthy industrialists from the North were frequent visitors, and the dining room at the Arthur B. Hotel was surprisingly lovely.

Arm in arm they entered the softly gas-lit dining room. John Wilpole abruptly rose as Berta graciously extended her ring-filled hand. She was indeed beautiful. There was not a head in the room that was not appreciatively turned toward her to drink in her loveliness, male and female alike, for Berta Norwood McRae Williams had a regal bearing, and all the guests there were chattering among themselves about her identity.

This room and these people with their plastered-on faces intrigued Berta. It had never occurred to her that she'd be allowed to play this role. She commanded, she demanded, and Layke vicariously absorbed her energy and instinctively followed her lead. All the while they were playing the game. They would, from time to time, glance at each other and know that later in the evening in the privacy of their suite they would relive the comedy of this eventful evening.

Berta had masterfully parried and blocked every dart extended by Mrs. Wilpole to Layke's delight and complete astonishment. He thought to himself as he observed his little South Spring wife that if he weren't careful, she'd be running for political office, and at the same time he secretly declared - after all, he was on his fourth bourbon - he'd be the first to vote for her, by gum!

Mrs. Wilpole was a pleasant enough woman; at least Layke had found her so when he worked for them, but now that this upstart cowman was trying to invade her sacred station, she had got plumb powerful in her one-sided opinions. He was grateful that Berta was putting the old gal in her place. God, his eyes must be glazed, and he decided to not accept John's offer of another bourbon. He knew Berta or any lady of the South would have only a light wine or a sherry - nothing stronger. Now his cow town girls...well that was another story.

When Berta turned to ask him to please order dinner, she almost panicked. Quickly she rose and asked the Wilpoles to please excuse them as they must speak to the chef; their dinner was long overdue and she wanted to be sure he had prepared the special sauce to her satisfaction.

She grabbed Layke's welcome arm and proceeded to the lobby, grinning up at his sheepish face and declaring to an amused Mrs. Lombard, "I've got the most entertaining husband a woman could have, Mrs. Lombard, but he's had too much bourbon, and I'm afraid those vultures in there are going to devour him."

She needed to say no more. Mrs Lombard, who allowed nothing to escape her regarding the activities in her hotel, had been privy to the episode when the cow town girls tried to make sport of Berta and had delighted in the results of her putting the riffraff in their places.

"Don't you worry, Mrs. Williams. The coffee is coming up, and I'll have cook start serving," she stated emphatically as she smiled her approval.

Berta turned toward Layke and asked, "Do you want to delay dinner, Hon?"

When he looked into her humorous eyes, he broke out in laughter, and that is how John Wilpole found them in the lobby of the Arthur B. Hotel - in each others arms, laughing and twirling around and around.

Mrs. Lombard immediately rescued the clinging couple. "Mr. Wilpole, dinner is served," and she turned toward Layke and said, "Mr. Williams, you have a telegram at the desk, sir. It would appear it is urgent."

Berta turned slightly, and realizing that Mrs. Lombard had diverted the enemy, winked at her. A short time later, after Layke had consumed almost a pot of strong coffee, he and Berta returned to the dining room.

When John Wilpole extended his arm and motioned to Layke and Berta, Layke apologized and said that he was sorry for the delay, that there had been a business negotiation that required an immediate response. He glanced at Berta for her reaction and found her already deep in conversation with Lucille Wilpole about the difficulty of finding good house help these days and about their youngest daughter, Aretha, who was making her debut in October. She wondered if the Williamses would be able to attend.

"Oh dear, Lucille, Layke and I are planning an extended trip, but if we return by - what date? - we would be delighted to attend. Simply delighted. It reminds me of my debut in Macon many years ago," she added.

Layke knew he'd have to restrain his laughter 'til later, but he was having one helluva time. He knew Berta was right, and so was Orlean. It was a game they were expected to play; so perform, pretend, give them what they expect, so you can dwell in your own soft cushion to ponder...to dream...to feel. As he looked at his much admired, beautiful wife, he thought, "Mostly, my darling, to feel."

As they slowly ascended the stairs toward their bridal suite they relived their eventful evening. She looked at him and in a very convincing voice said, "Layke, if you want to be king in this country, it is yours for a price." He couldn't see her serious face in the soft lamp light, but he knew she was absolutely correct. "My dear husband, anyone can be king."

"I'm obviously a novice at king making, Berta."

He lifted her effortlessly as he turned the knob, and once inside kicked the door shut with his polished boot.

"But you're very accomplished in other ways, my sweet," she teased.

****

Berta rolled over and looked at her husband and his disheveled brown hair. She was an early riser by habit, and as she relived the night before she was again exhilarated by the happenings. Her knight in shining armor had not been tarnished. He had been human, and, as she enjoyed the remembering, had eventually slain the smoking dragon.

Once Layke had overcome the strength of the bourbon, he handled John Wilpole masterfully. There would be an exchange of information between the ranchers, and Layke agreed to inform him of the results of the meeting at Bullseye with Pierce Garvin and Jordan Northrup. He appeared to be grateful to be allowed such privileged information, and when he shook Layke's hand heartily Layke knew he was sincere.

****

The roomette on the Florida Atlantic and Gulf Central Railroad was much the same as the Macon-Savannah Railway Berta and Reuben had ridden almost 18 long years before. This one, however, was decorated in royal blue brocade, and as Berta busily got them situated, she thought, "And it's just as noisy."

She searched in her trunk for her hand work. They curled up on the slightly faded, cut velvet bed, and by lamplight Berta with her deft fingers worked her miracles with ecru string. "Berta has the busiest hands I've ever seen," Layke informed Trudy one day. Layke just as adroitly did his figuring of how much they could spend for the additional cattle he hoped to purchase from Pierce Garvin.

Berta turned toward her deeply intense husband and remarked, "It didn't take long for the newness to wear off, Layke Williams. Here we are married not more than three days, and already you're immersed in your book work."

He smiled suggestively at her upturned, teasing face, kissed her on the tip of her nose and exclaimed in his affected African darkie sing-song tone, "Why, Miss Berta, I sho nuff could be tempted by yo bodacious woman's curves," and he turned her over his knee and caressed her outlined curves to the delight of Berta, who playfully pushed him backward to ward off his advances.

"Shush, Layke Williams. We're not the only ones on this train." He turned her over and they were soon in each others arms, the crocheting and figuring tumbling to the floor and forgotten.

The train pulled into the Jacksonville station, and while Layke summoned the porter, Berta searched for Uncle Jock in the awaiting crowd. Layke soon joined her, and finally she saw her uncle and waved to him.

After the introductions and the usual greetings they, Jock and his youngest child, Simon, who was twenty years old and one of three of his and Lawanda's children who remained in the family residence on Riverside, drove through the beautiful residential area. The sun had been up for only a few hours, but the heat was already oppressive. The tree- lined dirt streets afforded the loquacious foursome little respite.

Uncle Jock was explaining to Layke about the devastating fires that almost destroyed Florida's largest city during the War. "There are still, after all this time, entire blocks of rubble left to remind us of those heartbreaking times."

While Layke and Jock discussed the War's effect on the city, Berta engaged Simon in conversation with the usual inquiries about what work he was engaged in and teased him about keeping company with some, no doubt, lovely young lady, and as they chatted the buggy arrived at the Jensens' white wooden residence, that was built by ship's carpenters after the War.

There were front and back verandahs and an over abundance of gingerbread work bordering them. The white pillars were in need of paint as was the front door, where Aunt Lawanda met them. In her easy-going manner she made them comfortable in no time. The rest of the large, sprawling house was as the outside, in need of some attention.

Later, Berta told Layke in the quiet privacy of their once elegantly appointed room, "Ma and Aunt Bertrice always said that Lawanda left all her good upbringing back in Savannah when she moved to the uncivilized state of Florida."

When Berta parted the ruffled lace curtains on the east windows overlooking the St. Johns River, she called to Layke excitedly, "Hon, there's the St. Johns!"

He joined her and together they marveled at its beauty and tremendous size. "Berta, Jock said that in some areas it is five miles wide!" he exclaimed in disbelief. "It's more spectacular than the Mississippi! I had no idea!"

Situated on a high bluff on the river the back yard of the Jensen home was deep and heavily wooded with magnificent live oaks, their tendril-like limbs extending for fifty feet or more from their massive trunks. What the house lacked in attention the beautifully landscaped gardens made up for. They were breathtaking with sculptured boxwood in animal shapes lining the back stone wall overlooking the river. The flower gardens in the shape of stars were filled with impatiens of every color and roses of every hue deeply bordering the side yards. Azaleas as tall as trees had completed their blooming by July and the camellias in circled beds would not show their array of crimson, coral and deep pink until November.

Berta looked up at her handsome husband's face and saw his appreciation. His arm circled her small waist, and he said, "Hon, it is indeed majestic, and the gardens are lovely, but I prefer the sleepy, unpredictable Suwannee and the quietness and less formal atmosphere of our South Spring."

He kissed the top of her sun-lit hair and squeezed her to him. "We'd better make our appearance, or Lawanda might suspect what I'd like to be doing right this minute, my dear one."

Berta reached for her strong, amorous husband. "I agree, but I know full well Uncle Jock would know. After all, they had eight children," and they both emerged from their room chuckling at their private exchange.

An ancient-seeming Negro woman waddled down the hall toward them. Berta said, "I bet that's how Sadie looks if she's still alive. Oh, how I miss them all." When she got closer, and got a better look in the dimly lit hallway, she shouted, "Sadie, is that you? Are you my Sadie?"

The toothless grin with wide open arms enveloped her. The last time she had seen Sadie was when she and Reuben had married. When she returned five years later after the War, Sadie and Benge had moved to Washington, D. C., to be with her brother's family. She had always been free, but the pressure the Negroes felt from both sides, slave and free alike, right after the War was so unkind and unnecessary, not that they received anything but love and kindness from the Norwoods. It just wasn't the same as it had been.

Little Woman had started to work for Aunt Bertrice next door after Berta's pa had died, but Berta had heard no more of Sadie and Benge.

Standing quietly on the stair landing to witness the happy event were Jock and Lawanda, who had saved the surprise for Berta. Layke joined them and was enjoying his wife's and Sadie's moving reunion.

They all went downstairs together with Berta and Sadie arm in arm talking animatedly of times gone by. When Benge died about four years earlier, Sadie had written to Little Woman and told her of her loneliness. Aunt Bertrice, who was ill, had a constant companion caring for her needs with Little Woman running the household, so she had no need of Sadie's services, but she had just heard from Jock and Lawanda about the problems they had finding good help after the War. "Everyone wanting something for nothing. My, I don't know what's going to become of the Union if this shiftless attitude is allowed to continue. It'll be our very destruction...."

So Bertrice wrote Jock about Sadie's plight, and the letter exchange resulted in a very appreciative Sadie arriving in Jacksonville over three years before. Berta and Uncle Jock had written rarely, and when they did it was mainly to inquire of each other's health. After Reuben's death, Berta didn't have the heart or time to write, so Sadie's whereabouts was a complete surprise.

They retired to the terraced lawn, where Lawanda in a very Savannah-like manner, Berta observed, served tea in her finest English bone china, and the tiny lemon cakes had to have been lovingly prepared by Sadie's still dextrous, black hands. It was obvious that Aunt Lawanda had not left all her good upbringing in Georgia when she moved to this wilderness state of Florida, after all, Berta thought.

Uncle Jock, Aunt Lawanda and Simon accompanied them on the grand tour of Florida's most cosmopolitan city. Jacksonville was a bustling city. It was nearly devastated during the War, having been burned twice. Although the damage was still evident in some sections, it now enjoyed large residential areas, and the wharfs along Laura Street were back to their pre-War activity. Barges and tugboats, steamships and schooners occupied the St. Johns. But the cowmen still drove their cattle down the main dirt road to the slaughter houses on Lackawanna Ave.

To Layke and Berta, who were used to a very slow, unhurried life style, the stimulating hustle and bustle was a welcome addition to their already eventful honeymoon. The street vendors were out with their hot corn-on-the-cob and peanuts and steamy chicken pies sold from colorful carts and hawked by the sing-song chants of the Caribbean Negroes. There were warehouses, foundries, lumber mills, shipyards and every commercial structure imaginable, and Layke, immersed in conversation with Jock and Simon, was curious about them all.

"Layke will keep the people of Old Town entertained for an entire year with all the information he's storing away, and there won't be a vacant spot on a board of Stucky's front porch," Berta thought, as she continued to marvel at this fascinating man she married.

They rode leisurely through the stately tree-lined streets of two-storied homes. The Georgian architecture seemed to be the most popular, Berta noted, with large gardens, all formally planted, so unlike Melrose Street in Macon. Jock and Lawanda were very proud of their progressive city and sang its praises to Layke.

"The people have had a tremendous resurgence of energy since our near destruction. When Lawanda and I returned from the farm in Middleburg right after the War, we were met by a barricade of huge tree trunks, and every yard in our old neighborhood, Brooklyn, was just a mess of weeds. It was so disheartening. Most of the houses had been confiscated by the Federal Army, and some of our friends' homes had been sold right out from under them. Imagine! What really galled us was that some of the new owners were our old neighbors who had stayed here and played host to the Feds," Jock exclaimed bitterly. "Bought them for next to nothing, they did. Next to nothing."

"Now, Jock. You mustn't bring all that up, dear. Let's think of pleasant things for our guests," Lawanda soothed his tirade with her soft Savannah voice.

"We now have wonderful schools, and various entertainment troops are constantly visiting our city." he continued after he calmed down. "Lawanda and I make it a point to have an evening out every week. Why, only last week we saw "Macbeth" performed by a theatrical group from Washington. Wonderful, just wonderful, wasn't it, Lawanda?"

Before she could agree, Simon interrupted with, "And the traveling acts of Mr. Barroso's Circus were stupendous. Just stupendous." He waved his arms in youthful jubilance.

"How about the oyster roasts in winter, Ma? And "marooning" on the seashore in the summer - sometimes for two or three days," Simon continued.

"What on earth is "marooning", Simon?" Berta interjected with enthusiasm.

"Oh, a bunch of families pack lots of food and spend time at the shore when it's too warm for anything else. There's always someone who plays a guitar or banjo, and we always go on a full moon. It's fun to splash in the warm water or just jump waves like Marlene and Ovetta do. We dance in the moonlight and sing around a camp fire and sleep out under the stars...oh, it's lots of fun."

He began singing softly the popular song, "Lightly row, lightly row, as o'er the dancing waves we go; smoothly glide, smoothly..."

"You can see that Simon is the romantic of our family, Berta," Jock said, reveling in his youngest son's youthful fervor.

When the exuberant tourists returned, the ladies retired to their rooms to rest before changing for dinner. Layke, Jock and Simon went to the study, where Jock summoned Jasper for their drinks. He soon returned with them and a platter of Jock's favorite delicacies. There were smoked bay oysters and hot deviled crab on scones, sprinkled with pepper sauce. Thinly sliced breast of wild turkey, smoked just right, was wrapped around miniature sweet pickles, pungent with allspice.

The ladies soon joined the men in the study. Berta had changed into a cool peach sateen gown that was perfect for her golden coloring. She was amazed that it fit as well as it did. Gracious, she had purchased it when she went back to Macon after the War, but it was still fashionable, thank goodness. Lawanda introduced Ovetta, who was twenty-three, and Marlene, twenty-five. Both girls were lovely with a delightful sense of humor and a ready wit. It was a festive evening.

Jasper announced that dinner was served and soon entered carrying a heavy tureen of clear sea turtle soup laced with sherry and heavy cream. Lawanda was a polished hostess and while she ladled the soup, Gloria, the cook-housemaid's daughter, served the buttered cheese scones. Sadie and Edna, Gloria's mother, had outdone themselves in preparing a feast fit for royalty, Layke exclaimed to his beaming hostess as he viewed the feast before them. There was breast of quail wrapped in a paper-thin pastry and deep-fried with a tart apricot sauce; fluffy saffron rice, colorful with red pimentos, green onions and English peas; green cabbage wedges topped with a creamy horseradish sauce; a crystal platter of pickled beets, watermelon rind and peaches, attractively arranged with lemon rind curls and parsley sprigs; and Sadie's biscuits - no one, but no one could duplicate Sadie's biscuits. And for dessert, huckleberry jam filled tarts mounded high with mountains of rich whipped cream and finely chopped pecans.

The conversation was lively. Berta became acquainted with the three children and found them all fascinating...so unlike her friends in west Florida. They were more like her Macon cousins with their incessant chatter about every subject. Jock didn't feel his daughters should refrain from controversial topics, and their opinions were encouraged as were Simon's. She loved it and so did Layke, who found Berta not only intelligent, but she seemed to have an extra sense, a visionary approach, weighing each problem, then suddenly finding a solution. She continued to amaze him. He realized that her talents did not lie in hand work or the mundane chores of a rancher's wife - she was destined for greater things.

Jock was expounding on the merits of his daughters. Ovetta, according to her proud father, was a very accomplished pianist and taught piano and played for the First Baptist Church, a very large and beautiful church left - praise the Lord - untouched during the War. Marlene worked as a milliner in one of Jacksonville's finest shops, Furchgott's on Bay Street. Her creations were much sought after by the cream of society, Aunt Lawanda proudly mentioned.

After dinner Lawanda and Berta retired to the parlor to chat, and she told her niece about the effect the War had had on Marlene. It had left her extremely nervous, and after just one date the young men didn't call again. But she was the only one of their children who had suffered any visible effects from the upheaval. "Having to leave our home and hide out in the country in little more than a shack the last two years of the War and living off of anything we could grow or scavenge was terrible for all of us. Jock insisted that we leave, and of course he was right."

"That wasn't bad enough, Berta, but the Blacks had almost taken over the city when we returned. They were so insolent and unruly. They expected the government to feed and cloth them, and not a one of 'em would turn a hand. Of course, Edna had not deserted us and hid out with us in Middleburg. She's such a fine woman. I don't know what we'd have done without her when Jock was away. I don't think Marlene will ever get over it."

"Oh, Lawanda, I had no idea. Really I didn't. You had to witness even more than Mama and Papa did. I'm so sorry. We were the ones who were spared. Reuben was away only a few months at a time, and we always had enough food...not like it must have been here."

"We didn't know whether we'd have a home to return to," Lawanda continued. "The city was under siege, and just traveling a few blocks was a frightening experience for us. The time in the country actually restored our sanity."

"I pray my family and I never again have to experience the ugliness that emerges from otherwise nice people when their lives are threatened. Berta, you become suspicious of even your best friends when loyalties are questioned. Why, our next door neighbors were sympathetic to the Union and were not just shunned, but treated terribly by lifelong friends. All of them weren't thieves, as Jock would have you believe. He's so bitter, still, after all this time! I'm sure Lillian and Nordie must have been subjected to the same treatment in Macon. But the burning of our proud, beautiful city - well, at least, they were spared that horror and humiliation. If you could have seen the inhuman expressions on their faces as they went about their despicable acts..."

Berta was shocked. "We got so little news in Old Town, and the few papers we did get were so old by the time we read them that..."

"Aunt Lawanda, Jacksonville is a very active city. Perhaps Marlene needs a different, calmer atmosphere to restore her confidence. I don't thing Old Town is the answer. It's really too primitive for a single girl, but I'll look around Crescent City while I'm there; and Lake City is becoming much more cosmopolitan. Why, when Layke and I were there, I was amazed at how much it had grown in the twelve years since I'd last seen it. There are four entire streets of buildings; some even had two stories. Perhaps the horror of the War still visits Marlene here in Jacksonville. We'll keep in touch. She is such a lovely girl and so talented, I'd like to see her properly settled.

Lawanda rose from her deeply cushioned, rosewood chair and went to Berta and with shining tears of thanks reached down to her. They embraced and Berta realized that it was the first time she had ever felt close to her. She had been a child the few times she had been around Lawanda, except when she had made her debut, and was so preoccupied with being a new bride when she and Reuben came through Jacksonville that she had not made an effort to get to know her aunt. "I've missed a lot. She's a dear, sensitive lady, and I'm so glad I'm finally aware of it."

Their visit was all too short. Layke told Jock that he would like to have discussed cattle shipment with some of the steamship companies, that as South Spring grew there was no need to concentrate on the Cuban market alone. "I'll discuss it with Pierce and Jordan at our meeting," he stated emphatically to himself.

Sadie and Berta were in tears as Simon came around from the back with the buggy to drive Layke and her to the landing. She and Lawanda had spent a delightful morning in downtown Jacksonville at Furchgott's shopping for a new hat. Marlene had been so proud that Berta had selected one of her creations that the three decided to have morning coffee at the St. James Hotel tearoom as a sort of good-bye party.

"My, I haven't giggled this much in years, Aunt Lawanda. Oh, Marlene, I was speaking to your mother just a few minutes ago. Layke and I would love for you to come visit us at South Spring. Now, don't get too excited," she interjected as she could see Marlene's enthusiasm ready to burst out. "Old Town is just a tiny wilderness town, dear. Not much happens there, but we do have lots of fun, nevertheless."

Jock had to be at a very important cotton brokers' meeting, so he allowed Simon to drive the honeymooners to the wharf after he dropped Jock off at the building on Main Street. Invitations to visit were extended to the entire family before they departed, and Berta enthusiastically explained to Layke, "I think Marlene is interested in visiting us at South Spring, Hon. Do you know she will be the very first relative I've ever had visit if she does?" He nuzzled her cheek and squeezed her to him. Simon had a hard time keeping his eyes on the road and not looking back at the romantic couple. His father glared at him, trying to let him know of his displeasure, but Jock wore an understanding smile just the same. He was so happy for Berta. She had always been his favorite. He just prayed that this energetic, vital young man was what he appeared to be. He was so unlike Reuben, he thought. Jock was a very cautious man.

CHAPTER IV THE ROBERT E. LEE

Simon helped Berta and Layke get settled in their stateroom on the upper deck, hugged Berta, shook Layke's hand firmly, then bounced down the gangplank, stopping long enough to pat a young colored boy on his head before returning to the buggy on Laura St. The wharf was lined with passengers, some saying their good-bys to relatives and others alighting from the elegant coaches from the nearby hotels. He turned to wave his good-by exuberantly.

Because they were traveling all the way to Georgetown on Lake George, the port nearest the Garvin ranch, they had decided to spend the night in one of the lovely hotels at Palatka. Berta was sorry that they'd not have an overnight aboard the beautiful new ship; they would use the stateroom only for changing their clothing for dining and dancing on board. It was a beautiful room paneled in mahogany and yellow pine with a shell-shaped marble washstand in the far corner. The two berths, one above the other, were covered in a rich gold brocade; the upper one was arranged on hinges so that it could be turned up against the wall allowing more room for the passengers. A rich, dark red, figured Wilton carpet covered the small floor area, and an ornate, gilded mirror hung above two comfortable red plush arm chairs. Polished brass lamps with etched, red globes hung on either side of the mirror.

The deckhands were filling the hold and first deck with bales of cotton, turpentine and resin, barrels of nails and stacks of lumber. On the return trip from the upper St. Johns it would be loaded with the popular cypress and live oak lumber from the Palatka area, and later in the year crates of oranges and lemons for the growing northern trade. Layke informed his attentive wife that the river was one of the few that flowed north, and that at one time it was thought to have been part of the Atlantic.

"He has the same curiosity as Reuben," she thought. "Actually, that and his love of the land are the only things they seem to have in common."

Berta and Layke were fascinated by the activity on Laura Street; then they turned their interest to the Negro children who were performing for the boarding passengers on the wharf. There were tap dancers, harmonica and banjo players, and some actually danced and played their instruments at the same time. The delighted passengers would drop a few coins in the straw hats that were strategically placed beside each performer. The circus-like atmosphere brought smiles to their faces as they paraded along the deck of the 155 foot *Robert E. Lee*, one of the finest boats on the river, and certainly the finest of the Baja Line. It was the only one with an iron hull and deck beam frame with everything below the main deck constructed of iron.

Berta's enthusiasm simply could not be contained. She marveled at the size, then the appointments of the prestigious steamship. When she and her brother and sister had accompanied their parents to Savannah as children, her father had taken them to look at the large ships. But none could have been as majestic as this one...and on this one she'd be with Layke.

It was a warm July day tempered by a light, cooling sea breeze from the Atlantic, certainly welcomed by the many passengers. Berta was having difficulty keeping on her new, navy blue leghorn hat that she had purchased that morning while shopping with Lawanda. Finally she decided to remove it altogether. She stood quietly on the stern, holding on to the polished mahogany rail. The sporadic wind gusts loosened little sun-glinted, golden wisps of hair about her glowing face. The huge paddle wheel behind her began its hesitant, creaky revolution as it dipped into the dark amber river water, churning it to a bright yellow hue. Layke held her to him and whispered, "I wish we were going to be on the *Robert E. Lee* for at least a week, Hon."

Berta looked up at him and replied, "Did you know your eyes are the color of the Gulf, my love?" Ignoring the surrounding passengers, they were intent only on each other. They embraced while the amused on-lookers tried to look away, but their smiles conveyed their delight. Among them stood a tall figure in white, a black cheroot in hand. He was leaning against the wall, his polished boot resting on the deck chair beside him. He watched Berta's every move.

There was already activity in the men's saloon on the second deck. Some of the male passengers were engaged in card games in the smaller room that was set aside for them, and the room was heavy with cigar smoke. When Berta looked inside, she saw a handsome gentleman, all in white, seated at a table in the far corner playing cards with three other men, who appeared to be quite wealthy, if their expensive attire was any indication.

"Why is the man in white being so conspicuously brazen, staring at me in that manner?" she thought to herself. She purposely looked away and turned to leave, but she could feel his eyes follow her. "He does seem familiar, though," she thought. "Where could I have known him? His eyes are the most unusual blue I've ever seen, milky, almost opaque. Couldn't be Old Town. I've been away from home only once in seventeen years. Maybe Macon?"

A uniformed gentleman, obviously someone who worked on board, came toward her, and she decided to ask him who the man was. "I'll not rest 'til I know, so I might as well get it over with."

"Sir, I don't wish to be a bother, but I know I'll die of curiosity if I don't find out. I mean I'm ..."

He stopped and smiled slightly down at the pretty lady, who was obviously having trouble expressing herself.

"How may I help you, Madam? I'm first officer Evans, and I'm at your service."

"Oh, I know this is ridiculous, but there is a man dressed all in white in the men's saloon, and I know - at least I think I know him from somewhere. But for the life of me, I can't remember where. Why, this is only the second time I've been away from Old Town in seventeen years," she rambled, "and I know that's not where I've seen him. And before my first marriage I lived in Macon...you know, Macon, Georgia. I don't recall having known him there, either. But he keeps looking at me like he recognizes me, too."

Hurriedly she continued before first officer Evans spoke. "I hope you don't think this presumptuous of me. It's just that I'm so curious, and know I'll not rest 'til I have reconciled this matter."

"Madam, I assure you that I do not think you presumptuous. The gentleman you refer to is one Conner O'Farrell, a riverboat gambler, and I'm sure that you've had no occasion to be in Mr. O'Farrell's company. He's been on the *Robert E. Lee* since it was commissioned in Savannah, and before that, I've been told, was a frequent passenger on the *Delta Sun* in New Orleans. Now he did serve in Florida with Capt. Dickison during the War, but I don't imagine that you'd have known him from that."

Before Berta could answer he resumed..."No, Madam, I'm sure you're mistaken."

"I am not mistaken, sir," she wanted to say, but smiled her thanks up at him and continued down the passageway to the other small saloon, adjacent to the men's saloon, and used by the women and children. Rather than enter she decided to find out what all the commotion was at the opposite end of the deck. People were standing inside about three rows deep oohing and aahing at the rich appointments of the grand salon. It was a magnificent room, and she realized she had never seen such grandeur, not even in the fine hotels her family and she had stayed at in Savannah. Deep red velvet curtains intricately draped the doorways. Mirrored pillars were heavily encrusted with gold leaf designs, and in the center of the room above a highly polished, yellow pine dance floor hung a beautifully ornate chandelier, gold with crimson, etched globes. Small French gilt chairs with red velvet seats lined the large room, and round tables were strategically placed for dining. At the far end were comfortable-looking chairs in red plush, and the walls behind the mahogany grand piano were lined with magazines and books.

Every time she turned around there he'd be, the man in white, always with that strange expression for all to see.

"Is he following me, or is it just my imagination? It must be!" She decided to ignore him and also decided that she'd not mention her suspicions to Layke. She would never have kept them from Reuben. They would have analyzed the situation and discussed it until Reuben had decided on a course of action. But Layke was new to her, and she was hesitant to even mention her concern to him. He didn't seem to have the control that Reuben had. It delighted her...this intrigue. "My, my. Less than a year ago I was burdened with my tremendous responsibilities and not a reprieve in sight. Then my love rode into my life. And now, a stranger, an exciting, mysterious stranger, has surfaced." She laughed. "Orlean would say, 'Mees Berta, he come from one of your udder lifes, he does.' "

****

As beautiful as the grand salon was, Berta preferred sitting in a canvas deck chair on the open deck and watching the passing countryside. The perennial, unbroken walls of green lined the river's banks. The small towns of Magnolia and Hibernia had resumed their activity since the reconstruction days and were enjoying the golden era along with the larger river towns. As they slowly moved south, she watched their activity and thought, "They're not unlike Old Town - probably the same type of people, good, hard-working, caring. I think I'm homesick," and she laughed at her foolishness, but SuSu's haunting face appeared unexpectedly.

"I'm not going to think of home, and I'm going to concentrate on pleasant things, just pleasant things," she declared and resumed her handwork, forcing herself to relive her first meeting with her love and their amusing evening with the Wilpoles in Rowland's Bluff. But the sad image of SuSu kept entering her mind. "I've got to take hold. Nothing must mar this wonderful trip. Nothing! And why do I allow the pale-eyed stranger to keep interrupting my thoughts?"

The trip to Georgetown would have taken only about 12 hours if they had sailed directly and had not stopped overnight in Palatka. Pierce wrote that he would meet them when they docked at the Georgetown dock only a few miles from his Bullseye ranch and west of Crescent City. There were the scheduled stops at wooding stations and mail delivery at Magnolia, Hibernia and Green Cove Springs, a small, bustling town south of Jacksonville, and finally, Palatka, the up-and-coming town west of St. Augustine, that was vying with Jacksonville, 75 miles to its north, for supremacy on the river.

She put down her handwork and watched Layke, who was conversing with yet another gentleman. He had quite a group surrounding him, laughing sometimes, but mostly serious, deep in thought.

"I'm already expected to share him. It's not fair! Am I jealous of this ambitious man I married?" she questioned as she continued looking at the group. "He stands out even in a crowd. He'll be so excited when he finally remembers me, he'll want to share every morsel of their conversation and his opinion of them. But I want to be a part of it! I want to have my say," she thought, trying not to be envious.

"Berta should have been the boy, Lillian." she remembered her pa saying to her ma when she was not yet sixteen. "She's always so darned sure of herself and her direction, not gushy and silly like girls are supposed to be."

Her ma had replied in that softening tone, "Oh, Nordie, for

heaven's sake. Just because she can handle those high-minded politician friends of yours doesn't mean she's manly. Why, ladies from throughout history have been keeping you men straight." and she chuckled lightly as he cleared his throat in that special way of his, and Berta knew that that would be the end of the conversation, so she busied herself with something else.

As predicted, when Layke remembered his bride, he excused himself and joined her. He was so excited about his conversation with the gentleman in the dark brown suit, the one smoking the big cigar, that he began repeating it verbatim. He was from Baltimore on his way to Palatka to investigate some property for his company's expansion. As he animatedly repeated the conversation, she became just as enthralled with the expansion plans of the many developers on board as Layke. He said almost every man he'd spoken with all morning was on the same type of expedition, and some had discussed a plan to go all the way to the Everglades to investigate the possibility of draining it and making the land habitable," if they could get into it without being eaten by a gator," he laughed.

Florida was indeed booming. He knew Pierce and Jordan would be interested in the information he'd learned, and that they would no doubt use it to their advantage in making plans. After having enlisted the support of John Wilpole, Layke believed that now was the time to form some type of organization, an association, perhaps, of the largest ranchers in the state. They needed to work together. His years of study at The Citadel would certainly be beneficial in helping to formalize a draft to present to Pierce and Jordan when they got to Bullseye. He knew he was on his way. His wandering days were over. He sighed.

Before he could continue his conversation, a young Negro man dressed all in starched white with brass buttons announced, "Dinner is served," and struck the metal gong another authoritative blow as he marched importantly up and down the long deck.

Putting her crocheting in her bag, Berta and Layke joined the other hungry passengers in the grand salon. Marie and Harry Dunston from Virginia introduced themselves and asked if they might join them. When Layke saw the meager display of food he whispered in his low voice, "From the looks of it, I'll go to bed hungry tonight, my love," and Berta playfully kicked his ankle under the table and smiled at Marie, who was a large, affable woman, and had overheard Layke. She couldn't contain her laughter, and soon they were all immersed in light conversation. Seated next to them was the man in white. Berta decided not to acknowledge him, but she could feel his presence.

Harry was telling them about the steamboats of the northern line, the DeBary. He said that he and Marie had spent the night at the St. Jame's Hotel in Jacksonville, and that everyone there was speaking of the fine French food served on the DeBary ships, and that they had almost changed their minds and taken the smaller sidewheeler, *Rosa*, but when they saw the *Robert E. Lee*, they were so glad they hadn't.

The smoked oysters and clams and miniature crab cakes served with thickly buttered scones were only appetizers. When the soup course arrived, Layke happily realized his concern was unwarranted. They selected the cold cucumber soup sprinkled with freshly ground nutmeg. Berta was mentally storing up recipes for Trudy to try on the Old Towners. Miniature biscuits and thinly sliced pickled vegetables accompanied the soup course. Berta was eating sparingly, but Layke, who was a large man, consumed a great deal of food, and Berta thought, "He's just trying to keep up with Harry," who was heavy set.

Marie was quite genteel, although she spoke rather loudly. They were en route to Georgetown to visit her sister and husband, who owned and operated two ice plants on the large lake, and she and Harry were considering leaving Virginia and relocating.

"The War destroyed the friendly feelings in our town, Berta. Our children are grown and have moved away, and Harry and I don't feel comfortable there anymore, so we're looking for a place to settle for our sunset years. My sister, Olga, loves it in Georgetown. It's just a small village, but she says the area is growing rapidly, and for special activities there is always a steamboat leaving for Jacksonville and Palatka at least three times a week."

"Berta, I think I'll love it. We need a new start. As long as we stay home, the War and the hard times will remain with us, I'm sure."

As Berta looked around the salon she realized she was seeing the new Floridians. She avoided glancing toward the table next to theirs, but she knew he was still there.

"Oh no!" Marie exclaimed as the impeccably uniformed waiters arrived with huge platters steaming with sliced smoked ham surrounded by candied yams topped with broiled Florida pineapple and glazed walnuts. Baked tomato cups and baby yellow squash stuffed with sausage and bread stuffing and light-as-a-feather corn bread sticks were served next.

They decided to forego dessert. Instead they'd take a walk around the deck before retiring to their cabins for their naps, as was the custom in the South.

When they arrived at the fantail, Layke asked Berta, "Would you like coffee served, my Lady? Here, you and Marie sit down here, and Harry and I will do the honors." He bowed to the ladies, his dark brown hair falling over his forehead, and groaned at the difficulty of bending even that slightly after such a sumptuous meal. Berta and Marie began to laugh at his theatrics. Putting his finger to his lips to shush them, he and Harry abruptly turned and in military fashion marched off toward the salon to secure some coffee.

"Layke is such a charming young man. Harry and I were saying just a few minutes ago how much he reminds us of our son, Lamar. He was killed at New Market, you know. Layke has the same way about him, meeting people so easily and making you feel welcome. And oh, he is so handsome, my dear."

"She reminds me of Trudy," Berta thought. "The same caring." But aloud she said, "I do hope that after the ship docks at Georgetown, that we'll have the opportunity to meet you and Harry again, Marie. Our time together will be much too short."

Before Marie could answer, the men had returned, and with a great flourish Harry presented them with a napkin filled with assorted, jam-filled cookies.

"Oh, you didn't!" they cried in unison. Berta informed Layke that neither he nor she would indulge, and that she'd put them in her sewing bag for later, giving her husband a secretive wink.

They excused themselves and retired to their small stateroom. Before they entered, Berta saw a white figure leaning against the wall of the adjacent cabin, the cigar smoke spiraling into the air. Layke, only aware of his love, laughingly exclaimed that he wasn't sure that they would both fit in the cabin after such a repast. It was warm, but not too uncomfortable. Berta undressed slowly and put on her pretty, pink, silk brocade wrapper. She slowly sank onto the narrow berth, and Layke sat on the carpeted floor beside her stroking her loosened hair.

"I love you, Mrs. Williams. Do you know how important your happiness is to me?"

She took his strong, gentle hand and kissed his fingers and nodded. He soon fell asleep still on the floor beside her with his head nestled on her breast. She lay awake and saw only the tall figure in white, wondering who on earth he was and if her imagination was playing tricks on her.

****

Berta and Layke were enjoying their relaxing afternoon on the fantail. The seabirds were thick around the ship, and the passengers lined alongside the railing were enjoying feeding them bread crumbs. It was a bright, sunny day with not a cloud in the dark blue sky. The afternoon rains had not arrived and would perhaps give them a reprieve. Soon they would arrive in Green Cove Springs, where they and the Dunstons planned to have their tea in one of the small hotels.

Berta was teasing Layke about his politicking and reminded him, "As I told you in Rowland's Bluff, Layke, anyone can be king in this country - for a price," and tweaked his ear as she pecked him on his welcome lips.

"Yes, my dear, so you told me. Would you be interested in living in the governor's mansion, Berta?"

"Not necessarily, my dear husband. I think I'm more partial to the big house in Washington. But, then, we do have to begin somewhere, don't we?"

"Yes," Berta thought, "It's all for the taking, my dear husband. But the price would be my aloneness, my willingness to share you. I'm not sure I'd be capable of that magnanimous a sacrifice. We'll see. We'll just wait to see...but I'm sure you'll put me to the test," and they lazed away the afternoon visiting with the other passengers in a light vein to while away the time.

As they teased they both knew the possibility existed for whatever life they decided on. South Spring, with Layke at the helm, could one day be a very powerful ranch. His intelligence, his wit, his affable personality, his insatiable thirst for knowledge and, above all, his love for the land were all necessary ingredients for prosperity in this frontier, this last frontier.

They passed by a green sloping bank covered by orange groves, and in their midst were quaint cottages surrounded by oaks dripping with Spanish moss. Berta could see no shops or buildings other than the large structure that she overheard another passenger explain was the Magnolia Hotel owned by a Mr. Louis B. Brown.

A few miles up river and around a wooded point lay the quiet village of Green Cove Springs. They could see a group of active people alongside the landing but could not understand why they were so animated and what they were shouting about. When Harry and Marie finally joined them, they were closer to the dock, and the words could be understood. They realized that the colored men were vociferously shouting the praises of the Clarendon and Palmetto House Hotels, trying to coax the departing passengers into following them to their respective establishments for tea.

About a dozen passengers departed, and those who were staying the night handed over their small traps to the two colored gentlemen, who in turn led them to their hotels. As they walked down the sandy street they passed a high wooden fence that very obviously enclosed the famous Blue Sulphur Spring. The odor was unmistakable. The baths that the passengers planned to enjoy during their stay would nurse their rheumatic joints while the healing waters rejuvenated their tottering limbs and failing powers; or so the advertisements guaranteed.

When Berta, Layke and the Dunstons reached the gate to the Clarendon, they were impressed by the rows of orange trees heavy with the green fruit; it would be two or three months before they turned their bright orange. The northern tourists were childlike in their enthusiasm. Tea was soon served on the enclosed piazza, and before they were ready, the time to depart was near.

The foursome decided to return on another trip to take advantage of the bubbling waters that gushed from deep in the bowels of the bottomless ravine; the spring water temperature was reputed to be a constant 78 degrees. Marie and Berta insisted on peeking at the bathhouse. The enclosed pool was 60 feet long, and above the white sand bottom lay four feet of clear blue water. It was surrounded by a wooden platform and small dressing rooms, where the bathers could change into their costumes.

Marie turned toward Berta and whispered, "I am so glad that Harry and I decided not to stop for an overnight. I did not think to bring a bathing dress, did you?" Berta didn't want her to know that she didn't own one and had never even seen one except in pictures. When she and the children swam in the south spring, she usually wore an old chemise and petticoat. They thanked the colored woman who had allowed them inside without paying their twenty-five cents and quickly joined their waiting husbands. Across the street she caught a fleeting glance of the figure in white and quickly averted her eyes toward the river.

****

Berta and Layke and many of the other passengers had planned to stay overnight in one of the beautiful hotels in Palatka but would dress for the evening's activities on board in their stateroom. Berta had discussed with Marie Dunston what the dress would be, and after much deliberation and to the amusement of Layke she decided on the mauve faille she had worn for their wedding. When they arrived in the grand salon, she was pleased by her choice. There were grander gowns, to be sure, but hers was as pretty as any there and indeed appropriate.

Harry and Marie soon joined them, and Layke, being in a gala mood, ordered the popular Mumms champagne for their table. "Oh my, aren't you afraid to serve your bride the elixir of the gods, my dear husband?" Berta asked.

"You are the elixir of the gods, my dear one," he replied as he took her hand to kiss. Marie and Harry were delightfully entertained by their playful exchange, and their merry evening commenced.

There would be dancing into the night. The violins played, and a number of couples waltzed to their lilting notes. Berta and Layke had never danced. She whispered to him, "Let's retire to the deck, dear," as she took his arm and proceeded to the fantail. They were alone. The night was glorious. Every star in the heavens twinkled at them, and in the distance the lamp-lit streets of Palatka beckoned.

Layke took Berta in his arms stiltedly. Berta whispered, "Relax. Just follow me and try to keep time to the music." She showed him the step, and he began counting..one..two..three...and again he repeated the steps. Then he began whirling her around and around.

"Why, Layke Williams, you know how to waltz," and she

playfully hit him with her lace fan.

"My dear Berta, yours truly was a much sought gentleman and officer at The Citadel before he became a Florida cowman."

She stopped, held him away from her and said, "You should not have had to remind me, Layke. It would appear that we know very little about each other. I'm embarrassed at my presumption."

Layke looked at his lovely bride and taking her arm, put his strong arm around her waist and waltzed her through the open door to the salon. Her tiny feet flew happily to the strains of the lilting melody. Exhausted, they joined the Dunstons to rest.

"You're the handsomest couple on the floor, Berta," Marie gushed with a mother's enthusiasm.

"And the best dancers, by far," chimed in Harry.

Layke rose, reached for Berta's hand, and bid their goodnights to the Dunstons. They were surprised as the night was young and the evening festive. Layke explained, "It would appear that my wife and I need to find out more about each other," and Berta quickly pulled him to herself, and as she took his arm she smiled her good-by to their friends.

Marie and Harry could hear their peels of laughter as they went arm in arm onto the moonlit deck. She and Harry looked at each other and sighed, remembering when they were young and their love was fresh. Harry took her pudgy hand in his and brought it to his lips. She smiled warmly at her good husband of over thirty years, and they rose to join the other dancers. They paid no attention to the man who followed Berta and Layke out of the salon.

****

The town of Palatka was situated on a high shell rise above the river. Long wharfs lined Water Street, and wooden buildings stood beside red brick buildings, some three stories tall, that overlooked the river.

Layke and Berta and a few of the other passengers walked toward Lemon Street and were quickly met by the mule-drawn street railway, that would seat as many as twenty riders, to transport them to the various hotels. But they declined. It was too beautiful a night to ride, they decided. They walked hand in hand, not talking, and drank in the bright night, the fireflies lighting their way. In the distance a panther screamed, and Berta drew Layke closer to her. The noisy frogs cried for rain, and the screech owls were as loud as at South Spring, she mentioned as they turned onto Front Street. A wooden sidewalk lined with orange trees ran the length of Putnam House, which was the largest and most prestigious hotel in Palatka and covered an entire block with wide, landscaped grounds on both sides.

The large foyer was comfortable looking with plush chairs in gold and deep green. The leaf design on the patterned, Wilton carpet accented the gold and green colors, and large urns, that held miniature citrus trees were placed between the grouped chairs and love seats, affording the patrons some privacy.

Layke picked up a copy of *The Eastern Herald*, Palatka's only newspaper, that was universally known, because its editor was the very colorful Alligator Pratt, so called for the noted alligator stories he wrote, that frightened the readers from coast to coast.

While Layke registered them at the desk, Berta wandered over to the dining hall and peaked in. She was impressed by its size and elegance; it was as large as the one at the St. James in Jacksonville, she noted. The menu displayed on the brass stand at its entrance interested her. As Layke approached she motioned him over. The porter, who was a few steps behind him, carried their small traps.

"They are noted for their extensive wine cellar, I was told," Layke informed Berta, "and from the looks of this menu, honey, we're definitely not in the wilds of Florida, even if the panthers' screams do seem to be coming from just over the rise."

The stooped, colored porter commented as he waited for them to read the menu, "An' dey's got mighty good food here, I's been told - mighty good."

"Oh, I wish we could stay at least for another day, hon," she pleaded, her face turned up toward Layke, "but I know we can't - maybe next time. Layke, promise me right here and now that we'll return...promise!"

He was engrossed in the menu and answered her nonchalantly, "Of course. How good is your French, Berta? Mine's rusty. What does *a l'Anglaise* mean?"

"Gracious, I haven't read any French since Miss Horton's class, Layke, and that was over eighteen years ago. But I think..."

"Oh," he interrupted, "I remember. It's English style. *Fillet of*

Beef Larded, a l'Anglaise. I think I've been a cowman too long, my love.

"Well, Sir," she whispered low, "If you think you're going to entertain yourself this evening reading Mr. Alligator Pratt's paper, then I know for sure the honeymoon is definitely over."

She grabbed the paper out from under Layke's arm and quickly stuck it behind her as she teased him. The porter snickered at the two playful lovebirds while Layke tried to retrieve the paper from Berta, and she dodged his attempts, effortlessly running up the stairs toward their room.

The man at the foot of the stairs wore and amused expression.

"I feel like a new bride," she said breathlessly. "Gracious, I am a new bride." Layke grabbed her and wrenched the paper from behind, holding her arm hard. The porter left hurriedly. He could see the passion between them. Layke threw Berta on the covered bed.

"Yes, my sweet, you are indeed a new bride and I'm famished."

"Layke," she gasped, "You're hurting me!"

"Oh, God, Berta. I'm sorry. I'm sorry, my sweet. I'd not hurt you for the world. Here, let me soothe that hurt away...all away."

****

"Berta - stop! Berta, what's wrong?" She could hear herself screaming and felt his hand covering her mouth, suppressing the next outburst. She was enveloped by his arms, which were tight around her, trying to ease her fright. She was gasping for breath, and the tears began.

"Sweet, it was just a bad dream. Please, my dear one.. please. Everything will be all right. I'm here. Please."

A loud knock on their door was followed by "Is everything all right in there?" in an unmistakable Irish brogue. She shuddered, then gasped for air as Layke got up to get her his handkerchief. "Yes, everything is fine. My wife just had a nightmare. Thank you for your concern."

She could hear the footsteps retreat for a short distance but was so upset by the dream that it didn't register that the door which closed was next to theirs.

"Here, dear, blow your nose and I'll get a damp cloth for you."

He went to the gold-edged wash bowl, poured the cool water

from the matching pitcher and dampened the cloth. Turning he said, "I want you to try to remember the dream...all of it."

"Here, place this over your eyes." He handed her the damp cloth, and Berta held it over her face.

"Oh, Layke," she said heaving, trying to calm down. "It was so real! SuSu was in a sort of cloud, I thought. Her little face was contorted - like she was in great pain. Layke, I know it's a sign. I know something is wrong at home. I just know it!"

"Berta, stop right now, this instant. I want you to tell me your dream. Then I want to discuss it calmly and rationally. Now go on, hon," he spoke slowly - deliberately.

"Then I could see her in a sheet of water - like a waterfall. But there was no top nor bottom, just gushing water." Her hand went to her mouth to stop the scream she was afraid would come. "The water kept streaming from the sky, pouring over her...just going and going. She couldn't breathe, Layke. She was screaming and, Layke," she gasped, "she was drowning. All I could see was her frightened face and her mouth forming...Mama..Mama..Mama. Oh, Layke, it was so real!"

He held her close stroking her damp hair from her tear-streaked face. "It was a dream, a frightening dream, Berta. No more tears, my sweet. I'm here. You always worry about SuSu - ever since I've known you. I know she's slight, but she seems to be in good health, hon. Here, blow your nose and let's get some sleep. I'll tell you what. We'll have breakfast in the dining room. How would you like that?"

"You're soothing me with your charm, Mr. Williams." She kissed his hand that held hers and said sleepily, "I'd like that, Layke. I'd like that, hon, "and was soon sleeping soundly.

Layke lay awake for a long time. Berta's dream was troubling. He couldn't seem to get it out of his mind enough to relax. Finally, drowsily, he prayed, "Dear Lord, please let it be only a dream...Please..."

CHAPTER V CRESCENT CITY

When the *Robert E. Lee* docked at Georgetown, Pierce and Thom Garvin were waiting for the honeymooners. Berta had met Pierce only once many years before when he visited South Spring to purchase some of Reuben's stock. He had changed little in that time, a little more gray to his sandy hair, but he was still slender. Young Thom, whom she had never met, was a very good-looking young man with a beautiful smile, and he used it effectively to greet her when she thanked him for assisting her into the buckboard. She could readily see why Callie Meade was so taken with him. Layke had told her about the sport the other cowmen were having with them on the return to Tater Hill Bluff, and how the two of them seemed to have taken a shine to each other.

They had made their good-by to the Dunstons before departing and discussed plans for a visit if and when they relocated in Florida. Marie's sister and her husband had met them at the landing, and they were engaged in animated conversation as Berta, finally catching Marie's eye, waved good-by, and turned her attention back toward the ship to look for the figure in white. She did not see him behind the barrels on the lower deck, where he stood silently gazing at her.

"Good," she thought. "I've just got to take hold. This is ridiculous."

The countryside was not unlike the western part of the state except for the many orange groves that lined the packed sand road. The same stately pines and other types of vegetation grew in the sandy soil, she observed, as Thom made every effort to avoid the holes in the rutted road. Pierce and Layke were already deep in conversation about the upcoming meeting with Jordan, and Berta remained quiet in order to listen.

"Layke, my husband," she thought, "You have an uncanny way of seeking out power." Of all the men on the spring drive, the ones he was most taken with were Pierce and Jordan, the two most knowledgeable and influential men in the cattle business in the entire state. Jordan, or Prof, as his men called him, had been a college professor in Massachusetts, was an expert rancher, and Pierce, whose family was probably the oldest ranching family in

Florida, was also very political, having uncles, cousins and the like serving in the senate and legislature, and carried a lot of weight in Tallahassee.

The stock on the Garvin ranch descended from the cattle that accompanied Ponce de Leon's second expedition in 1521, as Pierce and his late father, Joe, had proudly attested. Their holdings began as a grant from England during the British occupation, and the original 20,000 acres had grown to the present 80,000. It had originally been an indigo plantation with some acreage planted in cotton and corn, and they had only a small herd of cattle.

Mary later related to Berta that there had been a Pierce or Garvin on the land ever since. Mary's family had migrated south from Virginia early in the 1800's to Palatka and were of Scotch-Irish descent as was Pierce's, whose ancestors had left Ireland and settled in Scotland before coming to America. Their acreage bordered the western side of Crescent Lake almost to the northern boundary of the beautiful, clear lake and was bordered on the west side by Lake George. Layke told Berta later that day that he'd never seen such lush pasture land, as deep as over at Payne's Prairie in some areas.

Mary was a lovely, quiet woman and the perfect mistress of their Bullseye Ranch. Their home was so comfortable, Berta thought. It had two stories and a wrap-around porch like she remembered seeing in Georgia, white with dark green shutters that also served against an unannounced norther or hurricane.

Berta and Mary were having tea on the shade-cooled front porch while Little Bit, the youngest child, was trying every antic her active young mind could conjure up to get their attention. She was standing on her head and tumbling and skinning the cat on the low oak branch while busily keeping a watchful eye out for their amazement at her daring, and listening attentively for their frightened outbursts.

"She's as active a child as I've ever seen, Mary, and about the same age as Wesley and just as towheaded. Now, those two would make a pair. She's just as outgoing as he. How old did you say Lucinda is?"

"She'll be eleven in October, but she's as tall as Sarah, who's almost two years older."

"SuSu is going on eleven, but she's very slight, like my Aunt Bertrice was at that age, I've been told. I do worry so about her,

Mary. She's not a sickly child, but she doesn't seem to have much strength." She decided to not tell her of the frightening dream she had had in Palatka or about the man who she was positive was following her. She couldn't get him or the dream out of her mind, and when she and Layke first arrived at Bullseye, she was afraid that a telegram would be waiting for them announcing the sad news of SuSu. Thank God there wasn't one.

"Oh Berta. Please put everything unpleasant aside... at least for this trip. We always make time to worry about our children, don't we? At least that's what Pierce says. Well, my mother was a worrier, so maybe I inherited it from her."

They continued to chat about their families on the shadowed porch. Mary finally got up enough nerve to comment about Reuben. "Berta, I know you are aware of how fond Pierce was of Reuben. It was such a shock to all of us when we heard about his sudden death, but when Pierce returned from the last drive and told me of Layke's feelings for you and the opposition your son felt, well, we were so in hopes you'd be able to resolve the problem." She took Berta's hand in hers. "When Layke wrote of your wedding plans, well, my dear, we were so pleased. I'm so glad you came for a visit. We ranchers' wives live in such isolated areas, I'll declare, we don't really get to know one another, do we? And we have so much to share."

"You're absolutely right, Mary. We really should make every effort to remedy the situation. But a solution, I don't have. Perhaps we can at least write more often. That would make it possible for us to keep up to date on each other's family happenings. Somehow men aren't that interested in our small talk." She laughed and added, "When they're discussing the cattle business, it's extremely important, but when we discuss our families...well, it's merely small talk." They both chuckled at the irony of it. Mary added, "And what's most important to both of them?...their families, of course."

Not only did Pierce raise cattle, he had huge pecan groves, some cotton, and in the low lying areas, rice, and he had begun putting in orange and lemon groves, that some believed would be in more demand than timber and cattle. The three oldest boys, Thom, Thurmond and Lanier, were of an age to help run the ranch. As Mary had confided in Berta, they were a tremendous help, especially during the cow hunt. Pierce had promised Thurmond that he'd also be allowed to go on the next drive, because Lanier was now old enough to oversee Bullseye.

As Mary was talking about her boys, Berta allowed an idea that had been in the back of her mind to surface. "Maybe now Young Reuben can come home to South Spring. I've missed him so, and seeing him at the wedding made me realize just how much. I'll speak to Layke about it. He'll certainly have need of him when we expand, just as Pierce does his boys." Just thinking of the possibility made her more animated, and Mary could see her relax and forget momentarily what had obviously been bothering her.

The Garvins had really gone all out to make the newlyweds welcome. Jordan Northrup would be arriving in two days from his "Big Lake" spread if all went well, but in the meantime they had the opportunity for a real visit. Mary had very good Negro help that had stayed on at Bullseye after the War. Berta resolved that that was one thing she was going to see to when she and Layke returned to South Spring. There was no longer any reason for her to do all the work now that Layke was taking over the operation, and she'd ask Willa to inquire when she went to church in town if there was some young girl who might like to be trained by them.

Lucinda rang the dinner bell out by the barn, and it seemed to Berta that children ran from every direction to answer it.

"I never have to make but one dinner call at South Spring, either. I guess it's the same everywhere. Now, when I call for chores to be done, well, I can call two or three times..."

"That certainly holds true at Bullseye, Berta."

Pierce and Layke joined them, and the couples went arm in arm into the spacious dining room. Mary proved to be a beautiful hostess. A soup tureen was steaming with corn chowder served with cheese scones. For the main course there was golden fried chicken and chicken perlo. Berta had never tasted it prepared that way, she told Mary. Her one Negro cook, Marisa, came from the Grand Bahamas, and, as Mary told the appreciative diners, "She has added a lot of her country's spices,ones I'm not familiar with. And Berta, she uses a lot of fruit juices and rind in her seasoning. For instance, she adds lime juice and rind to her perlo, and the small pickled seeds - actually they're flower buds - are known as capers. Mr. Baylor at the General Mercantile Store in town has been able to purchase them from St. Augustine and Key West. It seems that the Spanish use them in their cooking as much as saffron, I'm told."

"Oh, Layke, I'd love to take some back home," she said turning excitedly to her husband and gazing lovingly at him as she pleaded. All the eyes at the Garvin table saw and felt their deep passion as she and Layke looked at each other.

Pierce coughed, his hand hiding a smile, and Mary quickly broke the lovers' spell before one of her children made an uncalled-for remark. "Berta, I'll have Maccaw drive us into town to purchase some, perhaps tomorrow morning, before it gets too warm."

When Berta turned toward her, and in so doing saw all the Garvin faces staring at them, she blushed and answered Mary quickly, "I'd like that, Mary, if it's no bother." She said to herself, "If my legs were longer, Layke Williams, I'd kick you a good one, causing me to look at your handsome, devilish face like that and embarrassing me." She was anxious to finish the meal so she could tell him so in the privacy of their room.

Dessert and coffee were served by Marisa, or Risa, as the family called her, on the shady side porch. The dessert was a delicious ambrosia to which she had added small bits of candied citron and orange and lemon peel and grated coconut. Pierce brought fresh coconuts back to the ranch from Punta Rassa, Mary told Berta, and they grated and dried them for use all year long.

"I guess I'll be getting another order from my wife now, Mary. She does love to cook and is a good one, too," Layke said taking her hand and squeezing it.

Berta complimented Risa on her cooking. "I'm thanking you, Ma'am," she replied in her delightful sing-song voice and turned toward the summer kitchen behind the main house, where Holden, who was nine, was tormenting Little Bit, or so she said, as she ran into the protective arms of her doting father to avoid whatever Holden had decided to do to her. He was the impish one of the family, Mary had told Berta.

Little Bit yelled at him, "If you don't quit, Holden Garvin, I'll get Deut to put a spell on you." Pierce picked her up, her golden pigtails flying, and held her high so Holden couldn't reach her.

"Pierce, don't! Lawd, she'll get sick. She just ate. Pierce, for heaven's sake," lamented Mary.

"Sounds of home," Berta said. "Dear me, I think I'm homesick." SuSu's face appeared, and Berta had to force herself to not dwell on her.

Pierce let the squirming girl down, and she quickly outdistanced her freckle-faced brother, who was determined to catch her. He'd not be bested in front of company by any old girl, he thought, as he gained on her, huffing and puffing but determined. As they rounded the corner of the house he could hear the Williamses laughing at them.

"Layke," Pierce said, rising from the rocker, "after you and Berta rest and it cools off a bit, we'll ride out to the south pasture. I want to show you the pride of Bullseye...next to Mary and the kids, that is," he said playfully to Mary, who took her husband of twenty-plus years in her stride.

"If that bull wins a "diploma" at the State Fair next week, I do believe he'll mean it, Layke," she retorted.

There were four sizable bedrooms upstairs in the large white house. Berta's and Layke's room faced west, and as they climbed the wide staircase she told Layke that Mary had mentioned the spectacular sunsets to be seen on their spread, and she was looking forward to enjoying them during their visit.

"Is that all you're looking forward to at the end of our day, Mrs. Williams?".

"I'll declare, Layke Williams! Don't you think of anything else?" she teased as she slipped out of her brown twill skirt and beige blouse. Gently folding them, she put them over the blanket roll at the end of the four-poster bed so as not to wrinkle them while she and Layke rested after their heavy meal.

They lay on top of the colorful quilt, and she filled him in on her conversation with Mary, and he highlighted his morning with Pierce. But before he was halfway through they were in each others arms.

"Woman, you're the most desirable creature on earth."

"Why, Mr. Williams, how you do carry on," she cooed, stroking his face.

Later Layke poured the cool water into the wash bowl and she re-combed her hair. "We'd best be presentable for our host and hostess, Mr. Williams. After all, you're about to see Pierce Garvin's pride and joy."

"I'm anxious to, Mrs. Williams, and if you weren't such an insatiable wench, I'd already be feasting my eyes on the beast." He took the end of his towel and flicked it close to Berta's behind as she leaned over to button her shoe.

"Layke, you stop that this instant. I'll declare, you're like a frisky cowman after a pint."

They composed themselves as best they could and went downstairs to the large foyer. Berta looked in the parlor and saw no one, then into the dining room, but no one was around. She heard a noise on the porch and through the screened door saw Holden bedeviling one of the poor cats. He was startled when they closed the door to the porch, and quickly putting his hands in his pockets, he sheepishly averted his face while volunteering the whereabouts of everyone else. She and Layke could hear the animated voices of the Garvins as they hurried toward the barn.

It seemed that Jordan Northrup had arrived a day early, and the entire family was down by the barn looking at his entry to the State Fair, that was to be held in Gainesville the following week. Berta had never met Jordan, but was anxious to, for Reuben had spoken of the Yankee from Boston often and with a high regard. He was known to be extremely intelligent and, as Layke had said, very agreeable as well. She also knew that he had the respect of every cowman and rancher in the entire state, and she was excited to meet him at last.

Pierce and Jordan had been exchanging information ever since he bought and developed his Big Lake spread in '68, when there was virtually nothing in that section of Florida but miles and miles of sawgrass. He had told around many a camp fire that he'd not have made it without the invaluable assistance of Pierce and the Seminoles who lived near his holdings. They would not work for a White man, but they were very agreeable about sharing their knowledge, and Jordan had welcomed their hospitality. This was his first visit to Bullseye, and Mary was as excited as Berta about finally getting to meet him.

Jordan stood a good head taller than those surrounding him. He was at least six and a half feet tall, but well built rather than thin. He was a man in his mid forties with perfect, straight features, but as Berta and Layke approached the group she got a better look at him and realized that he was not a handsome man. He was more clean cut than handsome. As she studied him she decided that if he and Layke walked into a room together, every woman in the room would swoon over Layke, but Jordan would evoke maybe, "He's a nice looking man" and no more. There was something animal about her husband. He moved with such grace, despite his limp.

Layke soon joined the others, leaving Berta beside Mary, and warmly shook Jordan's hand. She was so deep in thought that she didn't hear Mary speak at first. "He's a nice looking man, isn't he, Berta?" she said again quietly, and Berta smiled, "Yes, he is. Layke said he's probably one of the most knowledgeable ranchers in Florida. He and Pierce are by far the most respected ranchers this state has produced. Reuben felt the same way, Mary. I know you're proud."

"It's his life. It's the only life he's ever known or wants to know. He was gone for almost four years during the conflict, but aside from that and the spring drive every year that's the only time Pierce Garvin has left Bullseye." Berta thought she detected some bitterness in Mary's voice.

"Thom is old enough to give us a chance to go away for a few weeks, but Pierce always seems to have a project afoot that he can't leave." Sighing, she continued. "I guess our chances of getting to South Spring for a visit are slim, Berta, but to tell you the truth, I'm in need of a change.

"From what you've told me of the marvelous trip on the *Robert E. Lee*, I declare I feel like taking Sarah and Lucinda and just sailing up to Jacksonville and Savannah on her. I'm serious, Berta. And a few days in Gainesville at the State Fair isn't a change at all. Heavens, we do that every year. I think everyone needs a real change, don't you?"

"I certainly do. Do you know that this is the first trip I"ve had since right after the War when I went to Macon 'cause Mama was so ill? I didn't get there in time, bless her heart. But, you're right, Mary. Why don't you do it? The girls would learn so much, and it would give you a chance to see some plays and shop in the delightful shops on the square in Savannah, and..." she caught her breath. "Oh, they're so much fun. Also, the shops on Bay Street in Jacksonville are elegant."

"I'm going to speak to Pierce as soon as he returns from Gainesville. He wants me to accompany him, but I declare, another State Fair isn't my idea of fun anymore. When we first attended them, I would enter the various contests, but I really don't seem to care whether or not my watermelon rind pickles get the blue or the white ribbon anymore. I've just lost interest, Berta. I know I need a change. Having you and Layke here with your fresh, young love so obvious has made me aware of how humdrum our lives have become. Now really, my dear, it's true," she said as she put her hand on Berta's protesting arm. "Pierce is a wonderful man, and a good husband and father, but we've just become dull...we might as well face it. I do have some exciting news though.

"Thom has been writing Callie Meade, Parker and Kate's daughter. My sister Beulah lives in Tater Hill, and she wrote that Callie has mostly put aside her tomboy ways and is much sought after by the young men there. He was so taken with her after the spring drive that he stayed to visit Beulah and George for three long weeks, and Parker gave him permission to call on Callie. Why, he's so excited about next week that he's been singing and is just so frisky, whereas up to two weeks ago he moped around just like an old hound dog. I do hope he's not disappointed in Callie.

"Pierce said she was more cowman than woman and that she could ride and shoot like the best of 'em, but Beulah said she'd turned into a beautiful girl when she got all dressed up."

They continued to visit while the others examined Jordan's entries to the Fair. He and two of his hands had brought his Brahma bull and a new mixed Brahma and Jaffarabodi, of which he was particularly proud, at grazing speed from Big Lake, and he wanted to pen them on Bullseye to replace any weight they'd lost on the trip. Pierce had put in velvet beans again this year, and that plus grain should bring them up to weight.

Layke, accompanied by Jordan and Pierce, joined Mary and Bèrta on the side porch for some of Risa's lemonade and coconut-pecan rolls that she had prepared, and they stopped talking about ranching long enough to comment on Berta's enthusiastic inquisitiveness.

"I might have to purchase a trunk to hold all the recipes Berta will be taking back to South Spring, Jordan."

""My Min will be happy to share her recipes with you, Berta," he commented enthusiastically. "She has quite a collection of interesting dishes she's got from the Seminoles. There are so many tropical and semi-tropical herbs and spices of which we were unaware, and Min has made quite a study of them. When my mother visited us for the first time, she was aghast at the un-Boston-like dishes Min served. She'd learned them from Lottie Tiger and was so proud of the concoctions, but Mother thought she was trying to poison her," and he laughed a hearty bass laugh.

"I like that man, Layke. He's fascinating and true," she whispered as he helped her take the empty tray to the sideboard in the dining room. "Oh, how I wish we could stay for the Fair. I know we can't, but please, my love, let's plan on it for next year. We can make it a family trip, and perhaps the deMoyas can stay at South Spring again. I know Orlean and Dom would welcome the change. They're getting much too old for all that wandering, Layke. Let's propose it when we return."

It was as if Berta had never left Macon, moved to the wilderness of west Florida and accepted her humdrum life. She was as surprised by her youthful enthusiasm as Layke and the Garvins, and Jordan delighted in her.

Layke kissed the top of her golden hair and whispered, "I love you, Mrs. Williams, and of course we'll go to the Fair. It should be great fun, and perhaps by then South Spring will have its own prize bull to show."

He looked off into space when he said that, and she knew he'd do his damndest to best Pierce and Jordan at the next Fair. That would mean she'd spend hours and hours alone. She already missed him.

"Well, Bertrice Lillian Norwood McRae Williams, what did you expect from such a vital man? Did you expect him to hold your yarn and chit-chat on the front porch?"

"No, I did not expect that, but neither did I expect to spend my evenings alone." A figure in white was allowed to enter her subconscious.

"I'll not have it. I'll just not! Go away...go away."

CHAPTER VI THE MISTAKE

The hot July days were drawing to an even hotter August, but the daily afternoon showers would give the fields and natives some relief. The watchful eyes of the Floridians were ever constant during August and September, for the advent of a hurricane was more likely in those months. Old Town vicinity had been spared the brunt of the last hurricane that had devastating consequences in the eastern coastal region, but the high winds and torrential rains they received had been destructive, none the less.

South Spring had returned to normal after Berta's and Layke's wedding. Orlean and Aimee supervised the children and house, and the men tended the stock. The daily tightrope practice continued. Juanita maintained her constant improvement to the surprise of Orlean and Pierre, and the rope had been moved up to an amazing eighteen feet in the air. Aimee was her constant companion, and Orlean wondered if she was her confidant as well.

A decision had to be made, and Orlean knew she would have to make it soon. She had noticed that Juanita had been late in awakening each morning, probably curled up with one of her books, but she had also been having difficulty eating when she first got up. She continued to observe her while Layke and Berta were on their honeymoon and declared that she would not allow the girl to mar their happiness on their return, so the expediency of her talk with Juanita was paramount. Just how she could confront her and not hurt her relationship with her devoted son was an unwanted problem for the very concerned Orlean.

After weeks of painstaking work Aimee had completed Juanita's costume, and it was indeed beautiful. The bodice was covered with hundreds of tiny brilliants and bugle beads in gold and silver, that also edged the tiers of the knee-length skirt with row after row of the shiny beads. When Juanita tried it on in Berta's bedroom, Aimee insisted that she close her eyes before looking in the tall dresser mirror. She spun her around and around as she counted. When she called out zero, she shouted, "Now, Juanita, you may look!" Juanita opened her eyes and her mouth flew open with disbelief. She couldn't get over the effect.

"I just can't believe it's me, Aimee. I just can't," she said in a whisper. She removed the heavy combs and loosened her hair. It caressed her shoulders as it cascaded down the back of the rich aqua and gold satin, tiered costume, her hair reaching its lower edge.

She bit her lower lip in amazement and quickly turned to view it from every angle, this way and that way. Aimee stood by apprehensively awaiting her comments, studying her expression for her reaction.

Mesmerized, Juanita stared at the girl in the mirror and couldn't utter a word. She surely didn't look like Juanita Jane Graves. She did indeed look like *Cherie, the Golden Girl.* "I just can't believe it. I just can't. I sorta wish R.J. and Joe Bob were here to see me. Why is it that every time something important happens you can't find a soul ya wanta share it with?" she wondered silently.

Aimee could restrain her questions no longer. "Well, Juanita, do you like it? Isn't it beautiful?"

She went to Aimee, hugged her and exclaimed in a low, subdued voice, "Aimee, I've never had anything in my whole life pretty like this, not in all my 17 years."

That is how Orlean found them, in a sisterly embrace. "Dat's very pretty, Juanita, but eesn't eet a beet snug at de waist, Aimee? Maybe you'd better put an eensert along de sides. I'll help you eef you'd like, eh?"

"No, Maman, I don't think so. Juanita, does it feel too tight?"

It did feel snug, but she wasn't about to give the old crow an ounce of satisfaction by owning up to it. "No, Aimee, it feels just perfect. Mrs. deMoya,"she said in her exaggerated southern lilt, "honestly, does it look too tight to you?"

"Jus' a leetle, but you have been puttin' on a few pounds seence you been weet us, an' I tought maybe Aimee should add an eensert before she feeneeshes de sewin' of de beads. Eet would be much easier, Aimee, eh?"

Juanita whirled around toward the mirror to see if the words Old Lady deMoya were throwing at her could be true. She stared at her image. Maybe she was right, but after all she had lived off of cold beans, corn pone and coffee the whole time she'd been with R.J. It's a wonder she hadn't turned into an old scrawny skeleton if the truth were known.

"It's gotta be that good cookin', Mrs. deMoya," she said sweetly, "and the good care Etienne is givin' me," she added with an extra barb that did not go undetected by Orlean.

But Orlean got in the last word. "I do hope dat's all eet ees, Juanita. I surely do, my dear." And on that she turned ...slowly...deliberately, and went into the kitchen to resume the preparation of dinner.

She called to Aimee to assist her. She wanted to allow the seed she had planted to take root and grow, and Aimee's constant young chatter might interfere. "Now," Orlean thought, "I weell have to be more observant dan ever." Juanita's ambitious, calculating mind took so many different roads it was difficult for her to keep up with her.

****

Deciding that she would not wait for Etienne, Juanita began the practice by herself. She climbed up the ladder that rested against the oak tree. She casually glanced at the kitchen window to see if Orlean was still staring at her.

"The old witch!" Juanita said to herself. "As usual there she is with her old crow-like eyes watching my every move. I just wish she'd say it and get it over with. She makes me so nervous. I know that's why my stomach churns to beat the band every blooming morning. How can a body think or do anything right with that old woman glaring and staring at your every move. It's a wonder I've not fallen off the rope and killed myself, she makes me so nervous. Oh, to heck with it. I'll just wait for Etienne in the wagon and read *Jane Eyre*."

She walked very erectly back to the already hot wagon and flopped down on her pallet. Her hand instinctively felt for her precious blanket filled with the doubloons that R.J. had given her before their capture. "My future," she thought to herself. "Even Etienne has been acting kind of strange lately. Oh well, I'll stick with these holier-than-thou Gypsies for just as long as it takes, and then I'm off to bigger and better things." She turned over on the narrow pallet and allowed her mind to wander. The cheering crowd she envisioned when she performed her glorious feat in Rowland's Bluff appeared before her, clapping, calling their praise for her bravery. But her mind could not dwell on it.

Ever since Orlean had said, "I hope dat's all eet ees," Juanita's mind had been working overtime.

"Not now, not now!" she declared bitterly as she pounded her stomach. "Not when I'm just starting to get my due," and she turned over and stared at the bare wood of the wagon. But she was almost positive the old crow was right. "That R.J. Skinner has had the last laugh, after all," she moaned and began beating her stomach so hard she hurt. "I'm not gonna have any stinking old 'Blessed Jane.' Not now, not ever!"

"What to do, what to do?" she pondered. She had not been intimate with Etienne. God, he treated her as if she were some kind of saint. Every time he looked at her she was afraid she'd sprout wings. "Oh Lordy, what has that devil, R.J. gone and done to me?" she thought angrily. "I've gotta plan something. I know I've heard of a potion you can drink, but I can't remember what. That old crow knows. She knows, and she knew even before I did. God, she must be some kinda witch with special powers or something. But knowing her, she'd be the last person in the whole wide world to wanta help me. She wants to see me get as big as a barn and ugly just like Bonnie did when she was carrying Blessed Jane. Oh...she was ugly! Her old legs and feet got as big as an elephant's. It's not gonna happen to me. It's not!"

Aimee began calling her but stopped when she heard Juanita's moaning. Etienne had sent her to fetch Juanita for their morning session, and it wasn't like her to not be there when he'd finished his chores. It was she who usually had to wait for him and Pierre, but of late Aimee and SuSu had to awaken her. They didn't know that Juanita had been so upset about what Orlean said that she had awakened early and gone out into the early morning to try to take her mind off of it.

"She sure is acting strange..snapping at me," Aimee confided to SuSu. "Why just yesterday she said, 'Why do you have to follow me everywhere I go? I'll declare you're worse than old Tag, Aimee,' and she said it in such a mean way. But then she said she was sorry. I guess she's getting nervous about her debut." But afterwards Juanita hugged her, and Aimee felt somewhat better and forgave her.

When Juanita heard Aimee pull the tarp back, she pretended that she had stubbed her toe, and that's why she was moaning. Aimee cautioned her about trying the eighteen and a half foot height if her toe hurt, but Juanita quickly assured her that it was better and was just a little ole stub anyway.

She slowly followed Aimee and Susu out to the side yard, and there was Etienne with a quizzical look on his dark face. "Ma Cherie, are you not well?"

"Oh, Etienne, I just stubbed my toe, just a little stub, mind you, and Aimee is making a big to-do about it."

She looked up at his handsome face and thought, "I wish I could love you, Etienne. I just wish I could, but you're getting me about as nervous as that mother of yours. At least she knows I'm not a saint. All my problems would be solved if I could just love you. Maybe if I try harder, and her hand instinctively rubbed her stomach. The gesture was not lost on Orlean, who was peering out the window at the scene.

"A ha...de seed was planted, an' now eet ees growing," Orlean said to herself knowing that Juanita was now aware of her condition. A satisfied smile spread across her wrinkled face. "Now, I'll 'ave to be very watchful or she'll do her deveel's work on my son."

"Do you think you should try the eighteen and a half, Cherie? We have time. We can wait a few days."

"Oh, no, Etienne. It was just a little stub. I'll declare, you're as big a worrywart as Aimee. I'll declare you are," and she reached up on her tiptoes and kissed him on his cheek. She raised her eyes toward the kitchen window to make sure Orlean saw her, turned toward the rope and said to herself, "Put that in your craw, ole woman. I hope you choke on it."

"Maybe I'll fall - just half way up the ladder, not too high - and it'll jar loose," she reasoned as she climbed the ladder with Etienne holding on to her hand so securely that a person would think she was a piece of glass. She'd have to be real careful how she handled it, she knew. Nothing, but nothing was going to prevent her big night. They were due to perform in Rowland's Bluff on August the 6th. It was located on the Suwannee north of Old Town about a day and a half away, and nothing was going to stand in her way, she declared. She'd worked too doggoned hard for this, and R.J.'s brat was not gonna rob her of her chance.

Then it dawned on her. Why hadn't she thought of it before? It was like she'd lit a lamp; her whole face lit up. Orlean could see the change in her expression and immediately put down her dish, moved quickly out the kitchen door and toward Aimee. Juanita continued to climb the ladder, ever so slowly and when she got to the top rung she feigned dizziness, holding her strong, small hand to her eyes and began to moan.

Etienne called to her, frightened. "Cherie? Cherie, are you all right?"

She answered in a weak voice.

"Do not move," he cautioned her, "I'll be there. Hold on."

As Orlean witnessed the scene she could not discern whether the girl was seriously faint or was faking. But no matter, Etienne thought she was faint, and that's the only thing that mattered. He helped the bent-over Juanita down the ladder. He was so concerned and tender with her that it angered Orlean, but she had to admit that she did look small and forlorn even to her suspicious eyes.

Aimee was beside herself with worry, and even Pierre showed concern. He had come to respect Juanita's tenacity, and the fact that she had not taken advantage of Etienne's obvious feelings for her had made him less suspicious.

When they got to the wagon, Etienne parted the tarpaulin, and Juanita looked into his worried eyes. She whispered that she wished to speak to him...alone. He turned to Orlean and said, "Maman, I'll call you if you're needed."

Gently he placed her on the pallet while stroking her soft, pale face. Then Juanita went into her act. She thought, "I'm glad he isn't R.J. R.J.'d be on to me in jig-time." She began to moan and then sob. Etienne could not bear to hear her.

"Shush, Cherie, my sweet. Please tell me what's troubling you." He kissed her hair, her cheeks, and continued, "You may tell Etienne anything, my love, my golden girl." He had opened the door as she knew he would.

"Oh, Etienne, I'm so embarrassed, so hurt, so afraid. He forced me. He told me all the terrible things he'd do to my dear ma and pa if I didn't..." and she hesitated before rushing into the unveiling of her plight "...submit!" I think I'm carrying that devil's - bank robber's - murderer's baby. And Etienne, I don't want it. You've gotta do something!" She became hysterical, and this time Juanita was playing her scene honestly. She had worked herself into a fit.

Etienne was a take-charge man. He was slow in the ways of seeing through cunning women such as Juanita, but he was very strong in his convictions and purpose. He took her into his comforting arms and held her close to quiet her, soothing her with caressing words. It was obvious to Juanita that he was upset, but she couldn't understand French, so she was not aware of his plight.

She did not know about his love of all life. Orlean and Dom referred to their children as gifts from God, and they meant it. Etienne, being the oldest and having been privy to the gifts of Pierre and Aimee, believed it to be true; whether the child Juanita was carrying was the child of a bank robber who had forcefully impregnated her was of little consequence to him. It still was a gift of God.

When she finally quieted down, Etienne spoke without much deliberation. His mind was set.

"Do not worry, Cherie. I shall love the child as my own. It shall never want and shall be well taken care of. I have not spoken of my feelings before because I was aware of your frightening experience, and I wanted you to heal." He took a very distraught Juanita in his arms and continued. "It is time we were wed. I'll speak to Papa and Maman tonight."

Never in her active imaginings had she thought Etienne would react as he did. She thought he would be angry, furious, at the acts forced upon her innocent body, and naturally would want the pregnancy terminated as she certainly did. She would just have to be honest and very direct with him.

She squirmed out of his protective embrace and said matter-of-factly, "But Etienne, I do not feel about you in that way. I love you as I would a brother, and I respect you, but Etienne, I do not love you as a wife should. Don't you see?" She held him away from her and looked up into his saddened face. "I cannot have that murderer's child. I know I could never love it. Don't you see, dear Etienne? The baby would be marked for life being a bank robber's child," and she began to sob quietly.

"Ma Cherie, I am aware that you do not love me as I do you, but in time perhaps you will change for the sake of the babe. You must think of the babe, my golden one."

Well that did it! How could he be so blasted stupid! Babe, my eye! She shouted, "But I do not want this...his baby. Don't you understand? He defiled my body, and I hate him for it, and if I have his bastard baby, I'll never be able to love a man, Etienne, not even a wonderful man like you. Please help me...please," she pleaded with her words and her sad face. But when she looked at his set jaw she knew in her heart her pleading was for nothing. She'd seen him when he'd made up his mind in the past, and there had been no dissuading him then, and there would be none now.

When he jumped down out of the wagon, Orlean was instantly by his side. "What ees eet, my troubled son? Ees Juanita eel?"

He took her hand and looked down into her sunken, wise old eyes. "We have been much blessed, Maman, have we not?"

"Yes, we have," she said slowly knowing her son was deeply concerned and was choosing his words carefully.

"And the meeting of Juanita, Berta and Layke and their family has truly enriched our lives, is that not so, Maman?"

She thought, "Oh, why does he have to be so, so...? Why can't he jus tell me what she said? But eet ees not hees way, so I must be patient." Aloud she said, "Yes, my son, eet ees so."

"My golden girl has within her a joy soon to be expressed by the birth of a babe, Maman. It is not mine, would that it were, but that of the hanged man, R.J. Skinner. He defiled her, and she does not want this babe, Maman. After all, she's very young - only a little older than Aimee. I have asked her to wed, but she has told me that I am but a brother to her though much loved, and she does not feel for me as I do her. Cherie is a very remarkable girl, Maman. She shall require special care now to protect the unborn and unwanted child. I put her in your expert hands, for I know you are wise in the ways of women who are in difficulty, and I am but a bumpkin, as I suppose most men are about such things."

Orlean was beside herself. She had known how Etienne would react about the baby, but to hold the girl totally blameless was beyond even her wildest imaginings.

"I weel do what I must, my son, but Juanita was honest weet you. She weel hate dat child and us as well for forcing 'er to 'ave eet. Don' you see, Etienne? She weel cause trouble een our family, mark my word, my son. Der weel be trouble where before der was only respect and love. I fear for de consequences of your deceesion. I fear for us all."

She abruptly turned away from him, and turning deaf ears to his pleading she rushed toward the house. "She 'as won! De golden trollop 'as won. Already she 'as dreeven a wedge between us," she spat out.

CHAPTER VII SuSu

"Now you wait, Wesley McRae. You just wait for me," SuSu cried out to him as her slight legs trudged to keep up with Wes. He kicked the loose sand out behind him as he ran just as fast as his sturdy legs could propel him, laughing at his older sister as he left her far behind. He turned to see how far she was and was delighted that he had outdistanced her that quickly.

"You just wait 'til Ma gets home, Wesley. You just wait," she struggled to catch her breath and decided to stop. She couldn't go on. Faltering, she decided to sit down beside the low willows. "Who cares if you get hurt, anyway? Who cares? I don't," she said tiredly.

SuSu had been keeping her eye on her baby brother since he was born, going on seven years. She used to love caring for him, but lately he was just too much of a handful, always testing the authority her ma had vested in her. Almost every evening - it seemed like forever - she had accompanied him down to the south spring to tend to his old turtle. He and Ezekiel had built it a cage, and because he wasn't allowed to go by himself, she had to go with him to feed the dumb old thing. She couldn't figure out why, 'cause he could swim much better than she. There were a lot of things she'd rather be doing, such as practicing her tumbling with Aimee deMoya. But, no, she had to tend her mean little brother while her ma and Layke were on their honeymoon.

Wes reached the spring area and immediately went to his turtle, Slowpoke. He wasn't even out of breath as he squatted beside the cage and began to search in his britches pocket for the bits of biscuit and hoecake Orlean had given him. He went to the blue-green spring and filled the bowl with its cold water. The sun was low in the sky, but there was plenty of daylight left. Even if there hadn't been, Wesley would have still dawdled. The only time he did anything rapidly was when he wanted to best SuSu. She had become so slow that she wasn't much of a challenge any more.

Slowpoke stayed in the corner of the cage, not moving. Wes could tell he, or maybe she (he couldn't tell nor could Dan or Zeke whether it was a boy or girl) was alive, for its hooded eyes moved from time to time. He was now on his stomach, lying down staring at the turtle. He wanted to watch him eat the biscuit but guessed he wasn't hungry, 'cause there he sat, not acknowledging the food.

He heard SuSu's labored breathing as she ran toward him. Quickly he dashed behind the low brush in back of the cage and decided to throw his straw hat into the spring. He sat, excited, expecting. No telling what she'd do when she saw his hat on top of the water. He bet she'd jump in. He placed his grubby hand over his mouth to stifle his laughter. Boy, his ma'd really be mad at her getting all wet in the cold water if she were here. His ma always worried about SuSu.

She came tearing around the sandy path, and before looking at the cage or even searching the surrounding area she saw the hat and screamed, "Oh, Wesley! I'll save you. I didn't mean it. Oh, Wesley..."

She jumped right into the deep water, her arms splashing wildly, calling him as she went down, up for air and under again. But she didn't see him anywhere. Under again.

Wes was getting scared now. He began calling her, but she was making so much noise she couldn't hear him. She went under again, and Wes panicked and started running the quarter of a mile for help, his young heart racing, tears of fright streaming down his freckled face.

He stumbled into Pierre's arms and jabbered unintelligibly. Pierre called Orlean, and she and Aimee rushed outside to the stoop.

"What's de matter, Pierre? What's wrong weet Master Wes, eh?"

Aimee reached Wes, and he grabbed her around her knees while calling SuSu's name. She and Pierre turned toward the spring, and before they could explain to Orlean began running. Wesley couldn't seem to stop crying and babbling, so Orlean hugged him to her, patting him on his back, trying to get him calmed down.

She coaxed him into the kitchen and had him blow his nose and wash his streaked face. Finally he was able to tell her what had happened.

Orlean immediately grabbed a quilt off of Jonah's bed. Dashing outside she called Dom and Etienne as she made her way to the barn. She glanced at the wagon, but there was no movement from the tarp. "Guess de girl ees reading as usual. Ees as well. She would be of no help."

Orlean, Dom and Etienne made their way quickly down the

deep sand path with Wes struggling to keep up with them. When they arrived at the spring, Pierre had SuSu draped over the barrel that was always kept beside the spring. Her head and legs were dangling, and her dark braids were dragging on the ground as he and Aimee rolled her, pressing her back trying to release the water she had swallowed.

"Make sure her tongue is disengaged, Pierre!" Etienne shouted as he rushed to help.

Orlean's hands went to her open mouth as she began chanting. "Oh, Mees Berta..Oh, Mees Berta," is all she could say as she knelt beside Slowpoke's cage. Old Dom's reassuring hand patted her bent shoulder as he stood beside her with tears streaming down his face.

BOOK TWO:

CALLIE AND THOM

CHAPTER I THE FAIR

Excitement was in every pore of Callie's long, muscled body. Thom would be at the fair. He had been very faithful about writing, and she had replied. The letters were mostly concerned with the crops, weather and ranch life in general and inquiring of her health, but in every letter he added his own brand of humor.

She knew his Aunt Beulah had been writing her sister about the goings on at Tater Hill Bluff, 'cause she told her so. There had been several frolics since Thom left, and Callie had attended them all. Buster Brewton and Bobby Hand had squired her to the ones at the Young Hotel, and that handsome Clay Willett asked her to the church picnic. Her ma made her a lavender gingham dress and braided her rich brown hair in French braids. She tried her best to smooth out the little curls that kept springing out all around her heart-shaped face, but as soon as they dried, they defied her efforts.

There wasn't a nicer young man around than Clay. His mother was widowed when he was but a youngster, and to earn their meager living she gave piano lessons and helped out at the school. She wasn't exactly a teacher, but she did assist Miss Taylor, and Clay had worked at Jeeters' Dry Goods store ever since Callie could remember. Mr. and Mrs. Jeeters had no children of their own, and the way they bossed him around you would have thought he was theirs. But he had a real good nature and paid them no mind.

Callie liked him 'cause he always treated her the same, even after she and Thom had discovered the doubloons and everyone else in town had made her feel like some kind of a celebrity. But not Clay. He was interesting to talk to and seemed to know something about most everything. Seemed to Callie that he'd read every book that had ever been written, and it was his dream one day to become a writer, and Callie for one thought he would, too. He was already writing articles for the *Sunland Times* in Tampa, and Mrs. Willett had a scrapbook plumb full of them with his name on them and everything.

But what Callie liked most about Clay, besides just looking at him, were the articles he'd written on Jay and his stuffed birds and animals. The paper had printed some of the pictures of Jay holding the great horned owl and the panther Slick had shot up near Palmetto Hammock. She just wished that Jay had smiled. He looked like he had been chewing on gall berries, her pa had said, and they all got a laugh out of that...even Jay. Because of the article the State Fair Committee had invited Jay to display his work at the annual fair all the way up in Gainesville, about an eight-day ride by wagon.

There wasn't much doing at the Tall Ten in early August. The crops had long ago been harvested, and they'd not be putting in the corn for some time, so Parker decided it was time for the entire family to take a trip. Slick and Jam could handle whatever came up, and Mattie would see to it that no one went hungry. It would give him a chance to see what the other ranchers were doing to improve their stock. He knew that Jordan Northrup and Pierce would be there - they'd talked about it during the drive. Jordan's Big Lake spread was the talk of the camps. It was not as large as Tall Ten, but his experiments with grasses and breeding were becoming known all over Florida.

Kate could enter her sunflower quilt in the quilt contest, and when he asked Callie whether she was going to enter the calf-roping event, she changed the subject real fast. Later in the quiet of the evening, when he and Kate first went to bed, he mentioned it to her.

She chuckled and said, "Why, James Parker Meade, you're getting old and forgetful. Don't you know that Thom Garvin will be competing in that event? Now, how would it look if Callie up and beat his time? You know she's sweet on him, don't you?"

"Oh, Kate, you women have always gotta have your daughters sweet on some no good lout. Why, the next thing I know you'll be saying she's sweet on Clay Willett."

"And why not, Mr. Know-it-all? I for one think Clay Willett will be quite a catch one of these days. He's intelligent, handsome, talented, and, mark my word, he'll be someone to be proud of. Why Callie said just the other day that he's planning on a writing career."

"Well, I surely hope so. If he's thinking of marrying my daughter, he sure couldn't feed her beans on what that skinflint Jeeters pays him."

"J. Parker Meade, now did I say or even hint that Callie had marrying on her mind? Why, she's just getting into the swing of courting, and here you go and get her married before she even learns the first thing about courting," and she turned over in a huff.

****

"Kate has packed enough food to feed hungry cowmen on a hunt," Parker said, as he and Slick loaded the wagon for their trip. Callie wondered if her ma was upset about leaving Tall Ten. "She sure is a bear this morning. It's not like her. Maybe she's tired or somethin'. She did stay up late finishing my new blue dress. I wonder if Thom'll like it. Lordy, I'm acting just as silly as one of those racey cow town girls on a Saturday night, whatever that means." That was one of her ma's favorite expressions.

Parker, with the help of Jay, had planned their trip to travel as direct a route as possible. They would follow alongside the Peace River to the east and skirt the Withlacoochee, then head more west to avoid all the small lakes, and before they knew it they'd be pulling into Paynes Prairie south of Gainesville, they assured Callie and her ma. They expected the normal afternoon rains of summer and took tarps to spread over the lead wagon to ward off as much as they could.

It didn't take much to excite Callie and Jay. They were just like two pups with a bone. "I'll declare, Jay, Pa has talked more today than he usually does in an entire week." She guessed he was as anxious as the rest of 'em, even if it did mean being away from Tall Ten for a while. Neither Callie nor Jay had ever left DeSoto County except when Callie went with her pa on the spring drive. They'd be visiting cousins up in Fort Meade that they had never seen before, plus Parker's brother and wife and their two boys, Gurley and Ned, who had lived on Tall Ten when Callie and Jay were young children.

Kate was pretty good about keeping in touch with both sides of the family and had written that they'd be stopping in Ocala about the seventh day to visit her Aunt Audry and Uncle Henry, who had helped raise her after her mother, Callie, had died. She hadn't seen them since before her own Callie was born. So the trip was not just for Jay and Kate to participate in the Fair events but to renew acquaintances and family ties, as well.

The previous week had been spent getting Jay's display wagon fixed up. He had painted the canvas backdrop to look like the sky and marsh land. The cattails did look real if you got back about three feet. He had got some brown croaker sacks and some old green cloth Kate had, left over from a skirt, and had fashioned a tree that came apart. When he got it all put together and put his birds up in it, it was really a sight.

Miss Taylor had helped him mat all his pen and ink drawings, and his pa had even helped make the easels for them to sit on. But the most special thing of all was when the day before they were to leave two wagons filled with folks came riding out to the house with Miss Taylor leading the bunch of 'em. They presented Jay with a beautiful sign that they had made after school had closed and before most of 'em had to return home to do their chores. It was made special to go on top of the display and had curlicues all over the place, and it said in great big letters, "JAY P. MEADE", and under that, "Tater Hill Bluff" in wee,tiny letters so as not to take away from his name.

When Callie saw it she sat right down on the porch edge and cried like a big dumb baby, she was so happy for Jay, and when she could get herself together, she noticed that he had tears in his eyes, too. Her ma must have known they were coming, 'cause from out of nowhere she and Mattie came up with two giant jelly rolls, all sugared up with mint leaves surrounding them, and some herb tea with cinnamon and lemon wedges to help wash 'em down.

They all gathered on the front porch, and Clay Willett made a speech the likes of which Callie had never heard. He quoted poetry, and he read about the famous painter, John James Audubon, whose pictures of birds and flowers hung in the big museum in New York City. And Miss Taylor even said that it was her belief that Jay Meade had as great a talent as Mr. Audubon.

"I don't think I'll ever be a witness to anything quite like it again, not if I live to be a hundred," Callie said to Mattie, who was also choked up and drying her eyes on her apron tail. They helped her ma clean up after everyone had gone home, and Jay went out to his workroom, and her pa had hurriedly gone to the bunk house so the ladies couldn't see how moved he was. Oh, it was a glorious occasion!

****

First thing Jay and Callie did when they made camp each night was to check his birds and animals. They had wrapped them securely in old newspapers and put hay all around them, and so far they were perfect - not even a bent feather. Jay was worried the whole trip that something was going to happen to them, and no matter how many times Callie reassured him, he was still a nervous wreck.

When they arrived at Aunt Audry's and Uncle Henry's farm north of Ocala late on the seventh day out, it sure was good to get off those hard benches. Kate had made some feather cushions, but the dadburned things kept slipping and sliding all over the place so they finally just took them off and used them as a foot rest. They left the next morning on the hungry side, and Parker said it was for sure that Kate hadn't learned her cooking from Audry. "No wonder Henry looks like a walking skeleton. Folks just can't live off of grits and corn bread and coffee, especially on a farm," he added rubbing his growling stomach.

But Kate said she remembered her aunt to be a right good cook and she was sure they'd all survive. "She's just old and forgetful, Pa," Callie spoke up in defense of her aunt. "I bet she called me four names every time she spoke to me, and each time I'd have to yell that my name was just plain Callie. But every time she'd do the same thing all over again."

After a while it got to be funny. Uncle Henry was as deaf as she, and they spent the entire day yelling at each other. It wore them all out, but Kate was glad that they had stopped by if even for only a short visit. They'd been real kind to her, and she had wonderful memories of them.

They drove up to the fair grounds that ninth day in the mid-afternoon. Jay was anxious to set up his display before it got dark, but Callie kept looking around for Thom, and Jay was really put out with her. "Good grief, Callie, either you're going to help me set up, or you're gonna crane your old stork neck after every cowman here."

"I don't have to help you one whit, Mr. Jay Parker. You'd just best keep a civil tongue in your head, Mister, or you can put up the blasted thing all by yourself."

When Jay quickly apologized, they both calmed down enough to finish up. "Oh, my, it sure looks nice, doesn't it?" Callie commented as she eased backwards and eyed it from every angle. People had begun to gather around to look, and Jay had to stop them from touching the panther and pulling at the leaves to see if the tree was real. They decided that one of them would have to stand guard in case some ragtag youngun started to get cute and tried to pull out some bird feathers, and Callie sure hoped she'd not be the one, 'cause she wanted to roam around to look for Thom. Their ma and pa had gone over to the livestock pens, and goodness knows when they'd return, she realized, disappointed.

The fair was to open officially the next day, and Governor Drew was to make a speech and cut the ribbon. "I wouldn't be a bit surprised if next year the President of the United States showed up," Callie announced to Jay. There wasn't a man, woman or child who wouldn't welcome President Hayes, her pa had said. At least he got the Federal troops out of the state. That's more than Grant did the whole time he was in Washington. But Callie and Jay were just as excited about the Governor's visit as they would have been about the President's, because they'd never seen anyone at all real important.

Callie was getting more antsy by the minute. "Now where do ya think two grown people would be?" Then out of the corner of her eye she saw her ma approaching. Not being able to contain herself any longer, she pushed through the crowd toward her.

"Callie, I just saw Thom," she said low. "And I finally met Mary. I can hardly wait to tell Beulah. She seems just as nice as Beulah, Callie. "Now, where are you off to?"

Callie turned around and called, "Where are they, Ma?" and had trouble standing still for Kate's reply.

"Well, if you weren't in such a hurry I'd be happy to tell you, young lady." She caught her breath and proceeded to give Callie directions to the arena fence, where the roping and riding took place, but before she finished, Callie was off like a deer.

She called loudly, "I was about to tell you that they know we're here, 'cause everyone is talking about Jay's wonderful display." She knew Callie had heard her - she'd slowed down to a walk. Kate shrugged her shoulders and began to work her way through the throng to give the good news to Jay, muttering under her breath, "I guess seeing Thom is more important than hearing how everyone admires her brother's display."

When Callie heard her ma, she pulled up short. "Well, if he knows I'm here and he's so all-fired anxious to see me, why isn't he here? That's just like an uppity man for you. Write you that they're about to die to see you again, and here you've been here for about an hour, and they just kick the dirt and fool around with dumb old horses and cows. If he doesn't beat all!"

Callie was about to blow a gasket when she saw those white teeth gleaming half way across the fair grounds. "Here he comes," she said to herself. "Boy, does he ever think every girl in the whole fair grounds is making a play for him, he's so sure of himself. Look at him swagger, would you just? Well, I'm not an easy mark, Mr Thom Garvin. Not Callie Meade."

She started walking back to Jay's display, acting like she didn't even see him. Kate looked at her, her brows raised, and started to ask why she had returned, when she saw Thom approaching. She immediately went over to their wagon and busied herself, motioning to Jay to follow her so Callie could handle the meeting all by herself.

When Thom got to their space, he bent from the waist in a grand gesture, removed his hat with a flourish and in an affected voice announced, "Master Thomas Pierce Garvin at your service, M'am."

And, trying as hard as she could, Callie could not hold her laughter, and when she swung around she got all flustered. "Now why does he always make me feel funny? Lordy, my rubbery legs are back." But aloud she said very proper like, "Why, Thom, I was hoping I'd see you while we were here."

"You knew dadburned well you'd see me, Callie Meade." And before he got completely bent out of shape, she smiled ever so sweetly and said, "I do thank you for your nice letters, Thom," so he calmed down.

"Hey, Callie, you gonna get in on the roping? Boy howdy, I bet you'd beat every cowman around...even me."

"Oh, I haven't given it a thought, Thom. I'd probably be the only girl, and somehow that doesn't seem right..."

"Heck no, Callie. Why, Horace Reynolds's two girls'll be competing, and so will Marthanne Greer."

It never occurred to Callie that other girls would be competing, so she decided that she'd better give the matter some serious consideration.

"How long do I have to make up my mind, Thom? I brought BeeBee, and boy, has he been itching to get some action!"

"Gee, I don't know. Come on, we'll go ask Stoker. He's got the list. It's gonna be a rip-snorter, Callie, a real rip-snorter.

"Boy, he can get excited about almost nothing," she thought, but her face was as flushed as his when he yelled to Stoker to tell him that he had another entry. Callie was about to protest - then she saw her competitor coming toward them from the arena. She had curly blond hair and lots of it, and big blue eyes, and both of 'em were aimed right at Thom, and her hips went swirley-swirley as she sashayed toward them. When she opened her rosebud lips, honey just poured out, and Thom's mouth was plumb hanging open.

That did it. Callie knew for sure that she and BeeBee were going for the blue. She wanted first to kick his shins and second to spit in the girl's China-blue eyes. Thom broke the spell by quickly introducing them, and both girls mumbled a "How-do-ya-do", not caring one whit how they did, and the darts flew between them.

****

"Now where did he get off to?" Callie asked herself as she searched for Thom. "I'll declare, I'll not be treated like this, Thom Garvin," and as she angrily whirled around, there he was with his ma on his arm, and they were coming right toward her. When he saw Callie's expression, he got real concerned.

"Callie, what on earth is the matter?"

She couldn't say, "Well, Thom Garvin you just walk off and leave a girl standing there to fend for herself, and here she is, a stranger, and....Oh, he makes me so all-fired mad!" So instead she gave Mary Garvin her sweetest expression, and Mary saw why her son was so taken with Parker's daughter. She had an open face and enough spunk for an army.

"Mrs. Garvin, I'm so very glad to meet you. I've heard your sister speak of you often." And to herself, "Lordy, I sound just like Ma. Why's he squinting those eyes at me, anyway?"

"Ma, don't let Callie's airs bother you. She just recently became a girl, and she doesn't quite know how to handle it."

That did it! Callie scrunched up her face and beaded her eyes, and before she could catch herself, she had hooked her booted leg around an astonished Thom's leg and had thrown him headlong into the sand spurs.

Mary had to turn her head, she was so tickled, and Thom was so surprised that he just sat there, and Callie was so embarrassed and so flustered that she stomped off as fast as she could to find BeeBee, so she could ride back to Tall Ten, where she belonged.

Mary bent down to help Thom up and berated him, "Thomas Garvin, you go after that young lady. You embarrassed her, and now her feelings are hurt. Right now, Thom. You go this minute."

He brushed himself off while ignoring the amusement of those who had witnessed the incident, but for the life of him he couldn't understand what he had said that provoked Callie to tumble him like that. "Girls!" He called after her, but she didn't slow down, so he guessed she didn't hear him.

She was dead set on getting on BeeBee and leaving this lousy old fair, and she'd never go to another one, either. Not ever. The tears began streaming down her face, and she didn't even try to control them, just wiped them away with the back of her hand.

Thom began running to catch up with her and called her, but his voice was lost. She could hear only the loud pounding of her heart and her sniffling. She was at the edge of the clearing, where the large hickories shaded the stabled horses, when he caught her arm and whirled her around to face him.

She fought, trying to free herself; her face was contorted, and she was crying so hard that Thom finally crossed her arms behind her, pinning them, and pulled her hard to him. He started talking to her in such a soft, warm and loving voice that she ceased to struggle. She shuddered a few more times, then went limp. He pulled her down on the grassy slope beside him, and took her heaving body into his caring arms.

"Callie, I wouldn't hurt you for all the world. You know how crazy I am about you. You've gotta know, Callie. Why a day doesn't go by that I don't wish I were with you instead of at Bullseye. Please stop crying, Callie, please."

Just an occasional sniffle escaped now, and she managed to speak. "Oh, Thom, I'm so embarrassed! I don't know what came over me. I know your mother must think I'm some kind of freak or something."

"Heck no, honey. She likes you. I can tell. Why, she likes you almost as much as I do, honest."

She turned her tear-streaked face up to his and said, "She does, Thom? She really does?"

He couldn't help it. He kissed Callie right on the mouth in the broad daylight. When he realized what he'd done, he quickly looked around, knowing full well half of Gainesville would be witnessing it. But no one was about, so he took a very willing Callie in his arms and gave her a good one that time. She felt so limp and helpless and girl-like. When he finally let go of her, he said, "Oh, Callie, I love you so. I just can't get you out of my mind."

"Thom Garvin, you best not be teasing me. I don't think I could stand it if you were teasing me."

"Good grief, Callie, I wouldn't tease about a thing as serious as love. Honest I wouldn't. Do you love me, Callie? Just a little bit, maybe?"

"I think I do, Thom. But I'm real new at, you know, being a girl," and when she realized what she had said, they both broke out in laughter, holding each other and howling. That's what Marthanne Greer saw and heard as she rounded the hickory trees in search of Thom.

"My, my, how you children do carry on," she said sarcastically. "Your mothers might spank you two if you get your britches dirty from playing in the yard," and she angrily swung around with her blond hair flying out behind her and hurried toward the arena.

Thom got up and prissed around Callie, mocking Marthanne by rolling his eyes and pursing his lips in such a funny fashion that Callie thought, "Lordy, if he doesn't stop making me laugh, I'm gonna wet my drawers for sure."

****

Pierce and Jordan both won "Diplomas" for their entries in their respective categories. Parker and Kate rushed to the judges' booth to add their congratulations to the other well-wishers' and decided to accept their invitation to join them under the big tent for the barbeque, that they'd heard was outstanding. The men were deep in conversation, and Kate whispered to Parker, "I'm going to look for Callie. I don't think I can stand to hear another discussion about breeding. I wish Mary had joined us. See you later," and she made her way toward Jay's booth. She managed to push her way through the large crowd surrounding the booth to Jay, who was explaining to them where in the state each specimen had been killed. She wanted to ask if he'd seen Callie, but he was so engrossed in conversation she decided to look for her herself.

"Well, she's probably at the arena." Kate was a little down, and just being around Callie with her fresh approach to everything usually perked her right up. Her quilt took only the white ribbon, and she couldn't help but be disappointed, although she did agree with the judges' decision about the quilt that took the blue; it had circles of rose garlands on a soft green background done in the feather stitch and was by far the prettiest thing she'd ever seen. A Mrs. Brubaker from Apopka made it, and she told Kate that she'd worked on it for five years. Kate later found out that she had eleven children, so it was obvious why it took her so long. But she did think hers was as pretty as the red-ribbon winner. The sunburst pattern was really very common, but she had to admit that the lady's stitches were certainly tiny and uniform.

"Oh, well, maybe next year," she thought. "Callie isn't the only one in this family who's competitive, and I saw how Parker's eyes shone when Pierce and Jordan got their diplomas, and he sure did question them about everything, even what they fed them. I'll have to work on him slowly, 'cause he's not one to leave home often, but I truly think we should make it a yearly event. Best not tell him, but I already have an idea for next year's quilt entry."

She went up to the gate to inquire when the calf-roping event was to start and realized that it would take her the half hour to find Parker and get back for the event. She'd have to hurry or they'd miss the first entry. She didn't see Callie anywhere, but knowing her daughter, she was sure she'd be with either BeeBee or Thom.

****

Callie and Thom were having to make a special effort to keep from looking at each other. They were outside the fence behind the arena, and everyone was having a good time joking and teasing, all except Marthanne Greer, who stood off by herself, very aloof.

It was a known fact, she found out later, that Marthanne Greer had her sights set on one Thomas Pierce Garvin. "And when Marthanne wants something, Marthanne gets it, and she'll cheat to get it, too. No doubt about it," Betty Sue Reynolds said as she filled Callie's ears full to overflowing with tales concerning Marthanne. The Greer spread was west of Palatka, and their holdings were almost as impressive as Bullseye or Tall Ten. Marthanne was an only child and spoiled rotten. The only friend she had was Marthanne, herself, Betty Sue said.

Callie liked the Reynolds girls. Shirley was the older and a rather pretty, dark-haired girl - seemed real nice. Betty sue was Callie's age, on the plump and plain side, with thin, pale brown hair, but she had a ready wit and lots of friends. She seemed to know every one of the contestants. Her family had a small farm and ranch south of Gainesville in the Micanopy area and attended the Fair each year.

"Boy, does she ever like to breath that high air!" Betty Sue whispered to Callie. "Don't let her fool you, Callie. I'd not put a thing past her. You'd be smart to keep an eye on your horse. Don't look at me like that, Callie. I'm for sure serious. She'd do anything to win, and it's obvious that she's lost Thom to you know who." She sidled her plump body up next to Callie and cupped her hand so no one else would hear. "When he looks at you, he could eat you with a spoon, and Miss High-and-Mighty knows it."

Callie was inclined to believe her. That girl acted like she could cut her heart out. BeeBee was moved to the closer pens with the other horses, and Callie had saddled him herself, so she didn't hold much store in Betty Sue's suspicions, but just to make sure she decided to check on him. She ducked under the fence undetected, found BeeBee and began to rub his neck. He did seem skittish. She ran her hand underneath the blanket under the saddle, and lo and behold! She couldn't believe what she was feeling. BeeBee whinnied and stomped as she loosened the saddle and removed the sand spurs from under the blanket. They were the big, devil-sharp, dried kind, and there must have been at least a dozen of them under both sides of the blanket.

"That does it, Miss Marthanne! I'm gonna out rope you and every blasted one of 'em here!"

Oh, was she angry! Most of all because of the pain it would have caused BeeBee. She sneaked out from under the fence and tapped Betty Sue on the shoulder to show her the mass of spurs. Betty Sue wanted to call Marthanne on it and wanted to report her to Stoker, but Callie said, "No, we don't have any proof, and we'd sure look dumb without proof."

She finally agreed but thought they should at least tell Thom. Callie decided that wasn't such a hot idea either, 'cause he had such a short fuse, she was sure he'd cause a commotion. "Don't worry, Betty Sue, she'll get hers. I'll make sure she gets hers." But Betty Sue wasn't believing Callie would give the varmint what she deserved and muttered words to that effect as she went to the pen for her horse.

There were sixteen entries in the calf-roping contest, and Callie drew #7, Thom, #10 and Marthanne, #5. Betty Sue was #2 and made a respectable time, but not nearly good enough to win. When she came out of the gate Callie rushed over to her and exclaimed, "Gee, Betty Sue, I hope you didn't do that on account of me and BeeBee."

"Callie Meade, no one likes to win better than I do. I'd never let you or anyone else best me on purpose. "Callie felt very foolish for even having suggested it, 'cause she knew she was a very honest and direct girl.

About then Stoker called out # 4's time and said it was better than last year's winning time by a whole second. "The next entry is #5 from Palatka. This little lady has a tough time to beat. Her name's Marthanne Greer, and she's riding Jester."

The audience clapped loudly, and Callie spotted her ma and pa sitting beside Thom's parents and Jordan Northrup. Jay couldn't be there 'cause he had to guard his booth, but Callie knew he'd be pulling for her. She looked at Marthanne and got a lump in her throat. She did look queen-like sitting on her beautiful chestnut mount. The gate opened and she was on that calf in no time, had him roped and tied and was throwing her arms up triumphantly and staring right at Callie as if to say, "Now, you upstart, let's see you better that one."

"Lordy, she's fast. She beat #4 by a whole second. Callie Meade, you've got your work cut out for you. Grief, BeeBee looks like a hand-me-down beside Jester."

It seemed that the time just evaporated, and then it was her turn. She couldn't even remember what # 6's time was. She nervously walked BeeBee into the shoot and suddenly felt a hand on her shoulder. She almost brushed it aside, but turned to see who it was, and there was Thom. He took her hand and squeezed it...said nothing...he didn't have to. His eyes said all Callie needed to know.

Betty Sue yelled, "Go for the blue, Callie."

She sighed and took three deep breaths. The wooden gate opened on the count of zero, and like a shot she was on her calf. Betty Sue turned to Thom and excitedly exclaimed, "I never saw anything like her, Thom! Boy, she's some kinda gal!"

"You're tellin' me, Betty Sue. I'm the one who's in love with her."

The crowd went wild, and Callie saw her folks standing and yelling and calling her name. She'd beaten Marthanne by a half second, the best time ever recorded for the state competition. She returned to the side gate with BeeBee, saw Marthanne off to one side avoiding her, but Callie walked right up to her, reached into her saddlebag and produced the handful of sand spurs she had wrapped in newspaper.

"Miss Greer, I believe these belong to you." Marthanne's mouth had fallen open to protest, but when she looked into Callie's steely eyes she decided not to respond, turned herself around and stalked off. Callie, her head held high, realized that she had never had so much pleasure. She put the spurs back into her saddlebag so she could show her ma and pa on the way back to Tall Ten.

Callie and Betty Sue were sitting on the fence waiting for Thom. She saw him walking Goldie over to the shoot and wanted to go over to him, but before she could jump down, she saw Marthanne rapidly making her way toward him. She decided to stay put, and Betty Sue was so put out with her that she jumped off the fence and called back to her, "Callie Meade, that Miss Priss is gonna beat your time if you don't do something. I can't believe you're letting her get by with this."

But Callie knew Thom knew where she was sitting and also knew he'd look in her direction before the gate opened...and he did. She waved and mouthed, "I love you."

He let out a "Yee Haw!" and the gate flew open.

"He's beautiful," she thought, "every bit of him. Every single bit of him."

He beat Callie by half of a second, and she was so happy for him that she jumped off the rail and unthinkingly ran right into the arena and kissed Goldie, shouting to Thom about how thrilled she was. "Well, isn't that a fine howdy do, Miss Meade; kiss Goldie before me," and he picked her up in his strong arms and kissed her right in front of the entire audience. Callie turned every color there was. She avoided looking in the direction of her folks as she ran from the arena for the sanctuary of the corral.

She wasn't exactly hiding, but she just wasn't ready to be seen by all those folks - at least not yet. She could hear all the commotion as she stroked BeeBee's mane and could hear the other riders' times called out. She prayed that Thom's nine seconds would hold and he'd win the blue. Oh, how she prayed!

She heard his name called and knew that he'd won. She jumped upon BeeBee and hugged him around his neck, and the tears rolled, she was so happy. Then she heard her name being called for the red, but she wasn't ready to leave her quiet refuge. Somehow she knew that her folks would understand and probably accept her ribbon for her, or maybe Thom would, or even Betty Sue. But she just couldn't leave the darkness just yet.

She heard him call her name, softly at first. She didn't know why she couldn't answer - guessed she just liked to hear him call. He got closer and called more fervently, and she answered ...cleared her throat and responded more clearly that time.

Thom grabbed her hand, and she could feel him looking at her in the dark. He called back to Betty Sue to say that he'd found her and that they had some talking to do..."Just the two of us."

They returned to the grove of hickories and sat down abruptly. "No, no, don't say a word. I don't want to hear a single word." He put his finger on her open lips, that were ready to protest. "Just listen, Callie." He took both her hands as he continued. "Now, I've been thinking about this ever since the Cypress. But, Callie, when I saw you in that blue-green dress at Aunt Beulah's, I was sure. I want you for my wife. I know I'll have to get permission from your pa, but I just couldn't 'til I knew how you felt about me, and when you said, 'I love you', well, honey, that did it."

"Why is he so calm," she thought, "when my heart's going lickety-split. He's so sure of himself. Why am I so scared?"

"Say something, honey; I can't see your face in the dark."

Her hands were sweating, and she was embarrassed - her mind wouldn't clear. She didn't know what to respond. She knew she loved him, but...

"Thom," she began slowly, "I'm just not sure that I'm ready to wed. Now, I love you, I really do, but I'm just not sure like you say you are. Heavens, I don't know the first thing about cooking or running a house or any of those wifely things. I'd make a fool of myself, just like I did this afternoon. I just know I would..."

"Oh, honey," he said, relieved, "you don't need to know all those things at first. Those things you can learn later."

"But Thom, I want to be a proper wife to you, and I do think those things are important. At least I think I do."

"All right. Why don't you go back to Tall Ten and have your

ma and Mattie give you some lessons in all those things. But I want you by my side as my wife by the next spring drive. Do you hear?"

"But, Thom, after we're wed, I can't go traipsing off on a cattle drive just like before."

"Who says? I want you right next to me in my bed roll. I don't ever want to leave you, Callie Meade. Not ever," he declared fervently.

Callie had never felt anything for Thom but pure, childlike love. She had never even entertained the idea of bedding with him as a wife. The very idea scared her half to death. She was naive about the ways of a man and a woman. She knew about birth - goodness knows she'd seen it enough on the ranch and had seen the animals couple - and she'd heard the girls talk at school, but she'd dismissed it as a bunch of rubbish. Her mother had never sat down with her and discussed her role as a wife. Gracious, she'd just started courting.

When Thom kissed her this time, passionately, she felt warm all over - she couldn't think, and a throbbing, stirring sensation intruded, unasked for, as she clung to him not wanting to stop...wanting it to last forever.

Finally, Thom pulled away, and said, "Grief, honey, it's hard for me to say this, but the way I feel about you, I'm having a difficult time controlling myself. We're going to have to be very careful so as not to get too carried away." He thought a while and continued, "Do you know what I mean, Callie?"

She wanted to say, "Of course I know what you mean. What do you think I am, some kinda dumb person?" but she couldn't answer that, 'cause he was right. She didn't have any idea what he meant, and she might as well confess that she didn't. She shouldn't story to Thom.

When she didn't answer right away, he realized she didn't know. "Callie," he said so gently, "what I mean is, I want to make love to you so bad that I know, if we're around each other a lot, I might not be able to stop...with just kissing, I mean. Callie do you have any idea what I'm talking about? Do you know what a man and woman do when they make love?"

Silence.

"Oh, I shouldn't have asked you that. I'm sorry, honey. I'm out of line, Callie..."

She didn't answer, and he took her in his arms and kissed her cheek. "My girl-woman, it'll be all right. I'll make it all right. I'm gonna talk to your pa this very night."

She shuddered and called his name, "Thom, thank you for being so understanding and patient. I know I have a lot to learn about being a woman...but Thom, I learned how to rope a calf and win a red ribbon, so I guess, by golly, I can learn to be a woman and wife."

"You're all the woman I'll ever want or need, Callie Meade," he declared emphatically.

****

Thom spoke to Parker that night on the boarding house porch. They had a man-to-man talk, and when he told Parker that Callie was unsure of her role as a wife and that they had discussed it, Parker was shocked.

"Thom, it wasn't your place to do that."

"What do you mean, sir?"

"I mean, Thom, that if Callie feels she's not ready to be a wife, perhaps you should consider waiting until she is ready. And I also mean that you should have discussed this whole matter with me before saying anything at all to Callie. That's what I mean."

"Well, Parker, I mean Mr. Meade..."

"Oh, you can call me Parker, Thom. There's no need to be formal."

"We'd like to be married before the spring drive, uh.. sir, uh, if it's all right with you," he quickly added.

"Well, it's not all right with me. Callie is very young, and as you just said, she's not sure of herself yet. She needs a lot of nurturing, Thom, and I highly suggest that you consider a period of growing up for her - say two years or so."

"But, Parker...there's no way we can wait two whole years." He was beside himself, but when he looked at Parker's stern face, he knew he'd have to.

"If that is your feeling, sir, of course, I'll abide by it."

"It is, Thom. Indeed it is." He put his arm on Thom's slumped shoulder, bid him goodnight and wearily climbed the stairs to his and Kate's room. He liked the boy and was in a way glad that Callie had the good sense to fall for a cowman. That certainly took a load off his mind, for he knew Jay wouldn't want to carry on at Tall Ten. But to give up his Callie...not yet. Not just yet.

****

Callie heard her pa's footsteps outside her door. At least she hoped that was who it was, so she opened her door just a crack and could see his long legs go to his and her ma's room and enter.

"I'd better let them talk it over," she said excitedly, but she was having such an awful time controlling herself that she finally gave in to her druthers, opened the door and ran out of her room, down the hall and on reaching their room stopped abruptly to compose herself.

"I've just gotta act grown-up enough to be wed. I've just gotta."

She rapped gently on the door, "Ma...Pa," she called hesitantly. When they responded she rushed in and hopped on the side of their bed. "Well, Pa. What did he say?" she blurted out.

Parker had just told Kate about his conversation with Thom, and as much as Kate hated it, she knew that he was right in his thinking. Maybe not two long years, but a delay was definitely necessary. Callie had been wild and free for so long that she would need a great deal of training to prepare to be a wife and homemaker before she would be ready to assume her responsibilities.

"He asked for your hand, as you said he would, Callie," he said, clearing his throat, but before he could continue, Callie in her uncontrolled excitement let out an enormous cowman's yell, "Yeeee Haw!" Kate's hand went to her mouth, and Parker just looked at his daughter and shook his head with amusement.

"Good grief in the morning, Callie Meade. Have you lost your senses? You'll wake everyone in the entire boarding house."

"Oh, I'm sorry, Ma. I'm just so happy - that's all." Parker had a hard time explaining his and Kate's decision and spoke so softly that Callie kept asking him to repeat what he was saying.

At first she was upset, then angry; then she was just relieved. She knew she wasn't ready to be Thom's wife, or anyone's wife. It was just that she loved him so much. But she felt it was her duty to protest their decision and began giving them all the reasons that they should change their minds.

When Parker asked her whether she thought she could run the house at Tall Ten, especially when her ma had the affluent ranchers and their families for weekend visits, she had to admit that she couldn't but quickly stated that she could learn. When Kate asked her whether she could do any of the wifely chores, she retorted that Thom just wanted her by his side, and that he said she could learn all those things later.

"Callie, your pa and I both like Thom, and we think it's wonderful that you've found a nice young man to like. But we know in our hearts - and I think you know it too - that you're not ready to make a home for him, and that's your first duty as his wife, that and bearing his children."

She hung her head low and began sniffling. Then she stood tall beside their bed and looked at both of them. Her mind was made up. "I know you're right, but if I learn real fast, promise that we won't have to wait two years, Pa. Would you please promise me that?"

Soon they were all hugging each other exclaiming that it would be all right, that she was a good daughter and that they knew what a wonderful wife she'd make Thom .

The Garvins and the Meades met the next morning for breakfast in the boarding house dining room. They quietly discussed their children's future and were all in accord. Both couples were pleased about the prospective union, and as Parker explained, he couldn't be more delighted and relieved, stating that Jay would never want to run the spread, so it would be up to Callie and whomever she married to carry on Tall Ten.

"I know that Thom is a very capable cowman, but his and Callie's happiness is much more important to us than having an experienced manager." They all agreed.

As Kate and Mary walked out of the dining room, Kate took her aside and said, "Callie and I have already set up a plan for this year. She's agreed not to participate in the cow hunt or the spring drive. That's a real sacrifice for her, Mary." She rushed to continue before the men joined them, "And she'll assist me in running the house and learn to cook and do at least some hand work, such as darning and mending..."

"Oh, Kate, don't get her too domesticated. I like her just the way she is, and so does Thom. Maybe smooth the rough edges - that's all. Frankly, dear, she's a breath of fresh air after having to be pleasant to that Greer girl and her parents. Those people have just about driven us crazy with their visits and invitations and ..well, shenanigans. Thom has not encouraged that girl one bit, but every time we turn around there they are with some excuse for visiting. Why her father's bought cattle and tried, I'm sure at her and her mother's urging, to ingratiate himself in every way possible. Oh, Kate..believe me, Callie is a breath of fresh air."

"And, Kate, Thom is certainly not the most polished gentleman I know. He has a lot to learn, too. Was Parker when you married him...polished, I mean?"

"Well, no Mary, he indeed wasn't. We both had a lot to learn, and," she laughed, "we're still learning."

Mary smiled and got a faraway look on her face as she remembered her early marriage and how thrilling it was to wake up every morning beside her Pierce. "I wish we could go back, at least for the good times. How I envy those youngsters...and Berta and Layke!"

She sighed as she walked toward the crafts booth, not that she was interested in even looking. She just had to be by herself, and there was no one there to interrupt her thoughts. Oh, how she envied Berta this new, vital love! She and Layke should be arriving back at South Spring about now, she thought.

"Well, the girls and I will just take a little trip on the *Robert E. Lee* to Savannah. I don't care if I ever see or smell another cow! It won't be the same as going back in time, but guess it'll have to do...at least for now."

CHAPTER II MATTIE AND HERS

Callie was going on five years of age when her pa brought Mattie and hers to Tall Ten. The War had ended the year before, and Tall Ten was getting back to normal. Parker had served the last three years of the War going as far north as Charleston, where he served as a clerk in the Confederate Army Subsistence Department. His main function was to supply the Confederate forces with provisions, and he served in that position for the duration of the War. But even so, Kate worried as much about him as if he had been in the thick of the fighting.

His brother, Logan, and wife Betts and their children, Gurley and Ned, stayed on the Tall Ten with Kate. Gurley looked just like a girl when he was born, and Betts knew that Logan would call that poor little thing Girlie for all his natural born life, so she told him, "This here child will not be called any Girlie, Logan Meade, do ya hear? Now, I know your temperament, so I know you'll not pay a bit of heed to me. So, Mister, I'll go along with the Girlie...but we'll spell it more dignified. How about G-U-R-L-E-Y?" So that's how it was, and Betts never introduced Gurley that she didn't spell it out for whoever was listening and added proudly that it was a family name. Wasn't no such thing, but everyone let her have her way. The second son was called just plain Ned.

Logan did not serve in the Conflict. He had been badly injured while trying to break a horse, and him just a youngster at the time, and was left with one leg shorter than the other and experienced terrible pain from that day on. He could still participate in the cow hunts, and no one could track down a "bunch quitter" better than Logan Meade. He did have trouble keeping up on a long day's hunt but was still able to run Tall Ten while Parker was gone.

Parker had wanted Kate to move up to Ft. Meade to be close to his family while he was away, but she couldn't bring herself to leave her first born's grave...she just couldn't. They had waited for four years before Henry Parker had been born. He lived for only a few days. Kate had not had Callie 'til three years later, and she was as healthy and active a baby as had ever been born and the apple of her pa's eye. It didn't matter one whit that she wasn't a boy, 'cause Parker treated her just like one anyway, and no matter how Kate protested, he had his druthers, so to speak.

About two years after Jay's birth, Logan and Betts decided to return to Ft. Meade. His crippled leg had become arthritic, and just mounting a horse was difficult and extremely painful for him. When old man Burton died up in Ft. Meade, his livery stable was put up for sale, so Logan and Betts decided to sell their share of Tall Ten, 10,000 acres, to Parker and buy the livery stable and move back home.

Parker hated for Kate and the children to be alone so much of the time while he was on the cow hunts and with no neighbors close by, so when he heard that Morgan Murphy's top horse trainer, Elmer, had been killed and had left a wife and a bunch of kids, he rode up to Bartow to see what Morgan planned to do with them. He knew Elmer's wife helped out on the place with the cooking and cleaning and that her older boys worked the stables.

There had never been a better horse trainer than Elmer, and his pa before him had been blessed with the same instincts and talent and had been owned by the Morgan and Murphy families since their arrival from Ireland, before the first potato famine devastated their land.

Morgan's wife, Nora, had passed away before the Conflict, and some said that's why he pulled up stakes and moved his entire horse farm from the Charleston area to Bartow. He had freed Elmer and Mattie before the War, but they had decided to move to Florida with him instead of relocating up north, as had the other slaves.

There were four boys and three girls born to Elmer and Mattie: Elm, Ash, Hickory and Sap; Camellia, Petunia and Zinnia. Elm was the first born, then Ash, Camellia and Petunia, called Pet, followed by Hickory and Zinnia, and finally Sap, short for Sapling, because he'd been born prematurely, and Elmer said that after having had three healthy trees this one was just a sapling. Mattie's love, besides cooking, was her flowers, so when her girls started to arrive she named them for her favorites. She had grown beautiful camellias in South Carolina; they wouldn't grow in South Florida, for they needed a colder climate, but colorful petunias and zinnias bordered her quarters in Bartow and Tall Ten as well.

Parker told Kate that they gave Ash the wrong name, that they should have named him slippery elm, 'cause he was as slippery a thieving nigger as he'd ever heard about. Poor Mattie and Elmer had had trouble even talking about him since he'd absconded with the best stud in the Murphy stable. They hadn't allowed his name said in their presence since the day he hightailed it out of Bartow. No one had seen nor heard of him 'til after the War, when it came out in the Tampa Tribune that one Ash Morgan, formerly of Bartow, Florida, had been hanged for horse stealing in Wildwood, New Jersey. Poor Elmer didn't even want to know where they had buried him. He was a proud man.

Parker had bought his horse Storm from Morgan and 'most every horse he owned, all Marshtackies or cow ponies, some folks called them, and they had become good friends. When he approached Morgan about the possibility of moving Mattie and hers to Tall Ten, he agreed to allow Mattie to make up her own mind. She decided that the family needed to start fresh after Elmer's death, so she took Parker up on it. Elm, Hickory and Camellia stayed on at the Murphy farm, Tralee. Camellia took over as cook for her mother, and both boys continued in their father's footsteps as trainers.

It was an exciting day when Parker returned with Mattie and children and all their belongings piled high in the ox-drawn wagon. Callie heard them approach and ran around the house to the front porch. She hung close to Kate when she came out to join her but got so excited when she saw the children that she ran out to open the gate. Pet, Zinnia and Sap, who was just two, still slight for his age but as bright as a gold doubloon, jumped down from the wagon and eyed her from behind their mother's abundant skirt.

Mattie saw Callie, shoulders squared and standing straight, measure up her brood as she held the gate open and thought but did not say, "That one will be spunky enough for my Pet. Yessam...that one has got the grit."

There had been no one for Callie to play with since Gurley and Ned had moved away, not that they were interested in playing with a little girl. They had been real good about letting her ride her pony Jumper along with them, but having a girl near her own age would sure be better, she thought as she looked at both the girls, up and down, eyes squinting, in the hot noontime glare.

It turned out that Zinnia, who was closer to her in age than Pet and as prissy as they come, couldn't or wouldn't ride a pony or play in the dirt or do anything Callie enjoyed doing. She had an old rag doll that Camellia had outgrown, and all day long she played house. Callie and Pet, who was going on nine, took to each other as Mattie had predicted. Pet liked to climb trees and ride and didn't give one whit if her drawers got dirty. They became inseparable, as did Jay and Sap. Parker and Kate often said that bringing Mattie and hers to Tall Ten was the best thing that they'd ever done besides getting married.

As Zinnia got older she became Mattie's helper in the kitchen, and by the time she was fourteen she had moved into town to be Mrs. Horatio Henry's house maid. Amelia Henry - before her marriage to Horatio she had gone by Maude - was as prissy as Zinnia, so Callie told her ma that those two should get along just fine, and she wasn't the least bit sorry when Zinnia moved into town. But when Pet decided to go back to Bartow to live with Camellia and her husband and their two children, Callie was fit to be tied. She stormed around the ranch slamming doors and cupboards and in such a foul mood that even her doting father couldn't stand being around her and suggested that she go fishing for a few days, so they could have some peace and quiet. She talked Pet into going with her for one last time, and they decided to head for Ole Piney Creek.

"Ya'll gonna stay fer a week or a month?" Mattie asked. "Here, Pet, let me hep ya with da rations. Maybe ya'd best take ole Lem so's to strop all dese on him," she chuckled as she added, "Bet he'd be one sway back mule when ya put all dis on 'im. Yep, Ah bet his ole belly near 'bout tetch de groun'."

"Shucks, Mattie, this ain't much. If we don't catch any perch or cats we'd near starve to death with this little bit of food."

Pet spoke up as she grabbed the croaker sack of supplies from her ma. "Me an' Callie ain't ever been wit'out 'nuff rations for our own good, Mama. Have we Callie?"

Before Callie could answer, Mattie chastised her daughter. "Pet, dat's "Miss Callie" to ya. Ya knows Ah can' stan' fur ya to talk lak dat."

"Yassam", but she and Callie rolled their eyes toward the heavens simultaneously and started giggling at Mattie as she clucked her disapproval at the two of them.

"Don' knows how to act, don' knows how to talk and don' knows how to treat yore betters - not a one of ya. Git outta mah kitchen dis minute. Go on...Git out!" But as they rushed out and closed the screen door Mattie stood looking at the two long-legged girls. Her Pet, copper penny colored and string bean skinny, and Callie, with her old felt hat pulled down around her ears and moving...always moving.

Kate joined Mattie at the back door. "Dos two gonna be so lonesome, Miss Kate. And would ya look at Miss Callie. Movin', always movin'. Now wouldn't ya tink dat she'd run down sometime?"

"She's been that way since before she was born, Mattie. I declare, she began kicking before I even knew I was with child." They stood watching the two of them mount their horses and head for the creek.

"Come on, Pet. We bes' hurry 'fore dose two try to spy on us," Callie said, referring to Jay and Sap, who were always causing them grief of some sort. Callie always talked "darkie talk" when she was with Pet and out of earshot of Mattie and her folks. Her ma would've skinned her alive if she had overheard her, but she was so comfortable with Pet that somehow it was the natural thing to do. There wasn't a girl in all of Tater Hill Bluff that Callie liked, even a little bit. But, oh, how she loved Pet Morgan!

Talking like her wasn't enough for Callie. When she was about ten and Pet was going on fourteen, the two of them had even tried to whiten Pet's skin and had tried every remedy they could conjure up to accomplish it. Callie knew that as long as Pet was black that they'd not be able to do things together for much longer. Heck, they couldn't even go to the same school or church.

One morning early before her ma and Jay stirred in the main house and after the hands had left for the hunt, they met out back of the barn on the far side and away from Mattie's sight - she was already in the kitchen. Callie had about twenty lemons she'd pulled the evening before, her pocket knife and an old sheet that she'd stolen from her ma's rag bag. Pet didn't care if she was white or black, but it did seem to rankle Callie, so she went along with her plan.

They began slicing the lemons open, and Pet stripped all her night clothes off, and Callie proceeded to rub lemon juice all over Pet's face, avoiding her tightly-closed eyes while she was holding her nose. Then she smeared her young, swelling breasts, arms and back and followed it with a heavy rub of salt. She exclaimed with wonder at the miracle that the lemon juice, salt and hot Florida sun were going to perform on her best friend in the entire world, and that included brat brother, Jay.

Callie began her magic chant, low so's only the folks who couldn't be seen, but who could hear their plea, would know how earnest and desperate she and Pet were.

"A little bit of juice from a lemon an'
stole salt on a sheet...a heap a da sun's
rays and a whole bunch a needin'."

With that she turned around and around as fast as she could and fell flat on the ground holding her ears cupped out so's she could hear one of 'em just in case they had any questions. When none came, she proceeded to turn Pet around just as fast as she could twirl her, and she too fell on the ground. Still no voices.

"Ah am satisfied dat we's been heard and seen, Pet. Now it's their turn to do de magic."

Pet lay on the raggedy sheet just waiting for the sun to do it's job. Callie spoke up, "Now when ya gits done and whitened to the right color, you's gotta turn ovah to do the odder side. Wees can' have ya two shades. Oh, Pet! This'll mean we won' evah be apart. Wees'll always be together," and they started to hug but remembered in the nick of time. "Don' want no zebra stripes on ya, so wees best be still an not streak ya up 'til ole sun does his job."

Well they waited for the sun to start bleaching Pet...and they waited. Callie was getting more impatient by the minute.

"Maybe we din put 'nuff lemon on ya." So she proceeded to douse her real good and rubbed it all over her top, and Pet, spread-eagled on the sheet, went fast asleep while Callie was at the house making her appearance, so her ma wouldn't come looking for them. But she mostly went back to get some biscuits and sausage from Mattie.

"Mattie, me and Pet are going fishing and probably won't be back 'til 'most dark," she called back to her as she ran from the stoop, the tea towel bulging with her acquisitions. "Tell Ma, all right?" And off those long legs went to behind the barn. She knew that in her absence Pet had surely turned color. Well, she had turned all right. A bright red rash had raised up wherever the lemon and salt had been, and when Callie saw it, she got so all-fired mad that she began to cry and storm around so vociferously that Pet didn't know what to do, so she just sat down and began to holler so loud that Callie had to shut her up.

Then the itching began. She had an awful time just giving it a little rubbing, 'cause Callie was so upset about their defeat that scratching wasn't nearly so important as soothing her best friend. She loved Callie more than anyone, even her ma or her dead pa, and down deep she too knew that they'd not be able to spend much time together as they got older. If Callie said "hop" she'd do it, and if Pet said "les do it", Callie'd go along with her.

****

"I'm not gonna think of her going back to Bartow - I'm just not - but whatever will I do without her? That brat Jay and dumb old Sap'll drive me crazy wanting to follow me everywhere. I just know it. If I know them, they'll be poking around us tonight.

She's as sad as I am," Callie thought as she studied Pet's outline in the dusk. The light was fading fast. Callie and Pet slowed their horses down to a trot and said nothing. The overgrown trail brushed their legs, tugging at their britches as they slowed down to a walk. "I'm not gonna make her leaving any harder than I can, so I'm just gonna think about all the adventures we're gonna have when she comes back, I am."

"Callie, Ah bets wees gonna catch us a mess a fish come mornin'. Ah bets we gonna catch us a cat so big dat it'll take bote of us to tote it home."

"Why's she talking about fish for heaven's sake? She knows I just wanted to get away from the house, that I couldn't be around all of them when I was so upset. She rightly knows it."

But she grunted in the affirmative to respond to Pet's declaration. She seemed to need to talk, so Callie let her ramble on. Pet knew better than to bring up her leaving. She knew Callie'd jump right down her throat, so on she rambled about almost anything else that came to her mind.

"Been meanin' to ax ya if you's goin' on de spring drive dis year."

"Good grief, Pet! Ya knows Ah'd nevah miss a drive. Good grief! Are ya daft?"

They pulled up to the clearing beside Ole Piney Creek, where they always came, got off their horses, and Pet jumped over the old oak log just like it wasn't four feet off the ground, while holding onto the sack of supplies, too. It was gonna be a dark night, she observed. Callie started gathering wood to put into the rock bed, and Pet added the lighter knot she'd brought from the house.

After examining the stack of old dried up palmettos that they'd previously used for a bed, Callie decided to cut some fresh green fronds to place on top, but when she dropped the first load on she screamed, "Good grief! They're full of palmetto bugs. I ain't gonna sleep anywhere near 'em. Here, give me that log so's Ah can squash 'em. Lordy, they stink. Watch out, Pet, or one of em will crawl up yore britches leg. Whew! Smell 'em, would ya now. Bet there's a million of 'em."

They decided to place their new beds as far away from the previous ones as possible and on the other side of the fire but close enough for the fire's smoke to chase away any insects.

Jay made sure that he stepped over the third step from the top - it was the squeaker. Didn't want to wake up his ma and pa. It was such a black night that he couldn't see Sap on the porch, but even if there had been a moon, he'd have been hard to see. He was as black as his pa before him.

He heard Sap's hog grunt, their signal, and followed the sound to the end of the front porch making sure that his responding grunt was loud enough for Sap to hear. The screened front door made such a slight noise that he didn't worry about it, and he managed to avoid his ma's fern stand at the end of the porch as he reached out to Sap.

Because Jay was allergic to horses and would sure as shooting start sneezing and awaken everyone around, they knew they'd have to walk, but they were used to that. Ole Piney Creek was about a mile and a half from the house, and the road was used often, but not enough to keep the rabbit tobacco and fennel weed from growing thick all along both ruts of the road bed.

"Did you remember to bring the coal oil and cattails, Sap?" Jay asked anxiously.

"Course, Ah did. Dat's mah job, ain't it? Don Ah always do mah job, Jay Meade?" he whispered low. There was no reverence between the boys. They were equals in every way, and no one told them otherwise. "Best friends to the end..", they had sworn on many an occasion.

"Well, yeh, guess you do. We better wait 'til we're past the barn to light 'em." Jay smelled the cattails and, sure enough, Sap had soaked them real good.

About fifty feet past the barn they came to the road to the creek. Sap lit each a cattail. They didn't want to come eye to eye with a panther. Didn't have to worry too much about bear or wolves anymore. They'd been hunted out of most of the close-in land on the Tall Ten. But the cats and wild hogs were thick, as were the gators and poisonous snakes; rattle snakes, moccasins and from time to time a coral snake showed themselves.

About a hundred feet before they turned the sharp bend to the north, Jay pulled out the water bottle and doused the cattails. They knew they'd be able to see the girls' fire from there as they had on other occasions. They were in such a good mood about the trick they planned to play on them that it was hard to stifle their delight. They stood for a while to get their bearings, but it was such a dark night that even after standing for 'bout five minutes or so they still couldn't see a thing - not even the girls' fire.

"What's dat?" Sap whispered hoarsely.

"Don't know!" Jay responded, his voice shrill with fright.

"Sounds lak something big ta me...lak maybe a bear or...oh, man, Jay. We'd bes' get outta here...an fast!"

Sap started thrashing down the road with Jay right on his heels. But even with all the noise they were making they could hear whatever it was right behind them. Then they could hear its loud grunt clearer, as it caught up with them. It was grunting and making such an unusual racket that neither one could figure out what on earth it was and didn't slow up enough to examine it. When Jay fell, he swore it's monstrous, big hairy leg kicked him. He yelled to Sap to wait up, that he was coming. But Sap had out-distanced him, and his gasping for air kept him from responding.

Finally they found the clearing to the spread. Exhausted they fell down and rolled over and over trying to catch their breath. Sap managed to say, "Ah knows it was a bear, Jay. Ah rightly knows it. Mus' a been a mama one, and wees got too close to her cub. Wees lucky to be 'live. Whew!"

Callie and Pet were laughing so hard that Callie wet her drawers, and Pet was coughing so hard that even with her hand held tightly over her mouth to restrain it she almost let it loose before Jay and Sap were out of hearing distance.

"Oh, whatta night!" Callie thought. "This has gotta be the best present Pet could've given me, the best good-by present in the whole wide world. That Pet has some rip-snorting ideas! Besting those nuisance brats will do me for all my life. Yep, that Pet has some dandy ideas."

Callie wanted to sit down and cry but knew she couldn't let Pet hear her, so she turned over in her old quilt and with her head under the covers sniffled herself to sleep.

Pet left the next afternoon to go to Tater Hill Bluff to take the steam boat up the Peace River to the landing in Bartow. She planned to spend the night in town with Zinnia and leave at first light. Parker decided that Callie should stay at home, and she was so glad when he said it that she didn't even bother to protest. She just went down to the willows beside the pond and lay there staring at the clouds trying to confuse her with their ever-changing shapes. Even Jay decided to leave her be.

Mattie had a hard time controlling her tears as she served their noontime meal, and Callie knew she'd not be able to eat a single piece of chicken, much less one of Mattie's biscuits. But when Jay sheepishly asked his pa if he thought that maybe there might still be bear around there, and her pa said that he didn't think so, Callie got the chance to add fuel to her and Pet's well-stoked fire when she said, "Pet swore that she heard one while we were at Ole Piney, Jay. Never heard such a noise - 'bout scared us to death."

Then her ma asked Jay where on earth he'd got all those scratches on his face and neck. Jay's lower lip was hovering around his collar; he was so scared that she'd find out that he and Sap had been spying on the girls and he'd been scratched up by the berry bushes when he fell. He lied, "Oh, me and Sap had us a big ole fight, Ma, but we made up already."

At that, Mattie rolled her big brown eyes toward the heavens. Sap had asked the same question that very morning. "Do ya tink dat der still be any bears 'round Tall Ten, Mama?". She began to put two and two together, and when she saw Miss Callie just about busting with laughter, the same reaction Pet had when Sap had asked her about the bears the day before, she knew or at least she suspected the trick the girls had played on the boys.

She couldn't let it alone. She winked knowlingly at Callie, and when she left the dining room, she heard Callie say, "Pa, would you please pass the rice and gravy, and oh, yes, some more chicken too. If there are bears around here, no tellin' when I'll get another one of Mattie's biscuits if one of 'em decides to make a meal out of me."

CHAPTER III CALLIE'S PERSEVERANCE

"If that old snaggle-toothed Slick opens his gaping yap just one more time, I'm gonna bop him one, so help me!" Callie declared as she brushed the flour off her soiled apron. "Tough as whit leather, my eye!" Her face and hair were dusted with flour, and the tip of her up-turned nose wore a smudge of the biscuit dough she was rolling out.

"One more week to go," she thought. "Just one more forever-seeming week 'fore Thom gets here."

Callie had been in training ever since the State Fair in August. Mattie and her ma had started her off on the simple chores: the proper way to dust, mop and make the beds, set the table, polish the furniture and the tedious job of mending.

"I never in all my born days saw anyone as clumsy as Callie when you put a needle and thread in her hands,"Kate told Parker. "You'd think she had a hand filled with rattlers, she's so shaky. Parker, I'm thinking it'll take longer than two years for that girl to be ready to wed."

As he tamped the tobacco in his pipe he smiled and continued to rock on the side porch. He thought Callie was going to cane Slick when he began to sputter and spew out her biscuit that morning and then had the nerve to ask her if she was trying to kill her pa's hands. Now Parker would admit that they weren't the best biscuits he'd ever had, but then again they weren't the worst either.

Kate glanced over at her husband of twenty-some years and inquired, "Just what is so amusing? You're the one who saddled that girl with a two-year sentence, J. Parker Meade. Now, I'm the one who has to help her every single day with her lessons, and you can't say she's not trying, either. Why, I never saw anyone try harder than Callie. She's up 'fore first light and in that kitchen just begging me and Mattie to teach her more recipes. She's got me plumb worn out, Parker - worn to a frazzle." She bit off the end of the thread and shoved her mending back into the bag before rising.

Slowly she turned toward the amused Parker, walked over to his chair and gently kissed the top of his thinning hair. Squeezing his shoulder she said, "If it weren't so amusing it would be pathetic, honey. I'm just glad we can see the humor in it. I'm turning in now, dear. Callie will have me up before I've had my rest, I'm sure. She's determined to fix a fancy dinner for Thom all by herself, and she's only got another week to practice."

****

The weeks had gone by, just dragging, since the Meades returned to Tall Ten. Callie gave up on counting the days and took to the endless weeks instead, but their slow growing into months did not add patience to her anxiousness. She was more frustrated than ever. The only respite from the tedium was Thom's wonderful letters. He had taken to drawing little pictures instead of words, and Callie would read them again and again before she could figure out their meaning.

The smiles around Tall Ten were confined to the "letter days". Jay told his ma that Thom would have to write more often so that they'd be able to put up with Sourpuss Callie and that he was sure tired of lumpy gravy, falling-apart biscuits, lead-filled pancakes and half-raw fried chicken; that as skinny as he was, he couldn't afford to lose any more weight.

The more Kate said, "Now, Jay, we must be patient," the more impatient he became, and he and Callie began snapping at each other, something they had never done before.

After four months Parker had had enough. "We never seem to be able to sit down to a quiet repast anymore," he said as he bored a hole in Callie, who was seated next to him at the dining room table; then he turned his attention to Jay and finally rested it on Kate's perturbed face. An impish grin transformed his usually sober face. "I've made arrangements with Beulah and George Young to save rooms for the entire family every Saturday night 'til the spring drive just so's we can have some smiles around here." He knew there'd be no sniping at each other at Beulah Young's table. He sat back in his straight chair, and while he let his announcement sink in, he asked Jay to please pass the rice.

As their mouths hung open in surprise, he looked at the gummy rice and said not a word, took the big tin spoon and served himself a mounded spoonful and suggested that Jay do the same. Then he asked for the gravy and doused the pathetic rice with the lumpy, no-color gravy and began to eat it just like he was enjoying it. Out of gratitude Callie did the same. Even Jay faked his enjoyment, all the while thinking, "At least I'll get a decent meal on Saturday nights - 'bout time!"

Since Callie and Thom had become betrothed, she could no longer receive callers or attend the many functions around Tater Hill Bluff with them. So on Saturday nights Kate and Parker accompanied her to whatever was happening at the Young Hotel, and more often than not, Clay Willett would be there.

It was obvious to the Meades that his feelings for Callie were not platonic, but their hints to Callie concerning the situation went ignored. "Clay Willett is just a good friend, the best friend a body could have. You and Pa are just imagining things, that's all," and Kate could see the ruff rise up on her back, so she quit bringing the matter up. But she noticed how Clay would practically leave a customer to fend for herself when Callie accompanied her into Jeeters' Dry Goods. Callie would get just as excited and flushed and babble away to the very receptive Mr. Willett. It was becoming a worry to Kate, she confided to Parker. "Maybe we'd better remain at Tall Ten on Saturday nights and just go to church on Sunday as before."

But Parker didn't agree. "If Callie and Thom are right for each other, Kate, all the Clay Willetts in the world won't shake her caring. Now you know that's a for-sure fact." But Kate knew Callie was new to the boy-girl relationship and in her naive way was actually encouraging Clay, so she worried.

The Jeeterses, who were like Clay's second parents, also began noticing his infatuation with Callie. Gus Jeeters was encouraged by his wife Ione to have a talk with Clay about his attitude toward a betrothed woman.

Gus did his wife's bidding, and before the Meades were due in on Saturday, he took Clay aside. "Somehow it don't seem fittin' for you to cow-eye Miss Callie just like before, Clay. Now I know she's a looker now that she's taken to being a woman with a woman's ways, but underneath that skirt she's still the same tomboy Callie Meade, and she's spoken for by Thom Garvin. You just gotta know yore place, boy," he said with his arm in a father-like fashion around Clay's slender shoulders.

Clay responded, "Uncle Gus, I'm well aware of Callie's position, and I indeed respect it. We are just good friends, and frankly she's the only girl in all of Tater Hill Bluff I can talk to.

She knows how to listen, and I admire her directness. We have a very special relationship," and as he explained on and on to Gus Jeeters that cool January day, Gus thought, "And if you had any kind of life to offer Parker Meade's daughter, Clay, you'd be the one betrothed to her and not that uppity Thomas Garvin. That you would, lad."

Instead of berating him further, Gus patted him on the back to let him know that he understood and that there would be no further need for conversation concerning Callie.

The very next Saturday when Callie and Kate came into Jeeters', Clay looked in her direction and smiled tentatively, but he continued to wait on Maude Jennings, when before he would have left her to take care of herself so he could visit and assist Callie. Callie lowered her eyes in disappointment, and she knew that Clay sensed it.

"Ma, let's go." Kate dropped the piece of blue gingham she'd been fingering and followed her. She could tell that Callie was upset. They walked across the sandy, rutted road toward the hotel, and Callie blurted out her frustration even before they got to the other side.

"I don't know what's the matter with me and Clay being friends. I just don't! He's always been my very best friend, Ma. Now you know that. Next to Pet he's just about the best friend I've ever had. Just because I'm spoken for shouldn't make one iota of difference if we talk with each other. It shouldn't. Heck, the whole world is looking on when we're together." And as she shook her chestnut curls uncontrolled tears began to stream down her face. A very unladylike Callie purposely took her dress sleeve and wiped her nose in a grandiose gesture for all of Tater Hill Bluff to see and defiantly glared at every person she could find.

"Callie Anders Meade, you don't have to make a spectacle of yourself right in the middle of town, young lady. Why, what on earth are people going to think?" Kate said in a hoarse whisper as she smiled and nodded at the passing townspeople, trying to appear unperturbed by her daughter's actions.

But Callie would not be appeased and ran up the hotel stairs bounding over as many steps as her coltish legs could reach to the sanctuary of her room. She slammed the heavy pine door and threw her sobbing body across the quilt-covered bed. Finally she calmed down except for a few shudders, and instead of Thom's flashing smile playing across her memory, Clay Willett's handsome, fine-featured face, so sensitive and intelligent, visited her every thought. She soon fell asleep.

Kate rapped gently on Callie's door. No answer. She called softly to her, and Callie stirred, responding in a hushed voice. It was dark as Kate entered the shadowy room. She eased onto the edge of the bed and began stroking Callie's forehead. She began to speak in a faraway voice about when she and Parker were courting. She hadn't thought of those days in many a moon and realized that she had never really had a quiet mother-daughter talk with Callie. Gracious! She'd never even told her about how she met Parker. Now seemed to be the appropriate time. Callie was so quiet it disturbed Kate, but she continued just the same.

Kate had been reared by her Aunt Audry and Uncle Henry after her folks took typhoid and passed away. She was about ten years old at the time. They lived outside of Ocala, about the middle of the state. It was a town very much like Tater Hill Bluff but on a smaller scale.

She was a pretty girl with dark brown hair and eyes and very popular with the young people of the area. She had a ready wit and kept them entertained with her piano playing. All any of them would have to do was hum a tune, and Kate could put the chords to it in no time.

She and Ben Chastain had been keeping company for it seemed like forever, and though they had not become serious enough for their folks to set a date, everyone, including themselves, knew they'd eventually marry. Ben was a perfect gentleman, church-going, serious and very industrious. His family owned the feed store in town and lived in the back portion of the building. He had a pretty tenor voice, and he and Kate were often asked to sing for various functions in and around Ocala.

One day shortly after Kate turned eighteen, J. Parker Meade rode into town on his way south. Fate played a part in that chance meeting. Ben had ridden out to the farm to fetch Kate - they were to perform at a revival that night, and Kate had insisted that they practice beforehand. He had forgotten something or other at the store, so they stopped by en route to the church to pick it up. Parker's horse had thrown a shoe on the outskirts of town, and the first building he came to was Chastain's Feed Store, so he stopped in to ask where he might find a blacksmith.

Ben had left Kate on the buckboard and entered the living quarters on his errand, and while he was gone, Parker and Mr. Chastain had come onto the open porch. Mr. Chastain nodded to Kate and proceeded to introduce her to Parker. She'd never forget that meeting for as long as she lived. She was immediately taken by the shy quietness of the tall and erect young man before her. He had smiling, blue eyes deeply set under reddish-brown brows and seemed to have difficulty looking at her as they were introduced; so she had to take the lead.

"Are you new in town, Mr. Meade?" she asked, looking directly at him, trying to engage him in conversation. Of course Kate knew he was a newcomer. Ocala was a small wilderness town, and she knew everyone around.

"Yes, Ma'm, I am. My horse threw a shoe a few miles back. I'm on my way south," he had said tentatively, but had gained strength in his voice when Kate smiled at him warmly in her engaging and most hospitable manner.

"I do hope you will be able to stay long enough to attend the revival tonight, Mr. Meade. There'll be a wonderful supper prepared by the town's best cooks and lots of singing and fellowship," she had said, her rich brown eyes sparkling with every word."

Parker not only stayed for the revival but found work on the Angus farm so he could court Kate proper-like; and one month to the day he and Kate became husband and wife and were en route to the Tall Ten to begin their life together.

Callie stretched her slender arms as she yawned and smiled resignedly up at Kate. They embraced and held each other close. Kate broke away first and patting Callie's shoulder said, "Enough of reminiscing, young lady. Your Thom will be arriving in no time, and I think you deserve a brand new dress for your first dinner together. Let's go back to Jeeters' and get that blue-green striped taffeta we looked at earlier.

Kate wanted Callie to know that she could change her mind, just as she had. There was no way anyone could rope Callie Meade in, and her ma understood that. She had never regretted changing hers.

****

Callie and Mattie were in the kitchen putting the last-minute touches on the tray of relishes. Her ma had taught her how to make radish roses and carrot curls, and Callie stepped back to inspect the results. Mattie nodded her head in approval and was about to finish clearing off the sideboard when they heard Jay shouting from the side yard.

"He's here, Callie." Thom was coming up the road from town in an anxious trot. "He's here," he repeated as he ran toward the porch with Kate hurrying out from the garden and Parker rounding the north side of the house.

Callie took precious time to try to smooth back her uncontrollable curls and remove her apron, only to toss it over the dining room chair as she dashed out the screened door onto the shaded front porch. They were all four standing stiffly in a row; that is, 'til Callie's ladylike demeanor was cast aside. She suddenly hiked up her skirt and petticoats and ran across the field calling his name, grinning from ear to ear with her chestnut curls loosening, then flowing out behind unrestrained.

Thom let out one rebel yell after the other and gave Goldie the spurs when he saw her excitedly racing toward him.

Kate and Parker just looked at each other, shaking their heads in resignation. Jay with his fourteen-year-old philosophy stated, "I knew you couldn't make a lady out of Callie, Ma, not our Callie, and I, for one, am glad. I didn't much like the new Callie."

Thom scooped her up, and she straddled Goldie's rump with her strong arms encircling Thom, her head held tight against his damp, muscled back as he sped her toward the isolated stand of willows beside North Pond.

"Callie...Oh, Callie" is all he could say as they slid off of Goldie. She said not a word as he enveloped her and gave her a kiss that made her toes curl. "I wonder if this is like dying." She just seemed to float away.

Kate looked up at Parker, pleading, and he answered as he squeezed her work-worn hands. "You can tell Beulah that we'll be having a wedding before the next drive and to start the preparations, Kate. We're gonna have us a shindig the likes of which this cow town has never been a witness to. Yessiree!"

They turned toward the willows but saw only Goldie, who was munching the bright green shoots of grass alongside the pond's edge. As they walked toward the house, hand in hand, both were remembering a similar night twenty years or so earlier. Their far-away expressions went unnoticed by Jay as he whistled to himself and entered the sanctuary of his workroom, his world.

Mattie resumed the cleaning of the kitchen and made clucking sounds of approval. " 'bout time they all got smart. There ain't never been the day that Miss Callie Meade would be a house woman - never been the day, nosiree!"

BOOK THREE:

JUANITA AND CONNER

CHAPTER I CHERIE

From the moment Berta and Layke boarded the *Robert E. Lee* for the return trip to Jacksonville Berta was unobtrusively looking for a white suit and black cheroot. But the mysterious man was nowhere to be seen.

"This is ridiculous!" she thought. "A grown woman behaving in this manner. I'm just glad that my bridegroom doesn't know he's married to a ninny. I can't believe I'm acting like this." But she continued to be watchful just the same.

They were met at the landing by Simon and Marlene, and Berta, anxious, was relieved that there had been no word from South Spring concerning SuSu. She relaxed as they visited on the lower deck while waiting for the porter to fetch their traps. Berta felt someone watching her. She was afraid to glance around for fear it would be the man, that Mr. O'Farrell, but her curiosity was more than she could handle. Ever so slyly she looked over her shoulder past the loading ramp, where the dockhands were busily unloading the cypress and live oak lumber from the mills in the Palatka area. He wasn't there.

"Berta, Simon has suggested that we have dinner at the St. James. What do you think, hon?" Layke looked down at his usually attentive wife only to find her not listening and definitely distracted.

He lifted her delicate chin and saw an embarrassed expression in her evasive eyes, "Lady of mine, perhaps you can tell me what's troubling you?" He laughed at Marlene and Simon and continued, "Well, the honeymoon is definitely over. My bride of less than two weeks has already learned to ignore her amorous husband."

"Why, Layke Williams! Now you know that is not the case. I declare, you make a fuss about almost nothin'." And she reached up on her tiptoes and kissed his cheek.

"I just thought that perhaps I would see some of our fellow passengers and would bid them good-by, that's all."

"Why am I lying? What on earth has come over me? First my terrible dream about SuSu and now this total stranger with the familiar blue eyes has usurped my usual good sense. I must be daft. Surely I'd remember if I had seen him before."

Simon and Marlene had the family carriage waiting only a few yards from the gangplank, and as they followed the Black porter Berta could not seem to restrain her desire to look back at the ship.

"I'll not! I simply will not, and that's the end of it."

"I hope you enjoyed your trip, Mrs. Williams," the porter said with a beautiful but unusual accent as he assisted Berta into the carriage. Before she had a chance to inquire of Layke how the man could possibly have known her name, she turned and instinctively looked up at the upper deck of the *Robert E. Lee*. She saw him. He seemed strange, this man in white. He was holding on to the rail very tightly, trying to steady himself, she thought. There were dark circles under his eyes. She gasped, and her hand went toward her lips as she quickly turned away from Layke.

"He's ill. Dear me! No wonder I didn't see him. He's ill." But Berta couldn't share her concern with the others, and as they drove away from the wharf she asked Simon to stop - she wanted one last look at the beautiful ship.

They were standing together, the porter and the man, the porter's arm affectionately draped on the gambler's bent shoulder. "Why am I so sad? Is this the last time I'll see him? Will I never know the part he's played in my life, or will I return to South Spring filled with curiosity? And how did the porter know my name? I thought that Layke's venturing into my life was the most excitement a person had a right to, but this mystery certainly adds sage to the dressing. Gracious me!"

She enthusiastically squeezed Layke's hand while a devilish smile played across her face. As she turned from her husband she allowed her bright blue eyes to question the stranger in white. He responded with a knowing smile.

****

Out of breath, Orlean and Dom had arrived at the spring, where Pierre and Aimee had already recovered SuSu from the icy water and had immediately begun to roll her slack body over the barrel as they had been taught. Pressing and kneading her thin back they rolled her up and down the packed sandy slope toward the spring. Etienne quickly checked her tongue to make sure it was not blocking her throat. At first nothing...eyes closed...no life...silence. But they did not give up and continued to press her as they rolled the barrel back and forth..back and forth...

She began to gurgle...then cough... and finally with a racking abandon she gave up the cold spring water that had filled her stomach.

Orlean and Dom grabbed her. Wrapping her in the quilt, they rushed for the warmth of the cabin. No one spoke. Dom knew what Orlean needed and left immediately for the wagon to fetch the spider weed powder. Aimee grabbed the powder from Dom as he rushed into the kitchen and added some to the water for the tea, while Orlean began rubbing the rest of the powdered root over SuSu's heaving chest and neck as she lay across Berta's bed. Dom brought her a sack for the poultice of spider weed to put on SuSu's chest to hasten the relief of the soreness that was sure to come. The deMoya wagon held many medicines, and spider weed, or antelope horn as some of the natives called it, was a favorite for fever or any breathing problems and had been used often by the family.

Aimee carefully spooned the steeped tea into the limp child, and with tears that were too many to remain in her big brown eyes, she sang a lilting lullaby from her youth while gently smoothing back the still wet strands of SuSu's dark auburn hair.

Go sleep..Go sleep..go sleep my little baby...
Bees and butterflies gonna peck out your eyes..
Poor little baby's gonna cry...
Poor little baby's gonna cry.

Over and over she sang the haunting melody. Orlean and Dom tiptoed out of the room and sat tiredly at the kitchen table unable to talk - unable to think. Finally Orlean rested her head on her boney arms, the arms that had held her three children as she sang the same lullaby to them on the bayou so many years ago, and sobbed with relief. Old Dom rose, walked 'round and 'round the table chanting, rocking back and forth, his bowed legs keeping time with the age-old rhythm, his arms extended.

****

Berta and Layke had decided to return directly to South Spring, driving through the Swede's land and not going to Old Town first, as they normally would. It would shorten their return by over two hours, and Berta was getting so anxious that Layke put the crop to Blackie. He knew that her horrible dream about SuSu had not left her and was concerned by her behavior on their return trip, especially on board the ship and again at the landing in Jacksonville. She seemed so remote. He had no way of knowing that Berta's unusual behavior was due to her curiosity regarding one Conner O'Farrell and not just her slight daughter, and had anyone told him that that was the case, he would have protested violently, blistering his ears.

They approached the south gate and heard Wes let out a war whoop announcing to all within earshot that they had returned. He jumped off Fiddlesticks and dashed madly for the gate and his mother's anxious arms, his towhead glistening in the bright sunlight.

Orlean ran out of the kitchen ignoring the door that slammed behind her, and Jonah rounded the back of the barn in a trot. Something was wrong. Berta could feel it. She quickly looked at Layke and could see that he, too, sensed it.

"Where is SuSu? Has something happened to SuSu? Wes, where is your sister?" she yelled. He lowered his head.

"Oh, thank God, there she is. She's just slower than the others." Berta held Layke's arm hard as she relaxed against his comforting shoulder.

"Why're her eyes so sunken, hon? She's been sick. I can tell."

"Berta, for heaven's sake! Take hold of yourself." He helped her down from the buckboard as Orlean, almost in a run, approached them. Soon they were all gathered around, sober-faced.

Layke said jovially, "Well, aren't you going to greet the honeymooners? A fine howdy-do. Gone for two weeks and this somber looking bunch..."

He didn't finish. Etienne interrupted him and as he held their hands explained the reason for their sadness. While he spoke in a controlled voice, SuSu's slight, listless arms wrapped around her mother's waist, and she began to sob. Berta couldn't stand to hear her. She hugged her as she patted Wes, trying to ease his whimpering. She asked Etienne to tell them the rest of the tale later, that she just wanted to hold her children close and talk of pleasant things, and that all that mattered was that SuSu was all right.

"That's all that matters, my dears," she re-emphasized. A relieved Orlean joined her as they wearily walked toward the house. Berta saw the girl, Juanita, her defiant chin lowered, leaning against the large oak in the side yard, and wondered what had transpired while they were away. When she glanced at Orlean, she could feel her bristle.

"Dear Lord! These two are like caged animals. The girl's animosity is aimed directly at Orlean!"

****

The dried corn scattered and bounced in the powdery dirt, some hardly landing before the hungry chickens' yellow beaks grabbed them. "Here, chick..chick..chick. Here, chick, here chick." It had taken Berta no time at all to get back to the business of being a cowman's wife. Diddle and Dumplin, Wes's pet bantams, were the last to find the feed. Berta wondered why they were always together and had not been accepted by the other chickens. Wes had raised them since they were just chicks. He kept them in a wooden crate beside the cook stove in the winter months and on the front porch when spring arrived. They helped him over his daddy's going, and even Berta had a special feeling for them, even though they were now grown. But it was strange to her that the other chickens knew that they were different. Didn't seem like chickens should be that smart. Wes said they were smarter than Old Red, and Berta was inclined to go along with him. He'd even taught them to play hide-and-seek, and they'd chase a pulled string all over the yard and even pull his paste-board box harnessed with string, like a mule.

"SuSu seems much better," Berta said to Orlean, who had joined her. She tied the sack of feed securely and leaned it up against the tools on the shelf of the barn. Mama Cat sat crouched behind it hoping one of the barn mice would take a hankering for some of the corn and proceed to gnaw a hole in the sack to satisfy his hunger. She was never far away from the feed sacks and had a fat belly to show that she could outsmart the unsuspecting rodents. As they walked up the path to the kitchen Berta said, "My, the honeymoon seems so long ago, but I'll have my precious memories, won't I, Orlean? They'll always be with me." The face of the man in white flashed before her. She shook her head.

As the two jabbered continuously around the kitchen table, Orlean finally let everything out, even though that very morning she had told Dom that she was going to wait 'til Berta and Layke were settled. But she had held everything in for too long. She had to unburden her concern about Juanita, to share her troubled heart with a compassionate and caring person, another mother who would understand her plight.

Layke soon joined the women, went to the stove and poured himself a cup of coffee. Standing attentively behind Berta's chair, first blowing then sipping the steaming liquid, he listened as Orlean related the news of Juanita's pregnancy and her understandable concern for Etienne's future.

Her work-worn hands clenched and unclenched nervously as she cried out her frustration. The girl had bested them all with her willful conniving, and Orlean did not like to be bested by anyone. She took pride in her position as matriarch of their family and despised the ignorant girl for shaking her self esteem. Berta made the appropriate, soothing comments. Orlean seemed to relax a little, and her fears began to diminish slowly as Berta and Layke quietly talked, trying to assuage them.

"We wondered why Juanita was keeping so close to the wagon since our return but thought it was because of the kidnapping and her terrible treatment of Jonah," Berta said. You'll have to be especially loving and caring of her, Orlean. Now, now," she said, soothing her, "I know it won't be easy for you, but as Etienne said, the babe is all important. You're a fortunate mother, dear." She patted Orlean's hands and continued, "Juanita is being honest with him. Frankly, I don't know of a single woman who wouldn't marry him under the same circumstances. Then you really would have a problem. He knows Juanita doesn't feel for him as he does for her, and I for one think it's commendable of her to tell him so."

"I know you be right, Mees Berta, but she'll hate de babe. She'll hate de babe!" She shook her tightly knotted, gray-streaked hair as she shouted vehemently toward Layke, who had decided to sit with the distraught women. "She already hates eet..." What was left unsaid was, "An' I weel hate eet, too - eet 'as dreeven a wedge between my first-born and me already."

"But as you said, I 'ave to be 'specially caring now. We leave tomorrow. Juanita ees ready for her debut, but Etienne ees 'fraid for her. He don' want her to walk de rope een her condeetion, but Pierre and Aimee agree wid Juanita, dat eet ees de teeng to do, and so do Dom an' me. She's worked very hard dese past weeks, an' she should be allowed her triumph. I say so, don' you agree?" Orlean deMoya was a good business woman and never missed an opportunity to fill their chests, even if the source was the hated pink and white trollop.

Layke finally spoke. "You're right, Orlean. If you deprive Juanita of her chance on the rope, she'll hate all of you, not just the unwanted child, but all of you. As you said, she has earned the rewards of her efforts. I don't think she's an evil girl. She just seems to crave excitement, or why would she have run away with a murdering gang in the first place? And she has been honest with Etienne."

Layke had risen from his chair as he spoke and came around the table to place his hand affectionately on her shoulder. Suddenly she inhaled deeply and stood erect, regaining her composure. "Berta is correct, Orlean. Just be patient and caring. It's the unborn babe who is to be protected."

But Orlean heard only her own silent declaration. "The trollop weel not ween...nevair...nevair! But how to best her? I must teenk of someteeng before eet's too late."

****

Jonah had arrived from Old Town the night before and was in the barn telling Pierre about some of his past hunting experiences. He had made up his mind long before he left town that he'd stay far away from Juanita and not let on to Etienne how she had treated him. The whole town knew how smitten by her Etienne was, and he didn't feel it was his place to enlighten him.

"Layke knows about her, and if he wants to tell his friend, then all right. But I'm not about to," he had told Young Reuben before he left to return to Rosehead. Reuben agreed with him but secretly wished someone would alert the Cajun. "I know I'd wanta know. But, shoot, as lovesick as he is, he probably would come up with a hundred excuses for her. I guess I'd be dumb enough to do the same."

Acknowledging Layke, Jonah kept on talking to Pierre. Finally Layke interrupted and said, "We've got a few hours before dusk, Jonah. Let's ride out to the spring to see about moving the beeves to the north pasture. Pierre, you wanta come along? We could sure use your help".

The three saddled up and rode the tall weed-lined, sandy path toward the south spring. Layke couldn't believe his ears. Jonah was whistling. He glanced at Pierre, who nodded to Layke silently acknowledging that he understood Jonah's new happiness. Out of the corner of his eye Jonah could see Juanita's outlined body at the tarp-draped entrance of the wagon. Tentatively, she ventured outside. "Guess she's staying clear of me, too. Good," and he resumed whistling. Blackie's tail swishing the flies was the only other sound.

Layke was amazed at the change in Jonah. He was talkative; he smiled readily. He thought as he watched the animated young man, "I guess Juanita is sorta like Jonah. She needs to be recognized, to feel special like Jonah was made to feel. I hope it'll be enough for her, but I doubt it. The more she gets, the more she'll want. On that I'd bet."

While the Williamses were gone, the deMoyas had freshly painted their wagons, using the same bright colors as before: red, blue, yellow and bright willow green. Etienne was ecstatic as he proudly informed Berta and Layke about the beautiful canvas backdrop he'd also had painted. The artist, Juan Escobar, one of the finest in that part of the state, had come all the way from Gainesville to study Juanita secretly, so her likeness would be exact. With Etienne's approval he had painted Juanita reclining on a rock beside a lively waterfall, her golden locks concealing her body and cascading into a shimmering pool of water bordered with colorful tropical flowers.

Etienne elaborated, "It will be unveiled as a surprise for her debut in Rowland's Bluff. Oh, I do so wish that you could be there!" he exclaimed in a whisper, so that the inquisitive Juanita would not hear - they stood beside the wagon. He had no way of knowing that her ear was pressed so tightly against the inside wall of the wagon that her entire head ached.

"Now, why can't he speak louder? I heard almost everything he said. Frankly, I'm sick and tired of walking on egg shells in this old place while everyone whispers about me, especially that old crow of a mama. I just wish we could leave this very minute!" She pounded her slightly rounded belly, and with a scowl on her pretty face she resumed her position against the wagon's side. As Etienne continued giving their itinerary to Berta and Layke, she pulled her knees up under her cotton skirt, hugging them to stop their shaking. She was getting more excited by the minute.

Etienne had finally succumbed to the pressures his family and Juanita had put on him and agreed that she could make her debut at Rowland's Bluff, their next destination. The route they would travel was the same one they usually took during the hot, sultry days of August and September. They'd spend a week in Lake City - then on to Jacksonville, where they always drew large crowds. If the rains held off they should pull into Palatka by the second week in September and stay a few days before going across the St. Johns to St. Augustine.

Etienne continued. They'd zigzag across the state, playing the small settlements, most of them like Old Town, just wilderness towns of about a hundred or so hearty souls. Slowly they'd work their way as far south as Ft. Pierce on the ocean. When he said that, Juanita had to quickly cover her outburst, she was so thrilled. She'd never in her entire life seen a big ocean. Then they'd head over to Ft. Basinger on the Kissimmee River before going south to the Caloosahatchee River, crossing at Ft. Thompson. They planned to travel through La Belle, not much of a town, just a few buildings that hugged the river and the nearest settlement to the small farm where Juanita was from.

"Now why on earth do we hafta go there? I'll just not think about it! I'll just not! By then I'll have had R.J.'s bastard baby." She listened...then they'd continue following the river route west to Alva, the next settlement, where they'd stop for a few days, and then on to Ft. Myers on the Gulf before turning north to the trail alongside the Peace River and on to Tater Hill Bluff. They planned to return to Old Town in June as they had in previous years.

She simply could not contain herself. She could not. Never in all her years had she really thought she'd be a part of such an exciting adventure. Running away with the Skinners had indeed been thrilling, but to go to all those strange-sounding towns and to perform on the tight rope in front of hundreds of people in her beautiful costume...her heart would not stop racing. She had completely forgotten the baby.

Slowly she ventured outside and pretending not to know that they were there, said, "Oh, there y'all are. I was just wondering where everyone was." Etienne immediately went to her and with a questioning look on his dark face asked, "Ma Cherie, have you been there all the time?" She asked why he wanted to know. Because she apparently had not overheard his conversation concerning the backdrop, he smiled as he squeezed her to him and responded, "Never you mind, my sweet, never you mind," and winked at Berta and Layke as Juanita squirmed her way out of his grasp, saying as she ran from him, "Oh, Etienne, how you do go on. I declare, you do. Please excuse him, Mr. and Mrs. Williams."

When Juanita was out of hearing, Etienne told them that he knew that Orlean had confided in them about Cherie's pregnancy and that it was his plan to remain in the Ft. Pierce area the latter part of February to await the babe. They could not believe how excited he was about the bastard child. Etienne hurriedly left to join Juanita at the rope.

"He'll love it enough for the both of them, my sweet," Layke said, "but I'll be very much surprised if Miss Juanita stays with the deMoyas after the babe is born. She does not want the responsibility. She'll not be visiting South Spring next June, and the deMoyas will have the babe. Mark my word."

Berta agreed, but she could not fault the ignorant girl for it. She wondered how she would handle the situation if she were in Juanita's shoes. "Would that I were." She patted her stomach and thought, "I hope and pray I can give you sons, Layke Williams. You deserve sons, my love. Would that I were."

It was a sad good-by. Wes and SuSu had become fast friends with the deMoyas. Aimee had taken a special interest in SuSu and had taught her many tumbling tricks and had started her on the tightrope the first week that Berta and Layke had been away on their honeymoon. As Berta and Layke joined Aimee in praising SuSu, she displayed her ability on the five-foot-high rope, her small feet fleeting across the rope as if she'd been born to it, and they were amazed at her adroitness. She'd regained her strength and come out of herself so quickly, Berta observed.

Juanita was lying relaxed on her pallet. She decided that she'd best mind her manners and join the others. The narrow wagon steps were not very sturdy, and as she placed her feet carefully she latched her small hands on to the sides to steady herself. Lowering herself she thought, "It'd just be my luck to fall and break my neck..just my fate, and wouldn't old lady deMoya be happy about that. She'd grin her old washboard face 'bout off."

She thanked Berta and Layke for allowing her to stay at South

Spring, and trying to not look at Jonah, who also had his face averted, she could see that Orlean was taking in her discomfort and enjoying it. Angrily she rounded the performing wagon toward the back wagon driven by Pierre. She had some tall planning to do and didn't want Orlean around to distract her.

"I am not going to have your bastard child, Mr. R.J. Skinner. I swear on your buzzard-eaten carcass, I'm not!"

But what to do to rid her young body of the unwanted child, she did not know. As best she could calculate, she should be approaching her third month. "I bet it's a boy, and it's already growing horns just like its father," she said as she pounded her rounded stomach, her white, angry fists practically bouncing off. She had tried jumping up and down as hard as she could when no one was looking, but nothing happened, and try as she might, she couldn't remember what the herb potion was for her to drink.

CHAPTER II ANGEL

Juanita was finally over her dizziness, so Etienne promised that she could make her debut in Rowland's Bluff as planned. She could hardly contain herself, she was so excited. When she asked Aimee how it felt the first time she had performed, she said that she had been so young that she couldn't remember anything but being scared half to death and the applause. She could best remember the crowd's applauding, so she had quickly forgotten about falling and breaking all her bones.

It should take two long, hot days to reach Rowland's Bluff. They'd follow the trail alongside the Suwannee and stop to seek shelter only if the afternoon rains, that were almost a daily certainty, were accompanied by high wind. Two days seemed like an eternity to the antsy Juanita, but the time arrived more quickly than she thought possible.

The town's excited children heard their approaching wagons and gathered at the end of the main road - boisterous - anxiously awaiting them. They were hopping up and down, shouting their enthusiasm when Juanita heard them. With the same child-like exuberance she came to the front of the wagon and joined Pierre and Aimee, who were smiling and waving to the people. They were singly spaced, hoping for a better view, all along the sandy main street.

The curious guests at the Arthur B. Hotel gathered on the wide porch to see what the commotion was all about, and in front of the Suwannee Saloon the cow-town girls were waving with their usual abandon. Juanita just knew her heart was gonna burst right out of her light blue blouse. When she glanced down, she could actually see the beat of her heart lift the fabric in and out.

Etienne turned around in his seat in the lead wagon to look at his Cherie's glowing face, and turning back to Orlean said, "The turpentiners will be in town by nightfall, and we should have a good take. We always do when we play the weekends, eh? And with *Cherie the Golden Girl* performing, our take should double."

Orlean bit her tongue to contain the outburst. "Why ees he so stupid? He ees so smart 'bout so many teengs but so stupid 'bout de trollop! Double de take, indeed. We be lucky eef she don' fall and break her neck." She smiled at the thought of it, but then remembered the babe. She could not bring herself to hate the poor bastard babe.

The family had discussed the split with Juanita and had decided that she should have a full share. Orlean figured that if she could work for two more months, she should earn enough to give the child a good start in life. After she became large with the child, she could still help with passing the hat, repairing the costumes and even the camp chores. She appeared to accept Juanita for all their sakes, and not even Dom knew of her growing hatred.

They pulled the wagons into the vacant lot between the Arthur B. Hotel and the livery stable, as they had in previous years, and before Etienne, Dom and Pierre had finished setting out the benches, the town's rowdy boys had scooted in to claim their spots while the girls pushed and shoved each other, fighting for the remaining seats. The posts for the hanging lanterns were set in place beside the stage, that folded out from the lead wagon. Pierre and Etienne strung the tightrope between the two buildings, testing it again and again for its tautness, and making sure that the platforms at the top of the long poles on either side of the stretched rope were properly in place and the knots were secure.

Etienne caught Aimee's eye and signaled her that she was to carry out their plan of taking Juanita behind the wagon on some pretence or other so he and Pierre could hang the new canvas backdrop. He wanted nothing to spoil the surprise.

It's a wonder she didn't become suspicious when the squealing young girls shouted, "There's the Golden Girl. I see the Golden Girl." It should have alerted the whole town about the unveiling. Etienne was so put out with them that Pierre said later it was a good thing that the preacher and all those church-going ladies couldn't understand French. He had never in all his life heard Etienne so upset.

The signal was given. Aimee and Juanita walked around to the front of the wagon. At first Juanita didn't know what all the commotion was and didn't even look at the canvas. Everyone kept looking at her and then back to the canvas. She was getting more nervous by the minute, what with Etienne grinning at her like a chessy cat, but her eyes soon followed the children's stares. When she saw it, she just stood there with her mouth gaping, feeling like some kinda nut or something, she was so astonished. Her embarrassment soon turned to pleasure; then the tears started welling out of her large, blue eyes, and with all those people staring at her she thought she was gonna die right there in the middle of Rowland's Bluff, Florida.

Etienne said if he lived to be a hundred years old, he'd never forget the look on Cherie's face. When Aimee looked at the tears escaping and rolling gently down Juanita's flushed cheeks, she started crying right along with her, and Juanita squeezed her hand about off, she was so excited.

Not a word could Juanita say - not a word. She went up on her tiptoes and kissed Etienne's cheek, turned and quickly ran around to the back of the wagon, jumping in so fast that she scraped her leg in the process. The uncontrolled sobbing was muffled by the blanket that she grabbed off of Aimee's bunk. "Why can't I love him? Why? He's so good and kind and thoughtful. Something must be bad wrong with me."

"Don't go to her, Aimee. She needs to be alone with her happiness."

"Oh, Etienne, she was so surprised! Did you see her face?"

"Oui, Aimee. I saw our golden girl's face, and I'll never forget it. Never. It told me that one day she will care for me as I do her." He wore a faraway look on his dark face, and Orlean, who was behind the wagon listening to them, shook her head at her foolish son's declaration.

"I would pray for you, my son, but am afraid the Deveel would be de one to answer eet. De girl don' have any love een her eveel heart. None at all, my poor Etienne." And she disgustedly spat on the ground.

****

"Juanita, quit fidgeting. You must hold still, or I will never get it hooked. Hold in a little more. Oh! Good! Now turn around and let's get a look at you." Aimee stepped back a short step. The wagon was so small that even that small step put her up against the bunk on the opposite side. Orlean was at the entrance and was amazed that the girl did indeed look like a golden girl. But her good sense returned in a hurry, and before Aimee let out another burst of praise, she told them that they must hurry, that the crowd was swelling and the turpentiners were in a hurry to view their big act. They liked Pierre's tricks with Delilah well enough, but they all knew why they were there, and it sure wasn't to see a man and his trick dog - they were getting very vocal about it, too.

But an exuberant Aimee could not restrain herself. On and on she gushed, until Orlean for once in her life felt like holding her old hand over Aimee's mouth to quiet her. "Oh, Juanita, you're so beautiful. Maman, I'm so glad you had me fold in the gusset. I'll have to let it out by next week, I'm afraid. Oh, I hope it's a girl! We'll have such fun with her, Juanita. You just wait and see."

"Dat'll take de honey out of her smile. She don' forget de babe now. My Aimee won' let her. No more smile from de girl tonight, I teenk."

Juanita, dejected, turned from them, and before she could warn Aimee to shut her babbling about the bastard child, Pierre stuck his head inside the tarp to call Aimee for her act. Juanita was to be the final act, the climax of the evening. Etienne said that Aimee would warm up the crowd, and then *Cherie, the Golden Girl*, would capitalize on it. He had told Dom and Orlean that he was sure that the coffers would be overflowing when the crowd saw the beautiful Cherie with her long hair flowing in the soft August breeze.

When Juanita heard the applause, she knew that Aimee had completed her walk and that she would be summoned. "Why are my hands so sweaty? Good grief! You don't think I'm gonna throw up all over those people, do you?" she questioned herself out loud. Pierre's calling stopped her. "Juanita! Juanita, Etienne is announcing you. Don't you hear him? Hey, Juanita!" She couldn't move. She couldn't move a muscle nor utter a sound other than the whimpering that she didn't recognize as hers. She just sat there in the back of that stuffy wagon and whimpered just like a sick old dog.

Pierre stuck his head inside the darkened wagon. At first he couldn't see her, although he heard what sounded like a mewing kitten. "Not now you won't!" he thought. "By God, not now! You'll not gain my brother's heart and make a fool of the rest of us, you little whore!" He took some deep breaths and calmed down enough to say soft-like, "Juanita, you need to come out of this old stuffy, hot wagon and into the fresh air. Aimee was just the same as you when she walked her first time," he lied. "Just the same. Now, come on out, and I'll get you some cool water and then go tell Etienne to do something to keep those turpentiners from jumping up on the stage and tearing his heart out.

Aimee came running back calling to her, "Juanita, hurry, hurry. Etienne has announced you."

When she saw Pierre's expression, she shushed. "Juanita needs some fresh air. The wagon was so hot she felt faint." He whispered, "Go tell Etienne to sing - anything - use the puppets. She has to relax and get her confidence, or she'll never perform."

Etienne used his head and announced that the golden girl was to perform right after he sang a song written especially for her in honor of her debut, and he proceeded to play the guitar and sing a tearful love song in French, that he made up right on the spot. Lucky for him there weren't any turpentiners from the bayou, or they'd probably have run him up a tree or something just as humiliating. He must have sung six verses and finally had to end it, because the yelling they were doing was drowning him out.

Aimee, who was standing behind the stage out of sight of the crowd, was waiting for Pierre to signal her that all was well. Nothing. She shook her head at Etienne; so in desperation he pulled out the puppets, Madam and Monsieur, and did an impromptu husband and wife spoof that seemed to assuage the loud men and children.

Finally, Aimee nodded and he held out both his arms to quiet the rowdy bunch and loudly said, "Ladies and Gentlemen. It is with great pleasure that.." but he couldn't continue as the crowd was on its feet and yelling so loud that Juanita became frightened when she heard them. But straightening herself up tall, she confidently regained her composure, climbed the ladder to the stage and with her head held high, queen-like, she stood beside Etienne. She was indeed a glorious sight to see - all aqua-blue and gold and sparkly all over.

Pierre was kept busy shoving the half-drunk men from the stage so Juanita could accompany Etienne to the ladder. Dom, Orlean and Aimee were standing below the taut rope, and the crowd sensed their anxiety and became quieter. As she climbed the long, wooden ladder to the platform in the sky, her hair held in a giant clip, Etienne prayed as he had never prayed in his life. So did Orlean, but her prayers were not as her son's. She didn't wish the selfish girl any personal harm, but she just wanted her to go....to go away so that their lives would be as before and her son's heart would not be broken. She was sure it would be if the girl's act was triumphant. Then, she would never leave.

There was a hush.

The stars were ignoring the onlookers. The clouds moved swiftly in the deep blue summer sky selfishly performing their own capricious patterns. The moon was nearly full and did not acknowledge any earthly happenings. But all changed when *Cherie, The Golden Girl* reached the platform, opened her sparkly parasol and released her glorious mane to flirt with the moonbeams and the star light. The audience went wild. She felt her power. "I'm alive. For the first time in all my seventeen years, I'm alive."

As Juanita lifted her beautiful head and looked toward the heavens the audience roared its approval. The moon lit her face, and someone in the audience shouted, "Look, there's a halo on her hair." Others shouted, "I see it. I see it."

"I'm as close to heaven as I'll ever be, and Preacher Catlett was right. 'The heavens will perform their magical feats, and you'll float gloriously amidst your fellow men. There will be no fear and no hunger - no want....'"

She took her first step, and she had never been more sure of herself and her ability than at that moment. She almost danced across the tightrope. She didn't sway from side to side to keep her balance as did Aimee. She glided across, barely touching the rope, it seemed. When she reached the other platform beside the Arthur B. Hotel, the audience stood, and their applause and words of praise filled her. She began to bite her lower lip and cry, and although she had never been a religious girl, she knew at that moment that there had to be a heaven, 'cause she'd just visited it.

Etienne was the first to reach her. "Ma Cherie, I love you so," he whispered holding her delicate hand as he helped her from the ladder. And carried away by her own exhilaration, she responded, not realizing how Etienne needed to hear her words, "And I love you, Etienne."

The audience left their seats. They crowded around her, and she couldn't move. Pierre helped Etienne lift her onto the stage, Dom began ringing the triangle and Orlean played the music box trying to distract them. But they did not hear; they did not want to hear as they, too, had experienced a bit of heaven and did not want to let it go.

Orlean and Aimee had long since been asleep on the narrow beds, but *Cherie, the Golden Girl,* could not let her evening go. "I can't believe it. I just can't. Why couldn't R.J. and Joe Bob or even Rose have been here to share it with me? I need someone I care about to share this night." She had finally had the recognition she wanted, she needed, but what good was it if she didn't have someone with whom to share it.

As she lay on the straw-filled pallet, her hand eased down to her rounded belly. "Baby," she said in a whisper, "Do you know that we were in heaven tonight? You and me in heaven. Imagine!" She stroked her belly in a rhythmic motion and began singing softly to it. "You've gotta have a name, baby, and it sure as heck won't be Blessed Jane or any such. How about Nita? No, it's gotta be special."

Not being able to sleep she worked herself to the wagon door, and, sitting, swinging her bare feet in the evening's cooled air, she leaned her golden hair against the tarp and wistfully watched the show-off clouds perform in the bright sky and tried to think of a special name for her new friend.

"I know! I'll call her Angel. That's what...Angel."

****

The deMoyas and Juanita extended their performance and stayed Sunday night, as well. Etienne telegraphed Lake City that they would be a day late arriving. The afternoon shower did not last long, and the crowd was even larger than on Saturday night. Orlean was still skeptical about the girl's popularity and told Dom that she thought that it was just a fluke, the extra large crowd, and that they shouldn't start counting their chickens just yet.

The turpentiners, wanting to make the most of their weekend of raising hell with their bellies full of shine and watching that Golden Girl in her skimpy costume walk the rope, did not return to their camp 'til late that evening. Boy, she was really something to see. Juanita was the talk of the whole county.

Lake City was also a triumph. The rains came earlier in the afternoon than usual, and after the others had retired for the night, Dom and Orlean, sitting alone on the porch of the store next door, discussed the amazing increase in their take and hoped that the rains would continue to arrive early to insure large crowds as they played the small settlements en route to Jacksonville.

Orlean would still not give Juanita credit for their improved financial situation, and when Dom suggested that her addition might be the reason for the hefty sack he held, she set him straight. It was just a coincidence, she said. They hadn't played Jacksonville yet, and because it was a more sophisticated town without the rowdy turpentiners' throwing away their money, it would be a better measure of Juanita's worth. She knew she wasn't fooling Dom, and she certainly wasn't fooling herself. The ungrateful girl was still besting her at every turn.

This was the first time that Juanita Jane Graves had ever earned money. Even her own ma had a can filled with doubloons from the sale of chickens to the trappers who camped alongside the Caloosahatchee. She couldn't believe it when Etienne showed her her share of the take in Rowland's Bluff and Lake City. She just couldn't believe it. But she quickly took it, putting it into a cloth sack and sewed it into the blanket alongside the doubloons and stashed it beside the books Etienne had given her. Oh, she liked having the doubloons that R.J. had given her, but this was different. A feeling of peace and satisfaction came over her, and she couldn't figure out why. But she couldn't allow it to creep in and change her plan. She and Angel would leave these Gypsies just as soon as they had enough money. Just as soon.

Pierre suggested that she spend some of her new wealth on a pretty, new dress, and Etienne teased her about all the bonnets she could buy in Jacksonville and how he'd like to take her to the St. James Hotel for tea, and, oh, how they did have sport with her all the way to Jacksonville! Orlean and Dom seldom addressed her, but it seemed to Juanita that even Orlean had warmed to her a little. Not that it mattered. She dismissed Orlean just like she would a pesky mosquito, and it was getting under Orlean's skin. "Dees trollop will not make a fool of me...not ever." But which path to follow even the tea leaves did not reveal. She must be cautious, she decided.

The closer they got to Jacksonville, the largest city on their planned route, the more excited Juanita became. It was early September but still warm. It wouldn't cool off until the end of October or early November when the maples, oak and cypress would blind you with their fall colors. She wished she could see the gold of the cypress along the St. Johns that Etienne talked of, but that would come later after she left the Gypsies. Juanita never doubted her ability to realize her dream.

Aimee had to let out the gusset so her costume would not bind her, but Juanita still got a thrill when she put it on. There would never be anything as beautiful, no matter how many gowns she owned, not ever, she decided, as she fingered the sequins and bugle beads. Although Angel had been allowed a position in her future plans, Juanita still had not addressed any change in her life...like caring for her. The day-to-day, unending caring of a helpless infant did not find a place in the romantic mind of Juanita Jane Graves. She thought of Angel as a companion...a friend. Never as a helpless baby suckling at her full breasts and dirtying diapers. Now, Juanita was not stupid. She knew that babies did these things. It just had not entered her dream that Angel would be one of those...

They rode down Bay Street, and it was as old Dom had told her. Even Orlean was talkative, and when she saw the St. James Hotel that Etienne had glowingly told her of, she actually shivered. She'd seen pictures of large buildings, but the largest one she had ever seen was two stories tall. If she hadn't run away with R.J., she probably wouldn't have seen even that one.

Her confidence began to ebb. The women on Bay Street were elegantly dressed, and as they alighted from their handsome carriages, Juanita realized that riding in a painted wagon was not as grand as she had formerly thought. Oh, it was better than riding in the old wagon her pa drove, but when she witnessed the prancing horses pulling the fancy carriages with the beautifully turned-out ladies, she got scared. She had to bring herself up tall-like and decide once and for all that she'd wear her hair proudly, dressing it like the women she had seen.

"Angel and me'll not be riding in a painted wagon for much longer. Oh, I can just see us now, my hair piled high with a little white bird perched on a big blue hat just ready to fly away...almost. And her, oh, she'll wear a cap with rosettes all over the place. Oh, we'll be a fancy sight to behold. Why, that old tightrope costume will look like a rag..."

****

Riding into Palatka was not as big a thrill as when they

approached Jacksonville. Although the towns were comparable in size, Jacksonville was more cosmopolitan. But the large boats moored at the wharfs off Water St. were almost as plentiful as in Jacksonville. The *Savannah* and *Robert E. Lee* were both in port to seek shelter, for there was word of a hurricane southeast of Palatka and headed their way. They were the largest ships Juanita had ever seen and dwarfed the side wheelers, barques and other small boats that hovered beside them.

"Shoot, they look 'bout the size of the wet-ass boats on the Caloosahatchee," Juanita said derisively. "Just like toy boats," she said to Aimee, who had joined her beside Pierre on the front seat as they rode along the busy street. Wood and brick buildings, some three stories high, prestigiously looked down at their upturned faces, their mouths gaping in wonder.

Juanita knew that this would be her last performance, because another eight or nine months would go by before she could resume her act. She was beginning to show, and even Aimee's magical needle could not hide her condition. She reluctantly agreed with the deMoyas that the Palatka shows would be her last. The take should be large - the big ships were in for an overnight and should add mightily to her hoard.

Continuing to feel the excitement of her performance, as though it were the first time, *Cherie, The Golden Girl* anticipated the evening's performance and knew that tonight would be no different if the dark clouds to the east didn't rain them out. She was getting anxious as she observed them. She wanted her last night to be spectacular, memorable, the most wonderful night of her life. But Etienne and Pierre were concerned, as were the townspeople. The stores along Water Street had already begun boarding the windows that faced the river in preparation for the expected hurricane.

The wind picked up, and a sheet of driving white rain accompanied it when they pulled into the vacant lot. Hovering inside the wagons they ate the cold corn cakes left over from their breakfast, and Juanita, with the tarp pulled back, cursed the storm's untimely interruption and prayed for her last chance, while the storm, ignoring her, continued to display its might.

It was September 8th and the middle of the hurricane season. The citrus trees, heavy with oranges and lemons, were waiting for the cold air from the north to sweeten their fruit for shipment to the hungry northern markets. Juanita had never seen the likes of them, lining the streets leading right up to the big hotels, that were already filled with tourists.

The southern part of the state was finally opening up to homesteaders seeking a new life. They sailed the St. Johns, stopping at the various towns and villages along the way, some settling even before arriving at their planned destination. Palatka was one of them. The St. Johns was but a meandering stream after Palatka, but soon broadened into vast lagoons, rich in a wild natural beauty, that had been only imagined by the passengers on board and certainly never seen. From Virginia, Maryland, North and South Carolina and states north, south and west they came. The upstream journey - for the St. Johns flowed north - was luxuriant with orange groves amidst the moss-draped oaks, that sloped to the water's very edge; their fragrance permeated the heavy, sub-tropical air. They were an adventurous people full of hope and high with spirit, and they were impatient to experience this verdant land.

Juanita, Aimee and Orlean were inside their wagon, solemn-faced. The rains had subsided, but the winds continued to move the tarp in and out, although they had fastened it as securely as possible. "I'll not miss our last walk, Angel!" Juanita declared to herself and her belly. "I simply will not, do you hear?"

As she silently declared her intention, Orlean was watching the girl. She knew that their take would lessen if the storm did not pass them by and Juanita was unable to perform in Palatka, but she'd not admit it to any of the other family members. There was no doubt that the girl had contributed, as Etienne had said she would, but Orlean was still watchful. Juanita seemed to have become more complacent, but Orlean knew her attitude had to be fleeting; her true self would emerge and cause her family the trouble that she had read in the leaves. She never doubted the leaves. But, desperate to find a solution to her problem, she had begun reading the cards, something she did only in moments of desperation. Old Dom was worried for his wife. He had never seen her so vigilant...frightened.

The winds lessened by early dusk, and the rains were reduced to a light drizzle. Only an occasional rustling of the fronds on the palms that lined their vacant lot reminded them of the blustery afternoon, but Etienne was adamant in his belief that it was too dangerous for Juanita and Aimee to walk the rope. The talk was that the eye of the hurricane was stalled off the Atlantic coast and that it would continue north. White-capped waves still pounded the wooden wharfs, their spray riding the winds to the opposite side of Water Street. But the excitement was high, and having two of the large passenger boats in was a bonus that they had not counted on, and Orlean was trying to convince Etienne that it was indeed safe for the girls.

"Juanita weel be very disappointed, my son. She 'as been very quiet all day...hardly spoke a word."

"I know, Maman, I know, but her safety and her babe's are more important than her desires. Don't you agree, Papa?"

Old Dom shook his head, then replied, "But she weel fight our decision, my son. She weel fight."

And fight she did. She stomped her feet. She flailed her arms around as she cried and stormed at Etienne. She cried torrents of tears, but the undaunted Etienne was not swayed by her tantrums. The decision remained the same.

As he jumped down from the dripping wagon, Juanita stuck her head out from around the tarp to blister his ears with one last outburst. "I'll walk that rope tonight, Etienne deMoya, and you'll see *Cherie, The Golden Girl* perform her greatest triumph. Yours is a heart of stone, Etienne, a heart of stone!"

Juanita got her way. The winds miraculously subsided but for a few intermittent gusts, and the anticipated hurricane was no longer mentioned by the huge crowds that gathered from the *Savannah* and *Robert E. Lee.*

There was not room for another living soul, Orlean commented, as she approached the wagon, where Aimee and Juanita awaited their summons from Etienne. Juanita sat inside the performing wagon behind the stage. No one could see inside the quiet darkness as she scanned the audience in anticipation of her walk.

"We'll be in heaven soon, Angel."

It was then she saw him. He stood taller than the others, although he was leaning against a tall sand pine at the edge of the audience. He was dressed in white from his Panama hat to his spats. She could feel the intensity of his presence and could not force her eyes to leave him. He smoked a black cheroot slowly, the wispy, gray smoke curled into the damp, pitch-black night, swirling lazily around the lantern light above him.

She stood, then walked around the painted canvas, and their eyes found each other - they just stared. Juanita felt warm all over. "Not now," she thought. "Dear Lord, not now. Don't let me meet him now." She had to get her thoughts together and concentrate on her performance.

Etienne called her again before she heard and responded. He assisted her, his muscled arm holding her protectively around her still small waist. The ladder was but a few feet from the tall, dark stranger. She could feel his eyes burning through her, and he seemed to know that she was very much aware of his presence with his heavy black eyebrow cocked and that inquisitive smirk on his handsome face.

"Who does he think he is - staring at me like that! I'm *Cherie, The Golden Girl*, mister. Don't you know who you're looking at in that...that..." She couldn't think of the word, so she shrugged and ignored the upstart.

Etienne's concern interrupted her thoughts. "Cherie, are you feeling all right? You look flushed."

"I'm fine. I'll be just fine, thank you."

"He'll not upset us, Angel. No matter what. This is our walk, mister, and you'll not be causing us any problems, will he, Angel?" But all the way up that long ladder Juanita saw those opaque blue eyes, and her keen instincts told her she had met her nemesis...her punishment.

When she arrived at the platform and opened the draped parasol, the slight gusts of wind from the storm still lingered and felt cool and clean on her flushed cheeks. Her performance began as usual. The swell of the crowd's roar bolstered her showmanship. As always, at the beginning, she would gaze into the heavens, and the audience would be on its feet, calling her, referring to her as the golden angel. She loosened her knee-length, yellow-white tresses to flirt with the evening breeze, and when she slowly opened her eyes toward the heavens, she saw the boiling clouds roaring in from the east.

"We'll not be frightened, my Angel."

She approached the rope, her head still raised. Her bravery is what delighted her subjects. When she glided across the rope the audience felt transposed. They walked it with her and thrilled to her every step and heart beat.

She challenged the storm clouds filled with their threatening wind and saw the stranger's image in every one of them.

"Why do I feel that this night is different? I feel so light...like I could fly right off this rope. Angel, do you see those clouds? We'll hav'ta be real careful, my sweet."

Pierre and Etienne saw the parasol tilt and knew that a gust of wind had caused her to lose her balance. "Am I floating? Is that screammmmmmm...?"

The screaming crowd blotted out her thoughts. Pierre was there instantly to break her fall. Etienne shoved him away and circled his arms around her limp body, calling to her in French, his tears bouncing off the gold and aqua costume.

No response. No movement. She lay crumpled in his shaking arms.

"Do not move her," someone said from behind him. "I'll send for the ship's doctor. Do not move her," he said again in his authoritative voice.

Etienne turned to see who was giving him orders. He stared into icy blue eyes, commanding eyes, and he could feel the tall stranger's power. From the back of the crowd they heard a voice pleading with the frightened, uncontrolled throng to let him through.

"I am a doctor. Please let me through." He called loudly and again repeated his plea.

The stranger in white leapt upon the stage and commanded the unruly people to allow the doctor to attend their Golden Girl. He had their attention at last. When the doctor reached her, he told Etienne and Pierre to get a blanket with which to make a stretcher. Orlean had covered the crumpled Juanita with her shawl, and Aimee just stood, staring, and as Dom held her she looked at her fallen friend and shivered in the balmy night.

Etienne and Pierre managed to get the stretcher holding Juanita through the curious crowd and into the back wagon. The ship's doctor turned toward the man in white and told him, "Announce that the girl is alive. Her pulse is not strong, but at least she's alive."

What he didn't say was, "Alive but not with a great deal of hope, I'm afraid." The blanket was covered with blood, and he listened to the announcement from the stage encouraging the people to disperse, to go to their homes or their boats; someone would keep them informed about the girl as soon as they learned anything. The doctor asked Etienne to leave the wagon; he wanted Orlean to assist him. He could see that Etienne was not capable of much more.

"He must love her very much, poor man, and I don't know if I'll be able to save her." He directed his concern to Orlean, who shuddered when she saw the blood and told the bald, middle-aged doctor that Juanita had been with child.

"Had been, is correct, Madam. She is no more." Orlean could not prevent the tears. "I do not like dees girl, but de babe...de poor babe."

Pierre and Dom helped Aimee, who was now shaking uncontrollably, into the performing wagon, and the stranger was again offering his help. "This should ease her shock, Monsieur," he said producing a flask containing whiskey. "Just a little, mind you," he cautioned in his resonant accent. Aimee sputtered as she fought for breath, pushing them away, but Pierre insisted that she sip a little more. He covered her with the warm blanket, stroking her tenderly to give her courage, while Dom sat weakly beside her with his bobbing head buried in his gnarled, tan hands.

The black, wind-filled clouds suddenly unleashed their fury causing the last of the bystanders to run for the closest shelter. Pierre invited the stranger to come inside. Etienne, who was right behind him, had not escaped the suddenness of the downpour. Once inside he, too, began shaking. The tattered blanket did little to allay his chattering teeth, and when the stranger in white offered him a swig from the flask, he shook his head negatively but managed to ask the stranger his name.

"I, sir, am Conner O'Farrell, recently of the steamship *Savannah* and formerly of the most prestigious ship on any waterway, the *Robert E. Lee*. I'm at your service, lady and gentlemen." He pretended to bow but could not because of the cramped quarters.

Etienne wanted to comment on the *Robert E. Lee* - Berta and Layke had told him of its magnificence - but did not feel the need to converse with this man. When there was no response from the overwrought foursome, Conner continued, trying to get their minds off of the golden girl. "I make the Savannah-Palatka run on the St. Johns River. You see, I am a gambler and the river is my home. Before I traveled the St. Johns I was privileged to call the mighty Mississippi home, but a distraught husband had the effrontery to accuse me of dallying with his buxom wife, so my man Harrison and I sought other ...shall we say, accommodations."

Etienne, concerned that Aimee was hearing this crude gambler's remarks, saw that she had succumbed to the shock and whiskey and had fallen asleep, so, anxious for any diversion to keep his mind off his Cherie's fall, shook the loquacious man's extended hand and encouraged him to continue. He was surprised at the man's hand. Its length and slenderness were unexpected. Conner was used to this reaction and said, "My hands are those of a gambler, Monsieur. Would that they could wield a surgeon's knife or play a musical instrument, as my dearly departed, sainted mother would have wished. But instead, they're happily at home with a deck of cards, a glass of good bourbon and a seductive wench to take for my pleasure."

Wanting to change the subject, Etienne said, "My dear friends, the Williamses of Old Town had the privilege of a trip on the beautiful *Robert E. Lee*. As a matter of fact, they were on their honeymoon and stayed at the Putnam House while here in Palatka." He did not see Conner's reaction at the mention of Berta and Layke. But Pierre did.

"Did you meet them - Berta and Layke - when they were on the ship?" Pierre inquired.

Conner hesitated, became very solemn but quickly recouped and with renewed energy answered, "But of course, everyone on the entire ship was aware of Mrs. Williams's beauty." His voice was strange, but he instantly changed and added with verve, "A man would have had to be blind and a fool not to have inquired as to her identity, and I, sir, am a man who appreciates beauty. I assure you that I do not wear the fool's mantle." He gave them his controlled grin, but his eyes were of stone, Etienne noticed.

"The insolence of the man...speaking of Berta in that manner." He normally would have said it aloud, he was so incensed. Had he not been so distraught about his Cherie, he would have reminded him of whom he spoke. But he replied quietly, "You, sir, no doubt also had the opportunity of meeting her equally handsome and charming husband, Layke. He is a dear friend of mine and a gracious host. My family and I enjoyed the hospitality of the Williamses at their ranch, South Spring, on the Suwannee."

The man abruptly rose. Rudely ignoring Etienne's chatter, he pulled back the dripping tarp and gracefully jumped down from the wagon alighting into the ferocious storm. He removed his rain-spattered hat, and having regained his composure, turned, shouting his words into the howling wind, "Gentlemen, if we're to converse in this bloody hurricane, yours truly needs another flask...or perhaps two would do me. I'll return in a moment with the Devil's brew." And with his bare head bent against the wind and rain he trudged through the foot-deep water toward the river front.

Etienne watched him and gazed at the wagon where his love lay, perhaps dying. He saw the tarp pulled aside, and the doctor stuck his head outside, his hand shielding his eyes, but, though he tried, he could not hear what he said to Conner.

"I know you're off the *Savannah*. I would like you to go to the ship's steward and ask him to give you my medical bag from my cabin. I am Dr. Wallace Young, and I'm in cabin No. 21 on the second deck. I'll also need some whiskey and laudanum, as well."

Conner grinned his approval when the slight doctor mentioned the whiskey. "I thought you wouldn't mind bringing the whiskey, sir," the doctor said sarcastically. Conner bowed. "You are very astute, Doctor."

The doctor then yelled to Etienne. "Are you the husband?"

Why does he want to know? Sweet Mary and Joseph! "No, would that I were," Etienne said weakly, then lied more forcefully, "She was recently widowed."

"She has lost the baby, I'm sorry to say, but seems to have broken only her left arm." Competing with the wind proved ineffective, so he slipped outside holding over his head the slicker Orlean had given him and approached their wagon. Pierre helped him inside. "You, young man, saved her life, breaking her fall as you did." He coughed, his hand instinctively covering his mouth, as he directed his comments toward Pierre, shook the slicker off outside the tarp and stored it in the back behind the bunk. A precise man. A methodical man. Tired, he spoke stiltedly. "She is to remain quiet, and I do not want her to be moved. We will just have to ride out this hurricane as best we can. I fear she has had a concussion, as well, and have instructed the gambler to bring my bag from the ship. Mrs. deMoya has my instructions as to her care."

Juanita slowly opened her eyes but did not speak. She ached all over and was very drowsy. Dr. Young was by her side but did not touch or console her. He quietly said, "You have lost your baby, I'm sorry to inform you, but you're very fortunate to be alive, young lady." He didn't understand what she was muttering about angels. She kept referring to angels. He assumed she thought she was in heaven. He ceased speaking when she drifted into unawareness.

When Conner returned, Dr. Young asked him to help Orlean into the other wagon, because she was near exhaustion. He didn't need two patients, and he would like for him to assist him in setting Juanita's arm.

Juanita slowly came to, her eyelids fluttering slightly, and when she opened them and saw Conner all in white, she thought she had indeed died and gone to heaven. Then he directed his devilish grin down at her, and she haltingly asked, perplexed, "Are you the Devil?" He threw his wet, rumpled, black hair back and roared with laughter.

"Yes, my dear Cherie, I am indeed...I am indeed." She drifted off again.

****

The wind's velocity began to increase, and the wagon that held Juanita, Dr. Young and Conner seemed to answer its roar with its creaking and rocking. Dr. Young turned to Conner and said, "We've got to move her to a substantial building, Mr. O'Farrell. I don't like the idea, but I doubt this wagon will stand much more."

"I'll go to the hotel next door and ask for help. I should have brought Harrison back from the ship but thought we'd just be getting the fringe of this storm. It would appear that I was wrong and that the hurricane has turned directly toward us." And with that, and before the Dr. could make an alternative suggestion, he leapt out into the driving rain.

The Putnam House was bathed in light, and the music from the secure, dry lobby was as if nothing were happening outside that beautiful room. Conner, soaked to the skin, had difficulty closing the heavy door against the strong wind. A porter was beside him immediately and presented him with a warm towel and whispered, so the hundreds of guests who were off the two large ships couldn't hear, "Is it as bad as Ah thinks, Suh?"

Conner looked down at the concerned man and shook his

head..yes. Then he added, also in a whisper, "Aye. This is only the beginning, I'm thinking. We need a warm, private place for the young colleen from the medicine show. You know, the lass who fell and hurt herself. The doctor has asked me to seek assistance. May I speak to your man in charge?"

"Oh, yessuh, you sho 'nuff can. Poor girl. Poor little thing." He took Conner to the desk and asked the night clerk to fetch the manager, and the arrangements to move Juanita were soon in effect. They secured a large tarp, some dry blankets and additional slickers from the hotel storage room, and together the porter, Conner and Dr. Young managed to move her through the back door and into the spacious linen closet. The deMoyas were encouraged to join them, for the wind had become much stronger, and the manager set up space for the entire family in the storage room across the hall from Juanita.

Conner followed Etienne and told him that he'd drop by the following day, if the weather allowed, before departing for Savannah, and on his return trip he'd like to visit to see how Cherie was progressing. He asked if he could bring them anything from the ship or the city while he was gone. He was enjoying watching the Cajun squirm and could not help but needle him. Conner was well aware of Etienne's jealousy.

He became very quiet, and instead of telling Conner that there was no need for a visit said, "You will be welcome, Mr. O'Farrell. You have been of great assistance to my family and my golden girl," he emphasized. "We do not have need of anything, but thank you for your concern."

Conner got his obvious message and silently said, "You poor Cajun bastard. That little trick has already got you tied up in a pretty pink bow and doesn't need or want you. And neither do I."

Etienne didn't like his condescending attitude. He felt threatened by his mere presence, but it was not in his emotional makeup to be rude. The man had indeed been very helpful, and Etienne wondered why. He wanted the Irishman to know that Cherie was his...that she was not one of the seductive wenches he could take for his pleasure, but he said no more.

"Sir, it is not advisable for me to return to the ship in this weather, and I am exhausted, as well," Dr. Young addressed the manager. "I wonder if I might rent a room until this dreadful hurricane has passed."

The manager was embarrassed. "We are completely filled, Doctor. He thought a minute and continued, "There is space that can be fixed up for you in my office. It won't be as comfortable as you're used to..."

"No worry. It'll at least be dry. Thank you." He turned to Conner to ask if he wanted to join him but saw only his back, his wet coat clinging to him, as Conner made his way toward the rollicking noise coming from the dining room and, the doctor presumed, the bar as well.

"It is as well. I do not like that man...nor do I trust him," he said aloud. To himself he wondered why the gambler had been so eager to assist him with the poor girl.

"Probably do anything for excitement," he sighed wearily and soon was fast asleep on the pallet behind the manager's desk.

When Conner awakened the next day it was almost noon. His first thoughts were how in this Devil's world he'd managed to return to the ship in the middle of the hurricane, and the second one was of Cherie and her welfare, which in itself was unusual, for Conner never thought of any female tenderly except his sister Maeve and his love...his only love from so long ago.

"Why did I have to pick last night of all nights to visit the Devil's den?" he angrily inquired of himself. He was startled by a persistent and disgusted Harrison, who pounded on his door and, once inside, informed him, "Ah ain't gonna put up wit much more of this degradin' actin', Mr. Conner, Suh. Ah sho 'nuff ain't!" The cool water splashed in the marble basin, and with his head held down Conner tried to ignore Harrison but laughed instead and said, "Aye, and that's a fact, Mr. Harrison...Suh," he mocked.

The only time Talmai Harrison slipped into his Darkie talk was when he was so put out with Conner that the easiest way to get his message across was by using the dialect. "Are we moving, Talmai? What the bloody hell...!" Conner opened the door to see the St. Johns swirl past the tree-lined banks.

"Are we moving indeed. Of course we're moving. Or rather sailing. This is a ship, Sir. A bloody ship. And if my memory serves me correctly we're supposed to be working on said ship, Sir." He was surly. Well, why shouldn't he be upset? They had missed a golden opportunity to increase their depleted stash when the ship's passengers decided to take their game to Putnam House for the duration of the hurricane. Instead of Conner's telling him about the game when he returned to the *Savannah* to fetch the doctor's bag, he proceeded to get roaring drunk, while Harrison, unaware of the situation, rode out the hurricane on the swaying ship. He got seasick right in port, and if that wasn't humiliating enough, that White, lily-livered first mate saw him and laughed like a blooming hyena. Yes, he was upset!

Conner realized the need for calm. Amused, he removed the towel from his face to look into Harrison's not very amused black one. He was a handsome Negro, features as fine as Conner's and a smile that seemed to want to keep spreading clean to the outer edges of his strong jaw. But there was no laughter on that face today.

"Talmai, my good man, there'll be a new man at the tables tonight and every night 'til Savannah. On that you can lay a wager. I'll make up for last night's omission." Conner usually knew when he had gone too far and when to appease his friend, for Talmai Harrison was his friend, and the only one he could lay claim to. He'd need a clear head and a great deal of luck for the remainder of their trip, for Talmai was correct in his account of their funds. There was enough for only a meager stake at the tables.

****

The citrus crop was ruined, and wind and water damage was widespread throughout the northeast area of the state. The deMoyas and Juanita stayed in Palatka for another week, and the men helped the townspeople with the clean-up. The new bridge over Rice Creek had been destroyed, and huge live oaks, sweet gums and cypresses had been uprooted all over town, where some areas were heavily flooded. There were so many homeless people that the warehouses on Water Street opened their doors to them until more permanent shelters could be erected. But everyone expressed relief that there were no lives lost, and they were soon in the business of rebuilding and forgetting.

The deMoyas used the time they were confined in Palatka to make the necessary wagon repairs, and Orlean, Aimee and Pierre were busily replenishing their dwindling supply of "Elixer of Life".

Their audience had grown so much since *Cherie, the Golden Girl* began performing that they had a difficult time filling the demand.

Juanita continued to improve daily. She was still sore all over, and the huge all-color bruise on her left buttock was adding new color every time she looked, she complained to Aimee. She tried to not think of Angel and to place her mind anywhere but with the medicine show. She had even begun to think of her folks in LaBelle, something she hadn't done since she ran away with R.J.. Juanita had left her dreaming back underneath the willow tree beside the Caloosahatchee and was becoming very bored. And when Juanita was bored everyone heard about it.

Etienne insisted that they carry out the doctor's orders to the letter, and she was furious with him. She begged him to allow her to watch the performance, but he was adamant in his refusal. "The doctor gave me express directions, ma Cherie, and we must follow them. He said for you not to be out of bed for two weeks, and that is precisely what we will do." He tried to smooth her damp hair from her beaded forehead, but she pushed his hand away.

"Just where do you get this *we*, Mr. Bossy Etienne? Huh? Where does *we* come into it. I'm the one havin to stay in this blasted hot furnace of a wagon. I, Juanita, am the one who is about to die of boredom, Sir Etienne. I'm the one who has read these books 'til I'm almost blind," she shouted as she began to throw them at him, then changed her mind. She turned away from him with a huff.

The week's end was approaching, and the deMoyas were preparing for the onslaught of the townspeople and the passengers from the river boats. The *Savannah* docked early Friday afternoon and would remain in port 'til Monday to make repairs and load the hold with a new supply of lumber for the demand up north. Lumber mills had sprung up all around the city since the War, and dressed Florida beeves were finding a hungry market up north as well. The south was alive with activity, and the remnants of the War flared only in men's minds and attitudes.

Juanita continued to beg Etienne to allow her to watch the performance. "But, Etienne, I'll not move, honestly. I'm so all-fired bored just sitting in this stifling old wagon! Please, Etienne," she implored. "I'll sit just as quiet as a little mouse." She turned to Orlean and in desperation asked for her intervention.

"My son, she 'as been a good patient. She 'as obeyed de doctor's orders, an' I don' feel eet weel harm her eef she watch for a leetle while." She was just as tired of having to listen to Juanita's complaints of boredom as Juanita was of making them. Her attitude toward the girl had not changed..softened maybe..but not changed. She felt bad about the babe and had noticed that the girl was saddened, too... something she had not expected from her.

So Etienne gave in to the two precious women in his life, although reluctantly. Juanita was thrilled at being allowed to join the audience. All day she hummed and was very pleasant to everyone...even to Orlean. No complaints about the heat or the food Orlean prepared for her, but the night seemed a million years away. When the sun finally set, Etienne and Pierre carried her to her chair that had been placed on the front row, right in the middle. She tried very hard to not get carried away with excitement, especially when Etienne was watching her, and managed to restrain her applause and laughter at Etienne's and Aimee's puppet play of Madame and Monsieur that had the audience laughing uproariously.

He arrived midway through the performance, the tall man in white. He leaned against the same pine tree as before, smoking his cheroot, but he was not watching the puppet performance. His eyes never left Juanita's delightful, child-like face. She sensed his presence, and her eyes were drawn to his. In the recesses of her mind she heard her hesitant voice ask him if he was the Devil, and the resounding timbre of his deep laughter came to her.

When Etienne finished his lines, he looked at Juanita for her reaction, but she was not smiling nor looking toward the stage as before. She wore a very strange expression. He followed her gaze and saw Conner with the same intense expression. Etienne felt sick all over. He should not have encouraged such a man to visit his family, no matter how helpful he had been.

His first instinct was to have Pierre assist Juanita back to the wagon under the pretense that she had been up long enough for her first outing, but Pierre was busily helping Orlean and Dom pass the collection hats, and Aimee was due to perform next. So he remained indecisive about his next move. Suddenly he decided to go to Juanita himself to ask if she was feeling poorly. Anything. Anything to break the spell.

Juanita asked him who the man was even before he sat down.

"I sorta remember him from the night I fell, and I can remember asking him if he was the Devil. Did I do that, Etienne?"

"Yes, Cherie, I am told that you did. Oh, he is just a riverboat gambler, who went to the boat to retrieve the doctor's medical bag, my sweet. That is when you saw him." He hurried with his next statement. "Cherie, Aimee will perform next. Please give her your fullest attention. She confessed to me earlier that she was a wee bit unsure of herself." And to himself, "Why am I lying? Have I sunk so low that I have to lie to her to get her to cease staring hungrily at that Irish Devil?"

Etienne did not like himself that star-filled September night. He did not respect himself at all. He lowered his head.

"Oh, Etienne, I'll watch Aimee very closely," she called as he resumed his position on the stage to announce the act. But when he finished and again looked at her, she was not watching Aimee, as promised, but instead was devouring the Irishman with her beautiful blue eyes.

The performance was over, and Conner swiftly made his way through the crowd toward Juanita. Etienne was announcing the show time for the following evening when he saw him approach her. His heart pounded heavily. Quickly, he thanked the departing audience. As he did, he saw Conner lift Juanita effortlessly and carry her petite form toward the wagon.

When Juanita saw Conner approaching and drawing closer, she thought, "I haven't had this glorious yearning since I first felt R.J. undress me with his very eyes...oh, so long ago."

He leaned down toward her, and said in his fascinating Irish brogue, "Conner O'Farrell, Cherie. I'll return you to the sanctity of your warm wagon. Dr. Young would not appreciate it if you caught your death of cold on top of your previous ordeal."

She could not speak. She could feel his long, muscled arms surround her, and she burned all over. A knowing ache again visited her, and she knew beyond a shadow of a doubt that she had found the man who could tame her fierce yearnings, just like in Wuthering Heights, her most cherished possession in the entire world. "Is he to be my Heathcliff?"

"Etienne, what's the matter?" a worried Aimee asked. "You look like you've just seen a ghost."

"Not a ghost, ma Aimee, but a devil." He spat it out so fiercely that Aimee was shocked by his vehemence.

****

The *Savannah* made port on its return trip from Georgetown. Conner wended his way to the vacant lot on Lemon Street. No wagons, and no Juanita. He then decided to inquire of the porter at Putnam House her whereabouts, thinking that surely he'd know of her, but the man he sought was no longer employed there. It was as if she had disappeared into the night.

He laughed a scornful laugh and said aloud, "The Cajun was so anxious to leave that he disobeyed Dr. Young's orders. My..my..my. Did he actually think that I had an interest in his ignorant golden girl?" But there was something about Juanita. He had no answer except that she seemed so vulnerable up on that rope. All alone with nothing around her but stars and clouds and the sheepish moon dipping in and out. And there she stood...so tiny...with just the parasol to spar with.

He shrugged, straightened his white panama and said, "There'll always be a Cherie. If not here, then in the next port." He walked back to the ship seeing her child-like face before him and knew he was fooling himself.

CHAPTER III CONNER

"I'll not, Mum - I'll not," the not-yet-six-year-old Conner had promised his mum. He knew full well that the minute she and Mrs. Leahy left for the evening devotional, he'd be out from under the drab woolen covers, his fever miraculously gone, and would stealthily make his way down the dark, narrow stairs to the freedom of Broad Street and its exciting activities, all the while keeping his eye out for his Uncle John and sister Maeve. And after the tolling Angelus bell had ceased, he'd scurry back into the downstairs shop, creep past the rolls of brightly colored felt and the bolts of Italian straw and snowy white silk to climb the stairs to his narrow bed, hop under his blanket and feign drowsiness on his mum's return. Young Conner loved to outwit even his beloved mum.

The shop was a wonder to Conner, and he never tired of examining its beautiful treasures. The ostrich plumes and pheasant feathers were reverently placed upon the top shelf away from his young, inquisitive hands and above the profusion of colorful silk flowers on his mum's work table. Una O'Farrell was a milliner, who had recently come to America with her two remaining children, Maeve Margaret and James Francis Conner, at the pleading of her cousin Claire and her husband, John Flanagan.

His father, Nolan O'Farrell, had left his young family. He left them while struggling for life, fighting with his considerable strength. But in the end the life was wrenched from his long, lean body by the fever and starvation. The potatoes in his fields had turned to the same black mush as his neighbors'. All over the homeland the tenacious blight crept, denying the oppressed people their nourishment, and so he died.

But Nolan left them so much more than the remembrance of his deep, lilting, happy Irish brogue and twinkling, bright blue eyes that you remembered long after having been with him. He left them his energy, his insatiable curiosity and his delightful humor; he could never pass a tree that he didn't drop Conner's small, slender hand, and around and around the gnarled trunk he'd dance, quoting the songs of the druids to ward off the lurking evil and inviting the sprightly spirits to walk the path with them.

Never would Nolan pass a singing bird without calling its name and in honest wonder discuss its ability to fly as it darted among the gorse bushes, building its intricate nest, and he instinctively knew its purpose in life. For Nolan knew not his own purpose and would discuss it with great relish and concern over a pint or two at Finnegan's at the end of his long day.

But leave them he did, and Una, or as she preferred to be called in America, Agnes, for Una is Gaelic for Agnes, wanting to put all but her precious memories behind her, took the children to America. To Charleston they came and were met by her favorite cousin, Claire, who had preceded her to America by five years, settling in the town of Macon, Georgia. Her husband was engaged as a clothier in his uncle's store at the corner of Broad and Monument Streets in the heart of Macon, a very prestigious location. They also had a part interest in the M.E. Grogan Millinery Shoppe next door, and when Mary Grogan became betrothed to a gentleman in Augusta, Claire wrote Una that there would be an opening for her and that the three rooms above the shop would be perfect for the family's lodging.

Una was frantic. She was afraid that the post would be filled before they were able to get passage on one of the lumber barques that left Ireland, Scotland and England almost every day. America and Canada had become interested in the lumber market in western Europe after the Napoleonic wars and diligently captured the eager market. But on their return trip to America there was a want of cargo required as ballast for the barques.

With foresight the ship owners saw that if they rigged up bunks aboard their vessels and allowed the starving, desperate Irish to buy passage, they could also garner several pounds' passage apiece from the human cargo. Thus Una and her children, after four long months of waiting, arrived in Charleston, all ill from the rough sea and half-cooked food that Una prepared in the sand-filled fire box.

Claire and John took the train to Charleston to meet them, and when she saw the two beautiful children with Una, not clinging as frightened children should, but looking about drinking in every ounce of excitement and activity on the wharf, she knew she'd not have to be concerned for the O'Farrell children; they were of the cloth of Nolan, who could never have his fill of the world around him.

"They'll be Americans in no time a'tall, John darlin', no time a'tall," she babbled and gave his large hand a squeeze. Silently she prayed, "Oh, but to have a one of 'em - just one, dear Mary and sweet Jesus. But it's not to be. I'll now have Una's boyeen to fetch my shawl and Maeve with the wide brow, so like my own father's, to fetch me a cup o' tea. Life is good. It is good indeed."

The settling in took no time a'tall just as Claire had predicted. She and Una became inseparable, as they had been before Claire's family had moved to Nenagh when the girls were in their early teens. Their activities at the church and with the ladies' clubs left Maeve and Conner with the most freedom they'd ever had, especially since John, who soon became Uncle John, was usually busy with customers and didn't keep his eyes on them as Claire suggested. They'd always be able to get to his soft heart and with a few pennies make their way to the Broad Street park for the hot roasted peanuts or to the sweet shop for pralines, delicacies never heard of in Ireland.

Una was a magician with her nimble fingers, and her light, creative spirit caused the customers to multiply rapidly. She had apprenticed under County Kerry's most sought milliner, Margaret M. Pierce, who was known all over that section of Ireland for her creations. And before her marriage to Nolan and her move to Athea to his father's farm, twelve miles away and in the County of Limerick, she had built her own considerable reputation.

After the death of their first born Una again took up her trade at Nolan's suggestion. And a good suggestion it was. Her heart became light once more, there were song and laughter in his father's house, and soon she was again with child. The saints were her constant companions, and her hands sang their praises in silks and straw and gauze ribbons of every imaginable color. Nolan had built her a work table on the west wall of their marriage room, and life was good.

Maeve was now her inspiration, her light to work by, and soon Conner joined his bright, healthy sister. He carried his father's saint's name, James, and the name of St. Francis to guide him, but Nolan decided that Una's maiden name of Conner should be added for balance - the Conners were clothiers and very industrious. But he was like Nolan in looks and temperament and soon was of an age to accompany his father to town. They walked alongside the rock-walled farms with their thatched cottages and sheep and cattle grazing contentedly on the emerald grass, and they, holding hands, would bid their neighbors, "A grand morning to you, Mrs. Murphy"...and, "It's a glorious day for the races, is it not, Seamus?..."

But the darkness soon came, and the carefree walks to town were replaced by shuffling feet laboring under the homemade, crude, wooden caskets as they trudged beside the blackened fields. Nolan no longer danced sprightly around the trees or wondered why the gorse bushes were so filled with the trills of the singing birds. The birds sang as melodically as before but went unheard. And he, too, was soon to sing no more.

****

Maeve and Conner were enrolled in St. Joseph's Academy, and the good sisters were to learn that one James Francis Conner found their regimen not to his liking - it interfered with his spirited nature, and he'd rather devise any means his clever mind could conceive to avoid their rhetoric and to *let the light in*.

Conner was not a leader among his classmates. He worked alone. Now, mind you, they would have liked nothing better than to have been included in some of the ingenious pranks perpetrated against the ever watchful Sisters of Mercy, but Conner neither needed nor wanted a partner.

He was quick with his numbers and letters and in the beginning gave the good sisters no problem at all. But by the time he was in the latter part of his third year and the boredom of their unimaginative rhetoric blinded his eyes and deafened his ears, for sanity's sake he had to take matters into his own hands.

And so he did.

"You must send for the Reverend Mother, Sister Bridget. You must!" exclaimed Sister Teresa, as excited as her wheezing little voice allowed her to get. "There is obviously something very wrong with the boyo. He was such a bright and serious student and the handsomest..." She quickly covered her outburst - she knew that one's appearance should not have any effect on one's opinion. "May the saints have turned a deaf ear!" she muttered silently not wanting to say it distinctly enough for even the dear saints to know of her observation. But he was indeed the most beautiful child she had ever seen, and if the Lord made him such, why should she not appreciate it? Sister Teresa tried not to dwell on the complexities of any subject for any period of time and so dismissed her frailties with a preventive sign of the cross.

After much prayer and with no obvious results, Sister Bridget did as Sister Teresa suggested and went to the Reverend Mother with her insoluble problem.

"Now, now, Sister Bridget, nothing could possibly be as serious as you have described. There must be an answer. Have you spoken with the young man's parents? You have. Well..?"

"You say the father perished in the famine, and his mother is a milliner on Broad Street, a very devout woman, never missing daily mass or the evening devotionals. Hmm.."

"And what did the dear woman make of young Conner's affliction, pray tell, Sister? Did he have a fall, perhaps? Or maybe he was ill? Surely she is aware of this unfortunate development and should be able to shed some light on the matter."

"No, hmm...Well, my dear, I suggest that we all pray to Saint Anthony for guidance. You know he never lets us down in time of need.

"Yes, I know you have been using a mirror to unscramble his work. You have informed me of every detail, but you've not given me a solution. So, dear Sister Bridget, I suggest that you hand the problem over to an even higher authority, Saint Anthony."

When the Reverend Mother's voice rose even one tone, it was time to retreat backwards with head bowed. Sister Bridget's shuffling feet moved quickly under the black habit, and praying every step of the way, she escaped the austere room. The Reverend Mother's impatience had always been quick to arrive even under the best of circumstances, and she should have known that an insoluble problem of this magnitude was always handed over to a higher authority without question.

The good Sisters of Mercy all prayed to Saint Anthony for Conner's affliction to evaporate as quickly as it had arrived, but after months of daily prayers and novenas nothing changed. His problem was magnified; even his numbers became as his letters.

Sister Bridget's class was one of the happiest at St. Joseph's, for she was a young, enthusiastic teacher totally devoted to her mission. The fact that she was an unimaginative instructor did not enter her mind, nor, for that matter, the other students', but Conner O'Farrell was not as other students. Having to attend school for interminably long hours five days a week instead of watching the locomotives' arrivals or departures at the train depot, or lolling in the park under a dancing willow with the mockingbirds displaying their enviable talent high above him or, even better, just remembering how his dada said Boyo, well that was as tiresome an existence as he could imagine. He needed excitement.

The late afternoons had recently become very important to young Conner. He had been accepted by a few of the other boys on Broad St. A game of ball or tag or the call of the close-by fields with their mysteries beckoned them, but it still was not enough for the high-strung Conner, and a diversion in the classroom had become an absolute necessity.

He didn't remember when he came up with the idea. It just happened. Having completed his lessons at the suggestion of his mum, later checked by his Uncle John, he retreated to the privacy of his small room instead of meandering down Broad St. in search of his friends. He began to doodle...or it looked like doodling. Actually he was writing everything backwards. He took his mother's hand mirror down from her night stand, the one that had graced her marriage room in Ireland, and began to read it plain as anything. Enlightened by this wonderful discovery, he re-did his hand-in work with an impish smile on his handsome face and wrote the entire assignment backwards. He really hadn't intended to turn it in, but he did and anxiously awaited the results.

It wasn't 'til Sister Bridget confronted him after school let out that afternoon that he realized just how confused she was. Enjoying her flushed face, bright under the starched white coif, and in such a disturbed state, he innocently went along with the notion that it looked just fine to him and that he could not see why he was being questioned.

She was truly perplexed, and when the other children saw them in a tight unit worrying over his hand-in, that nosey Jimmy O'Rourk decided to find out what was going on. He sneaked around to the outside window, and like a monkey's those long legs found their spot on the sill. With his gummy ear pressed against the window, he heard about the trouble. He jumped down smack-dab on top of Paddy Carroll, knocking him into the dirt, and after they got themselves unscrambled, they ran as fast as possible with the others on their heels to the high grassy field so they could be alone and not heard. He breathlessly told them about the problem.

"Was this one of Conner's clever tricks?" they asked themselves. Oh, it was an exciting time, much better than when

Joe Morgan put the biggest bull frog you'd ever wanta see in Sister Margaret's desk drawer, or when Paddy Carroll had to find a long tack, about an inch long, so's it would go through all of Sister Catherine Marie's habit; and it did, and the yelp she let out could be heard all the way to Cotton Street. No...this was the best one yet. That Conner O'Farrell was really someone to be admired and envied, they now knew.

When he walked out and closed the big oak door with authority and as straight as you please, head held high and at least thirty minutes after the bells had rung, the gang was there questioning him. They knew he'd be in a bunch of trouble with his mum, but it didn't seem to bother him a bit. That added even more praise to be placed on his already admirable shoulders.

Every day Conner handed in his work meticulously written - but backwards. And every day the entire class watched for Sister Bridget's reaction. She never let them down. First, the sign of the cross - then with head bowed she'd say a special prayer to Saint Anthony. The children snickered as they eyed each other and glanced at Conner with admiration.

This went on for the remainder of the term, but on the last day Conner suddenly, miraculously, became cured. Sister Bridget shouted her thanks out loud to Saint Anthony, and seeing the students' reaction, dismissed the class early, stating loudly that a miracle had been performed and fell down on her knees to pray more reverently. Then, running as fast as she could in the cumbersome habit, she first went to Sister Teresa's room, and together they ran with their habits flying out behind them down to the far end of the long hall and rapping lightly on the polished, dark door burst into the Reverend Mother's sanctuary.

"A miracle, Reverend Mother! A miracle," they both shouted. "Saint Anthony has intervened with the Almighty, and a miracle has been performed on Conner O'Farrell."

Outside St. Joseph's Conner was surrounded by the other students. His friends hit him on his back playfully - others punched him affectionately about his face - all were laughing and shouting, and the Reverend Mother and Sisters Bridget and Teresa watched from the window above with broad smiles at Conner and his, they thought, relieved friends.

"You sure pulled a fast one on 'em, Conner," shouted Paddy. "Aye, the best one a body ever did," said Jimmy, while the colleens measured him up with their shy eyes.

"We must always remember to turn our problems over to a higher authority, Sisters. The lad has been cured. The saints be praised," said the Reverend Mother.

Conner smiled smugly.

****

The sun was already high in the sky, and spring was awakening from its slumber the first time Conner saw Bertrice Lillian Norwood. The day was Sunday, and Uncle John declared, as he patted young Conner on his black hair, "This is the day that the Lord hath made." Una and Claire had been invited for a cup at Mrs. Cassidy's, and Maeve and Conner had promised their mum that they'd not get their Sunday clothes dirty, that they would just get a paper cone of peanuts and sit very nice-like to await the concert in the park.

Conner was going on eight and Maeve ten, and both were tall for their age. Maeve's large, gray-green eyes, wise beyond her years, stared out of her fair Irish skin. Only a hint of light ginger freckles dared to splash across her cheeks and upturned nose all under a profusion of dark auburn hair, glossy with health like the Conner side of her mum's family, for whom Conner was named. Young Conner was an O'Farrell with hair as black as any raven's, as was his dada's, with eyes that belied description. His dada's were small and bright blue and Conner's so pale that, as Claire told John when she first saw the boyeen, "Oh, Johnny, the lad has to have been touched by an angel's wing. See the eyes. May the saints be praised!"

Conner would later prove Claire wrong. As John often pointed out, Claire had got her angels mixed up, and one Conner O'Farrell was an angel alright, the fallen angel, Satan, himself. He said it teasingly and with a grin, but Claire was afraid that he was partially correct in his assessment.

A favorite pastime on a lazy Sunday afternoon for the Norwood family was the concerts at the Broad Street Park. After church, a light meal and afternoon naps, they'd be driven by Wesley Norwood to the park, 'cause Sunday was the day that Benge and Sadie also rested. Berta had just turned six and Lamorah was two years younger - Tad was just learning to walk. The girls would work their hoops and run and play with their parents' friends' children until the concert began.

Maeve was the first to see the beautiful blond child. Her long curls cascaded down her back and were held by a large, navy blue bow. Actually, she just about ran into her while trying to avoid Conner, who was fast on her heels. Maeve's coltish legs stopped just in time, but Conner tumbled into both of them, sending poor Berta tail-over-tin-cup into the grass. She wasn't hurt nor did she cry, but she was startled when the young boy grabbed her up and said breathlessly, "I'll be getting your hoop, Lassie. Don't you fear."

He seemed more interested in retrieving her hoop than questioning her welfare, and when her papa reached her and began brushing off his daughter's navy blue skirt, he started to chastise the flushed young boy, who was standing before him trying to apologize.

It was obvious to Wesley Norwood that the two ruffians were Micks. Not that he had anything against the poor things, but as he continued berating Conner, he became enraged at the surly attitude of the lad before him. His shoulders were squared, and he was not the least bit ashamed. Out of those eight-year-old eyes glared a man ready to do battle.

"That Mick will be in trouble before he's seen another year, Lillian. Did you see the Devil in his eyes? Young upstart glaring at me in that manner, and there's probably a dozen at home just like him."

"Now, Nordie, for heavens sake, I don't want you to speak in that manner in front of the children. Mick, indeed! Those children belong to Miss Agnes at the millinery shop on Broad Street, and they're kin to John Flanagan and Patrick Murphy. Now you know that there were never finer people in all of Macon."

Lillian turned to Berta, "You should have been watching where you were rolling your hoop, dear," and turning back to her husband continued, "The lad did try to apologize, Nordie. You just wouldn't give the poor thing a chance." Refusing to be pacified, he put the crop to Gus and was upset all the way back to Melrose Street.

It was almost a month later that Conner next saw her. This time he very carefully avoided her hoop as she worked it with her stick, skimming the boxwood hedge that led to the gazebo. He couldn't seem to take his eyes off the girl. As he stood quietly behind the high privet hedge that hid him, Maeve watched.

"Now why in heaven's name does he think the lass to be pretty? Pasty faced, I'd call her." But Maeve knew Berta was beautiful. She just didn't appreciate anyone who had no freckles a'tall and eyes so blue that they defied description. She leaned against the weeping willow and through its blanket of leaves watched Conner. Her instincts told her that there would be trouble to bear if the boyo took a fancy to the pale lass from the uppity family. But what to do?

The musicians marched ceremoniously up the walk to the band shell, holding themselves proud-like in their bright red uniforms. They were men from all walks of life: farmers, merchants, railroad men and Father John from St. Joseph's, who played the trumpet loudly and almost always in time.

The concert began and Conner positioned himself directly behind the Norwood family, so he could get an unobstructed view of Berta. When Wesley Norwood glanced around and saw Conner, Conner shifted his eyes instantly and gazed nonchalantly over the man's hat pretending to not recognize him. It soon became a game. Wesley would quickly turn, and Conner would look down or up but never directly at the Norwoods, certainly not at Berta.

"What is it, Nordie? Why are you wearing such a scowl? I declare your face is red as a beet. Don't you feel well, dear?"

"It's that young Mick again." He gestured with his head to where Conner sat beside Maeve. "I caught him staring at Berta. The upstart!" He said it loudly enough for them to hear, and both Conner and Maeve smiled sheepishly at his frustration.

Exasperated, Lillian Norwood clucked her tongue at her foolish husband and added in a whisper, "And the next thing you'll be saying is that he's asking to call on her and her not yet seven years old."

She took her husband's hand and patted it maternally. "I'll declare you're just too protective of her, dear. Now relax, and let's enjoy the rest of the concert," she said turning and smiling at Conner and Maeve, who were both wearing their most angelic expressions.

Berta had heard her father, and when her parents were engrossed in *Flow Gently Sweet Afton* that the band was enthusiastically playing, she squirmed, straightened her blue lawn dress and slyly turned to get a look at a Mick. He was indeed looking right at her, and she felt herself begin to smile. Then she remembered her papa's dislike of the boy, changed her mind and resumed watching the musicians. But she wondered just what a Mick was and why he was different. He looked the same as any other boy to her except he was more handsome.

Maeve teased Conner unmercifully all the way home about the blond-haired girl. She knew he'd get even with her and that she'd have to be very watchful, for Boyo, as she called him, never forgot an injustice, and when she let her dukes down he'd best her. It was a game they had grown up with. He'd also never forgive the gentleman for calling him a Mick, and Maeve wondered just what he'd do for retribution. It was sure to come. She knew the boyo's mind, worried over him much more than did her mum and loved him with such a ferocious passion that it was a concern to her Uncle John and Claire.

It seemed to Wesley Norwood that everywhere they went in downtown Macon there would be the Mick. He swore that Conner was following them, but Lillian reminded him that the poor lad had no place to play except the street and that his mama's shop was close to the Broad Street Park, so naturally that is where he would play. But Wesley was not convinced.

The years passed, and the older and more beautiful Berta became, the more protective became her father, and the more Conner worshiped her. Wesley no longer saw the Mick hanging around the park as before, and so gratefully put him out of his mind. But Berta would catch a glimpse of the young man from time to time and knew he was admiring her from afar. He had just become more clever in his observance. She enjoyed the game and on occasion would smile at him, letting him know that she understood, and never once let on to her papa.

Conner had taken a position with his Uncle John in his shop when he was fifteen years old, over six feet tall and much older looking than his years. In his naivete he felt that if he acquired enough wealth, the Norwoods would have to welcome him into their family. It never occurred to him that his being Irish and Catholic were more against him than his lack of wealth, for he was a proud Irishman, and this was America, where prejudice of that magnitude was impossible, at least in his child-like observation. Maeve could have told him differently, for she was very astute and aware that the social and political position of an old protestant family would not look kindly on the boyo as a match for their darlin' daughter. But she watched and said nothing while waiting for Conner to make his move. She was positive he would no matter how long it took.

****

Conner looked up when the bell rang on the shop's front door announcing a customer. He was taken aback when he looked straight into the cold grey eyes of Wesley Norwood. The man almost turned around to leave, thought better about it, and when Conner approached him, he immediately put up his hand to stop Conner and said, "It is John Flanagan I want, young man." His attitude told Conner that he was not to touch him even for the measuring of a suit.

Conner was incensed, and when he pulled back the curtain that cordoned off the showroom from the storage room and office, where John was busily going over the accounts, he babbled so that John had to stop him.

"Let the old man fry in his spittle...in his spittle!" he said not caring if he heard him or not.

"What is it, Boyo? What in the name of sweet Jesus are ya blitherin' about?" When he turned and saw Conner's anger slowly gaining momentum, and knowing the lad's ferocious temper, he was concerned that it would ignite and there'd be the Devil to pay.

"Now, now, Boyo. There's nothin' in heaven or on this earth worth the anger you're spewing. Leave the Devil in his den, and tell me the trouble you're havin'."

"It's the girl's da!" he blurted out. "And he's not allowing a Mick to measure anywhere near his aristocratic balls!"

"Shush, Boyo. Who is it...?" John pulled the curtain back a crack and saw Wesley Norwood, one of his best customers, pacing up and down trying to make up his mind whether to stay for his fitting or to leave. While he peered out he extended an arm toward Conner to still his rage, then went to him whispering, "'tis the Norwood man. I'll tend him, but I want ya ta stop with this tirade 'til I'm through." He had his heavy arm around Conner's shoulder and could feel his anger subside with every deep breath.

Conner looked down at John, who had been a father to him, and they heard Wesley Norwood pounding his cane loudly on the floor and calling to John.

"I'll return in no time a'tall. You wait right here - now don't ya move, lad. We'll be havin' a lengthy discussion about this." He added gently, "Whatever it is, Boyo, we'll lick it...the two of us will lick it." To himself he said, "Just like we've licked every scrape you've got yourself into, and no doubt there'll be aplenty more." But John smiled even as he thought of it. "So it's the blond colleen, is it?"

Conner and Maeve were the children he and Claire had been denied. He'd helped them through the fever and intervened when Father O'Hara threatened to flog young Conner; he couldn't even remember what the lad had done that time.

"He's changed," he had told Claire over the stew that night. "Oh, mind ya, his temper would frighten Satan himself, but girl, the lad's changed. I can see somethin' going on in those strange eyes, somethin' deep, fearful.

"The boyo's probably found a colleen to his liking, dear. He's got that faraway look about him, and he's of an age to be lookin' at the lassies."

"Sure and he is, girl. Sure and he is. Me thinks you've placed your finger on it. A lassie, is it now?" He did not tell her who the lassie was nor of Conner's frustration.

Conner had stopped his trips to the fields outside the city, and the street boys had ceased coming 'round asking for him, so John knew the boyo was on a different track. Conner had stopped hanging around them, because he had a plan. Oh, it was a grand plan, an ambitious plan, a plan befitting the cleverest strategist. And it was all for his love, his Berta - his bride to be. He thought of her day and night. Her golden image awakened him of a mornin' and placed her angel's fingertips on his eyes at night. No one knew of his obsession but John and Maeve, who suspected something was going on, and felt sure that the Norwood lassie was right in the thick of his impossible dream, and his dislike of her father not far behind.

Maeve didn't hate Berta. Heavens, she hardly knew the girl. The few times she had attended her and her mother in the shop, Berta had been very animated and friendly. Easy to laugh usually meant easy to cry, she had heard. She seemed to have a mind of her own, though. When her mum asked about trim or flowers for her bonnets, she was never wishy-washy, changing her mind over and over again like most young girls. She'd point to the silk flowers and feathers and even climb up on the stool to retrieve the gauze ribbons from the high shelf.

But she knew the girl spelled trouble for Conner. She also knew that Berta was aware of Conner's interest in her. Maeve had noticed how alert she had become when she had mentioned the boyo and explained to her that boyo meant boy in Ireland, and that she was referring to her brother. The girl turned every shade of red, so Maeve became cautious. Loving him as she did, she would do anything she could to save him pain.

When the letter came from cousin Denis Sheehan from New Orleans telling them of his wife's death of yellow fever, and with her, four of their seven children, and his need of help with those who were miraculously left for his enjoyment in his old age, Maeve saw her chance to take Conner away from Macon and Berta. She had known from her birth that a milliner she'd one day be, and her own shop was her desire. Though Macon had become more cosmopolitan, the idea of having a shop in fascinating New Orleans was thrilling beyond belief. She plotted...she manipulated.

Her mum had always loved Denis, and to help him with the poor motherless children in his time of need was very appealing. Besides, Una's eyes weren't as they once had been, and she seemed to tire more easily. Denis owned a fine, but small hotel in the heart of the city, and there would be space for the entire family, Maeve pointed out, and Una could see the wisdom in her argument.

Though Claire and John would miss them terribly, they encouraged them to make the change. John was concerned with Conner's obsession with Berta, and had he thought any good would come of it he would have alerted Claire. They both could see how captivated Maeve was with the venture and were delighted with the prospects that New Orleans offered her, and so they made the way easy for Una to accept Denis's proposal.

Una had been able to put aside some money, and with the sale of her share of the shop should have enough for Maeve to realize her dream. Maeve's excitement was not a guise with which to lure Conner away from Macon. It was real, and although he was, at first, against the move and loudly decried for an entire night that Macon was their home, that it would be like starting over for all of them and that he absolutely would not accompany them, he eventually gave in when Maeve advised him of the vast amount of money he should be able to make in a short period of time. The realization that it would accelerate his plan convinced him that he could eventually return to Macon a rich man and claim his bride. Conner didn't understand that no matter how much wealth he accumulated he would never have enough for the Norwoods to allow a Mick to marry their precious Berta.

Maeve knew it...and she wasn't telling.

****

He was almost nineteen when he returned to Macon. His Uncle John had been very ill that fall, and Claire pleaded with him to return to spend some time with her Johnny, who had been asking for him and who had not recovered as rapidly as she and the good doctor wished.

Conner arrived, a man grown, and Claire hardly recognized him when he got off the six-o'clock train from Montgomery. He had filled out, face fuller but still chiseled finely with an aristocratic aire of assurance that had been missing from the boyo who had left Macon almost four years previously.

She got a lump in her throat and under her breath said, "He's Nolan all over again. May the saints be praised." As he brushed the cinders from his deep gray frock coat, beautifully tailored, she noticed, and looked up, she could see how wrong she was. Nolan had been a sensitive, philosophical man with charm that had every colleen in Athea swooning before he even became a man. The man before her had a cautious, animal awareness, and a chill ran the entire length of her spine; and when she opened her lips to speak, only a tiny squeak tumbled out. Then he grinned, and his entire countenance changed.

"Johnny was right. The boyo is no angel! He wears many a face."

Conner stayed in Macon for only two days. When he found out that Berta had married the previous month and moved to Florida, he was so shocked and upset that he left on the next train to return to New Orleans. It had never occurred to him that she'd wed another, and certainly not at such a young age. Claire could not understand why he left so suddenly, and Johnny was so upset at his own stupidity for not having warned him of the news of Berta that he died of a broken heart the following month, never forgiving himself.

He loved the boyo so...

BOOK FOUR:

BEGINNINGS

CHAPTER I THE BIRTHING

Berta read and reread the long letter that Orlean had Aimee write, telling them of Juanita's untimely fall. As she told Layke later, she had all along had a feeling that the baby would not be born, and in a way it was a blessing. The letter was written while they were in the town of Ft. Pierce on the Atlantic Ocean, and she said that their next performance would be in Ft. Basinger.

It had been over a month since Juanita's fall in Palatka, and she was very sullen and had not recuperated as quickly as the doctor had predicted. She never spoke of returning to the tightrope, and they were all concerned about her, especially Etienne.

Aimee wrote: "We expect to return to Old Town in June again next year, and Dom and me are looking forward to staying at South Spring. We would be privileged to stay with your wonderful family again, so you and Mister Layke can take a trip as before."

Berta smiled when she read that. "Now is the time to tell him. Now is the perfect time."

She put the letter down on the kitchen table and rose to pour her husband a cup of coffee. "I don't believe I'll be able to accept the kind offer Orlean made, my husband."

He looked questioningly at her. "Why might that be, Mrs. Williams?"

"Because, Mr. Williams, if all goes well, I'll be nursing a beautiful baby of our own."

"Oh, Honey, are you sure?" he cried as he went to her.

"I'm sure, my love, and I hope and pray it's a big wonderful male just like his father."

Layke kissed her hungrily, and then held her out from him. "I'll have to be gentle with you now," he said as he kissed the tips of her fingers, her closed eyes and the top of her golden hair.

"Nothing need change between us. This babe will not come between us, Layke," and she looked into his quizzical face.

"We will love as before," she said emphatically.

****

The cow hunt, penning, branding and marking began in early

March as they did most every year for the ranchers and cowmen. Layke, Jonah and the hands would be gone for weeks on end combing the open range for the beeves. The yearly roundup was a very time-consuming operation for the ranchers.

Berta's due time was thought to be after the spring drive to Punta Rassa, toward the first of June. Layke had become the typical, about-to-be father in his protective concern for her welfare. He had engaged Karine Haglund, Emma's youngest daughter, to stay with her while he was gone, and another long year would go by before Jonah would be allowed to participate in the drive. He was obviously disappointed but seemed to understand the necessity of remaining with his mother during this critical time of her pregnancy.

Berta had tried, to no avail, to dissuade Layke, but he was adamant in his decision. He had a long talk with Jonah, and on the surface there seemed to be no bitterness or resentment from Jonah for her to fear. He knew it was necessary for a man to be at South Spring in the event someone needed to go for Miss Trudy to help with the birthing. Big Dan and Zeke were just too old and feeble to be given that responsibility. She could have mistaken her due time, or the babe might decide to make an early appearance. Jonah felt Layke's reasoning to be justified, and Berta was obviously very proud of her son's newly embraced maturity.

As she had promised Mary Garvin, Berta had written often, and Mary had responded in kind. Receiving a letter from her became a high point in her day-to-day sameness while Layke was away during the hunts. Berta made it a point, as did the other wives, to visit in town on the days the mail boat made its weekly delivery, and Trudy's porch was filled with their excited chatter. The letters would be even more welcome with their husbands away on the long drive to Punta Rassa.

The deMoyas were en route to Ft. Basinger when Berta received their last letter. They had mentioned the possibility of stopping in LaBelle, and Berta was anxious to hear how Juanita's family reacted to her. Orlean and Aimee had been as faithful about writing as Mary. Berta responded immediately:

My dear Orlean et al,

How wonderful to receive your newsy letter. It was with heartfelt sorrow that we read of Juanita's loss, but we are so relieved she was injured only slightly.

We expect the entire deMoya family and, of course, Juanita, if she is still traveling with you, to be our guests at South Spring again in June. Layke and I extend our thanks for your kind offer to stay with our family to enable us to make a trip, but, my dear one, we are to be blessed with a child the first part of June, and of course a trip would be impossible. As you can well imagine, we are delightfully pleased with the advent of this most precious gift.

We are in the middle of the cow hunt and are separated a great deal of the time. This is difficult for us both, but it does make our time together more precious than ever. We remain in good spirits and health and pray for you the same.

Please let us hear from you soon. I remain your most true friend.

Berta

Postscript: Aimee, SuSu continues to practice her tumbling and rope walking. Jonah has strung a permanent rope between the two pines on the north side for her practice.

April arrived too quickly for Berta and Layke. He and half the men in Old Town would be making the final preparations for the long drive south to Punta Rassa. They would be away five or six weeks, depending on the weather and the arrival of the schooners.

Aimee had written that they would be performing at Ft. Myers at the time the men would be returning from the drive and that they would welcome a visit by Layke. She also stated that Juanita had reluctantly resumed her practice on the rope, but her fervor was not as before the accident.

****

"But, Etienne, why do we hafta go to dumb old LaBelle? Why?" Juanita asked for the umpteenth time, but he got that same old sweeter-than-honey look on his face and answered just as always, "Ma Cherie, you know why." When he'd try to hold her, she'd squirm from his embrace, and he'd add, "You need to let your parents know that you're all right. You know that they must have been worried about your welfare, Cherie. It is the proper thing to do."

"Proper...proper, my eye! They think I ran off with R.J. of my own free will, and you know it. I'll just spend the whole time trying to explain everything to 'em, and they'll just look at me like I'm some kinda ...oh, I don't know. But they will. I just know it," and she continued to sulk in the back of the hot wagon all the way from Ft. Thompson.

To take her mind off her problems she'd dream of the exciting riverboat gambler in Palatka and what her life would be like riding up and down the big river with the breeze blowing her hair and wearing beautiful dresses and eating fancy foods while he escorted her here and yon. Oh, what a glorious life it would be!

She did have to admit that she was getting excited about seeing her folks again and was about to bust to show her ma her beautiful costume, to tell her pa about how she felt up on the rope and about all the things she'd seen. But the closer they got to their road, the more nervous she became about how she'd explain her running away. Should she tell them the truth, that she just couldn't stay in that dumb old place and marry a smelly old cracker, or should she lie and tell them that she was tied up with a big old rope and gagged and slung up on a horse? Oh, what a dilemma!

She could feel the wagon slow to a halt, and not being able to stand it any longer she pulled the tarp back and peered out. They were too far from the house for her to see anything, so she eased herself out to the step and looked all around before Etienne could get down from the wagon seat. She didn't want him or the others to know of her excitement. She saw no one in the pasture, not even the Brahma bull. They're probably feeding the old chickens, she thought. Juanita sensed something was amiss but couldn't put her finger on it. When Etienne and Aimee got to her, she blurted out, "You stay here...right here. Do ya hear?"

She hiked up her old blue work skirt and ran through the tall weeds beside the pasture fence, her skirt catching the sticky beggars lice with every anxious step. That was it, the high weeds. Everything was overgrown. When she stopped to listen for the cackling chickens, there was no noise - nothing but silence. "Why is my heart beating so hard? Why don't they come out of the house? Why...?" she asked, panting hard, as she swung around the custard apple trees beside the out house and ran almost to the kitchen stoop before stopping.

There were no chickens to cackle, just a weed filled yard, and her ma's beautiful flowers around the stoop were covered with vines. That told Juanita that her ma hadn't been there in a long time, 'cause she never let even one single little old weed mess with her flowers. Not ever.

She didn't bother even to call their names. She turned around, saw a blue tailed lizard sunning itself on the stoop, and not knowing what else to do, kicked some sand at it. It scurried off into a clump of sand spurs that were still green. Juanita reached down, pulled them up and threw them onto her pa's high trash pile as she walked away. She could see that it hadn't been burned in a long time. Sighing, she slowly walked toward the wagons.

Etienne, brushing the clinging sand off his brown boots on the Burns Dry Goods step, winked at the old hound dog, that didn't even bother to raise his other eyelid as Etienne stepped up onto the worn, wooden porch. Mr. Burns acknowledged him as he entered and asked how he could help him. He could see that he was foreign and thought when he spoke that he was another French trapper. They were his best customers, so he was more spirited than usual as he went around the pine counter.

After ordering the salt pork and meal that Orlean had requested, Etienne casually asked about the family that he said had sold them chickens the last time they traveled through LaBelle. Juanita had suggested that he lie to get the information and had given him several suggestions and specific instructions about not saying that she was traveling with them. He absolutely was not to mention even her name, and he had promised, for she did need to know her parents' whereabouts.

"Oh, so you knew the Graveses? Too bad about Ben, I'll declare it was. Now that was one man who knew his chickens. Why, he won ever' blue ribbon in the entire county..." and on he droned. Finally, Etienne asked what did happen to him and his missus, who had been very kind to his family in the past, selling them chickens and eggs.

"Oh, he died. Just up and died. Ovella said that she called him to come for dinner, and when he didn't come, that she went to the coop, and there he was face down in the yard. Must've been his heart. Too young to die, I said. Yep, too young to die. Couldn't 've been more'n fifty, give a day or two," he shook his head as he wrapped up the side meat.

"You be needin' anythin' else, young man?" Mr. Burns asked as he studied the stranger. He sure talked fine for a foreigner, real fancy like. Maybe he was a teacher. They could sure use another one. So hard to keep a teacher out in the wilds like this. He got up his nerve, and before Etienne could inquire about Mrs. Graves, Mr. Burns asked, "Now don't go to thinkin' I'm nosey 'bout your business, cause I'm not, but it's for a reason that I'm a askin'. You wouldn't happen to be a teacher, would ya?"

Etienne smiled as he replied, "No, Mr. Burns, indeed I'm not. But if I ever sought another profession, other than the one in which I'm engaged, I would definitely consider it. My brother and sister and I were very fortunate to have an excellent tutor, who traveled with us in our medicine show. You see, sir, I'm an entertainer, and my family and I are on our way to Alva to perform."

"Oh, my...oh, my! Wait 'til I tell Elvira who you are. She'll have a fit for sure. Well, you know I haven't seen such a show since we moved from Baldwin ...that was way back in '58 before the War. My, my!"

As he excitedly turned to go to the curtained-off room in the back of the store, Etienne stopped him, and asked, "I would like to know what happened to Mrs. Graves. What did you say her name was?"

"Oh, you mean Ovella? Oh, she up and sold the chickens to Walt and Mamie Harris up the Caloosahatchee on your way to Alva. Yep, when Ben passed on, she moved in with Bonnie and Randolph and helps Bonnie take care of her two little girls. The new one, Charity Sue, is the spit'n' image of Juanita when she was that age. Now some folks think that Juanita's runnin' away with that Skinner Gang was the cause of Ben's passin', but then others say that it was just his time... Elvira...oh, El, honey, come on out here. You're not gonna believe who is here. Just not gonna believe. Nosiree"

Etienne barely escaped the Burnses without extending them an invitation to visit the wagons. When he told Juanita about her folks, she took it very well, but she was fit to be tied when he told her about how much the Burnses had wanted to visit his family. He decided not to tell her what Mr. Burns said: "Me and El will do our darndest to get over to Alva to see the show and to meet your folks, won't we, El? Why, this is almost as excitin' as when Randolph Martin came a ridin' up yellin' that the Skinner Gang was over at the Graveses'. Whew! That was some kinda excitin'!"

"Grief, you'd think that you were some kinda celebrity or somethin'" Juanita said disgustedly. "Haven't these people ever been anywhere or seen anything before? I'll declare to you right here and now that I'm just glad I don't hafta live in such a dumb old place, I certainly am," and she waltzed herself right back to the darkness of the wagon.

"She needs to be alone, Aimee. She'll be all right now that she knows about her folks. Just give her a little while," Etienne said as he restrained her.

Juanita curled up in a tight ball on her pallet and pulled the narrow sheet over her head.

"Charity Sue! Grief! What a stupid, dumb old name to give a baby! Bet she's as ugly as that Blessed Jane. I'll just bet." Rubbing her flat stomach, she was soon asleep.

The dry goods store in Alva hadn't changed even one iota, Juanita noticed as she ducked into the shaded room. "Miss Tatum must be out back weighing up someone's catch," she thought, 'cause there was no one there. From around the barrels of salt stacked on the top platform on the river side came a dark-haired girl, who was startled when she saw Juanita.

"Oh, I didn't hear ya come in. Can I help ya?" she asked in a hesitant voice as she studied everything Juanita was wearing.

"I was wondering where the girl with the light brown hair was. I can't remember her name. She was here the last time we came through."

"Oh, you must mean Rose...Rose Shorter. Well, she up and moved all the way to Ft. Basinger on the Kissimmee. Miss Tatum almost had a fit, she did. Just up and came in one day and told her that she was gonna move there and live with her cousin Thelma, you know, her Uncle Jimmy's daughter. Sure took us all aback."

"I didn't know her, exactly..." Juanita explained, but before she could continue her lie, the girl interrupted.

"She never was the same after that Joe Roberts just up and left...no notice or anything. Miss Tatum always thought he'd come back - anyone could see how much he thought of Rose - but he never did, and didn't write neither. I said that maybe he couldn't write, you know. But Miss Tatum said she knew that I was wrong, 'cause she seen him. She thinks that some harm come ta him, and so does Rose."

Juanita thought, "Some harm came to him, alright. Mr Joe Roberts Skinner was hung from a tall oak tree." But she said, "Is Miss Tatum around? "

"She's around, alright, but is laid up with the grippe, so I'm heppin' her out 'til she gets to feelin' better. I'm Lucy Hawks, just a friend. I ain't kin or anything like that."

Juanita was relieved that she wasn't around for fear that she'd recognize her, but after what Lucy said it would appear that the folks in Alva, except Rose, of course, didn't even know that Joe Bob Skinner and Joe Roberts were one and the same.

"Miss Tatum got a letter from Rose 'bout two weeks ago, ya know. She's doin' jus' fine and is working at the boardin' house, cleaning and cookin', and said she's really enjoyin' Thelma's little baby. Named him for Rose's pa Seth, and I think Thelma's husband must be named Robert 'cause that's what else she named him. Seth Robert. That's a pretty name, ain't it?"

"Yes, that's a right pretty name. When did you say the baby was born? My sister just had a baby girl, born in February."

"I believe Miss Tatum said somewheres around mid February. Just about the same time as yore sister's, I'd say."

Juanita calculated rapidly and smiled as she realized why Rose had to leave Alva. She introduced herself. "Oh, I'm Cherie, and I'm performing with the medicine show. I sure hope you can come out to see the show tonight."

"Oh, I wouldn't miss it for the whole, entire world," and she looked admiringly at Juanita. "You sure are pretty, Miss Cherie. I never in all my life saw such pretty hair. Oh, I wouldn't miss it for the world."

Juanita had a smirk on her face as she left the store and laughed all the way back to the wagon. "So, Mr. Smarty Pants Joe Bob Skinner, you planted your seed, and your sweet Rose is bouncing your baby boy. I should have known that the world would have another Skinner. I should have known. Bet you're down in hell laughing your head off, and that brother of yours is, too, and hitting you on the back trying not to wet his britches. I'll just bet."

****

Aimee wrote Berta that they again looked forward to being with her and her family. Dom had almost convinced the boys that a settled existence was one of worth and that they would speak to Layke of the arrangement they had discussed last August.

Juanita's performance, even though for such a short duration, had swollen their savings enough to make settling down possible this year, if they could get the boys to make a commitment.

When Berta received that good news, she and Layke both felt a tremendous relief. Jonah was a big help, but Layke wanted him to continue his schooling, and they both wanted Young Reuben to return to South Spring. With Pierre and Etienne to help it could now be possible. Layke promised Berta that he would make Etienne and Pierre a proposal that they could not turn down and added that Orlean's presence would be needed, because the daily chores would be increased greatly with a new baby. Willa could always assist, but Berta had noticed the fire going out of her this last year. She couldn't even get riled up about Zeke's laziness any more. Well, she was over seventy, so it was time for her to take it easy, Berta conceded with a warm feeling. She loved all of them so, and their time was not much longer, she could see.

She was large with child when the third week in April arrived. Layke was very concerned. He was positive she had miscalculated, but she felt well and had had none of the physical problems she had been plagued with when she carried Wes. His had been a very difficult carrying time and delivery, but she had never felt better during a pregnancy than she did now, she kept reminding him. But he was still a nervous wreck. The wife of a cowman did not have an easy life; it was lonely and hard. He wanted his Berta to have a better life than before, and he was going to do his darndest to make it a reality.

A very sad-faced man held her in his arms that misty dawn. The Haglund boys had arrived the night before, accompanied by Karine, who would remain with Berta. It was the most difficult time in Berta's life, she confessed to Karine after Layke left, almost as difficult as when Reuben died. At least then she was in shock and remembered so little of that period. But the emptiness was the same. She felt numb all over.

The spring rains continued to cause concern for the Old Towners, especially Miss Trudy, who kept in very close touch with

Berta. If there was a flood, then it would be difficult for her to get to South Spring. The Suwannee was always a threat in the spring, and she was afraid that Berta had miscalculated her due date and that the baby might arrive before Layke's return. She had attended Berta with all her births and remembered Wes's arrival vividly, having almost lost both of them, but she'd refrained from mentioning that fact to Layke; he was worried enough, goodness knows.

Three weeks had gone by when Frankie Brewster rode up to South Spring with word from the cowmen. They had arrived safely with no mishaps, and the schooners were supposed to start arriving within two days. Layke should be returning in less than two weeks. Berta was relieved - she had begun to feel so weary, she tired easily, and her anxiety made her even more subdued.

Karine was also getting very concerned but tried to make light of the situation. "Berta, that babe will weigh at least ten pounds, I bet."

"I was almost this large with Wes, and he weighed over nine pounds, so I guess this one will be huge," she laughed, but soon became quiet and reflective.

The evenings were filled with handwork and talking, and the long, weary days went by slowly. She and Karine began preparing the homecoming feast for the cowmen the day before their expected arrival. Big Dan brought up the largest ham in the smoke house for roasting, and Karine helped Berta bake a burnt-sugar cake topped with finely chopped pecans. They had planned the menu carefully, and Berta was more animated than she had been since Layke left, Karine noticed.

"I just know they'll be home today," Berta said over and over again. She had awakened early, and there was humming in her kitchen even before the first cock crowed. The day just dragged with no sign of them, and as dusk fell Berta took to the porch, her eyes never leaving the main road. Finally, she lost the battle with the hungry mosquitos and slowly left the porch, latching the door behind her as she eased into her lonely bed.

She couldn't get to sleep. The baby had dropped, and the swelling in her legs and feet was so distressing that she couldn't find a comfortable position. As she lay awake, tossing and turning, she thought of the past year and all the worries and triumphs, of new friendships and losses. It was almost first light when she finally dozed off.

****

Layke swatted Barney's cow pony Poker on his rump and said, "I'll catch up with you by tomorrow night, probably around Tall Tree Hammock. Just keep an eye on my doubloons and Tag, hear?"

He turned Bucko toward Ft. Myers and the deMoyas' campsite. He wanted to pay a personal visit to make sure that they understood his and Berta's invitation was sincere. "Won't take me but about five or six hours longer than if I follow the others back," he rationalized. "Hold on, Berta, I'm just doing what you made me promise."

He left the deMoyas' the next morning before first light. It was going on dusk, about another hour and a half of good light left, when he and Bucko came to the scrub country. He thought he could see the chuck wagon in the distance but couldn't be sure. Pierce and his men had split and headed east toward Ft. Pierce before returning to Bullseye, and Parker, Callie and Thom had gone on ahead to the Tall Ten in Tater Hill. Only Silas and his hands from Split Creek and the Old Towners rode together, their sacks of doubloons thrown carelessly into the back of the wagon along with grits, coffee, meal and Tag.

They were not concerned about their safety - the only robbery ever made in that section was the one by the Skinner Gang the year before. As he rode, his mind not on the successful sale of their 1200 beeves at $20.00 a head, not on Callie and Thom's obvious love, nor on the rumbling thunder he could hear in the distance, but on his anxiousness to return to South Spring in time for Berta's delivery.

"I don't care if I ever make this drive again. I've been on every one for thirteen years, and enough is enough." His mind was wandering all over the place when he heard shots ring out.

"Good, I hope they got something that cooks fast. I'm starving."

When he heard the Winchesters rapidly fire, he realized that something was up and put the spurs to Bucko. "What in hell...?" He could see three riders about a quarter of a mile ahead and heard the shouting. He recognized Barney's voice and thought he heard

Swede. When he looked up again they had gone into the brush - even the wagon was gone.

Layke couldn't tell what was going on but knew something wasn't right. The Swede's three sons carried Winchesters and so did Barney, but Sam, the cook, and the others wouldn't part with their Henrys from the War. Again, eight or ten shots rang out. He hit the brush beside the trail and hung close. There hadn't been many times since the War that he had wished for a gun but now was one of them. He had his whip out but no target in sight to strike. It was darker in the brush, but he could make out the wagon that was pulled up in a thicket of palmettos and scrub oak.

"Where's Tag?" he wondered. Surely he'd have heard his master and found him. But he was nowhere. Layke dismounted and crouched low as he came around a stand of pine beside the wagon. "Where's Sam? God! Where is everybody?"

A barrage of rifle fire hit all around him, and he hit the ground. His hand felt something furry and wet. He knew it was Tag and that he had been hit. He felt around his neck, but nothing...not a movement. "Damn it to hell!" he shouted and rolled over toward the wagon and saw Sam. His eyes rolled to the top of his bloody head. "I don't believe this...I don't believe this. When is the killing going to stop?" he shouted.

"Layke, it's me, Silas. It's me, Layke." He spun him around to face him. "We've been bushwhacked!" he said, shaking Layke trying to get through to him. "There're three of 'em, and they're totin' Winchesters. Hit the wagon from the back and would've got by with it, but Swede and Barney came back to tell Sam that we'd make camp up under those oaks on the ridge. They just missed gettin' their heads blown off but at least got in some shots. Barney thinks he got one of 'em."

Layke didn't even think to ask about the gold, and Silas didn't think to tell him. Another burst of gunfire, this time on the other side of the clearing and about two hundred yards ahead of them. "We'd better get around them on the other side," Silas whispered. Then he realized that Layke didn't have a gun and wouldn't be of any help.

Layke reached into the wagon, avoiding looking at Sam's head, that was almost blown off, and got his Henry. He turned around to Silas and said, "I'm right behind you." He got the bullets out of the box under the front seat, where Sam always carried them in case he saw a deer or plump rabbit for their supper, and running low they circled south and into the first clump of saw-tooth palmettos. "I'm gonna be one big scab by the time I get to Berta," he thought. "God, these things could kill a man."

It sounded like Swede, Barney and the others were bunched together across the trail in some low scrub and that the bushwhackers were across from them exchanging shots and getting no place fast. Layke tapped Silas on the shoulder and said, "I'm gonna go around behind them. They don't know we're here, and I'll need you to cover me. We've gotta draw 'em out."

"Gawd, Layke. Don't do anything crazy. It ain't worth it."

"Don't worry! I'm not stupid enough to get shot. I've gotta see my first born, and that's a fact."

Silas saw him run through the thorny smilax, its needle-like thorns tugging at his heavy pants, but Layke didn't notice. He was intent on the business at hand. His years of army training had conditioned him, and he went about the job methodically, his heart racing a mile a minute. The sweat was pouring off his face as he came upon them. Silas was right. There were only the two of 'em. Didn't look like they were more than just kids.

"Why'd they make me do this? Why?" He automatically pulled the whip out of his belt and unleashed it at the one leaning behind the big pine. His shirt ripped down his back and blood spurted. As he spun around, Layke pulled the trigger of the Henry with his left hand, sending the Winchester flying out of the boy's hands.

Silas yelled, "I've got the other one, Layke." The boy put down his gun and didn't even try to turn around.

They sat around the fire slowly sipping their coffee and eating the cold corn dodgers. No one spoke, just sat there puffing on their pipes and brushing away the insects. The dangling bushwhackers hung from a laurel oak not fifty feet away. Their once spirited, beardless faces hung motionless, cocked to one side. Layke finally spoke. "I'll stay tomorrow just long enough to say my good-bys to Sam and Tag, boys, and then I'm heading for home."

Silas held Barney's arm, restraining him, as he started to follow Layke. Quietly, he said, "He needs his grieving time, Barn. We all do. Sam Jones was a friend to us all, and Tag a good cow dog."

Layke lay beside the banked fire, his arms behind his head, remembering the first time he saw Tag. He had been just a ball of black and white fur - you could hardly see his eyes - and when he began petting the puppies in Sadie's litter, Tag came to him immediately and followed him when he left. He remembered turning around and telling Joel Wilpole that he'd like that one. He named him on the spot.

The tear he brushed away was followed by a few more before he could give into his grief. He'd sleep close to the wagon where Sam and Tag were wrapped in the tarp and would keep an eye out for any hungry wolves. He'd not be alone. Not much sleep would visit the cowmen that dark night.

****

When Karine awakened she was surprised that Berta was not up, a fire already going in the cook stove and the coffee made. So she got the fire going for the coffee and the corn dodgers fried up...but still no Berta.

"I best look in on her to see if she's all right." Berta was sleeping fitfully, and Karine became concerned as she stood there watching her toss and turn, the covers all askew. She hurriedly went to the barn to alert Jonah.

"I think your Ma's time has come, Jonah. You gotta go to town for Miss Trudy!" She calmed down, and following him to the rain barrel, where he splashed the cool water on his face, rambled on a mile a minute about her concern. Jonah dashed back into the barn and returned with Blackie and the saddle.

"Now, I might be jumping the gun, but I don't think so." He followed her back into the house to see for himself, and by then Berta had awakened but seemed lethargic.

"Berta, I'm sending Jonah to town to fetch Miss Trudy. I don't like the looks of this at all, and I'd feel better if she were here."

Berta did not protest as Karine was afraid she might. When Jonah realized that she wasn't going to, he grabbed a couple of corn dodgers from the iron skillet and ran to get Blackie saddled. On the way out he turned to Karine and said, "I know Layke will be fit to be tied if he's not back for the birthing. I never saw anyone as worried as he was when he left, did you, Karine?"

"No, and I wish you'd have Frankie ride down to Fannin Springs to telegraph south. If he's near, he can ride back real hard. I'm thinking your ma's gonna have need of him, Jonah. Now make tracks. If she goes into hard labor before Miss Trudy gets here, I'll really have my hands full." SuSu and Wes came out sleepily rubbing their eyes to find out what all the commotion was, and Karine told them to wash up for breakfast and to be quick about it. They couldn't understand why she was such a grump. Usually she was kind and gentle.

Karine saw their reaction and went to them, put her arms around both and said, "I think your ma's time has come, and SuSu, I want you to go to Willa's to tell her. Maybe she can help until Miss Trudy gets here. Wes, be a big boy now and get dressed."

She went into Berta's room and sat on the edge of her bed and asked, "Berta, have the pains started?"

"No, but I feel peculiar. I've never felt like this. The baby has calmed down, so I don't feel life like I did. Why, yesterday morning it was dancing a jig, but today... nothing. I'm worried, Karine. Oh, I wish Layke were here. If he were here, I know everything would be fine."

"I wish he were here, too," Karine thought as Berta began to cry, and because she was young and inexperienced in handling situations like this, cried, "Oh, Berta do you hurt?" not knowing anything else to ask.

"No, I wish I did. If I hurt, then I'd know everything was all right. It's just like there's nothing there."

"What'a ya mean...nothing there?"

"I feel numb ...oh, I don't know, Karine. I just don't know."

Karine escaped into the kitchen and put on the kettle for their tea. She could see SuSu and Wes outside the kitchen window coming back from Willa's, and even their presence relieved her somewhat. She went to the door and called them...anything to take her mind off of her predicament. Then Berta called. She went hurriedly, but Berta had stopped crying and only wanted to ask for the children.

"I'm fixing their breakfast, and then they can go back down to Willa's. She said it was all right. Berta, how about a nice cup of tea? Here, I'll fix it, and in no time you'll feel better."

SuSu and Wes had finished breakfast and were playing outside as Karine finished washing the breakfast dishes. She thought to herself, "Jonah'll be riding up to Stucky's about now. Miss Trudy will be gathering her birthing gear and scurrying around telling everyone in town that Berta's time has come and giving everyone orders as to what their jobs are while she's gone." She chuckled, but then thought, "I hope they hurry. It'll take at least an hour and a half to get here in the buckboard."

Karine heard her fall, then scream. She ran to the door and cried, "Berta, oh Berta, now don't you move. Here, let me help you." Her water had broken. Karine looked down at the puddle on the floor. Berta wearily climbed into bed without protest. Karine went into the kitchen for some rags and to get the kettle boiling. "Where on earth is that Willa? She said she'd be here, and just where is she, I wanta know."

"Oh, dear Lord, I'm scared. I've never attended anyone by myself before. I need your help."

She heard Wes and SuSu shout, "They're here! They're here."

"Oh, glory be," Karine said as she ran into the bedroom. Berta's contorted face told her that her pains had indeed started, and they were already hard.

"They're here, Berta. They're here. Thank God." Berta smiled and went into a contraction that turned her knuckles white.

When Karine ran out the back door she saw Layke instead of Trudy and exclaimed as she looked at his grin, that had to be at least a mile wide, "Grief! I thought you were Miss Trudy! Now what'll I do?"

"What'll you do, young lady? I'll show you what you'll do. You'll take some lessons. Out of my way, and you'll watch a master."

Karine ran into the bedroom before Layke and announced, "Berta, it's Layke. He's here, Berta, he's here," and she sat down hard on the first available chair, exhausted.

"Her pains started coming hard and fast, Layke. They just started out hard and close together. No warning. Her water just broke..."

"We passed Jonah on the way to town. Trudy will be with us directly...Karine?" No answer as she looked into space in a daze.

"Whew! I'm glad I'm back. The girl's vacant upstairs." He pushed past her, threw his dusty, sweat-soaked hat on the rack, went to the wash bowl, rolled up his dirty, torn shirt sleeves, changed his mind and ripped off the shirt. He turned to Karine and said as she sat there staring at him, mesmerized, "Get me a clean shirt," and running his damp hands through his rumpled brown hair said, "I don't want this babe to get its first look at its father when he's dirty and half naked."

"God, he's beautiful! Why on earth am I thinking that? And he's so happy...and at a time like this, especially when I believe we're in for a rough time of it," she thought as she stared at Layke's scratched, muscled back.

He washed up, put on the clean shirt she handed him and went into the bedroom. Berta tried to smile but grimaced in pain instead. Layke turned to Karine.

"Have you checked the baby's position?"

She shook her head. "No, there wasn't time. It all started so fast!"

Layke turned to Berta and explained what he was doing. "Now, honey, I'm not an expert at human births, but I've helped many a colt and calf enter this old world. So until Trudy gets here, you're going to have to do with your tired old husband."

After examining her, he turned toward Karine and whispered, "It's breech. I'm gonna hafta turn it."

He sat down beside Berta. Her face was beaded with perspiration. He explained what he was going to attempt to do, that he had done this many times on the range and that every cow he had assisted thanked him personally. He was trying so hard to make Berta relax with his poor jokes that Karine got the nervous giggles, then the hiccups, and Layke finally sent her from the room under the pretense of seeing whether SuSu and Wes were all right. "That girl makes me more nervous than if she weren't here, my sweet."

"Be brave, my love. Together we're going to bring this newborn into our wonderful world to share our joy," and as he talked softly, confidently, to Berta he managed to turn the infant.

"Give it a good push, my precious one. This babe is anxious to be born to join our family."

Layke talked and Berta pushed.

Karine ran inside, "I see the dust flying, Layke. I think it's Jonah with Miss Trudy."

Berta let out a loud moan. Layke said, "That's my girl. That's my best girl," as he helped Karine with the soiled rags.

A very excited Trudy Stucky moved her heavy feet over the brushed path like a fleet-footed deer. When Berta heard her voice, she managed to smile.

Trudy put her head inside the room and saw Layke deliver

Berta of a red, squirming baby girl. She stepped inside as he started to get pale. "I'll take over now, Daddy. You've done yours and then some. Karine, get Layke a chair and be quick about it."

As Berta asked what it was, she heard Trudy slap its behind, and a lusty cry escaped as the babe took its first breath. Layke just sat there grinning. Berta's face began to contort again, and Trudy turned to Layke and let out a yeehaw!

"We're not through yet, Mr. Williams. It would appear that this little girl baby is gonna have a playmate."

Ten minutes later Layke was presented with his son. Berta tiredly smiled as Trudy and Karine cleaned up the infants. They were not ready for the bright May sun streaming into Berta's kitchen and scrunched up their closed eyes even tighter.

Jonah, Wes, SuSu and Willa and the Haglund brothers, who had ridden back with Layke, were standing in the kitchen all in a row when Layke emerged with a babe cradled in each arm. Jonah was the first to speak. "Grief! There's two of 'em. We've got twins...grief! Wh-wh-what are they?" He was so flustered with excitement, everyone laughed at his stuttering.

"A gentleman and a lady, I am pleased to present to you: Tucker Layke Williams on my left, I think, and on my right, Lorraine Trudy Williams, I believe." He held them down so Wes could see closer, and SuSu stood quietly beside him and, not being able to restrain herself any longer, took the baby girl's hand in her slight one. She looked up at Layke, and he could see the love in her enormous brown eyes.

"Tucker is named for my captain, who saved my life in the War, and Lorraine was my mother's name, but she was called Raine. It seems that her brother, Harmon, couldn't say Lorraine when she was born but did manage the Raine part. So Raine and Tucker Williams bid you adieu so they can thank their mother properly for such a splendid entry into God's wonderful world."

Layke proudly handed a happy Berta her babes and leaned over to kiss her forehead. Trudy and Karine tiptoed out of the room and quietly closed the door, so they could have some privacy. He sat and looked lovingly at his Berta. "I don't ever want to leave you again, my sweet. Those were the longest five weeks of my entire life. The trains will be coming to the central part of the state in a few years, and there'll be no need for the long drive south.

The other cowmen are in accord. Pierce has decided to ship his up north after next year. Our world is changing, Mrs. Williams, and Tucker and Raine will find it a lot different from how we know it now. By next spring Pierre and Etienne should be ready, with the help of Young Reuben, to run the beeves, so I can spend my every waking moment with you, my own sweet one."

She answered drowsily, "That's good, dear." He held her hand, and the tears unashamedly ran down his handsome face in gratitude. "You must rest," and he left the room, while Berta, with her babes on each side, tiredly slipped into slumber.

Trudy had his strong black coffee poured when he joined her and Karine in the warm kitchen. As Layke relaxed, he told them of visiting the deMoyas in Ft. Myers. It was then that he found out about Juanita's leaving them. She had taken a stage in the middle of the night - only Aimee knew of her plans. The note that she left for Etienne was very caring, he was told. She said that she planned to return to Palatka to start a new life. She thanked him profusely for all his help and understanding and said that she would always love him in her own way, but his wife she could not be, and the longer she stayed with them, the harder it would become for her to leave.

Etienne was devastated and went into a deep depression. They were all worried about him, and when Orlean told him what Aimee had confided in her, of Juanita's infatuation with the Irish riverboat gambler, he took to his wagon, and not even Dom could get him to come out. He stayed inside for two days with no water or food, and when he finally emerged, Orlean saw that the fire had gone out of her first born. "He'll nevair be de same. Not evair. My poor boy...my poor Etienne. De trollop 'as won!" and she, too, took to her wagon.

Layke had decided to wait for a while before telling them of the ambush, Sam and Tag. The Haglund boys had agreed that it was best. "The Lord giveth and the Lord taketh away."

Layke gently put his hand on Trudy's tired shoulder, and she raised her sleepy head from the kitchen table to his happy face. "Layke Williams, what on earth? Letting me fall asleep when my namesake might need me?" She brushed back her hair as she got cool water from the dipper to remove the sleep from her eyes. Berta and her babes were fast asleep when Trudy rushed into the room. Layke, with a grin from ear to ear, chuckled at her frustration.

She turned and whispered, "Mr. Smarty Pants, you should be mighty pleased with yourself," and they were soon in each other's arms. Trudy thought, "You are my children. The Lord in all his wisdom gave me many, but you are special in my heart and in my care, and now I have two more to fret over. I have a feeling they'll need me more than the rest. Their pa will be a big man in this state some day. He still has the gnawing...that hungry look is still in his eyes, and Berta will be right beside him, mark my word, right beside her man just as she was with Reuben."

Layke was sitting on the side of the bed when Berta awakened. The babes had begun to stir, and Raine was the first to let her know how hungry she was. She was already the hungrier and louder. "They should be opening their eyes today, dear," Berta explained as Raine suckled strongly. Tucker was larger but required more sleep. He squirmed in Layke's arms and seemed to be waiting for his sister to finish. As Berta gazed at her two men, Tucker opened his still swollen eyes, and she got a catch in her throat when she saw the pale blue color. "The Boyo!"

"What did you say, dear?" Layke asked.

"I said, boyo." When she saw Tucker's eyes she instantly knew who the man on the boat was. She shivered.

"What's wrong, honey? Are you cold? Here, let me get your shawl..."

"Oh, I'm fine, its just that Tucker's eyes are the color of a young boy's I knew when I was growing up in Macon, that same pale blue. His sister called him Boyo."

"Well, there'll be no nickname for Tucker, honey. He carries a proud name, and I want it used."

"I know, Layke. It just slipped out, that's all." After Layke left the room to join Trudy in the kitchen, Berta tiredly closed her eyes, and as Tucker suckled she squeezed him to her saying secretly, "Go to sleep my little boyo."

CHAPTER II THE SAVANNAH

Juanita had difficulty lifting the heavy valise that contained her blanket filled with doubloons. The hot, tiring trip north took over two exasperating weeks, and she was not only hot but ill-tempered and thoroughly exhausted by the time the dilapidated old stagecoach rattled up to the impressive St. Johns Hotel in Palatka.

She stamped her small, boot-encased foot and snapped at the driver, "Now why on earth does a lady have to tote her own gear, Mister?" All the while she was brushing off the white dust of the old military trail they had just traveled. Seemed to her that they had stopped in every village from Ft. Myers to Palatka. Her dark grey traveling skirt, that she and Aimee had so painstakingly fashioned, looked like it was last year's rag, she angrily realized.

The toothless, dirty, tobacco-stained face appeared from under the floppy, brown felt hat and told her, "Little lady, jest hold yore horses, and Geek'll get his bent legs unscrambled to be heppin' you."

She continued to brush the road dust off her skirt and to straighten her dark grey felt hat with the ruby-red pin perched on the taffeta bow. She had been so proud of her new finery. She'd never in her whole life had anything so fine. Now, look at her. She might as well have worn her old work hat from La Belle instead of her new bonnet from Lady Isabelle's in Ft. Myers. Just the most exclusive shop in the entire town, it was. She just might as well have.

Geek finally unscrambled his arthritic, bowed legs and bent his creaking back to assist the pretty, fired-up lady with her gear. When he tried to lift the heavy valise, he let out an expletive not fit for a lady's ears and turned to apologize to her. She couldn't help but get tickled at his antics.

"He's just trying his best to make me feel sorry for him so he can extract a larger tip from me," she thought. "Mr. Geek, there isn't a trick in the book that Juanita Jane Graves hasn't pulled on an unsuspecting fancy Dan, so don't think all your moaning and groaning will get you another doubloon, because it flat out won't!" she informed the doubled-up little man confidently. He smiled at her with his toothless grin, the sweat pouring off his hairy chin.

When they first pulled up in front of the large three-storied hotel, she barely glanced at it. All she wanted to do was to make a presentable entrance and not shame herself. After Geek finally got his wobbly legs to cooperate, she followed him up the flower-lined brick walk. It curved so prettily up the sloping, green lawn, dotted with little white iron benches with curlicues all over, just sitting empty in the bright afternoon sun while the heavy limbs of the live oaks hovered above, the Spanish moss fanning the imaginary guests as it gently swayed over them.

The closer they got to the stately hotel with its imposing white pillars and the dark green double doors with their massive brass lion-head handles, the more frightened and unsure of herself she became. Geek dropped the heavy valise down on the red brick porch and let out a sigh of relief that could have been heard clear to La Belle, she thought, disgusted.

"I just wish the dirty old goat would behave himself. Lordy, he's got everyone looking our way. Now, why'd he have to go and act like that, anyway? He'll probably really put on an act when I don't tip him handsomely."

Juanita noticed a rather nice-looking young man seated beside one of the fern-filled urns. He was smoking a pipe and reading the paper, so gentleman-like. He tipped his dove-gray bowler, and she smiled a very tiny smile and averted her curious eyes quickly so as to cause as little commotion as possible.

The Geek didn't protest too loudly when she reached into her black velvet purse for coins. She was so relieved, she almost popped a stay in her cinched waist.

When she let out the sigh, the gentleman hurriedly approached her and said, "Here, let me assist you. It's not often that I'm able to help a damsel in distress."

He lifted the heavy valise effortlessly, and Juanita thought, "Oh my, how strong he is."

She thanked him coyly when they arrived at the crescent-shaped desk. It was covered in dark red leather, and the brass nail heads that secured it shone like golden stars, she thought.

Never in all her wild imaginings had she dreamed a room could look like this. There were massive, white columns that reached majestically to the third floor in the center of the red and green carpeted lobby, and white balustrades connected them, creating a rotunda. Handsomely dressed ladies and gentlemen sat quietly discussing she knew not what on the dark red, leather benches that circled them.

"Imagine not having anything to do all day long but get all dressed up and sit in a beautiful room like this," she observed naively. "I will be doing just that one of these days. And soon is not quick enough."

The young man excused himself and offered his services if and when she might have need of them in the future. She thanked him sweetly, and when she turned to follow the Negro boy in his spotless white uniform, she saw out of the corner of her eye a brown-haired girl about her age take the gentleman's arm possessively as they joined another couple. She turned to see if Juanita was watching, and seeing that she was, triumphantly hugged him closer to her.

When Juanita arrived at the first landing, she halted, looked toward the long French windows in the lobby and saw the couples seated outside at the tiny tables placed all along the brick porch. The Negro boy turned toward her and followed her studied gaze.

"It's tea time, Miss. Would ya be havin' tea in yore room, or would ya lak it served on the verandah? If'n you'd lak ta see the boats on the St. Johns, Ah could serve ya on either the second or third story balcony. They are plumb stupendous comin' around Forrester's Point."

She excitedly asked that he serve her on the third floor balcony - surely she could see more from there.

"Yes'm dat's for shore you can." Once inside her room, she reached into her drawstring purse and tipped him extravagantly with the doubloon. His white teeth shone brightly against his ebony skin, his eyes all a'dancing. "I'se be back in no time at all, Miss," he said as he started to open her valise filled with doubloons.

"Oh, don't bother with that, young man. I'm just returning some of the family heirlooms to a relative, who is down on his luck," she said, using her practiced and affected speech.

His big brown eyes got saucer-sized as he stared at Juanita with awe. "Dat's real kind of ya, Miss, real kind. I'se be back directly wit yore tea, Miss," and he quietly tiptoed out of the room, gently closing the heavy door so as not to disturb the young missionary. As he walked quietly away he shook his kinky head in disbelief. "Now dat's a fine young woman wanting to take care of de poor lak dat. Yessum, a mighty fine lady."

The gold satin canopy and the heavy ecru, lace-draped posts encased her as she fell on the massive bed, laughing uncontrollably.

She'd never in all her life had so much fun. She wished that R.J. were there. How he would have loved the comedy of it all! She hadn't thought of him in such a long time. She missed him...she truly did.

Her mind flitted from one happenstance to another. She was restless. "What if he's not on the *Savannah*? What if he's on a great big boat sailing up and down the Mississippi River, taking his pleasure with every wench in New Orleans?" She jumped up, smoothed out her skirt and hair, took the pale pink lace shawl from her bag to drape around her and her copy of *Wuthering Heights*. She had to be doing something. She could not let her mind dwell on the past or the future. "I can't think of R.J. I can't think of Etienne. Now is the time...Now."

She closed the door behind her, locked it securely and sought the stairs to the third-story balcony. The Negro porter was waiting just inside the French doors. He had placed the tray on the small, round table. The fragile, pearl-white service was set for two. Juanita thanked him and took the long-stemmed, pink rosebud from the crystal bud vase on the tray, holding it tenderly as she smelled its delicate fragrance.

"I guess my destitute relative is supposed to have tea when he arrives for his heirlooms," she thought as she glanced at the second place setting. She wanted to laugh out loud, to throw her unleashed hair to the wind and summon Conner. There...she said his name. All day she had been unwilling to say his name, even to herself.

She had not allowed her analytical mind to dwell on Conner. She knew if she did she would not be able to carry out her plan, for it was presumptuous to believe or even imagine he was as drawn to her as she was to him. But it was those icy blue eyes that she could not erase, not his rich Irish brogue or his tall, proud bearing that had haunted her every waking moment, and she with her romantic curiosity had to know why. What hold did this man have over her that she could not erase for six long months?

When Juanita checked into the hotel, she had asked the desk clerk when the *Savannah* would arrive, and he had told her that the *Savannah* and the *Robert E. Lee* were expected at one and one-thirty P.M., respectively, the next afternoon. She had this forever-seeming time to be nervous. Drinking her cooled tea she gazed over the shimmering blue of the wide river and agreed with the porter in his observation. This was indeed a spectacular panorama of the meandering river. The small shops dotted the north bend with their boardwalk overlooking the river, and from her high perch on the balcony the strolling couples were but colorful dolls in miniature, enjoying the cool breeze.

She could hear voices floating upward from the second-story balcony, but she was alone. She liked it that way. She had shared a tiny room in a small house and then a tiny bunk sandwiched into a small wagon. She felt gloriously free with the endless expanse of the hotel's long, empty balcony.

Suddenly she was tired, very tired. She finished her tea, tucked the remaining cookies into her bag and slowly went downstairs to the quiet sanctuary of the large, high-ceilinged room. It was cool, tomb-like, and Juanita welcomed it. She unbuttoned her skirt and blouse and released the corset. She curled up on the gold satin coverlet, and holding her book clasped to her chest, fell exhausted into sleep, not to awaken 'til the early morning light peeked through the lace curtains, creating snowflake patterns on the pale walls.

As she lay lazily beneath the cool sheets she realized that it was the first time in over a year that she'd slept in a bed. "Never again, not ever again will I live like that. Not even for Conner O'Farrell."

Her active young mind began jumping from one "what if" to another; "What if he's not on the *Savannah*? What if he doesn't remember me? What if he's not interested in getting to know me better?"

She startled herself by jumping up from the sanctuary of her bed so quickly. "I must make my very best impression," she thought. "I'll have to ask the desk clerk where there's a smart dress shop to buy myself the most beautiful outfit I can find. And some new slippers," she added as she danced barefoot on the deeply piled wool rug.

Slipping into her gray skirt and blouse she quickly brushed her hair, braiding it into two huge braids and expertly wrapping them around her head. Reaching into her bag she retrieved the tea cookies that she had taken and began munching on them, her heart thumping hard. Her fingers were all thumbs when she allowed herself to think of Conner. "I can't get these blasted old things to fasten!" she exclaimed loudly as she tried to button the tiny black buttons on her worn shoes. Finally she was put together enough to satisfy even her careful scrutiny.

"I'll not eat breakfast until after I've visited the shops," she said aloud. The truth was that she was not sure how to order her meal, and she knew that her table manners were not genteel enough for such a beautiful and fancy dining room. If Etienne had been with her she could have followed his lead, but to venture into that elegant room all by herself scared her more than even she would admit.

When Juanita approached the desk clerk, she saw the young man from the previous afternoon. He tipped his hat and began to come toward her. Juanita was amused when she saw the brown-haired young lady quickly descend the stairs and call to him. He changed his direction abruptly and smiled charmingly toward the girl, ignoring Juanita.

"He's probably promised to her...or married," Juanita thought, as she resumed dealing with the man behind the desk.

He gave her excellent directions to the dress shop. She realized that it was one of those that she had seen the day before from the balcony. "What a glorious sight," she thought, as she stood on the boardwalk gazing out over the rippling water of the river. The vendors were already hawking their pastries, pushing their colorful carts along the boardwalk. Everything smelled so fresh and new, and the aroma from the pastries made her realize that she hadn't eaten anything but the tea cookies since dinner the day before at the stage stop in Welaka, and she had been so apprehensive about arriving in Palatka that she had taken only a few bites.

A brass bell tinkled as she entered *Monique's*, a small shop. Gilt chairs tufted in royal blue velvet were placed around the shop. Large pink paper camellias in gold oriental jars of varied heights sat in front of the bay window with a breath-taking view of the river as a backdrop.

An attractive, middle-aged lady, very tall with beautiful auburn hair and smartly dressed, asked if she could assist her. Juanita could feel the woman evaluate her and became nervous. She talked just like Etienne, so Juanita knew she was French. She brought out three lovely outfits, and when Juanita saw the sky-blue, polished twill with the navy blue ribbon trim, she knew she had found her dress. The ribbon edged the deep, rounded collar, and the tiny buttons of braided ribbon matched perfectly. It had a small, unpretentious bustle and short train. "A matter-of-fact dress," she observed. "Just smart enough."

Monique cried out delighted, "Mademoiselle, I have found the most perfect hat for your costume, the most perfect." She had selected a dark blue hat with navy and white trim; a white egret plume circled the tailored bow.

Monique was suggesting various ways she could wear her hair with the new hat, but Juanita barely heard her. She just stared at her image in the long, oval, gold-leaf mirror. She could hardly believe it. She did not look like herself, and there was certainly no resemblance to *Cherie, the Golden Girl.*

She looked so sophisticated, said Monique, who was mostly concerned as to whether the young country girl had wasted her time and perhaps would not purchase anything. She looked at the gold watch on her lapel and realized that she had spent over an hour with the blond girl.

"It'll take more than one of my creations to make this pathetic creature a lady," she thought. "My, how condescending my attitude has become. I'm becoming shallow and bitter. I'm glad the boyo isn't here to witness this."

She turned toward Juanita and smiled warmly, but Juanita's only concern was whether Conner would approve of her new image. When Monique continued complimenting her about how lovely she looked, Juanita made up her mind. She turned slowly to her and in her most affected voice informed Monique that she would indeed take the hat and dress, "And I'd like the undergarments that I examined earlier, too, please... also, the slippers."

Monique's expression abruptly changed - Juanita could see that she was relieved - and babbling all the while in French, she quickly wrapped the purchases before the girl changed her mind. Juanita was not misled by her change in attitude. She knew what she truly thought. She had seen her superior attitude many times in the past and, frankly, found her amusing.

As Juanita turned to leave, she deliberately turned around and thanked her in French using her most sophisticated aires. All the way back to the hotel she saw the astonished woman's face, and it delighted her. Etienne had taught her a lot of French phrases, and she was now glad that he had persevered. Had she glanced back she would have seen Monique's amused expression.

"This one lives by her wits...interesting..." she mused as she watched the petite girl swish down the boardwalk.

Juanita hurriedly went into her room. She had to study her image once more to be sure. Her new slippers were already beginning to pinch. "I'll be just one big old blister by the time he arrives," she said, kicking them off. "The hair's all wrong," she cried, gazing at her image. "I'll do a low French twist. I need hair below the brim." She tackled the braids passionately and with her small hands worked miracles with the profusion of hair. Gingerly she placed the new hat to the side of her coiled braid and stood back. "Oh, yes, that's much better." She found one shoe and anxiously searched for the other. She wanted to be at the dock at least half an hour early to compose herself.

She had begun to feel light-headed at *Monique's* but did not want to purchase the mouth-watering pastries that the Darkies were selling in front of Monique's patronizing eyes. "Oh Lordy, I could eat a whole Plymouth Rock and all its feathers," she said, laughing. That had been one of R.J.'s favorite sayings. "Why am I thinking of him so much lately?" she wondered. "Grief! I wonder if he can see me?" She thought a while and concluded that he wouldn't be able to. "Shoot, he's frying in old Satan's big fire," and began to giggle in her nervousness.

The walk to the wharf where the *Savannah* would be docking was only a few blocks long, but when Juanita got to the bottom of the high bluff, she was out of breath and her feet were throbbing. She found the vendor with the pastries and also bought a limeade. His colorful sing-song chanting as he rolled his brightly painted cart along the boardwalk reminded her of the deMoya show wagons. It was the very first time she had allowed herself to really dwell on her life with them. They had been so caring after she fell and had encouraged her to stay, but she just couldn't - she had to keep searching, to keep moving.

Attractively dressed couples were beginning to arrive on the wharf, and the dock workers were lined up along the water, smoking and laughing to while away the time 'til the ships arrived and they'd have to begin their back-breaking job of unloading the heavy freight. She brushed off the wooden bench underneath a giant magnolia and sat, munching her delicious pastry and observing the other ladies present. There were none any more smartly dressed than she, she decided objectively.

A large, white ship rounded Forrester Point, and the seated

relatives and awaiting tourists called excitedly to each other. Juanita bounced off the bench and quickly walked over to one of the dockhands, her hurting feet forgotten, and asked which one it was and found to her delight that it was the *Savannah.*

She wanted to jump up and down and wave, but instead walked sedately along the boardwalk. "I absolutely cannot be so anxious. I must calm down. There's a good chance he'll not be on it." She worried and fretted the long-seeming time 'til it docked.

"As tall as he is, I'm sure I'll see him towering over the other passengers," but she did not. He was nowhere in sight. She felt empty.

"Why did I have to get myself so all-fired sure that he'd be on it?" Then she remembered that he said he worked the boats, not the boat.

"Maybe he's working the *Robert E. Lee* this trip," she said, sighing with relief.

She retreated to the shaded bench and was angrily brushing off the pastry crumbs that had found their way to her beautiful new dress when she looked up and saw him. He was leaning against the second deck railing, dressed all in white, smoking his black cheroot, just as she had remembered.

"Oh Lordy, he doesn't recognize me. I can't wave, not even one little wave. It's the hat. He doesn't recognize me in this dumb old hat. That's what it is."

She hurriedly removed the hat pins, pricking her finger in her haste. Frustrated at not being recognized even bareheaded, she angrily thought, "I just don't care whether he sees me or not. After all, I've just ridden half way across the entire state of Florida to be here and spent part of my stake to buy these dumb old clothes." She abruptly sat down.

"Confound you, Conner O'Farrell! What's a lady gotta do to get you to notice her...get naked?"

It was when she thought *naked* that he recognized her. "That's just what I thought. A lady has to get plumb naked before you see her," and she lifted her small gloved hand and wiggled her fingers just a little bit and allowed herself just a tinge of a smile. He gallantly tipped his white straw hat and slowly walked down to the gang plank.

Every eye on the dock was on the mysterious man. She knew he could have any woman there, but he made his way straight toward Juanita. "Right toward me..."

He smiled that remembered smile and lifted her hand, holding it tightly 'til it hurt and then, ever so gallantly, kissed it.

"We meet again, Cherie. Are you performing here in Palatka?"

"Oh no. I was visiting my mother's sick sister, but she died, and before returning to the west coast, I thought to myself, 'Juanita, you've never even been on a great big boat before. Why don't you just take a boat ride before returning to...'

He interrupted her at that point. "The *Savannah* is a lovely boat, Cherie, or is it Juanita?"

"Oh, Juanita is my given name, but Etienne thought Cherie sounded more professional-like."

"To me you'll always be Cherie," and he lifted her hand again, hurting her in the process, he held it so tightly. He relaxed his grip when he saw she was not going to acknowledge the pain. "Here, I'll walk you to the...in which hotel did you say you are staying?"

She proudly informed him, "The St. Johns," and forgot her sophisticated role with her enthusiastic chatter about how beautiful it was and the big bed in her gorgeous room, and when she looked up at him, she saw such a soft, warm, unexpected expression.

"Mr. O'Farrell, why I'm babbling like an excited child." When she looked for his reaction, the warmth had disappeared, replaced by his mocking grin.

"We'll be seeing a great deal of each other on board, Cherie," he said sternly. "I suggest that you call me Conner."

"Why, thank you, Conner, that would make me feel more at ease," she said honestly.

They arrived at the hotel, and Conner informed the desk clerk that Juanita was checking out and to have the porter bring her bags downstairs. Juanita flushed with embarrassment when the clerk raised his eyebrow at her, and she hurriedly explained that she had decided to go on to Jacksonville on the *Savannah*, because her aunt was very ill.

Conner was so amused by her obvious charade, he quickly fled the lobby to the fresh air of the front porch. She could hear his laughter, as could the suspicious clerk.

"I could gladly kill him! I could just murder him! Why does he have to embarrass me so? Why he's just as common as that

R.J. Skinner ever was. He is just!"

The same young Black porter brought her bags, and in the presence of the clerk told her, "I'm shore relieved that yore relative arrived, Miss. Now, y'all have a nice trip on the *Savannah*, heah?"

She could have kissed him. Triumphantly she smiled and thanked him profusely. "Yes, Cousin Conner will escort me to my dear aunt's in Jacksonville," saying it loudly enough for the clerk to hear.

Conner, still wearing a mocking grin on his face, summoned the driver to carry Juanita's bags. When the driver tried to lift her valise, he let out a groan. "Hey Lady, what ya got in here...gold?"

"Would that it were," she said, "but alas, it's only silver flat wear from my recently deceased aunt."

Conner looked down at her with that questioning look, brows raised. "Well, Conner, frankly it was none of his nosy old business what's in my valise," Juanita abruptly said. "Why are you looking at me that way, anyway?" she asked, getting more flustered by the minute.

In a sincere, fatherly voice he replied, "I'm enjoying your play acting, Cherie, and find it highly amusing, but in the future you need be only yourself when you're with me."

Juanita, biting her lower lip and looking down dejectedly, finally replied, "But I don't know who I am, Conner...I mean...I don't know how to be just one person."

At that declaration, he put his arm protectively around her. All the way back to the *Savannah* he held her in that fashion, not saying a word. People turned toward them and smiled, vicariously enjoying the young lovers, who were out for an afternoon ride.

When they walked up the gangplank, they were met by a nice-looking, middle-aged Negro man dressed in a neat, dark blue uniform. Conner introduced Juanita to "my friend, Harrison." "The *Savannah* doesn't operate without his expert assistance," he stated proudly. What he added under his breath was, "And yours truly doesn't, either."

"Now what is he up to?" Harrison wondered, as he watched the two of them walk toward the men's saloon. "That's all I need, him bringing another wench on board and getting us in a jam we can't get out of. But maybe with this little trick around he'll stay sober until we can build up our stash. Unfortunately, she looks so ignorant that she'll probably get us into more trouble than during the hurricane, and Maeve will have to bail us out again."

He put Juanita's bags in Conner's cabin and went below deck, his mind reaching for a solution to how to get Juanita off the *Savannah* so he and Conner could resume their daily card games, Conner playing and Harrison signaling his partner. He hit on an idea that might work, if only Maeve would cooperate.

"You shall now be introduced to the world of James Francis Conner O'Farrell, Cherie. And I most sincerely seek your approval, as I would be honored to assist you in finding out who you really are." Before she could protest he whirled her around and around and in an almost boyish manner laughed uncontrollably.

Juanita thought he was teasing her, making sport of her, and she was hurt...saddened. He was not at all like she thought he'd be.

The room, with bottles of every description lining an entire wall behind the mirrored bar, was centered with a massive crystal chandelier. The sunlight reflecting off its thousands of tear-drop prisms created dancing fireflies on the polished floor. Leather-covered tables were jet black as were the captains chairs that surrounded them. The only color in the entire room was on the red and black checkered carpet that encircled the room. She was impressed. She knew that there was money to be made in this room.

Conner confidently walked over to one of the two wing-backed chairs. He bowed low, ceremoniously gestured toward the chair closest to the corner table and with great pomp announced to the empty room, "The throne for my queen, Cherie."

When he saw her expression of chagrin, he bounded gracefully across the large room and swept her up in his strong arms whispering, "Cherie, I want you by my side. Do you understand?"

She did not. He was unlike anyone she had ever known, and her ignorance frightened her. R.J. she understood. Heavens, she could have almost read his mind. And Etienne, so loving and simple and good. "Why couldn't I have loved him? Something terrible must be wrong with me that I'm so attracted to this man. He must be very evil, or why would I feel so...so...but also excited. Gracious, I can't even think straight. My mind's all a jumble."

The curious passengers strained to see who the lady was that the gentleman in white was carrying, but her face was buried in his broad shoulder.

She opened her eyes when she heard the cabin door close behind her. She gasped in surprise. Conner warmed at her appreciation of the heavy oak and walnut inlaid paneling. "I won it from a high and mighty Bostonian lawyer," he spat out. "He's probably working the docks, the poor stupid bastard! It once decorated his prestigious law offices. Harrison helped me install it."

One wall was lined with more books than Juanita had ever seen, even in school. There weren't many to choose from in the one-room school house in La Belle. Before she could say anything, Conner answered, "Yes, Cherie, I've read them all. Some, more than once."

The dark green, plush couch was fashioned after the beds on a train, he proudly informed her, and the ornate brass oil lamp with dancing cherubs around its base had come from the president of the Savannah-East Coast Railroad as a gift.

He was obviously proud of his magnificently decorated cabin, his home. As he turned, she felt his energy heighten, and even with her eyes cast downward could feel his eyes pierce her very soul. She was having difficulty swallowing. Her back was toward him. "I'm trembling..why am I trembling?" She removed her hat with nervous fingers. When she finally replaced the hat pins and laid the hat on the polished oak chest, his arm swiftly encircled her, and he wrenched her head around, holding her hair tightly with his long, gambler's hand.

"He'll not see my pain...not now...not ever!" She forced her eyes to open, and when she saw his face, she saw the hate and anger. But she also saw the pain. She wanted to ask, "Who has hurt you so, my darling Conner? I know beyond a doubt that it was a woman. I can see the gaping, unhealed wound she has carved in you."

He relaxed his arm. She eased around toward him, and taking her free hand began stroking his face murmuring that all would be well. "Don't fret, my darling one...all will be well.." she said, soothing him. And when their lips found each other, there was no waiting.

His passion was overpowering. They said not a word. The intensity of their exploring, discovering, caressing each other was deafening.

She exploded, "Conner!" and went limp against the soft oriental rug.

They lay spent. He finally spoke in his appealing Irish brogue. "If I were wearing my hat, Cherie, I'd take it off to you," and roared with laughter as he stood.

Looking not at her soft, alabaster, perfectly rounded woman's body, but deep into her dark blue eyes, he announced, business-like, "There will be new blood at the gaming tables tonight, Cherie. You'll be by my side." He was arrogantly confident, stern. There would be no compromise with this man, she realized.

He turned gracefully and proceeded to anoint his body, enjoying the ritual of his toilet.

She rose slowly, opened her case and chose the seafoam, lace-edged wrapper that she had purchased at *Monique's*. She sat curled upon the bed, mesmerized, witnessing the celebration. In silence, so as not to interrupt the flow of his movements, she said appreciatively with her eyes, "You are the most beautiful man I have ever seen or ever hope to see, Conner O'Farrell, and I want to spend the rest of my life finding your heart, if you have one. And if I'm fortunate, extremely patient and am allowed a long, long life, perhaps I'll discover your soul as well.

Conner approached the cabin door, turned and flippantly said, "I think I've found my match, Cherie." Abruptly he turned, and as he eased the door closed after him he said more soberly, "As a matter of fact, I know I have." But in his mind's eye, he still saw Berta.

Stillness - she lay quietly still barely breathing, her full breasts rising..shuddering..then falling as she gasped for her next breath.

"You have indeed, my darling Conner...my Heathcliff. You have, indeed."

Preview

The continued romance of old Florida
in the compelling series

The Floridians

By: Ann O'Connell Rust

Volume III Kissimmee

(to be published in the fall of 1990)

The author cleverly intertwines the lives of these daring pioneers, who courageously attempt to tame the last frontier — Florida

Kissimmee

SOUTH SPRING:

Doodlebug, doodlebug, come out, come out
A big ole snake's gonna grab yore snout.
This here stick goin' 'round and 'round
gonna be yore way outa this here ground.

Wes chanted the old Darkie saying over and over as he circled the heavy straw into the mouth of the dry sand mound where the doodlebugs lived at the bottom of the inverted cone underneath Aunt Willa's and Big Dan's front porch. He was flat on his stomach and would spend hours fishing for them. Patiently he waited for one to latch onto the straw. When he caught it, he'd pull it out and place it in the clear jar of sand so he could watch it later.

As much as he liked his twin brother and sister, he couldn't seem to get used to his new position of not being the baby of the family. He'd always played well by himself, but since the deMoya family had moved to South Spring and SuSu and Aimee had become inseparable, he felt left out for the first time in his seven years.

"Dan, hey Dan, is dat Master Wes Ah heahs unnerneath de house callin' out dose doodlebugs?" Willa called. "Dan, you be dere?" She spent most of her time these days resting on the feather bed that she and Big Dan Roker had shared for over fifty years. Its heavy cotton ticking was stained and patched in more places than she could count. But Willa didn't notice the new tears nor the feathers that had worked their way out of confinement, especially on her husband's side of the bed. Her eyes didn't focus clearly anymore, and her breathing had become especially labored.

She turned on her side and looked for Dan past the only table in the small, square bedroom toward the kitchen and the only other room in the cabin. The kitchen also served as a parlor with its fireplace and clay and stick chimney. The big, square scrubbed-clean pine table and benches and three rockers, made soft by the cotton-filled cushions placed on their corn husk seats, were the only furniture in the room. Next to the door was a two-foot-wide wooden ladder that led to the sleep loft, that their four children had used after they were old enough to leave their cradle.

It about broke her heart to see Wes so down, so out of sorts and lonely. He had always been such a happy, open child, unlike the others but more like Young Reuben in temperament. Raine and Tucker seemed to take up all their Mama's time even with the deMoyas' help, and Willa was concerned for him.

Willa took the long gnarled cane that she used to assist her arthritic legs to steady themselves and began pounding the floor so Wes could hear her. He responded by knocking on the underneath side and soon was bursting into the kitchen door past the rockers and into her raised arms.

She hugged him to her and brushed his damp hair back from his freckled brow and asked, "How much do ya luv yore Aunt Willa, Master Wes? Hummm? More dan Fiddlesticks? More dan dark syrup candy? Honey, what's de matter wid ya — don' ya feel good?"

She began rocking back and forth humming an old hymn while stroking his saddened face. She thought, "Somethin' gotta be done 'bout ma chile. Somethin's gotta transpire."

She made up her mind that she'd make the effort to climb the knoll to the main house to speak to the Missus and Mister Layke. Her chile wasn't gonna put up wid no more of dis loneliness. Nosiree!

TATER HILL BLUFF:

Callie paced back and forth on Jeeters's porch. She just couldn't seem to get a handle on the new way of acting now that she was a betrothed lady.

"Why can't Clay and me be just like we've always been?" and she glared at Old Gus Jeeters. "He gives me the willies everytime I look at him. Why, it's barely more than a year that he couldn't do enough for me after Thom and me found the doubloons. Boy howdy! He couldn't say enough sweet, gushey old things to me then. And now...well, he glares those old bug eyes at me just daring me to give even one little smile at Clay. I'm sick of it. I'm sick of the whole blessed thing!"

Callie was in Tater Hill and it was week's end. The Meades spent Saturday night in town at Thom's Aunt Beulah's and Uncle George's hotel and would return to Tall Ten after church on Sunday. Since her betrothal she had to be accompanied by her folks to all the shindigs, and the restraint had taken its toll. Callie had always been free.

As she looked at Clay stock the canned goods on the shelf behind the counter, she was aware that he knew she was watching. He'd glance her way once in a while, smile, then resume his work. He wasn't ignoring her, and he wasn't shy, but he'd been warned by his Uncle Gus and Aunt Ione that he had to *know his place* with Callie now that she was spoken for, and he felt that out of respect he should abide by the custom. But the more he felt her watching the more he wanted to drop everything and head for the porch.

She looked so pretty in the soft, gold, polished cotton dress. He remembered when Mrs. Meade had purchased the fabric and was glad that she had decided on the beige lace that she had sewn around the deep bertha collar and the leg-o-mutton sleeves. Callie was so soft and feminine looking. He could even smell her jasmine perfume that he knew was a gift from Thom. He'd given it to her before the drive to Punta Rassa, and she was especially fond of it.

Clay was taller than Thom by a couple of inches, slender but not skinny, with intelligent gray eyes and thick, wavy, reddish brown hair above a strong, square face. His hands were manly but somehow pretty; they'd never worked a whip nor rustled a calf to the ground and were more at home holding a pen or pencil. He wore a plain blue work shirt and overalls and was neat and clean.

He seemed to have always been a lot older than Callie. If anyone needed to know anything they'd ask Clay, or if they needed advice he'd be asked — even by the oldsters. But when it came to Callie Anders Meade, he was jelly. She was truth, honesty, strength and beauty, and he had worshiped her from the minute she kicked wet sand onto his new overalls her first day at school; she was but six and he an aging nine.

He somehow knew he'd never have Callie, not that he felt unworthy — Clay knew his worth — but, for whatever reason, he felt that if he pursued her he'd be interfering with a master plan.

He saw his Uncle Gus go to the back. "If I walk out onto the porch...Why am I analyzing this? Why can't I act spontaneously? Must I always evaluate everything?" He became mellow. "Callie is sun — she's light — she's energy — she's all the things I'm not but would like to be. Why can't I just walk out there and say, 'Hi Callie, I'm going to walk down to Big Spring, wanta join me?' Why can't I say that?" But he couldn't.

PALATKA:

Frightened! Yes, frightened! Juanita had at last realized fear. Not the cold-all-over fear she'd felt when she first saw the black, devil eyes of R.J. Skinner, but a new, unexpected, even more exciting fear. The fear of loving a man as awsomely complex as Conner O'Farrell.

Her vision blurred. Not truly comprehending her situation nor her newly felt emotions, she was hesitant to act. Doubt invaded her stout reserve that still day, and as she lay motionless in the soundless half-light of Conner's cabin she systematically took stock of her situation.

Conner was everything she had ever dreamed of even in her wildest imaginings. She was overwhelmed by his intensity, his animal strength. But she doubted.

"I have just gotta get up from here, " she said to herself convincingly. But Juanita Jane Graves was not convinced. So again she said louder, "Cherie, you have gotta take hold," thinking that if she said it real loud that she'd pay head to the declaration. But she did not, nor could not move from her reverie. Slowly she was released, released to the quiet slumber of his warm, airless cabin where her demanding inquiries went ignored as she floated into non-awareness.

The cabin door shook with heavy pounding. Again and again he knocked as he tried to turn the black iron latch on Conner's cabin door. Harrison's black, furrowed brow was beaded with perspiration. His obvious concern distorted his otherwise amiable features as he again pounded on the heavy oak door.

She stirred and stretched lazily toward the low-paneled ceiling. Not quite awake, she was startled by the incessant pounding. As she became more fully conscious she realized where she was but was hesitant to answer the persistent intruder. Tying her soft, muslin, seagreen wrapper more securely around her tiny waist, Juanita leaned against the door and answered haltingly. "Yes — yes, what could I be helping you with?"

So it was the girl. He should have realized. A very relieved Harrison answered her, "Oh! It's you, Miss Cherie. It's Harrison. I'm sorry to disturb you, but I thought Conner was there and I wanted to waken him." He neglected to add that he had made it a habit of awakening Conner every afternoon so he could have a light supper before the games began, and that for the past year it had become harder and harder to arouse his friend. The emptied whiskey bottles had multiplied steadily, and he was concerned for his friend's welfare. It was a self-imposed labor of love on his part. Conner O'Farrell did not want nor would he tolerate any show of concern from him, and yet theirs was the only close bond either had ever experienced. Not since their youth in the black bowels of New Orleans had they been separated.

About the author:

Ann O'Connell Rust is a native Floridian, a "cracker". Her parents were pioneers in the Everglades in the early part of the century. Her father, Frank O'Connell, moved to Canal Point on Lake Okeechobee to work on Conner's Highway—the first hard road into the Glades. Conner was a friend of the West Palm Beach O'Connells, and young Frank wanted to be a part of Conner's thrust into the mysterious Glades. There he met Onida Knight, one of the beautiful Knight girls, whose father had homesteaded their land the previous year, and opened his own Knight's Grocery and Dry Goods Store in Canal Point. Luther Knight ultimately became a farmer/rancher and her father, a farmer, deputy sheriff and chief of police in Pahokee.

After schooling in Palm Beach County schools, Ann embarked on a very successful career in modeling—in Miami and New York City, where she met and married Allen, an FBI agent, and followed him to Puerto Rico, New Mexico, Washington, D.C., Mexico City and finally back to her love — Florida. She has had an on-going love affair with romantic old Florida all of her adult life .